Free book!

To keep up with latest release news and receive an exclusive subscriber only ebook,
DATING SUCKS: A Supernatural Dating Agency prequel short story, sign up here:
geni.us/andiemlongparanormal

HEX FACTOR

Chapter 1

Noah

"It's so cold out here, my balls are disappearing," my friend and fellow band member Zak announced to the three of us and half of the people in the queue surrounding us. We were waiting in turn for our audition for Britain's Best New Band, a reality show that could take unknowns and send them stratospheric.

Being a top rock band was our dream and had been for years.

"Are you not cold?" Zak leaped from foot to foot rubbing his hands.

"Idiot, I'm always fucking cold, I'm a vampire." I eye-rolled him. He was off his game today and I could hazard a guess why. The guy was knackered from his extra-curricular activities.

"Well, you must be cold, because you're not able to put your furry coat on," Zak pushed at Rex.

Rex didn't move, despite the shove. "Even when I can't have my fur on the outside, it warms me on the inside. PS, if you push me again, I'm going to knock you the fuck out." Ever the alpha wolf, Rex growled at Zak. "There are loads of women here. Go warm yourself up by screwing a few of them. Get some extra credit."

Zak's shoulders slumped. "I'll not stay awake for the audition if I do that. I need to have a word with Abaddon, seriously. My quota is too large. I could hack it when I was eighteen, but I can't now."

Roman, our lead guitarist, took a swig from the bottle of scotch he seemed to have permanently attached to his hand. "I feel lovely and warm."

"Fuck off, Satyr. That's because your blood is almost 100% proof."

"Can you keep it down, Zak?" I narrowed my gaze at him. "I don't think we should be broadcasting our paranormal status to the two thousand humans we're sharing the queue with."

"Excuse me?" A slim blonde tapped Zak on the arm. She was wearing a fluffy blanket around her shoulders. "You can share my blanket if you like?"

Zak ran a hand through his hair.

"Oh look, he's responding to the female. The penis flytrap is about to ensnare another victim," Rex scoffed.

Roman almost choked on his mouthful of whisky. "Penis flytrap. That's fucking fabulous."

Zak gave us all a withering glare, then turned back to the blonde. "Thanks, doll. I'd like to take you up on your invitation to share your blanket another day, if I may? Perhaps you could give me your phone number?" Then he yawned. It didn't put the blonde off though. She gave him a beaming smile and her contact details.

*

Five-and-a-half hours later, we were through the doors and waiting inside to see a producer. An older guy walked up to us.

"Okay, *The Para-not-normals*?"

"That's us," I confirmed.

"Great, well sing away." He looked back at his clipboard.

My mouth dropped open. "Here?"

"Yeah, here," the guy replied, looking bored.

"Okay, let me just get us organised."

The producer shook his head. "Nope, sing now. Yes or no from me, and then we're done." His fingers tapped his clipboard in impatience.

Shit, we'd better hurry up.

"After three, guys," I ordered the others.

We sang one line of Ed Sheeran's *Shape of You*, before the guy yelled. "Okay, that's a yes. Here's your ticket. Go through that door for the next stage of the competition."

"Will I get to meet Carmela?" Zak now looked much more alert considering he might be about to share the same oxygen as the former girl band member Carmela Toto who was on the judging panel this year.

"You're joking, mate. She doesn't turn up until we start filming. It's another producer again. One higher up the food chain though." The guy walked off.

"We got through to the next round." I raised my hand up to the others, but every one of them left me hanging while looking at me like I was a wally. "I'm hurt," I told them. Things like this reminded me of my teenage years at school; times I did my best to forget.

"I'm still defrosting," Zak replied. "Oooh, they're selling coffee over there, thank fuck. Back in a sec and then we can go through and wait for another billion years, although at least this time we'll be in the warm."

When we eventually got into the other room, we had another two hour wait. Now I was starting to feel pangs in my stomach that let me know it was time to feed. As soon as these rounds were done, I'd need to find a willing participant for a blood donation. I didn't usually have a problem. Given I was tall, dark, and fangsome, usually I had women falling at my feet, especially after I'd drained them to the point of anaemia.

We'd been ignoring carnal glances from women and a few men since we'd arrived and given some of them would be devastated at getting to this second round and getting a 'no', later I could give them a 'yeeeeesssss'.

This time we had to stand in front of a producer in a room by ourselves. The female redhead had the same bored personality as the man before her.

"And sing."

We began singing, our voices harmonizing, although Zak was the lead. The producer's face became more animated, a brow rising.

"It's a yes. Let me have your details and we'll be in touch about the next stage of the competition."

"You mean I don't get to meet Carmela today?" Zak whined again.

"Nope. That'll be next time." She licked across her top lip. "But if you're free for a drink, I'll be finished in..." She checked her watch and sighed, "about another six hours."

He shrugged his shoulders. "Probably a good thing. I'm exhausted. Maybe another day?" Once again he secured a telephone number.

As we walked out of the audition room, a runner came towards us with a tray holding tea, coffee, and water. As she passed by other people, drinks were swiped off her tray and by the time she got to us, she was empty. "Can I get you any refreshments?" she asked, super-enthusiastic. "I'll just have to pop back to the kitchen to re-stock."

"Yes, please. I'm parched," I told her. "I'll follow you there."

We didn't get to the kitchen. The show's runners were supposed to keep everyone happy and the dark-haired one now sucking my cock was doing just that.

"Yeah, baby, just like that." I grabbed the back of her head, fisted my hand in her hair and thrust myself closer so I went further down the back of her throat. Her eyes watered a bit, but bless her, she carried on like a trooper. Before long I was emptying my load down her throat. I looked at the runner's lanyard. Her name was Jan. By tomorrow I'd have forgotten it, but right now that shit was important.

"Hey, Jan, baby." I beckoned her up to me with my right index finger and she scrabbled up from her knees to come closer.

"Yes?"

"I think you have something on your neck. Let me see." I did my best concerned gaze as I pushed my hands, one on her temple, one on her neck slightly to tilt her head, so I could peer closer.

"What is it?" Jan trembled a little which made my cock harder.

"Me," I growled as my fangs descended and I bit through her skin. Her lovely human blood sang to me as it rose in a merry dance into my mouth. I greedily took what I needed before my tongue licked the wounds closed. Jan's eyes were lust-filled as euphoria hit her system.

"Fuck me," she whimpered.

So I did. Bending her over the sofa in the empty dressing room she'd taken me to, I pulled her panties down and off and then thrust straight into her wet heat. She groaned as I took her further towards paradise. Being drained and given multiple orgasms did that to a woman. After I'd come in her (no babies from this undead guy), I laid her on the sofa in the room and whispered in her ear. But these were no whisperings of love, rather those of vampire compulsion to tell her that she was feeling ill and needed to rest.

When I made my way back to the audition room there was no sign of any of my bandmates. We were used to each other's different ways after meeting at college years ago.

Feeling on top of my game now I had recently fed, I allowed myself to get excited about the fact we were through to the judges rounds of Britain's Best New Band. My teenage dreams could potentially become a reality.

Leaving the building, the smug smile I was wearing slid

straight off into my boots as I came face to face with a contestant making her way inside.

Stacey Williams.

My ex-girlfriend.

The girl I'd loved, but who I'd given up in order to pursue my dreams of fame.

Her eyes met mine and her mouth turned down in a sneer. Then she pushed past me, knocking my shoulder hard and was gone inside the building.

She was entering the competition?

That meant she was *my* competition.

My rival.

There was a fine line between love and hate and it appeared Stacey had come down on the side of vengeance.

The worst thing? I couldn't blame her.

I sped back to my apartment, thankful of my inbuilt vamp speed, sat straight down on the sofa and thought about how fucking delicious Stacey had looked. Long dark hair, a cracking pair of tits that her tight grey t-shirt ripped over the midriff hinted at to perfection, thighs that would squeeze the life from me were I not already dead. But whereas her green eyes used to sparkle with love, now they'd been crackling with pure venom. It was a long way from how we used to be around each other. But I couldn't change the past, and Stacey had every right to look at me that way after how I'd treated her.

I let my mind drift back.

Weston Senior School – eight years earlier

"Come on, choir. This is our last rehearsal ready for the end of year show. So pull out all the stops for me now and sing your hearts out. Pretend this is the performance to the parents."

Stacey, my girlfriend of the last year, rolled her eyes at me. The choir was where all the losers who could sing ended up. The ones where they didn't want us visible, but appreciated we had a good voice. All the adored kids had parts in the actual school play which this time was a production of Grease. Well, Stacey was my Sandy, and I was her Danny, so I didn't care.

Except I did. I was sick of being picked on by the cool kids at school. They permanently took the piss out of the fact I wasn't able to wear the designer stuff like they did. I had cheap non-branded shoes —the only ones my mother could afford as a single mum—and they called me things like Coco because I had clown feet; any damn thing to make themselves feel better and popular.

Where Stacey got completely ignored by everyone, like she didn't exist at all, I was a target for all. Sneered at, despised, told I stank, all because I couldn't wear labels and I had braces on my teeth that weren't invisible.

Finally, the bell rang signalling the end of the class and we pulled on our coats and left the building.

"Another exciting day at Weston complete." Stacey linked her arm through mine.

"Oh look, Granger's carer is with him again." Jack Brooks, my main enemy, sniggered as he stomped past, knocking my bag off my shoulder as he did. *"Ever want a real man, come look me up."* He winked at Stacey. *"My mum said it was important to do charity work."*

I hated the fact that I couldn't stick up for my girlfriend. The last time I'd tried, they'd held me down, stripped me of my trousers and pants, and tied me to a lamppost outside school by my own belt. I didn't know what Stacey saw in me.

"Stacey—" I began, but I saw her mouth twist in annoyance.

"Noah, you are the kindest soul I ever met, and I love you. I

*don't want anyone else. It's their fault they can't see what I see, and it's my gain. It's their loss and that's because **they** are losers."*

I smiled a half-hearted smile. "I love you too, Stacey. You are the strongest person I've ever met, and the most talented, with the voice of an angel. And one day you'll get your place in the limelight, I'm sure."

Stacey squeezed my arm with hers. "One day, Noah, we'll show them. We'll be the ones on top and they'll have a house in Loserville. Together we are invincible." She kissed my cheek. "Now come on, I might even let you feel my boobs."

Now my smile became genuinely wider.

Maybe I could turn things around? I had one more year at this damn school and then college beckoned. Perhaps I could reinvent myself?

Truth was, I wasn't sure I'd survive another year.
Funnily enough, I didn't.

Chapter 2

Stacey

I couldn't say it was a surprise to have bumped into my ex. I'd known it would happen sooner rather than later. Appeared it was sooner. The Para-not-normals were extremely talented, and let's be clear, I was talking about musically here. But so were my band, The Seven Sisters. I'd fully expected both our bands to advance beyond the first rounds of the competition. What I hadn't expected was to bump into Noah just outside the building on the very first audition day. My prayers had been to not see him until we'd hopefully got through to the live finals. I'd have liked my appearance there to have knocked him on his arse.

His really fucking fit, tight as a peach in my gentle hold, arse.

Bastard.

He'd looked so good, and I hated him for it. That dark spiked hair. His dark-brown eyes, like pools of chocolate sauce. You wanted them on you, like syrup drizzled down your naked body.

Come on, Stacey, stop this, I urged myself as we waited to sing for a second time. I was genuinely here for a chance to win the talent show and get my career on a high, but I'd be lying if I didn't admit revenge on Noah was a close... second. Yes, second... just.

Seven Sisters needed to win this whole competition, and

although we were all witches, I wouldn't use a single spell to advance us to the final and to win. I wanted us to win on our talent alone. Then not only would my dreams come true, but it would show Noah 'fucktard' Granger that when he'd made his choice years ago, he'd made the wrong one.

His dark-brown eyes reminded me of how bitter I was still, all these years later. Like 100% cocoa solids.

I spoke to the rest of my band. "We have to get through this round. We have to win this show."

"You got it, sister! We're going to be the next *Little Mix*, but with seven of us!" Donna said with gusto. At five foot one she often jumped up and down a little when she was excited.

We called each other sisters as we belonged to the same coven. When I'd been at my lowest, I'd found solace in spells and had found the local coven. They'd become my family, and I loved them all as if they were my biological brood.

Though I smiled, it wasn't worn on my face for long. I'd never confessed the truth to my bandmates about the other reason I wanted to win. Mainly because at least one of them would find a way around the 'harm no others' rule and turn Noah into a literal toad, rather than the metaphorical one he was. So, it was my secret to keep for as long as I was able.

Until our paths drew back closer together as the competition progressed, when I'd find it hard to cover up my true feelings for the idiot.

I'd loved that boy. Not the man. The boy. Until he'd changed, and it had been a long time until I'd found out why.

Noah and I had dated in school for a year. He was in the year above me and I'd thought he hung the moon. I had no interest in the self-appointed kings and queens of our school and their simpering subjects. I'd recognised what a kind, loyal boy Noah was. We'd met when he joined the school choir.

Being in the choir was more time we could spend together. We made plans for our musical future beyond the choir, and as a duo. I'd fully intended to give him my virginity at sixteen.

But before any of that happened, he'd finished with me. The boy I loved had changed in front of my eyes. Grown in appearance and in confidence. Instead of being the school joke, he'd become popular.

I'd waited, hung on, in the hope he'd change his mind. Because the boy I'd loved wouldn't do that to me. He was too kind. He must have been having a breakdown. He'd come around if I held on.

But finally, partway through my final year, I'd seen him, in an alleyway near the local tattoo parlour, with an older woman with dark brown hair. She was caressing his face with her fingers with such love. I'd turned and run back the way I'd come, tears streaming down my face, as I realised that it was really all over, and Noah was never coming back. Was not going to say he'd made a mistake.

Stacey Williams clearly didn't fit in with his image anymore.

At sixteen I'd given my virginity to Jack Brooks instead, who'd been sniffing round me in forever. A large error in judgement. It's not every day you have to confess to a one-night stand in front of your mother and two detectives when your one-off crap shag goes missing. He was never found.

It was a long time before I found out the truth about the woman with the long, dark hair. A drunken mistake a couple of years ago. I wouldn't let my thoughts go there now. I'd pushed the memories deep inside the locked compartment in my mind.

I shook myself down as if spiders were in my hair. My focus needed to be on this final and in forgetting Noah Granger once and for all.

Once I'd beaten him and taught him a valuable life lesson of course.

That ditching me had been the worst mistake he'd ever made, and one that he'd regret for the rest of his undead life.

And that was a fucking long time.

Chapter 3

Noah

Eight years earlier

On my way home after the end of school concert, I found the cool kids waiting for me. Stacey's mother had picked her up after watching her performance. No such luck for me; my mum had been working late.

"Hey, loser." Jack Brooks, the most popular guy in school swaggered over to me. Dressed in Hugo Boss and wearing D&G shoes, he looked every inch the rich kid, in contrast to my hand-me-down threads that ran an inch too high up my ankles and an inch too long at my wrists.

"I dare you to rough him up," one of his posh friends said, and I groaned inwardly, because if someone said 'dare' to Jack, he couldn't say no.

He laughed, looking at me like I was scum. "Fucking pansy singing in the choir. Let me give you a hand reaching the high notes." He kicked me in the balls; so hard I dropped to my knees seeing stars.

When I opened my eyes, it was to see Jack's fist coming towards me. A sucker punch that had darkness descending. The last thing I *remembered was being dragged behind some bushes and their laughing as I gave in to unconsciousness.*

When I woke up, I was no longer in the bushes. Instead, I found myself lying on a sofa in a house I didn't recognise. A woman who looked several years older than me sat near me as I came around.

I tried to sit up, but pain had nausea hitting my system and I stayed where I was in case I might pass out again. "W-where am I?" I managed to croak out.

The woman stood up and placed a cushion behind my neck so that I could sit up slightly. As she touched me to help me move, I flinched as her skin was so cold.

"My name is Mya," she said, in a soft, and caring voice. "I discovered you unconscious in the bushes and so I brought you to my home. You have a black eye and some other bruising which would suggest that you were the victim of a beating or mugging."

It came back to me. The hate from the kids in my school who I'd never done a thing to.

I looked up at my rescuer. At her dark hair; her almond-shaped, brown eyes; her full pink lips. She was enchantingly beautiful. Even her voice was hypnotic.

"How did you get me back here?" I asked, "and are we far from where you found me?"

"Err, a man passing helped to get you to my car, and no, you're not far. About five minutes from where I found you. Once you're okay I can take you home."

I'd started to think it was a little strange that instead of calling for an ambulance, she'd brought me to her house. Plus, she kept looking at me like she was studying me. I hoped it was in an 'I hope he's okay' way, rather than an, 'How many pieces will I need to chop him up into to fit him in the freezer' kind of way.

"I think I'm okay now. But I really appreciate what you did for me," I said politely.

Mya sat on the sofa arm at the side of my head. "Tell me about these bullies. I may have a proposition for you."

I wondered if her husband was an ex-wrestler or something and would beat the shit out of Jack Brooks for me.

"Gosh, I'm so sorry. I never asked if you'd like some water. Where are my manners." Mya stood once more. "Look, I know what you're thinking. About how strange it is I brought you here. Let me get you a drink and I'll explain. I promise if you want to go home at any time, you only have to ask. I've not kidnapped you." *She laughed and it showed her perfect teeth.*

"I'd love some water please," I answered.

She patted my arm. "Everything will be okay. I want you to tell me exactly what's been happening when I get back. I can't stand bullies. I was bullied myself in the past and so if I see one, I can't help but intervene."

While she got my drink, I reflected on the fact that Mya was not only beautiful, but she seemed to have her heart in the right place, even if she did appear slightly quirky.

I'd find out shortly that although her heart was in the right place, it no longer beat.

She passed me my water and sat next to me on the sofa once more and I told her about my life at school. It was so strange. Like I didn't want to tell her everything, but it all came out: about Stacey, about bullies, about the dare that had led to my beating. I know now that she used compulsion on me, but back then I had no clue that Mya Malone was a vampire.

"I'd like to make you an offer," *she said. By this time, I was in dire need of painkillers and had half started to wonder why she'd not offered me any.*

*Turned out **she** was the painkiller.*

"You say your life is miserable and you're bullied daily. What if I could make it that you became strong, desired, had everything you wanted, and even better, you could get rid of any bullies once and for all, easily?"

A life without bullies? Without being beaten up? A life I could live without fear?

"I'd say yes please and how?"

"Have you heard of vampires, Noah?"

My eyes widened. She was a crazy woman after all. Fuck. I'd thought being beaten and left on the street was bad enough, but now I was trapped in a house with someone who thought they were undead and drank blood. Where were the exits and could I manage to get to them given the pain I was in?

Looked like I'd fucked it. Life sucked right now, and so apparently did the woman staring at me with a smirk curling her lip.

"I can read your mind, Noah. It's perfectly normal for you to not believe me. Just humour me a moment. Let's go along with me being a vampire. The fact is that I have the power to change a human to be one too. It's called siring."

"Let me out of here," I yelled.

She came closer to me and looked me directly in the eyes.

"Noah, you will become calm and not panic. You will accept what I tell you and make an informed decision."

I could feel my heart rate slow down and the mad beat in my chest disappeared.

"Good, good. Now, I was turned myself in 2011. I didn't have a choice, not really, but it actually turned out to be good for me. I don't regret becoming a vampire at all. I've never sired anyone before, but I think being a vampire would benefit you too. Anyway, I'm going to let you access my memories a little so you can see how it's been for me."

This head injury was obviously more serious than I'd initially considered. Maybe I was actually still in the bushes unconscious?

"You're not. You're here, with me." Again, with the weird thought reading. *"To let you access my memories though I need to do this..."*

She lifted my wrist and turned it so my hand was palm up, and then bit down.

Euphoria hit my system. A feeling I had never experienced in my life. I felt no pain whatsoever and began to see flickers of images and felt pieces of knowledge come to me. Mya being turned. Living in a mansion with a dark-haired male, being happy. I saw her vampire family: the Letwines. Then the feelings settled, and I just felt calm.

"The feelings you experienced, the rush, the bliss, are all part of the vampire world, Noah," Mya explained. "What you just experienced will not happen again as a human. "This is what I'm offering. Strength... transformation... an extended family. Protection for life, or should I say unlife. Now, take time to consider my offer."

She left me and did various tasks around the house until eventually, after time spent thinking things over, I called for her.

"Mya."

She came towards me. "Yes?"

"I want it," I told her. "Make me a vampire."

Mya asked me questions and I could see she wanted to make absolutely sure I knew what I was asking for. That I couldn't go back to being a human. That I would be the first person she'd sired.

"I'll need to call my own sire to help," she explained.

I nodded. Though my hands and mouth trembled a little, I was determined to go through with this.

A blonde-haired man arrived and introduced himself as Lawrie. He and Mya went into the kitchen. I could hear low mumblings of their conversation, and knew just as Mya wanted to make sure I wished to be turned, Lawrie was checking on Mya's own decision to turn me.

Then they both returned.

"Okay, Noah, time for Mya to sire you," Lawrie said.

I didn't realise that to do so, Mya would have to drain me to the point of death.

♪

It took the next six weeks—which thank fuck, coincided with the school summer holidays—to recover from my turning and to adjust to my new life. Actually, life was completely the wrong word—my new death. I explained away not leaving my house due to being attacked.

Stacey tried to visit countless times, but I kept putting her off, talking via social media instead. I felt guilty about how I was treating her, but I was starving and surviving on bags of O-neg Mya kept me supplied with.

Thank goodness the whole vampires-couldn't-go-out-in-the-day thing was no longer the case; although being a teenager, I rarely surfaced until late afternoon at weekends and during holidays anyway, so my mum wouldn't have noticed.

As my fledgling status progressed over those following six weeks, I became the full adult male I'd been destined to become. Mya tried to act like a mother figure, although to me she seemed more like a bossy older sister. As my sire, we shared a bond that would never break until one of us died a vampire's death. I could always contact her through our mind link, though she taught me how to close my mind and keep myself safe. Mya taught me all about being a vampire, and she showed me how to find blood banks to get the blood I needed to sustain me.

My mum was shocked at the change in me. One minute I was a dweeb, the next I was six foot two, athletically built, and looked in my early twenties. But I wasn't the first teen male such things had happened to. One of the lads in my class had done the same at thirteen and luckily, she remembered. I did keep seeing her staring at me from time-to-time though and saying things like, 'How can you be that little boy I gave birth to, Jeez'.

I'd left school, had passed my exams, and it was time to start my first year of college.

A new place of education for a new Noah Granger.

I needed to think about Stacey. Now I'd be back going out on a daily basis, she'd no longer keep her distance while I 'recovered'.

But I knew we could no longer be together. She wasn't safe around me, and anyway, I needed to get used to the new Noah Granger.

The one who could now freely make choices without worrying about bullies.

I'm not proud of the decisions I made, but in my defence, I was sixteen years old and well, a dickhead. And I decided that singing in a choir was not what I wanted any more.

I didn't want to be unnoticed at the back.

I wanted to be at the front, but not quite centre.

My dreams had been of being in a band. All the time I'd spoken with Stacey about our future duo, deep inside I'd wished to be part of some rock superstardom, and now that was a goal I could reach for.

Love could wait. I thought.

Plus, the boy Stacey said she loved didn't exist anymore, so in a way I was doing her a favour wasn't I?

Selfish.

Selfish.

Selfish.

But teenagers are, and that's ones that haven't suffered their own deaths at sixteen and been reborn a bloodsucker.

So Stacey was out and my search for my new bandmates was on.

I soon found out, by the power of my newfound vampire enhanced sense of smell, that I wasn't the only supernatural who walked the corridors of Greystone College. There were other quiet kids who hung around in the dark corners hoping not to be seen.

That was all about to change.

🎸

A parking garage, three months after Noah's turning

I looked around at my friends' perplexed faces as they stared at the music and fitness equipment I had placed in the garage of Mya's property. She didn't need a car due to being able to whizz where she liked at speed, and so she'd told me I could use it. She'd even got someone to soundproof it.

"Time to become rock gods," I declared. "Maybe we aren't allowed to use our supernatural abilities in front of humans, but we can certainly use our musical ones."

"God, it's not fair. I'm the only one still human," Zak complained. His long blonde hair hung over his face in greasy ringlets. He looked like something from a horror movie with his scrawny frame and hunched over shoulders. Like he was about to slither out of a gutter and bite through your ankle.

"You can still use your God given talents—and a shower—to raise your game." I wrinkled my nose in disgust near him. "It starts today, my friends. Look around you. Treadmills, weights, a drum kit, guitars, a microphone. I've fixed them up the best I can. It's a start."

"Where'd you get all this from?" Rex asked, out of his pouty mouth. I was sure he was the secret lovechild of Mick Jagger, but I wouldn't dare ask his mother. As a wolf-shifter, she wasn't someone to piss off.

"It's what the ultra-rich have dumped in the last few weeks. Most of it wasn't even broken, just not the most expensive toy to show off anymore. I've been doing a nightly tour. Vampire sight, strength, and speed are no match for the refuse collectors."

"I hate that you don't need more than an hour's sleep." Roman yawned after speaking. He was a Satyr which meant that in his true form he had the horns and legs of a goat. On maturity he was likely to become a wild womaniser. Right now, him being horny was just his natural virginal, biological state.

He was right. I was lucky. The development of medication meant that my species could now be out in sunlight whenever we liked, and an hour's power nap was all we needed to re-set ourselves at some point during the dawn. It also meant it was not so easy to recognise vampires anymore, something else that was of huge value seeing as being awake all night and sleeping all day was a bit of a giveaway to any enemy. All they needed was a piece of wood to finish you off and a vacuum cleaner for the dust of the undead and it'd be like you'd never existed. Thank goodness there was a huge 'save the trees' and recycling initiative at the moment meaning wood was a hot commodity in London.

"*So what is the actual plan?*" *Zak picked up a microphone and even moved the hair out of his face to look at it more closely.*

"*We're going to work out, and we're going to form a band. Completely in secret. Then we'll book ourselves in with a hair stylist and a clothes stylist and relaunch ourselves on the world. It'll take us some time, and we'll need part-time jobs to save up for the hair and clothes, but we're no longer going to be the victims, we're going to be the victors. Who's with me?*"

"*You don't need to work out or have a makeover. You just look like that anyway. It's not fair,*" *Rex moaned. "I have to run about in the woods all the time to work off all my energy. I'll probably break these machines if I try to use them.*"

"*Okay, they're for Roman and Zak then. You go jogging.*"

Rex growled and I laughed.

"*What are we going to call ourselves?*" *Roman asked.*

We debated different ideas for a while but nothing good surfaced as a potential winner. And then Zak said. "How about an in-joke? We're all paranormals; well, all of us except me. So how about The Para-not-normals? I'm the 'not'."

"*I love that,*" *I said.*

"*Me too,*" *said Roman.*

Rex held up a drumstick. "Me three."

We high-fived his drumstick.

So The Para-not-normals were formed. Rex on drums, Zak with the microphone, me on bass guitar, and Roman on lead guitar. The rest of us could hold a tune and provide backing or occasional lead vocals.

Of course, my vamp speed meant I learned to play the bass guitar in super quick time. Rex was growly enough that banging on drums came naturally to him; and Roman had been forced into guitar lessons at a young age, by a father who believed all children should learn an instrument. Roman was keen to learn how to use an instrument all right, but one that laid between his legs, not against them.

Zak would later lose his 'not' status, but the band name remained for a long time.

Chapter 4

Stacey

Seven-and-a-half years earlier

It had been six months. Six long months where I'd cried enough to fill several rivers. But the six-month anniversary was the day I drew a line through Noah and Stacey, literally, on my wooden maths desk. Scored it out with the pointy end of my compass.

"You want to go shopping after school?" my classmate Fiona asked. We'd ended up hanging out together over the last month or so. We didn't particularly have anything in common bar loneliness, but it beat being on my own. She helped take my mind off things given she was a chatterbox and rarely needed an answer to her incessant spewing of words.

"Sure," I answered. I'd been saving my pocket money and birthday money and finally had enough to buy what I wanted for my newly decorated bedroom. I'd seen a beautiful blue and green dreamcatcher in a small store hidden down a side street in the city centre, and some gorgeous cushion covers in the same hues.

My mother had decorated my bedroom. No doubt in the hope of bringing me out of my lovesick gloom. To an extent it had worked, as she'd let me choose the colour scheme of blues and teals, something that made me realise I was growing up. Now sixteen, I *was in my final year of school and needed to study for my exams, not continue mooning around over my ex.*

He certainly wasn't mooning around over me.

In his first year of sixth form, Noah was unrecognisable from the boy I'd shared a year of my life with. In body and in soul.

I'd see him with his friends as his college was only around eight minutes' walk away from school. He'd grown to over six feet tall and he looked so much older than most. I reluctantly had to admit to myself that he seemed far better suited to the dark-haired woman I still occasionally saw him hanging around with than little old me.

My boobs were growing, but I remained five feet five. I'd never really bothered over my appearance, still didn't wear make-up, and now I kept my hair up in a messy bun. Wearing it down and long belonged to the old Stacey and I wasn't her anymore.

Noah now hung around with three other guys who he must have met at college because I'd not seen them around school.

They walked the streets like they were the fucking Beatles or something, having formed a band. No one had heard them play yet, but Rex Colton sauntered around with a drumstick in his hand all day, every day, and Noah now had a plectrum hanging from a chain around his neck. Zak would sing and hum to himself as they walked along and he could definitely hold a tune. The last one of them, Roman, remained the quieter of them and sometimes I'd catch him looking my way. He'd give me a sympathetic smile. That let me know that they all knew who I was—the ex-girlfriend. I ignored Roman, resisting the temptation to stick my middle finger up in his direction. It wasn't his fault his friend was a fucktard.

I knew far more about them all than I wanted to because they were all the girls in my year talked about now. If I heard 'your ex' one more time in a sentence I might strangle somebody.

Girls followed them around, giggling behind them and accidentally bumping into them. Occasionally, Noah would look my way, but I'd just turn my own gaze in a different direction. He just wasn't the guy I'd loved. I presumed puberty had hit him late and at times wished I had.

Last night The Para-not-normals had played their first gig at Rex's little sister's sweet sixteenth. A few of my classmates knew Paloma Carlton and had attended, and it was all I was hearing about.

"Oh my lord, they could really sing. Zak is so fit and he has the voice of an angel."

"But the body of a devil, right?"

"They're going to get famous. I just know it."

I wanted to put my hands over my ears, but not so much as when I heard, "Sonia says they're entering the Velvet Throat Lozenges, Voices of Tomorrow competition."

Anger coursed through my veins, burning acid coming up the back of my throat. He'd promised me we'd enter competitions together. As a duo. Now it was clear—though I'd known it as soon as I'd heard he was in a band—I'd been double dumped. Not good enough to be his girlfriend and not good enough to take over the charts.

Jack Brooks walked over to me while I was in the lunch queue waiting for my cheese flan, chips, and beans, my ultimate favourite food.

"Do you fancy going out tonight? We could go watch a film or something," he said, leaning in a little too close.

I wouldn't have ordinarily touched Jack with a ten-foot bargepole. In fact, I'd have rather touched a turd, but I knew he had a dislike of Noah, and for that fact I agreed to meet him later that night to grab pizza. Hopefully, the rumours wouldn't take long to get back to my ex. I hope they hurt, like he'd hurt me.

After school, I met up with Fiona and we headed off into the city centre. In Primark after she'd insisted I bought a cute little jumpsuit for my date, she bumped into another couple of friends who started banging on about last night's concert. I made my excuses and left to go find the shop down the side street that I loved: **Wiccan do it.**

I loved the title. It was so kitsch.

Pushing open the door, a little bell rang and the scent of patchouli and sandalwood drifted up my nostrils. I couldn't put my finger on why, but it smelled like home. Sighing with happiness and contentment at all the gorgeous items around me, I wandered around the shelves and stands. I was definitely going to make my bedroom have this kind of feel to it. Sauntering over to the book section, a book called **How to Hex Your Ex** caught my eye and I picked it up.

"You know that's just a joke read, right? Us Wiccans agree not to cause harm." A female voice from behind me made me jump. I turned around to find the short, blonde-haired shop assistant there. She'd moved from behind the counter without me noticing.

"Oh, don't worry. I don't think witchcraft is actually real," I informed her, watching as the smile left her face for a brief moment before it came back. It wasn't the same smile though. The genuine one had been replaced by the 'are you going to actually buy anything' smile.

Fuck. She must actually believe in it.

"Sorry, that was rude of me. Should I say, I've seen no evidence to suggest witchcraft is real, but you know, I keep an open mind about things."

Her genuine smile returned. "That's okay. I'm Donna by the way."

"Stacey."

"It's just I can tell that you have the source within you. The link to the old ways." She handed me a leaflet. "We meet at six pm on a Wednesday after the shop closes. You should come."

I opened my mouth, but she carried on talking.

"Keep that open mind."

I nodded.

"I love this shop," I told her. "Have you worked here long?"

"A year, since I left school. It's my mum's shop."

"Well, I've decided to take inspiration from this store for my bedroom. There are a few things I want, if you can help me get them?"

Donna nodded enthusiastically and she helped me gather the mirror, cushions, and dreamcatcher I'd chosen. Then she showed me a few candles and jewelled candle holders. By the time I'd finished there wasn't much of my birthday money left.

Reaching under the counter, Donna took out a book. **Introductory Guide for the Interested** *was the very vague title.*

"This one's on me for how much you've spent in store today," she explained. "Something to have a look at, and then maybe we'll see you on a Wednesday. No pressure though," she rushed out. "We're not a cult. Just people with a natural inclination towards the old ways. We don't turn people into frogs, no matter how tempting that can sometimes be."

I laughed, thinking about Noah.

"Yeah. Very tempting."

I went home and got changed for my date with Jack. My dad said he'd hang up my new mirror while I was out. I didn't want him worrying about me being out on a date, so I told him I was meeting back up with Fiona.

When I got to the pizza place, there wasn't only Jack there, but a whole group of his friends, both boys and girls. The boys just said hello and chatted like I wasn't anyone new, while the girls looked me over with curiosity, no doubt wondering why I'd suddenly become Jack's new interest. One of them asked where my playsuit was from. It sounded like she was genuinely asking, but the girls glanced between themselves when I answered, their looks clearly saying I wasn't good enough. That I shopped on the High Street FFS, so what was Jack doing with me. They could take their judgy stares and stick them up their tight arseholes.

After sharing pizza, one of the guys, Jed, declared his parents were away and it was party time back at his house. Though the majority of my brain was telling me to go home, the other part said to go to the party and see what happened. Jack had been attentive, putting his arm around me, and had whispered that he wanted me to come along.

So I did. I went to the party. I had a couple of vodkas for Dutch courage, and then I slept with Jack Brooks in one of the upstairs bedrooms.

Jack had acted amazingly gentle as he took my virginity. Then he took his own pleasure, discarded the condom, sat back and laughed.

"Well, well, well. So you never gave it up to that loser Granger? Could he not get it up?"

Even though revenge on Noah had been at the back of my mind throughout all of this, I was insulted that having just slept with me, all Jack could think about was Noah.

Standing up and hutching off the bed, I turned to Jack. "Thanks for a nice night. I'll get cleaned up and see myself out."

He was already texting, and I knew what it would say.

I was no longer thinking this had been a good idea.

When I got home, I placed my other new purchases around the room, lit a sandalwood joss stick, climbed into bed and opened the book Donna had given me.

Maybe I needed to know how to turn people into frogs after all.

The following Wednesday I returned to the store, and I never looked back.

Chapter 5

Anonymous

Seven-and-a-half years earlier

Jack Brooks was drunk. I watched as he staggered down the path towards the recycle bins where he was about to put the bottle of vodka Stacey had drunk from.

I knew because I could smell her scent around it and around him.

Knowing what he'd done, what he'd claimed, disgusted me. Bullying a guy was bad enough, but to take advantage of a vulnerable female did not sit well with me.

"Hi, Jack," I sniggered at my own joke. I was about to hijack him away from here. He just didn't know it yet.

He turned to me, his eyes narrowing. "What do you want?"

"I have something for you," I told him. "But you have to come get it. If you dare..."

He'd never been able to resist a dare.

I drained him of his blood even though it tasted of weed and cigarettes. Then I flew to the nearest tip and dropped him under an old pile of rubbish like the trash he was.

Chapter 6

Stacey

We were through to the next round of auditions. The part where we would get to sing in front of the actual judges. Donna was like a Jack-in-a-box, she was so excited. She had sugar daddy fantasies relating to the main man, Bill. Each to their own.

To celebrate, we'd all come to our favourite place, the Rock Hard Bistro. Anyone who loved music, loved the bistro. They had a mix of live bands and themed evenings, and the atmosphere was always positive. The food and drink were excellent and reasonably priced, and the owner and manager, Stu looked a little like Idris Elba which didn't hurt business.

On a Tuesday evening, the place was getting busier, but the music was background rather than the main focus, the food taking centre stage.

We'd ordered lots of things to share: nachos, ribs, chicken wings, pizzas, wedges, along with some large pitchers of beer and a few cocktails. I was usually quite partial to a whisky sour, but on this occasion had decided beer went better with the food.

"So I know you're through, but how did it go?" Stu asked me. "You reckon there's a real chance I might lose my favourite waitress and bartender?"

Yep, I worked there, and ate there in my downtime. I told you I loved the place.

I shrugged my shoulders. "We got through to the next round, but after that, who knows? Could be sent packing and then that's the end of that."

Stu tilted his head looking at me. To say he was only about five years older than I was, he acted like my dad.

"'Keep a positive mind. Negativity attracts negativity'," I mimicked in his voice. "I'll meditate on manifesting my success later." I rolled my eyes at him.

"You can scoff. I manifested my entire business and I'm loaded. Both in money and down my pants, so mock me. I'll stand throwing dollar bills at you."

"We're British."

He shrugged. "One pound coins would hurt, and then you'd sue me for a workplace injury."

I laughed.

"So when will I see you on the television and be able to tell all my friends I know you?"

"There are the live auditions after this. If we get through that it's then the judges' choices for who goes through to the live finals. So don't be advertising my job anywhere just yet."

"One day you'll make it, Stace. Whether it's now or later. You've an amazing voice and it'll happen for you, I'm sure."

"If it's meant to be right?" I said. He nodded, gave me a squeeze and went back to work.

I sat looking around at the rest of the band. As well as Donna, there was Dani, Kiki, Estelle, Shonna, and Meryl. We ranged in age from twenty-three (me) to twenty-eight (Meryl and Estelle) and in the main got along really well.

"So, Donna. What's your plan to ensnare Bill then?" Dani shouted across the table, her brown curls falling in her face.

"I'll bewitch him," Donna replied.

"You can't use your powers," Estelle said bossily.

"I'm not going to use my powers. I'm going to use my innate charm."

"You mean, you're gonna flash your tits?" Dani laughed.

"You betcha." Donna giggled.

This was why I adored them. The banter and the closeness formed by a bond of women who'd come together with a love of witchcraft.

Speaking of which, I'd make sure to put a hex on Noah that meant all my coven sisters found him repellent. You weren't allowed to use magic for your own personal gain, so I'd make the spell to protect my fellow witch sisters from him sucking their blood.

Simple.

Britain's Best New Band was run by the same team as those that ran the X-Factor, and a thought came to me to make me smile.

Maybe we'd picked the wrong show.

Because Noah had the ex-factor and would soon have the hex-factor.

I sniggered into my beer.

That was not how this was meant to play out, but it sure was punny.

§

Two years ago – Rock Hard Bistro

"I'll have a glass of champagne please and the blackened salmon. What would you like, Aunty?" the customer said in a cut-glass accent.

I took both orders. It was a rare quietish night due to the fact it had been raining solid for three days and people were no doubt choosing to stay in and order takeaways.

After I'd delivered their drinks to the table, the younger one, who I'd noted was uber-stylish with her sleek bobbed hair and gorgeous green silk wrap-dress, clutched her head.

"Are you okay?" I panicked. The last thing I needed tonight was drama. I just wanted to do my shift and get home.

"She's fine. She has visions," the older lady said, as if she was stating the younger woman had epilepsy. It was a good job I was a witch and knew other things walked the earth than humans or I'd have been sending for men in white coats. "Ebony? Ebony. Are you seeing something?"

Ebony had been looking like she'd already had several glasses of champagne, but as I watched she came around. Then she grabbed my wrist, making me jump.

"You have to enter a competition. Britain's Best New Band. In 2022. It's your destiny."

I stared at her for a long moment. She knew I was musical? Or was this a hoax as you could take a guess that a person working in a rock bistro liked music.

"You need to listen to her," the other woman said. "My niece doesn't come to London very often these days. She lives near the beach in a place called Withernsea, so you're unlikely to get her advice again. Enter the competition."

"O-okay," I answered.

And that was that. The two women continued with their evening like nothing strange had happened at all, and I knew that it was time for my band to practice, ready to enter their first serious competition.

Because my destiny was there.
Whatever that was.

Of course, I suspected part of that destiny would be tied up with Noah Granger. Finally, it was time to get my revenge or to put the past firmly in the past.

And now here we were, through to the next round.

I was meant to be here. I just didn't know why yet.

Chapter 7

Noah

We were through to the first round of the auditions with the judges. It was everything I'd hoped for and more. We'd spent years gigging and being talent-spotted, only for something to not work out at the last minute. The Para-not-normals had endured many highs and lows over the last few years, but now I hoped we could finally catch the break we deserved.

I wasn't being egotistical. We were that good.

If you'd told me about destiny a few years ago, I'd have thought you were a crazy person. But that was before I learned about the supernaturals living amongst us. Deep inside, I knew this band was meant to be, and I had three friends who meant the world to me. Were my brothers in every way but biological.

"The Para-not-Normals," the crew member shouted to us as we sat in the seating area with hundreds of other people.

"Do you think their clipboards actually have anything written on them, or just make them feel important?" Zak mused.

"Nick one and have a look," Rex suggested.

"No one will be pinching anything. We need to keep professional. Now let's go and show the judges and audience what we're made of," I said sternly.

"What bit your arse?" Zak huffed.

"No one in a long, long time. That's probably his problem." Rex guffawed.

We followed the clipboard guy up some steps and backstage where Zak's eyes immediately landed on the blonde haired, blowjob lipped co-presenter Harley Davies.

"Oh my. I need her on my dick," he mused. Clipboard guy gave him a dirty look.

"Concentrate, Zak," I admonished again.

"I thought the presenters announced us and then we went on stage?" he replied, with a furrowed brow.

He had a point. When we'd seen the show on television, the presenters announced you coming on for the judges. Come to think of it, no one was filming either. Harley, and the other presenter, Dan Trent, were chatting in the corner. Just before we went on stage, I saw Harley look pissed off with something Dan said, and she stalked off giving him the middle finger. Hmmm, looked like they weren't as friendly as they would no doubt act later.

Clipboard guy turned to us, looking smug. "You audition for the judges in front of the audience. If they like you, you do it again for the camera. If they don't—if you're terrible—then you also might do it again for the camera. If they're not interested, because you're entirely average, you go home. Stage is set up for you. When I indicate, follow me."

He walked out onto the stage, announced the band to the judges and then nodded to us.

Walking out from the darkness of backstage to the heavily lit area and the sea of faces in the audience, I felt both anxious and exhilarated. In front of us sat the four judges.

From left to right on the panel there was talent scout Maxwell Johnson; pop veteran Marianne Moore, who'd represented the Eurovision Song Contest in the sixties; Carmela, who'd fronted a girl band, but liked the attention on her alone and so had left to present instead; and Bill Traynor, CEO of Deep Heat Records.

Bill, the multi-billionaire who could launch us into worldwide stardom.

All four of them looked bored, though that could be due to overdoing the Botox that the showbiz brigade were so fond of.

"This is The Para-not-Normals," Clipboard guy announced.

Bill nodded. "Okay, sing."

Once again there was no pomp or ceremony.

We began our version of Taylor Swift's *Wildest Dreams*. They listened to thirty seconds and then Bill raised a hand and stopped the music.

"Okay. Here's what's going to happen," he told us. "You're good enough to go through."

We all beamed, and Rex growled, "Yes," only to receive a withering look from Bill. I glared at Rex hoping he realised it meant *shut the hell up*.

Bill continued. "Make-up will change your image a little before you come back on. Also, I'm going to suggest a name change, nothing too different, just taking the 'not' out. You'll agree." He scratched at his chin. "You know *Paradise City*?"

We nodded.

"You'll do that first but not well. I'll stop the process and ask if you have anything else. Then you'll blow the roof off with Wildest Dreams. Okay, thanks."

And that was it. Clipboard guy took us back off-stage and through to meet the team from make-up and hair.

"Right, I'll leave you here. Congrats, guys," he said and with that he was on his way.

We all stared at each other speechless.

"What just happened?" Rex eventually muttered.

"I think we just got to see a glimpse of what really happens behind the scenes of a TV Talent Show." Roman sighed. "No one said the path to the top was paved with gold."

Indeed, it was not. It was paved with going along with a reality show script and we agreed between us as we progressed through hair and make-up that if it led to the glory of a recording contract, we'd do whatever it took—within reason. Like Zak said, he'd already sold his soul to a devil so what did he have to lose?

Hair and make-up parted Rex's hair down the middle so he had curtains. I could see that after this he was going to have to let off some major energy and probably hunt because I just knew that deep inside his wolf was growling for permission to take the hair stylist guy's head off. Zak's was crimped, and mine was gelled so much it looked greasy. They put clear round glasses on Roman, making him look like Harry Potter's older brother and then finally they dressed us in clothes that took me right back to my old days at school, pre-turning.

"We don't say a word about this. It's never, *ever* mentioned." Zak glared at us all. "Not one word."

"Okay, all done." The head of the department radioed through for us to be collected and then we waited until it was time to film.

This time Harley walked over to us and said hi. She had perfect white teeth and gorgeous blue eyes and was the epitome of friendliness, unlike her co-host Dan who stood having his make-up retouched and shouted for her to hurry up.

"Sorry, guys. I must go do my bit. Good luck. I know it's all a bit smoke and mirrors, but it makes for great viewing and ultimately that's what you want. Thousands of people supporting you to win."

She went on her way, her arse bouncing around in her capri pants.

"Do you think they'll believe me if I say it's my microphone in my pocket, only I'm rock hard." Zak groaned. "And I've got to look at Carmela yet."

"Look at yourself in the mirror instead." Rex shoved him in the arm. "Not gonna score many chicks looking like that."

Zak smirked. "Now you know I can appear in their dreams

any way they like. But you've given me an idea. I'll look at you and those curtains you're displaying. Thanks, mate. I'm already limp as days old lettuce."

This time as we approached the stage we were stopped and filmed as Dan talked to us, Harley standing alongside him.

"Hi, guys, so you're The Para-not-normals. How did you four get together?"

I talked a little about us having met at college and how we'd formed the band, practising in our spare time.

"Well, the judges are waiting for you. Good luck." Harley smiled and then we made our way onto the stage.

From there on we did as directed. Firstly, we sang *Paradise City* and had to look worried when Bill held his hand up and stopped the music. Then Bill asked if we had a different song to sing and we performed our Taylor Swift song. It was soul destroying (well to those of us who still had theirs) as the audience cheered like crazy *because they were told to do so.*

Then it came to the judges vote on whether or not we went through to the next round, where the judges whittled down the acts and got their 'teams'.

Maxwell spoke first. "I think you have potential. It's a yes from me."

Then Marianne. "You remind me of The Rolling Stones in their early days when we used to hang around together. Great times. It's a yes from me."

Then Carmela. "I like you. You have a great energy. Yes, from me."

And finally, it was Bill's turn. "I like you guys. There's something about you, but I'm not sure..."

The pre-empted audience began to protest and chanted, "Yes, yes, yes."

Bill looked back at the audience and then at us. His tongue poked in his cheek. "I think with a little image styling and some expert advice you could have something. One thing though. Your name. I'm not into it. I'd prefer just The Paranormals. We can work with that. Get you looking like you're too fantastic to simply be human. I think we could have a little fun with that."

We had to converse with each other a little while the camera kept recording, as if we were deciding on the changes.

"What do you say? Ready for an image and name change?"

We said yes.

"Then that's four yeses. You're through to the next round. Congratulations, guys," Bill said.

The crowd roared their approval as directed and then we left the stage. Harley and Dan met us again backstage and once more they filmed our 'reaction' to being put through.

We were directed away from the presenters by another Clipboard guy who told us we could leave and that someone would be in touch. I was about to ask if anyone fancied a beer when I realised Stacey was waiting to go on stage with her band. I ran my eyes over them all. Seven altogether and all so very different. They didn't look like a band, but then again, neither did we after make-up and wardrobe had finished with us. Stacey was wearing her hair down and had barely any make-up on. She looked so like the Stacey of my past that for a moment it hurt.

Whose fault's that? I berated myself.

As if she could feel my eyes on her, Stacey looked over and met my gaze.

Her eyes widened as she took in what they'd made me look like, and I knew she'd had the same thoughts I'd had because she let her guard down and clear as day I heard, 'Fuck, it's Noah. God, he looks like he used to, but older'.

Quick as a flash she blocked me out, flashed a look of fury at me, turned on her low heels and walked out onto the stage.

"Was that Stacey?" Rex elbowed me.

"Yup. She's in the competition too."

"Did you hear that guys?" He got the other two's attention. "Shit just got more interesting."

"I'll catch you guys later," I told them as I began to walk away. "I'm going to check out the competition."

"I'm going to check out Harley," Zak added.

I walked around to where the audience was, but I stayed in the wings where the crew would let us stand to watch as long as we were quiet. Carmela asked Stacey about the band.

"We're called the Seven Sisters. We're not related but we are such close friends that that's how we feel," she explained. "We got together after a difficult time in my life, and I'd do anything for them."

"Okay, if you'd like to sing."

Stacey addressed the judges. "This is a song I wrote myself. It's called Regrets."

Carmela nodded. "When you're ready."

The song began calm and steady and like a ballad.

Once upon a time there was you and me.
Never thought back then there would ever be
A life without you...

The audience were quiet and although they'd been directed to be so, I knew that Stacey's soulful voice would have had them enraptured anyway.

Once upon a time there was them and us
Never thought back then there would ever come
A time without you...

Her voice picked up on the *you* and it made the hairs on my back stand on end. Her voice was incredible and had only grown better with age.

> *But you took yourself away*
> *Never gave me a say*

Then she went into a rock style and her voice picked up and growled out the next two lines.

> *Didn't give a damn, when my life broke down*
> *Just ran around all over town.*

I knew this song was about me. And she had me in her thrall. I could do nothing but stand there and listen to every word as the lyrics imprinted in my mind and my non-beating heart.

> *I hope you miss me every day.*
> *I hope you want for me to say*
> *That I forgive you...*

> *But my love for you went away.*
> *Tired of the game you played,*
> *I could resist you...*

> *You left me, not the other way around*
> *I hope you enjoyed the new life you found.*

> *Regrets*
> *Oh yeah*
> *Re-grettttttts*

> *Secrets*
> *Oh yeah*
> *Secrettttsss*

> *Our time is done*
> *Now I've moved on*
> *I'm here... ready to sing a different song.*

It then went into a rousing guitar solo before Stacey picked the chorus back up again.

> *Regrets*
> *Oh yeah*
> *Re-grettttttts*

> *Secrets*
> *Oh yeah*
> *Secrettttsss*

No time for the past to show up now.
I've shown I can survive without.
Regrets.

The other band members had played instruments and provided backing vocals, but my eyes were nowhere but on Stacey, whose eyes went straight to me as she sang the last word straight at me. She knew I was there.

Of course she did.

Where else would I have been?

The audience and the judges were on their feet, and this was not scripted. She was just that good. *They* were that good, but especially my ex. And I realised that once more I was in a position where my ambitions for my band were on a collision course with Stacey's life.

Phenomenal.

That was the word every single judge stated, and they were right.

I disappeared into the corridors of the auditorium lost in thoughts of times past.

Chapter 8

Stacey

I'd dreamed of singing that song to Noah so many times and the moment had finally arrived. I hoped every word had hit him like a shard of glass, but I doubted it would actually do anything at all. He'd left me without a second glance, and I needed to remember that. I had to keep putting one foot in front of the other until the blisters he'd left me with were gone and I could move on without pain. I'd dated since him, but there'd been no one who'd come anywhere close to my first love and I hated him for it. Hated that for some reason my mind wouldn't completely let him go. Hopefully this competition would bring me closure and then I could get on with my life, being 'fingers crossed' the winner of a million-pound recording contract. Even if not, at least I could have a chance of moving on, with the past finally buried and a peace of mind I'd been seeking for the last eight years.

And maybe things were already changing, because at the first round of auditions I'd bumped into the lead singer of another rock band, and I'd noticed he'd also hung around to watch us perform our audition.

After we'd finished filming and we were making our way towards the dressing rooms, Drayton walked towards me, his eyes running up and down my body. But then they also ran up and down several of the other women at my side's bodies too. Huh. Didn't look like he was ideal future-husband material, but he might do for right now.

He handed me a towel so I could dry myself off, given that the heat from the lights was fierce and made you sweaty, and then he took the towel and passed me a glass of water.

"Thanks. You trying to impress me or something?"

"I know how hot it is on stage," he said. "But now you mention it, you looked hot out there in another way entirely. I'd be rooting for you to win if I didn't want my own band to do so."

"You're honest. I'll give you that." I laughed.

"Do you like me enough that I could take you out to dinner, right now?" He put his hands in front of him like he was praying. "I'll totally get on my knees if you don't say yes."

I laughed again. "Why not? Woman's got to eat, right?"

"Yeeasss." He punched the air. "And you never know, maybe later a man's gotta eat too." He winked.

Drayton Beyer's band was called Flame-Grilled Steak, an apt name for the five beefy men of the band. They were all muscle and long-hair and if he'd told me they were bikers, I wouldn't have been surprised.

We swapped numbers and I arranged to meet him later that evening. Then I went into the dressing room and got showered, ready to head home.

※

"We need to talk," a cold but still enchanting voice sounded out as Noah stepped out from an alcove.

"I'm on my way home, Noah, and I need to hurry as I have a date." I picked up my pace, trying to leave him behind me, but in mere seconds he was at my side.

"You can't ignore me forever. We clearly have things to discuss."

His hand caught my shoulder and I flinched at his cold touch.

"Sorry," he uttered.

"You're either telling me sorry about the fact you're so cold, or about the fact you had the audacity to touch me at all. But really, the word sorry has no effect on me when it comes to you."

"Bullshit, Stace. That song says otherwise. You clearly needed me to hear it, and now I have. I know you'll never forgive me, but I still think we need to talk. After what happened the last time we met, and I don't mean at the audition, we still have—"

"Stop!" I interrupted his blast of words. "Don't call me Stace. You lost the right to that years ago. And don't bring up three years ago because it's been a long time since then and that was what got you out of my system once and for all," I lied.

"But you're not out of *my* system."

"Okay, Noah." I decided to call his bluff because I couldn't take this a minute longer. "Withdraw from the competition. Your band can find another bass guitarist. Give it up... for me."

His jaw set taut, and I saw the fight leave him. "I can't do that to my bandmates. You know how it is. They're family. We've got so far. They'd be devastated."

"So why are you here then, standing in front of me saying I'm not out of your system? Do you think I'm going to say 'oh, no worries about dumping me, it's all water under the bridge'? Or is this just to let me know once more that you think I'm not good enough? That you choose your new life. *Again*." I narrowed my eyes at him.

"Why do I have to choose? You have your band. I have mine. We can find a way."

I needed this man away from me before I broke the Good Witch Code and fried his balls with a spell. "Leave me alone, Noah. For good. I'm moving on and I've met someone else. I suggest you do the same. There are plenty of other females around the place."

"I don't want them," he said, and fuck me, if he didn't pout too, but I couldn't deal with another word from him.

"You can't have me," I said. "Regrets, remember? What a bastard they are."

I ran ahead of him, through the doorway and when I stopped and turned around, he'd gone.

I was surprised to find myself actually looking forward to my date with Dray. Though I hung around with the coven, I lived alone in a small studio flat in Bayswater. It was nothing fancy, but it was mine. I liked my own company most of the time, and playing pubs and clubs provided a modest and irregular income, so I needed small and cheap.

Noah waiting for me like that had put me in a bad mood, so when I'd got home I'd lit a Sandalwood joss stick that reminded me of a calmer, peaceful state, and breathed calmly and deeply until I felt like myself again.

After grabbing a quick shower, I dressed in black skinny jeans and a fitted red t-shirt and put my black hair up in a high ponytail. A quick spray of *Si* perfume and I was out of the door and on my way back to the bar and grill where Dray had suggested we eat.

Dray was waiting outside the entrance when I got there, leaning back against the wall, the sole of one foot up against it, looking like he was oozing testosterone where he stood. I saw one woman nudge another and nod her head in his direction as they went inside. Dray noticed too and gave them both a head tilt and a dazzling smile.

He was such a lead singer. Born to command an audience.

Whereas me? I'd found myself centre stage reluctantly. Put there by the others due to my voice. However, once I began singing, the audience and everything else just fell away and it was me and my music. It bewitched me, held me in its thrall.

When I sang, it felt like home, like everything was as it should be.

And I craved that feeling, mainly due to the fact that I rarely felt settled anywhere else.

"You look good enough to eat." Dray pushed off the wall and swaggered towards me. He was wearing dark blue jeans and a faded grey concert t-shirt of a Thunder gig from the nineties. It stretched across his wide shoulders. The guy was built.

"I'm hungry myself." I looked him up and down slowly. "But it's a burger I want."

"I can supply the buns," he said, turning around and twerking.

He made me laugh and I liked it. Didn't hurt that he looked good too.

I was surprised when he did the gentlemanly thing and held the door open for me. Then he spoke to the waitress who greeted us, and we were escorted to a table. I asked for a whisky sour and when they said it was two-for-one, I decided why not? Dray ordered a beer, and we checked out the menu. Or rather I checked out the menu and Dray checked out my tits over the top of his menu. His legs were thick and huge and as he was so tall, they rested against my own under the table.

"So tell me a little about yourself," Dray said. "I'm guessing witch or Fae, but I'll put my money on witch."

My mouth dropped open. "W-what?"

He leaned closer. "I'm a bear shifter myself."

It wasn't often I was lost for words, truly, but I found myself stuttering. "Y-you're a shifter, and y-you know I'm a w-witch?"

He tilted his head back and forth. "As I said, I was between the two, but you look more witch. The Fae seem to prefer their bright shades of hair."

"So I'm not only a witch, I'm a stereotypical witch?" I'd gathered myself now, back to my usual sarcastic self.

Dray pointed to himself. "I'm built like a linebacker, with long-brown hair, if we're going for stereotypical."

"How did you know?"

"I have a heightened sense of smell. It's genetically there for seeking out prey, but it doubles as a species sorter."

At that comment I snorted whisky sour out of my nose.

"Species sorter?"

"I can also smell arousal. My nose is telling me I need to work much harder," he drawled quietly and huskily.

I'd just taken another mouthful of my drink and this time I choked a little. I did not want to think about creaming my knickers and him being able to tell. No way.

"Could you just give me a moment?" I said, excusing myself to the bathroom.

It was the first time my pussy had been subject to a spell, other than a dry one.

Suitably reassured that I'd blocked off any chance of Dray smelling me, other than if I let him later, I took my seat.

He sniffed the air. "Cheat."

The evening passed quickly with plenty of pleasant banter between us. I did like him, but there was no way he was coming back to my place or I to his.

"So, can I see you again?" he asked as I stood next to a waiting taxi, Dray having opened one of the rear doors for me.

"Maybe." I smiled.

Leaning forward, he pressed his lips to mine. They were coarse, but warm. I let him kiss me and I kissed him back. He tasted of beer and Panna Cota. It felt nice, but that was all. Just nice.

God, if he could have read my mind, I was sure he'd have

picked me up and crushed me against the nearest wall to make sure I changed mine. I broke off the kiss.

"You have my number. Use it," he growled.

And I did.

We had a few dates, and they were as enjoyable as this one had been, but I didn't let things go beyond kissing and a quick feel of my boobs. I did grab his arse—his buns were worth a squeeze—but I knew I was holding back, and goddamn it, I also knew why.

My ex.

Chapter 9

Noah

I shouldn't have waited for her. It was a mistake.

She'd quite rightly challenged me and what could I offer her?

Nothing. A big fat zero.

I couldn't get her out of my system and that was my problem, because after getting this far, I wasn't going to leave my friends behind. This was the dream I'd sold to them when I'd been turned, and we'd first got together.

I owed them.

I'd already abandoned one person who now clearly despised me. No sense in adding another three people to the mix.

Stacey Williams wasn't mine.

But my brain wasn't getting the message. Neither was my little brain, because it remembered a random night three years ago... when just for a moment, I'd thought everything might work out. I should have known it wouldn't be that easy.

Three years earlier.

"There's been a change to tonight's line up," Zak said, as we prepared to go on stage at The Limelight, a club in North London.

"So?" Roman shrugged his shoulders. "Nothing new there. As long as it doesn't affect us."

"It's a band called Seven Sisters. They're following us on. The thing is, I just saw the lead singer..." his voice trailed off as he looked at me. "It's Stacey."

"Stacey? Noah's Stacey?" Rex clarified.

"She's hardly mine, is she?" I huffed. "We split up a long time ago, remember?"

We went out on stage and like usual I lost myself to the music, forgetting all about my ex. That was until she went on stage to do her own performance.

The girl I'd split from had been beautiful back then, but she was now all woman. Her brown hair was now a deep purple and rested over plump breasts encased in a leather bodice. Leather hot pants hugged her arse, and fishnets failed to cover shapely thighs and calves. She was spellbinding. The voice I knew had matured and learned its craft and Stacey sang like a powerhouse, the audience erupting in applause when the band finished.

I couldn't keep my eyes off her and as hers finally found mine as she left the stage, what felt like electricity shot through my body at our connection. But then I realised it wasn't electricity. It was magic. As she came nearer to me, I could smell it on her skin, could smell it on the other band members. They smelled like rose petals with an underlying hint of sage. However, as she finally approached me and stood right in front of where I was, her hand on her cocked hip, the intoxicating aroma of adrenaline danced in front of my nose, along with the sweet scent of her blood.

I picked her up and threw her over my shoulder and walked out of the club.

She beat at my back and then when that didn't work, she made an illusion of stakes all pointing towards my heart.

"Nice try, but the only wood around here right now is tenting my trousers."

I did however place her down on the ground and I turned to look at her, my arms folding over my chest.

"We can talk now. Or I can fuck you now and we can talk afterwards."

"Afterwards," *she said, and we made our way into the nearest hotel.*

"I'm going to use you for sex and then this time I'm leaving you," *she told me, stripping out of her clothes and revealing that hot body in all its glory.*

"If it'll make you feel better, then be my guest." *I shrugged off my own clothes, picked her up and threw her on the bed.*

"How did I not realise you were a vampire?" *she said.*

"Because you weren't a witch then. You were human. In order to protect you, I had to keep away from you." *I let my fangs descend and I bit her nipple. Then I sunk myself inside her.*

She arched under me.

I moved my head under her ear and trailed kisses down her neck, smelling the blood that sang to me. "When did you become a witch?"

"After you."

"Ouch."

"Don't flatter yourself. I meant I found my calling and a new set of friends. Not that you drove me to look for how to turn you into a frog."

I stared at her and arched a brow. "You telling me it never crossed your mind?"

"Well, maybe every time I saw you with that other woman."

I thrust inside her again. "What other woman?"

Stacey stopped me from moving and stared at me. "The woman I first saw you with in the doorway. You seemed very close. I kept seeing you together."

Smiling, I shook my head. "Mya is my sire. She made me a vampire. Nothing more. I've only ever kissed the neck of one woman." *I licked up hers, feeling her skin goose bump beneath me.* "Though I've bitten many to feed."

"What does it feel like?" Stacey gasped, and so I showed her.

I pushed deep inside her and then I bit down on her neck. I thrust and sucked, thrust and sucked until she came hard, her pussy clamping around my cock and making me spill inside her. I licked the bite wounds, closing them and moved to her side.

"That was..." she said, and I waited for her to finish. To tell me how good we were together. Maybe this was our fresh start now we were talking about the past.

"Okay," she added, pushing off the bed and gathering up her clothes.

"Okay? What do you mean okay?" I scrabbled to get off the bed, trying to work out what she was doing.

She pulled a bored face. "I meant it was adequate. I got off and the bite was a nice touch. I'll just go freshen up now, excuse me."

I watched, my jaw dropping as she sauntered away from the best defining moment of my life.

After she'd been in there a few minutes, my ego decided that this wasn't how we were leaving things. I'd have to continue fucking her until she admitted it was perfection. But when I walked into the bathroom she wasn't there. There was just a hint of the scent of rose and sage and a message on the mirror written in bright red lipstick.

Fangs for the memory.

Even now, the memory came back to me like it happened just yesterday. That was the thing about being a vampire. Time had a different meaning. Stacey had left and at first, I'd considered finding her and begging for her forgiveness. Then I'd decided I deserved it all, and that if she'd really wanted me back she'd have said so. The woman was not shy. Plus, I had other thoughts and feelings of why it was better to just leave it be.

A day later a talent scout had approached us with a promise of a recording contract which we came so close to signing, until a recession hit and we were dropped like a 100% mortgage offer. The interest had been enough for me to distract myself from Stacey. That was the excuse I gave myself anyway.

Deciding we just weren't meant to be.

That she was better off without me.

Deserved someone who put her first, always.

So, I let her go.

Again.

Chapter 10

THE DAILY NEWS

SHOWBIZ EXCLUSIVE

<u>BACKSTAGE FEUD THREATENS BRITAIN'S BEST NEW BAND SHOW.</u>

25 August 2022

It looks like it's not just the bands who are wanting to take centre stage this year. Our showbiz insider tells us that Dan Trent, last year's solo presenter, is becoming increasingly frustrated at being pushed to one side while TV favourite Harley Davies gets more filming time as they record the heats for *Britain's Best New Band*.

It's a step into the spotlight for Harley, who rose to popularity as the only female presenter of *Ride On*, the show for motorcycle enthusiasts.

"He's livid," our source says. "He's being treated like a support act after being the main attraction."

Our source went on to add that it's hard not to warm to and admire Harley, 26. "Her smile is infectious. She's just so nice and has the most dazzling blue eyes. Everyone loves her. Dan is threatening to walk out if he's not given the largest share of the co-presenting time."

You heard it here first folks.

Will Dan survive through to the live finals?

Chapter 11

Stacey

The acts had been sent to six separate rooms to await the judge's verdicts. Four of the six rooms housed winning bands that would go on to the live finals. Two rooms full of acts would be sent home. The live finals started in a month's time. The show had already begun on TV, and audiences were catching up with the audition rounds.

My throat was dry. This was it. Either my usual life, or the live finals was my future. In one month's time, I could be singing live on television with my band and be one of twenty acts battling it out for a million-pound recording contract.

Whether we won or not, life could change from that first live show. There were plenty of finalists who'd gone on to amazing things, sometimes better than even the winning acts.

"Okay, everyone. The judges are going live," we were informed.

Me and the rest of the band members held each other's hands.

The judges were sitting in a room in front of a table with photos in front of them of the thirty acts who had got this far.

Bill was the first to talk.

"Okay, so my team is up first. We've been battling it out

behind the scenes deciding who would get which room. I'd like to congratulate this room who are now Team Bill." A countdown appeared on the screen moving from the numbers five down to one and then the camera focused on room one, the room containing The Paranormals. I watched as the room erupted into screams and shouts of delight and I saw the four guys hug each other.

Noah was through to the live finals.

Marianne picked her room next as room five cheered and whooped. Donna squeezed my hand as the first room to be sent home was about to be announced.

"We'll be okay," she said.

And we were that time, as room two became a scene of devastation as dreams were crushed.

Maxwell was next and he choose room six.

There were just two rooms left and one of those rooms was the winning one. I felt sick inside as the time passed, and they dragged out the announcement of the winning room.

Room three.

We were in room four. Three of my coven sisters burst into loud sobs as they realised our dream was over. There was just an awful silence in the room, other than weeping. The emptiness of misery and shock.

We weren't through.

It was over.

We had to go home.

The cameras who had been showing room three's joy suddenly panned back and there we were on screen. Devastated entrants about to go home, dreams destroyed.

And then it panned back to the judges and Carmela was sat pouting.

"What's up with you?" Maxwell said.

"I'm not happy with one of my bands. There's another group I wanted, but someone," she side-eyed Bill, "put them in one of the losing rooms."

Ears perked up all around our room. Was there a chance for one of the losing bands after all? "I'm sorry, but I'm having six final bands and we can lose two at the first live round. I'm going to go get my other act."

She left the room and a discussion ensued between the other three judges and I realised then that this was part of the act, part of the hooks to entice viewers. It was all a ploy.

Carmela burst into our room. Cameras following her every move.

"I've come to claim my final act," she announced. "Seven Sisters, you're through to the live rounds."

A huge breath of relief whooshed through my body and then the next thing I knew I was fighting for my next breaths as my fellow band members squeezed and hugged me tight.

Carmela also hugged us all. As the cameras stopped filming, she turned to me and whispered into my ear. "Sorry about that, Stacey, but it made for great TV. If it's any consolation, your band is my absolute favourite and if we play this right, you can win."

Then she walked away as if she'd never said a word to me at all.

"What did Carmela say?" Kiki asked me.

"She said she was looking forward to working with us," I answered, because after what had just happened, I didn't want to give false hope. Not when we'd just got a little back.

We were about to leave when Dan Trent came storming out from a side room.

"Save it. Let me guess, you're screwing her? You're certainly giving me one up the arse. You can talk to my agent. This is not what I signed up for. My solicitors will be going through every line of my contract. I will not share the stage with Harley Davies any longer."

He stomped off, swearing under his breath.

But he was right. He wouldn't share the stage with Harley any longer.

Chapter 12

THE DAILY NEWS

FRONT PAGE EXCLUSIVE

DAN TRENT MISSING

26 September 2022

Speculation is mounting as to the whereabouts of *Britain's Best New Band* co-presenter Dan Trent who hasn't been seen since leaving the London Landmark Exhibition Centre after filming yesterday afternoon.

Rumours of an argument between Dan and TV execs were played down today as nothing more than a misunderstanding over recording agreements, with producer Everly Timms stating, "We hope Dan is safe and has just taken some time out for a couple of days. I urge him to get in touch with family or friends just so we know he's okay, and we'll welcome him back with open arms as soon as he feels ready."

There have been rising amounts of friction reported backstage since our first exclusive back in August. Rifts between Dan and co-presenter Harley Davies had seemingly turned increasingly bitter.

Harley was unavailable for comment, but her agent said her thoughts were with his family.

With the live shows due to start in a week's time, Cat Purr Productions, who own the show's format, said it was too early to comment on whether or not the first live show would go ahead.

THE DAILY NEWS

FRONT PAGE EXCLUSIVE

THE SHOW MUST GO ON

2 October 2022

Cat Purr Productions has taken the controversial step to go ahead with its live shows in the wake of presenter Dan Trent remaining missing.

Producer Everly Timms said she had spoken with his parents who firmly believed that by continuing with the series, it would help to keep the search for the presenter at the 'forefront of people's minds'.

The last known sighting of Mr Trent was of him walking down Sandbank Street towards an old abandoned industrial area, known largely for drug dealing and prostitution.

There is no suggestion Mr Trent was involved with either of these activities, and CCTV in the area was not working at the time.

Harley Davies will present the show solo.

Chapter 13

Noah

I was a mess. All the times I'd hassled my bandmates about reaching for the top and now I was rehearsing for the first live auditions while internally having an argument with myself about whether a vampire, who would never age, should pursue a witch, who would.

Finally, I was facing up to the truth I'd buried deep down for years.

I was in love with Stacey Williams. Always had been, always would be.

But forever was a long time in a vampire's world, and the other reason I'd let her go after our tryst three years ago...

Stacey would not be able to have children with me. Vamps were sired, rarely born. As I'd exploded within her warm depths without the need for protection, I'd rejoiced just at being inside of her at last.

But after she'd left and I'd laid in my empty bed, and I pondered pursuing her, I knew I could never give her everything she deserved.

A happy ever after with children and real love.

"Fuck me. He's off in a dreamworld again. *NOAH!* Get your arse in gear or fuck off and feed, because if Bill comes to check on us and sees you spacing out, he's going to turn you inside out from your arsehole," Zak yelled.

I may have formed the band, but once Zak got into rehearsals, his adrenaline gave him laser focus.

"I'm sorry. Okay, I'm in the room now. Tell me again what we're doing."

Bill had told us our first song to sing. I'd thought he'd be here to encourage us and give feedback, but instead he was home in the US. He would Skype us later in the week he'd said, and 'We'd better have nailed the song'.

We were doing a male version of *Toxic* by Britney Spears. Zak's drawled singing was sure to wet the panties of the entire adult audience.

The door to the rehearsal room pushed open and a fresh-faced Harley came in. It was strange to see her with no make-up on, her hair in a ponytail, and her dressed in a pale blue Nike tracksuit with white trainers. Her cheeks had a healthy pink glow. She was naturally pretty, and I saw Zak look at her like she was an ice lolly, and he was hot and thirsty.

"Hey, guys. I just thought I'd pop into rehearsals today and see how you were all doing. Is it okay if I sit and watch for a while?"

"Sure, as long as you don't put us off," Zak told her, moving clearly into his 'treat them mean to keep them keen' mode.

"I'll just watch and keep quiet, promise." She smiled. True to her word, she sat on a stool at the back, watched, listened, and her foot tapped with the beat.

When we finished, Harley clapped. "That's amazing. Keep up the good work," she said, and then she got up and walked towards the door.

Zak wasn't happy. He liked women falling at his feet and Harley was firmly on hers. "We're about to take a break. Can I get you a coffee?"

"No thanks," she said, "I don't drink caffeine, or hang with contestants. Would look like I was playing favourites, wouldn't it? Oh, also, the police are around. I'm not sure who they're going to speak with, but they're trying to see if anyone can shed any further light on Dan."

"Must be strange, him not being here," I probed.

"Yeah, very. Okay, I'd better get on." She waved and left the room.

"She didn't seem all that bothered over Dan, did she?" Rex looked over at the door Harley had just exited. "In fact, she was rather buoyant. I mean, whether she likes him or not, he's gone missing. You think she'd be scared over her own safety, and have extra security, wouldn't you?"

"I never thought of that." Roman walked to the side of Rex. "She was in a great mood. You reckon she had something to do with it?"

"Let's not rush to conclusions." I attempted to stop their imaginations running riot.

"Well, there's definitely something wrong with her." Zak pouted. "Because I asked her to have a drink with me and she said no. Something's fishy."

"What's fishy? The fact there are plenty in the sea, and you can't land this one?" Rex howled with laughter.

"We need to keep an eye on Harley Davies." Zak chewed on his bottom lip. "I'm telling you, something's not right."

When we left rehearsals, we called into the canteen for the guys to grab something to eat and drink. For me, it was a blonde called Mae. I returned from the staff bathroom with a pink tinge to my cheeks and a pleasant ache in my cock.

I felt wholly satisfied until Stacey walked into the canteen accompanied by the lead singer of a band called Flame-Grilled

Steak. She was looking at him and grinning, and he was looking at her like she was prime rib.

"Calm down, bloodsucker." Rex put a hand on my knee which was basically like fixing me in place with a boulder.

"Don't look at her, dickhead," Zak added. "She'll know she got to you."

I affected a nonchalant stance. "Stacey's my past. She can do whatever and whomever she likes."

"That why I'm holding your knee to stop you from ripping out his jugular?" Rex waggled his brows. "Look, pal. Just remember Drayton and his pack are bear shifters. You go for them and they're going to gang up and swat you off like an annoying midge."

"I wonder how long they've been a thing?" Roman pondered and we all snapped our heads to look at him. He took a drink from his coffee, which he'd topped up with some whisky he was carrying in his backpack.

"For God's sake, Goat-boy. We're trying to calm him down here." Zak glared at him.

"Sorry. But am I missing something? She's Noah's ex, right? He's moved on. He let her go, not once, but twice. I'm not understanding the problem with her walking in with Drayton. They look good together. I wish them every happiness and I also hope that their extra-curricular performances affect their live ones, so that we can take advantage. I wonder if swallowing affects a vocal?"

"We'll find out soon if you don't fucking shut up because I'll put my own dick down your throat to quieten you down," Zak threatened.

That shut Roman up. In fact, he started to look quite sick.

"Not without six billion washes of disinfectant and several rounds of antibiotics, stinkubus."

Rex's other hand shot out and now rested on Zak's knee to stop him from launching at Roman.

And that was when Drayton decided to look over at us,

taking in the four of us seated at a table, Rex's hands on mine and Zak's knees.

"Oooh, I didn't realise you lot had a kinky threeway going," Dray's voice boomed out so the entire cafeteria could hear.

Stacey left him looking over at us and walked towards the counter.

"Gotta go, the missus is hungry." He pointed after Stacey. "We worked up quite an appetite this morning." He winked.

"Gah," I shouted out at Rex. "You should not be able to hold me down. I'm a newly fed vampire."

"Come on, Noah. Do you think I've not worked out your weakness after all this time?"

"I don't know what you're talking about," I huffed.

Rex let go of my knee. "If I mention Stacey the fight goes out of you, dude. Might as well change her name to Stakey."

I scowled.

"If you want her, then why not fight for her?" he asked me quietly, which for Rex was a feat in itself.

"Because it's not that simple."

"Is love ever simple? I'm supposed to choose a wolf shifter from my pack. That's why I stay single. You seen what I have to choose from? Most men have a preference over bare or Brazilian; my lot are hairy everywhere."

That broke my pity party as I sniggered. "Fuck, Rex. I need to bleach my mind."

"You're welcome. Now, please tell me we can go to the club tonight because I need to party."

"We can go to the club tonight." I high fived him.

"Great, just what I need, to see the boss tonight," Zak groaned.

"I'll have a word on your behalf. See if we can get this month's quota cut seeing as we need you energetic for the live rounds. If I explain about the amount of pussy that'll be available if we win, surely he'll consider a reprieve," I said.

"You think a demon is going to have some sympathy for the

person whose soul he took?" Zak shook his head in disbelief. "How you've managed to survive since your turning is nothing short of a miracle."

While the others finished their food and drinks, I couldn't help but keep glancing over at Stacey. The other band members had joined them, and tables had been dragged together. It was a noisy gathering, but the sounds of laughter coming from there gave me a pang that hurt more than a bloodthirst.

"Leave him," I vaguely heard a voice say. "I don't mind him spacing here, but we need to discuss what we're going to do with him long-term."

I soon came to when Stacey's gaze met mine and narrowed on me. She turned to Dray and ran her hand through his hair. He turned to her, smiled, and nuzzled her neck. Closing my eyes, I wished for something, anything, to break them apart.

"Bloody hell, what's happening over there?" Roman gasped.

My eyes opened and I watched as two police officers walked towards Stacey.

"What on earth for?" I heard her snap at them, and then with a deep sigh, she got to her feet and followed them out of the room.

"What do you reckon that's all about?" I asked the others.

"Harley said the police were here to investigate Dan's disappearance, so my guess would be that it's about Dan's disappearance," Roman said, grimacing.

"No way Stacey had anything to do with that." I stood up. "I'm going to help."

Rex stood up next to me. I felt my jaw tense.

"Are you going to tell me it's not my business? Because if you are, we're going to have a problem."

"Nope," Rex said. "I'm here to offer my assistance. Let's follow and see if we can do anything to help." He turned to the others. "You two stay here."

We made our way outside of the canteen and began following Stacey and the policemen from a distance. I had superior hearing being a vampire and although I wasn't able to hear things from miles around, I could hear through a wall. So once Stacey had been led inside a room, I positioned myself outside and began to eavesdrop.

Stacey's bandmates had also made their way outside, but a show runner had told them that they needed to head to rehearsals as the room was booked for that hour and that Stacey could join them if she got out on time. Once more, I could thank my hearing for that.

I listened as the police told Stacey that it was only a few quick questions they wanted to ask her, that she was free to leave at any time, and could have someone with her if she wanted.

"I don't need anyone with me because I haven't done anything," I heard her say spikily. Good to see she wasn't being any less Stacey just because she was sitting with police officers.

"Could you tell us about any dealings you've had with Dan Trent," one officer asked.

"All I've seen of Dan is when they have filmed us chatting with him for the show. I don't know him at all."

"You're absolutely sure about that? You've never seen him outside of the show?"

"Most certainly not."

"Okay. Miss Williams. Part of our investigation is to look into the backgrounds of anyone connected however loosely to the missing person. Do you recall the name Jack Brooks?"

"What's that got to do with anything?" I heard her ask; her voice slightly raised.

"Well, Mr Brooks went missing shortly after spending the evening with you, didn't he?"

"That's right, and I had no part in his disappearance."

"And now another gentleman has gone missing, and once more you're around. You can see why we're asking questions can't you, Miss Williams?"

"I can see you're adding up two and two and making four hundred and twenty-six. Do I need a solicitor?"

"No. That's all for now. Thank you for talking to us. Enjoy the rest of your day," one of the male voices said.

Rex had stood there patiently while I'd listened. "She's coming out," I warned him.

As she opened the door, she huffed a large sigh as she spotted me. "Not now, Noah, please." She stalked past me. But I was hot on her heels.

"Stacey, what happened with Jack Brooks? I know he went missing, but what do they mean that you'd spent the evening with him?"

She stopped and turned around to face me. "Oh, Noah. They say eavesdroppers never hear good things about themselves, or in your case things they'd rather not hear. I was the last person to see Jack Brooks before he went missing."

"He went missing after a party, right, so you were there?" I clarified.

"Oh I'd been there, at the party... and in a bedroom with him."

I felt my eyes flash red as I lost it for a brief moment.

"I gave my virginity to Jack Brooks, Noah. Not that it's any of your business," she spat out, and then she stomped off.

Chapter 14

Stacey

Oh God. If things couldn't get any worse right now, the police were suspecting me of bumping off one of the presenters. Plus, my ex was trailing me because I'd just told him something I knew would drive him crazy.

"You slept with Jack Brooks? How could you?"

Oh, that was completely the wrong thing to say to me, and as I whizzed back around, I think Noah realised that.

"How could I? What the actual fuck does it have to do with you who I've slept with? Who I gave my virginity to?" I snarled. It was a good job I wasn't a vampire because his jugular would have been out and on the floor.

"He was the main bully of me through school. You know that." Noah had the audacity to look hurt.

I shook my head in disbelief. "You're still not getting this are you? You hurt me far more than Jack Brooks ever hurt you. And maybe I did sleep with him to get back at you in some way. I was a sixteen-year-old teenager and made teenage mistakes, but ultimately, it's not your business."

"How come you can make a 'teenage mistake', but I can't?" he snarked back.

"Because you're dragging your mistake through adulthood. You put me second and you're still not willing to put me first."

"I could quit after we win. Just get the band on the map and then leave. They'd find another bass guitarist."

"*HAVE YOU HEARD YOURSELF?*" I stood in the foyer apoplectic. "After you win? You're so fucking sure of yourself. There are another nineteen bands in this competition. And you're telling me that if you do win, you're going to drop the band? I'm not buying it. It would be, 'I'll just do this one tour'," I said it in a simpering, whiny voice. "Anyway, I'm going to do my damn best to make sure my band win this competition and that you're left with nothing but regrets, Noah Granger. No contract, no future in music, and certainly no Stacey Williams in your life."

The next thing I knew I was crushed against the wall and if the shock didn't mean I was overpowered, the fact Noah was a vampire certainly did. His body was up close and personal, and his mouth was crushing on mine.

And damn my fucking body because it completely betrayed my mind as it quivered under his touch. I couldn't help it. My body remembered how it had felt that night three years ago and it wanted more. My mouth opened and his tongue snuck inside tangling with my own, until finally, as I felt his hard length against my stomach, my brain caught up.

"Aaargh," Noah reacted as my knee came up. He clutched at his privates. Then I slapped him across the face for good measure.

And, of course, the two police officers chose that moment to come out of the room they'd interviewed me in. They walked past us both, and as they did, one of them said. "Don't leave London, Miss Williams, will you?"

"Kicking someone in the balls does not mean you're responsible for the disappearance of a well-known TV presenter," I yelled, as by this time I'd had enough of everyone.

The police officers didn't even turn around at my outburst. They just carried on out of the building.

"Is everything okay?" Harley made her way towards us.

"Not really," I said honestly, as Noah told her everything was fine.

"Come with me to my private dressing room. You can take a break there away from everyone before you go home or whatever. You can talk or not. It's up to you," she offered, along with a sympathetic smile.

Thank the lord. I needed away from all the people here, away from the police, and away from Noah. Harley was offering me sanctuary and I was taking it because as soon as I got back to the rest of my own band there would be six women asking me a barrage of questions and giving me a headache.

Harley's dressing room was down a private corridor at the back of the auditorium. There was a comfy red velvet sofa; a large dressing table and mirror, with a red velvet stool in front of it; and a rail full of clothes at the far end. There was also a fridge and a trolley full of goodies, plus glasses, mugs, etc. As I walked inside, it smelled of Harley's signature perfume, like sherbet.

"I love it in here. I'd never want to leave," I told her, sinking into the luxurious softness of the red sofa and thinking that when I had enough money saved, I needed one for my apartment. Oh, who was I kidding? It would probably cost two months' rent.

"Believe me, luxury only seems luxurious when you're not used to it," Harley said, and I noted the sadness in her tone. "I've always wanted to be famous, yet now things finally seem to be coming together for me, I'm lonelier than ever. Plus, now I'm being suspected of being behind my co-presenter's disappearance because they think I'd do that to get this gig on my own." She sighed and dropped onto the seat in front of her dressing table.

"They think you're responsible for Dan's disappearance?"

She shrugged her shoulders. "They didn't accuse me outright, but the underlying tone was that because it was known we didn't get along and that Dan seemed jealous of me, I might have motive." She stood up and opened a bottle of white wine. "Want one?"

"Why not?"

She handed me the glass and sat back down. "So I heard what they said to you about you not leaving London. What was that all about?"

I debated telling Harley for a moment, because what if she had bumped Dan off and then tried to frame me?

You're being utterly ridiculous, I told myself.

"When I was sixteen, the boy I slept with went missing. The police have found this out and so because of that and the fact I'm yet again in the vicinity of someone who's gone missing, I seem to be a person of interest."

"That's ridiculous. You live in London where tons of people go missing. Have you been responsible for all of them?" She took a sip of her wine. "Dan's a twat and he's probably sitting in five-star luxury accommodation somewhere, with a spy camera on me, laughing his head off, and planning his return for the quarter-finals where he'll get all the attention. That's how he is."

I giggled.

"Is it bad I just said that when he could have actually been hurt?" she asked me.

"No. We don't have to like people, do we? I'd find it a lot more insincere if you were doing some dramatic 'oh where is my co-presenter' fawning to the reporters."

"Don't get me wrong, I hope he is okay. I'm not that mean. But he's been super horrible to me and continually trying to get me fired, so I'm not going to pretend I'm devastated."

"Good for you." I took a large glug of my wine. I wasn't a huge wine drinker, but this was nice. Fruity and smooth. I could see it going down well.

"So, tell me about you and Noah Granger."

My mouth parted in an 'O'.

"I saw him plant one on you and at first it didn't look like you were too disappointed. Then you nailed him in the nuts."

"He's my ex."

Her eyes widened at the potential gossip there. "Ooooohhh."

"From school. I dated him from being fifteen to sixteen. He was a year older. Then he dumped me for his band. The one he's entered the competition with."

"Oh boy. This just got interesting. And do you still like him?"

"Truthfully? I can't deny there's still something between us. But it's not happening. I'm going to do my utmost to win this competition: for my band, my future, and for the sheer satisfaction of hurting Noah Granger as much as he hurt me."

"Oh?"

"No contract, no Stacey. Just a heap of regret. That's what Noah's future needs."

"Harsh."

"It's no less than he deserves."

"Only you know the answer to that, but it'll certainly give me something to stop the boredom setting in. I can watch the real competition now. Noah versus Stacey."

"Glad I can be of entertainment," I said sarcastically. "Anyway, what about you? Got your eye on any of the talent here?"

"Huh. I can't go there. For one thing I'd be accused of giving someone a helping hand, and how do I know if they're trying to score with me to get further on in the competition? So, I'll just have to stay my single self for now."

"I never thought of that. That sucks."

"Hey, I'm the career woman remember? Determined to get to the top, even making my co-presenter disappear. If you want a new friend, I'm available. Because you're a suspect too, so we have a lot in common." She sniggered.

I held out my glass towards hers in a toast. "To new friendships and to sisters doing it for themselves."

She clinked her glass against mine. "So now tell me about Dray because I've seen him hanging around you like a dog on heat."

I sighed. "I like Dray. We've been dating. I've kept it all

second base and fun though because he flirts with other women. The guy is clearly not a one-woman man, and while I'm not averse to a bit of fun, I'm concentrating on the competition from a musical rival standpoint, not a romantic one."

It was true. I had zero interest in climbing between the sheets with anyone right now. I wondered if Noah was the same.

Stop thinking about Noah.

"If you could date anyone from one of the bands, who would you go for? I promise not to tell. Only I feel you know far more about me than I do you," I asked her.

"That's because I'm so boring." Harley laughed. "Actually, I quite like one of Noah's friends."

"Oooh, who? Let me guess. Zak. Everyone gets the hots for Zak."

She turned her face up. "Not me. He's too much. One minute he's being rude to me, one minute nice. Far too high maintenance. I like a quiet man. I think Roman's really cute."

"Roman, huh?"

She raised a brow at me. "Don't you dare try any matchmaking shit. I can't date them. Not as presenter of the show. I'm serious."

I held up my hand. "I swear I won't do anything..." I trailed off. "...while the show's happening, but after... well, I can't promise."

She laughed.

"Oh." I thought out loud. "If you can't be seen to be hanging around with contestants, doesn't that mean people could say I was trying to get a helping hand?"

Harley's smile dropped clean off her face.

"Oh fuck. I never thought of that." A deep sadness hit her features. "Thanks for the gossip and the drink. Maybe we can be friends after the show finishes?"

"I'd like that," I told her honestly. I passed her a card with my phone number on it. "If you need a friend, call me, okay? Fuck the media."

"Stacey?"

"Yes?"

"Think carefully about the competition. It's going to lead to fame and with that comes a price. There's more to life than an amazing dressing room."

"Are you considering quitting?"

"No. I'm not cut out for a boring, ordinary life. One day, hopefully, I can find some happy medium between fame and a family, but for now I'm pushing through until I'm the household name I always wanted to be."

"A happy medium. That sounds good." I left her dressing room, feeling sad that we couldn't hang together because I liked Harley. What I didn't know was I was going from *talking* about a happy medium to meeting one.

The rest of the coven sisters had left by the time I finally exited the building, and there was also no sign of Noah, or Dray.

Good. I fancied a hot bath and an early night.

I soon saw that wasn't going to be happening though when I found Donna at my door.

"Finally. I've been messaging you. I was worried. Where have you been all this time?" She did look worried as well, bless her. She was rubbing her face and clasping her hands.

I took my phone out of my bag. Dead battery. "Oh shoot, my phone ran down. I'm so sorry. It's been one heck of a busy day."

"The last time I saw you the police had escorted you out of the canteen. I thought they'd flung you in a cell."

I laughed. "No, thank God. Anyway, I appreciate you looking out for me. Do you want a hot drink before you go?" It was a hint I needed time to myself, and I'd thought it was pretty clear.

"Yes, and then I want you to tell me everything that's happening. We're all worried about you."

Inwardly, I let out a heavy sigh. Outwardly, I smiled and

invited her in. Then while we enjoyed a coffee, I told her about the police and about Jack Brooks. I didn't tell her about Noah, or about Harley, as although we were all close, I was getting fed up of everyone knowing everything about me.

I was starting to crave space and alone time. Things were changing within me, and I wasn't sure how I felt about it. Harley's statement about if I was sure this was what I wanted was weighing deep, and possibly why I felt I needed a bath and some space. Time to think.

"As if you'd do anything to harm anyone. We need to know if we're around danger though, so I brought some things with me." Donna reached around for her backpack and opened it up. "We'll start with a protection spell and then I'm going to demonstrate my new talent, because I have a secret." She smiled coyly.

"Oh yeah?"

"I've been practicing mediumship," she told me matter-of-factly like she'd been learning Spanish.

"Pardon?"

"I've been practicing mediumship."

"Under whose guidance?"

Donna's voice and demeanour got haughty. "I borrowed two books from the library. I know about protecting myself."

"We know about spells and protecting ourselves from the harm of spells. Not from the harm of wayward spirits," I reminded her.

"That's why I got books from the library. They told me what to do. It's all fine. Stop panicking. I know I'm small, but I do sometimes get a little frustrated when you talk to me like I'm a baby. I'm a year older than you and brought you into this fold, remember?" She scowled.

Oh God. I'd really fucked her off and she'd just been concerned for me earlier.

"I'm sorry, Donna. It's just been a stressful day. I think it's great that you're trying to add another string to your bow as it were."

Her face relaxed. "Thanks. So I'll get everything prepared and then reach out. I was going to see if I could contact Dan Trent because then we'd know he was dead, but I can also try to contact Jack Brooks too. If they don't answer, we know they're alive and well."

*Or you can't contact the dead because you've tried to learn through **Mediumship for Dummies** or something similar,* I wanted to add, but didn't as otherwise I'd be the dead one.

It therefore transpired that rather than enjoying a hot bath, instead, I had to move my coffee table off my grey rug—the only decent thing I owned and that covered up a threadbare carpet—so she could lay out Scrabble letters in a Ouija style arrangement on top of an upside-down Monopoly Board. I daren't question her about any of it because I'd opened my mouth once to ask if we were going to have a 'yes, no, and a proceed to go', and she'd not found it as amusing as I had.

"Okay, everything we need is now here. As you can clearly see we don't have a glass out because we aren't having a séance. Through mediumship I will invite anyone to talk through me. The letters are laid out simply to let the spirits know that we are open to communication."

I needed a glass out and to commune with spirits, but vodka and whisky were my preferred options.

"Okay. Please sit with me and hold my hand. When I have said the spell, you can let go. We don't need to remain tethered in the real world as we will still be tethered in the astral realm. Time for a protection spell."

I was really unsure about this, but I'd known Donna a long time and she was a very competent witch, so against my better judgement I sat and held her hands.

"Goddess of darkness, Goddess of Light.
Trust in me with your blessed sight.
Protect both of us here tonight; have our back.

But let me be a conduit for Dan and Jack."

She let go of my hand and we waited. And then we waited some more. Five minutes passed and Donna began to look glum. "Huh, no one wants to talk to me."

"Erm, don't you like have to ask them or call to them?" I offered.

She slapped a hand across her mouth. "Of course, silly me. I forgot!"

Sitting cross-legged she closed her eyes and spoke. "Dan Trent from the television show Britain's Best New Band. Are you there?"

There was no reply, so she tried Jack.

"Jack Brooks, who slept with my friend, Stacey Williams. Are you there?"

Again, nothing happened, and I was truly tired and fed up now. I wanted my bath, and I wanted my friend to leave.

"Let's leave this, shall we?" I suggested.

Then Donna's eyes went jet black, and her head cocked towards mine.

"You like leaving, don't you, Stacey?" a weird, croaky voice came out of Donna's mouth and a small trail of blood slipped from her left nostril.

I scrabbled back a foot in shock.

"You left me last time and I came looking for you. It's your fault I'm dead, bitch." Newly possessed Donna looked around the apartment slowly, her skin a pale grey that showed veins underneath. "I thought you'd do better for yourself than this, Stace, but it's better than where I'm stuck. Where I'm stuck is complete garbage."

He leaped forward.

"You need to help me, Stacey." Donna pitched forward further but then jerked and her colour came back to normal.

Gasping for breath, she retched and threw up all over my prized rug. There was no way I was keeping it any longer anyway. It had that weird blood on it.

"I f-felt him, Stacey. He's passed. Jack was murdered." She shook. "He's gone now. He tried to touch you and it's not allowed, so he was cast out. Can I have a glass of water and then I'm going to go home. I need to go think about the picture I saw in my head. Where his body might be."

My voice rose in pitch. "I don't like any of this, Donna. I mean, what happened was some scary shit. You went a weird as fuck colour, your nose bled, and you talked strangely. Please don't do it again, will you?"

"I do feel a bit woozy. Maybe I'd be better off practicing piano. I was between the two."

Heading to the kitchen on now shaky legs, I returned with a glass of water for my friend. Her colour was fully returned, and she looked better than I reckoned I did. "Look. It's not going to hold up in court, is it? That you saw a vision. Why not just forget about it all?"

Donna's mouth twisted. "I will try to find the place Jack showed me he was dumped. I didn't get a clear picture, but it smelled vile. But if I can't bring the images forward then I'll just have to let it go. Hey, at least it looks like Dan Trent is still alive, because he didn't answer." She smiled.

"Great. Jack's dead, Dan's alive. All's sorted and now you can go home, because after all this I need a bath and a stiff—"

"Cock?" Donna asked.

"Drink," I corrected her.

"I don't understand you. Drayton would be round in a flash if you called him, but you'd rather have a brandy. Who ditches randy for brandy? You're not normal."

She eventually packed everything into her backpack and left.

Once she'd gone, I picked up my once beautiful rug and threw it down the rubbish chute, and then I went and got in the bath.

Had she really contacted Jack Brooks?

I mean, I suspected he was dead because I'd never seen him again.

Even though I'd seen spells performed and I knew of the supernatural, I was finding it hard to accept that Jack from school had spoken through Donna, but why not? And if so, then I'd actually missed the main question I wanted to ask him.

But if I got the chance again, would I *really* want to know whether Noah had been the one to end his existence?

Chapter 15

Dan

Stupid dozy bitch.

Dan had not been dead long. In fact, he was only just getting used to the idea that he'd been bled dry by more than just his agent. But he'd always been savvy. It was how he'd kept ahead of his rivals in the entertainment industry. Until that bitch. Harley fucking Davies, with her sweet smile and no doubt even sweeter pussy, had come along. He'd put money on the fact that she was getting her top position from getting in an on-top position.

While his unsettled spirit wandered around the auditorium where he'd once ruled, his body rotted somewhere that smelled indescribably bad. No one had heard his cries for help. Even if he had been audible, there were twenty bands practising for a start.

He'd heard his name be called, and suddenly, he was there in that small woman's body. He'd recognized the woman sat opposite him from the audition interviews because she had great breasts. Dan had had a hard time not reaching forward to feel one. You were a long time dead after all. But no, he knew that the woman who'd called him could just as easily cast him away, so he lingered to see what would happen. And what did happen? She called on someone else. There wasn't room for the two of them, I mean three's a crowd, right? So as soon as the other guy entered her, he got ejected. It was the first threesome where he was glad another guy got the girl. So now there he was, back where he'd been hanging around, at the auditorium, but now it seemed he could pop where he liked. And of course, he knew that his rightful place was presenting a top television series.

Dan Trent's spirit went looking for Harley.

He was going to take over the show in more ways than one.

Chapter 16

Noah

"Well, mate, I think it's good we're going to the club tonight, so you can talk to me about what the heck is going on with you and your ex, and why you just almost banged her in the corridor." Rex fixed me with a look that said, 'you will tell me all'.

"We're men. We don't talk feelings and shit. She kneed me in the balls and made it clear we're most definitely done. That and her being with Drayton. I had a lapse of sense because my blood had diverted south. There's nothing else to say." I stalked off ahead of him and left the building.

"I'll see you at the club at ten," Rex said. "You'd better be there."

"I'll be there. If for no other reason than to make sure Zak behaves himself. The last thing we need right now is our lead going off the rails."

With that I drove to my flat where I downed two bottles of O-neg to quench the thirst Stacey had set off inside me, and then I went in the shower and jerked off thinking of how she'd felt held tight against my body.

The warmth of the club was in stark contrast to the cool night air as I stepped inside *Sheol*. Walking towards the bar, I saw my bandmates were already there. Zak seemed antsy, hopping from foot to foot, and it wasn't in sync with the beat of the music playing.

"He's waiting for a meeting with Abaddon," Rex explained as I shrugged off my jacket and laid it across a bar stool. "And he wants someone to go with him. I've told him he's twenty-four and last time he showed us, had a fully working set of balls."

"I'll go with you," I told Zak.

He leapt up and hugged me. "Thanks, Noah. I knew I could count on you." He side-eyed Rex.

"And with that, I'm going to get another beer and then I'm going to go looking for some pussy, rather than spend my time with this pussy." Rex pointed at Zak.

A tall man dressed in a suit approached us. "Abaddon will see you now." The guy, who was called Aaron, had taken the whole *Men in Black* image a little too far, with his suit, tie, and shades, bearing in mind we were in a dark basement club in the centre of London. He'd knocked into two chairs on his way over.

"Thanks, Aaron." We set off walking behind him. "Now keep your cool, Zak, or you'll get nowhere. Let me handle it."

"I'm fine. I know how I'm going to play it. I just need you there because Abaddon tries to trick me all the time."

"He is a demon," I reminded him.

Getting in the lift, we went down six floors, coming out into a dimension hardly anyone in London knew existed beneath the ground: the seventh hierarchy where the demon Abaddon ruled. Zak had traded his soul as a randy eighteen-year-old virgin as well as agreeing to keep supplying Abaddon with a quota of other souls. In return, Zak had become an incubi. At eighteen he hadn't thought he'd get bored of unlimited sex.

At twenty-four while trying to become a rock god it was a whole different matter.

We followed Aaron into Abaddon's office where he sat behind his desk gesturing to the two seats in front of him. "I'd say it's good to see you, Zak, but given it's only the beginning of the month, I'm inclined to think there's a problem?"

In his actual form, Abaddon looked like a bright-red, ulcer-festooned slug. In front of us now, he was mistaken a lot for Brendon Urie.

"I have great news, Boss," Zak started. Inside, I groaned.

Abaddon—or Don as he called himself because his real name was a mouthful—sat back, crossing his arms over his chest, a bemused smirk curling the corner of his mouth.

"You do? Fabulous, let's hear it."

"We made the finals of Britain's Best New Band, and do you know what that means?" Zak ploughed on even though I could clearly see he was on a one-way trip to Loserville.

"I don't. Tell me." Don wiggled a brow.

"It means that every week we progress, more women are hanging around us. If we reach the final, there are going to be so many willing women whose souls I can plunder. So... I thought maybe you'd agree I need to concentrate on my music and then do a double whammy next month...?"

Don stared at Zak and time seemed to stand still. Then he threw his mug from his table which just missed the top of Zak's head before smashing into the wall behind with such force it created a hole. He'd deliberately missed and that was to show Zak how close to losing his own head he was.

"Nope. But it is fabulous news. You can get this month's quota as normal and then next month bring me more and I might let you have Christmas week off."

"I should get holiday entitlement anyway," Zak mumbled under his breath.

"I'm the leader of the seventh hierarchy. My name means The Destroyer," Don reminded Zak for what was no doubt the billionth time. "You will bring me part of the souls of satiated women as we agreed. You get your part of the bargain do you not?"

"Yes, Boss."

"Is there anything else?"

"No," Zak said sullenly.

It was my turn to try. "Zak's falling asleep all the time which means our chances of winning go down considerably, which means his chances of going down could also reduce considerably if you get my drift," I told Don. "He doesn't usually make much sense, but if he does have less to do now it would help the band. I think we have a pretty good chance of reaching the finals. We're 3:1 at the bookmakers right now and the press stuff is looking good."

Don tapped his fingers on his desk and his gaze went to the side for a moment, before returning to me. "I'll reduce his quota by half in October. In November I expect triple numbers, whether he's through to the final or not. Deal or no deal?" Don guffawed. "I always wanted to say that. Where's a red box when you need one?"

"There'll be plenty of red boxes if Zak has to satisfy triple the number of women in November," I quipped.

Don laughed again. "Oh, Noah, you are such fun, and of course I can't touch you seeing as you have no soul anyway, so you are as close to a friend as a demon can have. Great to touch base. Zak, cat got your tongue?" Don turned to me. "The pussy will have it soon, right?"

I laughed back.

Zak pouted. "Deal." He held out his hand. Don shook it and there was a loud bang and a sizzle, along with the smell of burned flesh, although when Zak removed his hand there was no damage or burn marks.

"Good luck with the contest. Tell the other two I said hi," Don said. Then he turned to Aaron, who'd been standing in the corner like a statue. "Well, go and bring my mug back, Aaron, or get me a new one if I broke it, and a fresh hot cup of tea. Do I have to remind you of your job?"

"No, Boss," Aaron said. "I'll show these two to the lift and then I'm on it."

"PG Tips. I can tell when you're pissed at me and try to sneak an own brand in. My poker has a very red-hot tip you know?" Don yelled at him, then he winked at me. "I don't get off on it sexually, but from a pain point of view, it's exquisite."

Yep, it was definitely time to leave, before Zak pissed his pants in fear.

On our way back up in the lift, Zak kept huffing and puffing.

"What the fuck is wrong with you? You just got your workload cut in half. Celebrate. Be happy."

"Why does he take no notice of me, but is all pally-pally with you?"

"He said why. I have no soul. He deals in them. I'm of no use to him so he may as well be friends with me. I'm sure if he found a way to screw me over, he would."

A voice came out from the top corner of the lift. "Yep, I would. Sorry, pal."

Zak jumped. "You have the lift bugged?" he spoke to the lift walls.

"I'm a demon. I have everything bugged. Zak, you really are going to have to wise up when it comes to demonology."

"Like I have time to study anything except the female body," Zak whined.

I gave him a dirty look. "It's not going to get you much sympathy, that line, mate."

"It sounds a lot better than it is. Trust me."

Having stepped out of the lift, we re-joined our bandmates. Rex was back and I caught him licking the back of his hand.

"Stop preening."

"I'm happy. I just got some in the ladies bathroom."

Roman, as usual, was drunk as a skunk. Two women came up to him and whispered in his ear. "I'm off to dance," he told us, before heading towards the floor, an arm through each female's folded one.

"Let's go dance too," Zak yelled over the music. "Because tonight I don't have to satisfy a woman and take her soul. I'm having the night off."

"You do realise we have the first live round tomorrow, don't you?" I pointed out. Sometimes I felt like their father.

"It's eleven o'clock. I promise to be in bed by midnight." Zak crossed his heart. "And for once I can categorically state it will be my own. I can't wait. Proper rest. A full night's sleep." He stood still for a moment thinking.

"Night guys," he said and with that he left.

I shook my head at Rex. "Let's get another drink, keep an eye on Roman, and make sure we're out of here by twelve. Tomorrow's a big day."

"Agreed. I'm off to get a pint. You having one?"

I shook my head, looking at one of the women Roman was dancing with. "Not a pint, more a quick shot."

Chapter 17

THE DAILY NEWS

FRONT PAGE EXCLUSIVE

THE H-EX FACTOR

3 October 2022

As tonight's first live rounds get under way, we can reveal that The Paranormal's bass guitarist, Noah Granger, was the childhood sweetheart of Seven Sister's Stacey Williams.

A source close to them said, "They dated for a year in school, but then Noah ditched Stacey to form the other band and pursue his musical dreams."

Suddenly, it seems there might be more to watch the live shows for than just the music. Especially when Stacey has recently been seen in the company of Drayton Beyer, lead singer of Flame-Grilled Steak.

Chapter 18

Stacey

We were backstage and waiting to go on stage for the first live show. With twenty acts, there were ten on a show today and ten tomorrow (a scandal had meant one of Carmela's other bands had been disqualified so all judges had an even amount of contestants again). Both my band and The Paranormals were appearing tonight. Drayton's Flame-Grilled Steak were on tomorrow night's show. Drayton had sent a bouquet of flowers to me. The note with them was as endearing as I figured he was going to get.

Stacey,
Good luck. I hope with all my heart your band are the runners up in the competition. But you're getting my D when this is all over, so you're a winner anyway!

Dray xo

Who said romance was dead?

The press were having a field day over my past relationship history with Noah, and Donna was fucked off with me for not having told her about him. The more time that passed, the more I wondered why I'd entered this competition at all. I'd been leaving rehearsals to find press hanging around the doors asking me if I was enjoying a threesome. I kept with my stock answer of I 'preferred a sevensome'.

Tonight's mixture of bands appeared to be human apart from us and The Paranormals. It was a live audience and after an emcee had been on stage to warm them up and tell them the do's and dont's of the evening, the judges came out to whoops and hollers from the studio audience before taking their seats. Carmela and Marianne were wearing outfits to try to outdo one another in terms of flashing the flesh and shock value, but they may as well have not bothered. Harley went out on stage to a loud chorus of applause far louder than theirs, and as the cameras flashed to the audience, I noticed a tightness around both of their mouths that no amount of Botox or fillers could disguise.

Harley faced the cameras.

"Hello and welcome to the first live final of Britain's Best New Band. Before we carry on with the competition, I would just like to take a moment to bring everyone's attention to the man who should be standing here tonight by my side."

The audience went quiet as a picture of Dan flashed up on the screen behind, along with a telephone number.

"As you know, our friend and colleague Dan is still missing. Dan, if you're watching, our thoughts are with you. Please get in touch and let someone know you're okay. Our best regards go out to Dan's family, and if anyone at home has any information on his whereabouts, then please ring this number that goes to the team working on locating him. Thank you."

Marianne stood up. "Dan was the best fucking presenter ever." She kind of fell back in her seat and then looked around at the others, a dazed expression on her face.

Harley smiled. "Indeed, he *is* a fantastic presenter. On behalf of the show and to anyone offended by the use of language, I apologise."

"What the hell just happened then?" Kiki said to the rest of us.

"Looks like Marianne's had too many uppers before she came out." Shonna laughed.

The cameras went back to Harley. "Our first band tonight are on Team Bill. So, Bill, would you like to introduce your band and tell us a little about their song tonight?"

The camera panned in on Bill. "My first band on stage tonight are called The Paranormals." There was a cheer from the crowd. "These four guys definitely have what it takes to go the whole way through this competition. Tonight's song choice shows the lead, Zak's, vocal talents in all their glory. They will be singing *Toxic* by Britney Spears."

"You heard it from Bill. Tonight's first act, singing *Toxic*, is The Paranormals." Harley held up a hand to the side of the stage and the band walked on stage while she walked off.

When the live shows happened, everyone got a makeover. From the lame looking act that had gone through the auditions, Noah's band had now been primped and preened to perfection. Zak's hair was short, dyed platinum blonde, and hair paste had been used to create a spiked effect. He was dressed in tight, black leather trousers that left nothing to the imagination, along with a white vest top. It showed off his muscled arms, and the tattoo of a death eater on the top of his right bicep.

Rex had taken to the drums at the back, his large body like a shadow of a boulder. Just his head and massive corded arms visible. His hair had been cut into his neck, but curls hung over one side of his face.

Roman wore tight silver jeans, a baggy black t-shirt with Alice Cooper on the front and the word Poison across it, and he had silver jewellery that ran from his ear to a nose stud. Against his dusky skin he looked electric, and I loved the poison/toxic connotations that wardrobe had put in. Like as if they were saying, *warning: this band can get in your bloodstream*.

Noah certainly seemed in mine.

I finally allowed my eyes to rest on him as he took his place and began to strum the guitar. All I could think of was those digits on my body instead. His dark hair was spiked like Zak's, but buzz cut below, rather than short. They'd put him in faded blue jeans that hugged his thighs, and a black short-sleeved shirt open at the neck. His chain hung down with the plectrum on it between the sides of his collar, taking me back to seeing him walk past me and ignore me when we were young. It still hurt. I wished with all my heart it didn't, but he still made me feel things I should have got over by now.

As their performance began, every one of them lit up like they'd been plugged into Blackpool illuminations, especially Noah. His dark eyes seemed to spark under the lights, the music seeping into his very being, and I realised that it would be wrong to separate this man from his music. So very wrong. Because although Noah was to all intents and purposes dead, with music he became very much alive.

It hit me then that Noah was married to his music. He'd made that commitment long ago, in the days when he'd left me behind. Some part of me now understood as I watched him work the crowd, giving them a cheeky smirk. Not because he was flirting with them, but because he was so happy to be standing where he was.

I had an amazing vocal. I knew that. And my band were good. But I also knew that next to The Paranormals, at this moment we weren't going to win. Because you had to give it your all up there, and some of me still belonged to the man on stage.

The audience went insane as the band finished their number. The judges went wild in their feedback, with Bill becoming increasingly smug.

Harley went to join the band on stage. "Wow, The Paranormals. What a first performance. What do you think to the judge's feedback... Zak?"

Zak stroked a fingertip across his eyebrow. "We are truly

honoured." He did a thank you, clutching his chest. "It's a privilege to be on this stage performing in front of so many people."

"And, Roman?" Roman looked shocked that she chose him to speak to, although I knew why. "You seem to be the quietest member of the band. Is that true or are you a dark horse?"

"Wrong animal, right, kid?" Zak sniggered, and Harley looked at him with a creased brow.

Roman leaned closer to the microphone. "It's hard to get a word in edgeways with Zak here, but I'm so happy to be in the band, and thank you to all the judges. We hope we'll be able to entertain you all again next week."

With that they made their way off stage.

We were the closing act and so I didn't know what possessed me, but I decided to go through to their dressing room and congratulate them on their performance. The corridor was busy, and I could see people going in and out, but I carried on, walking forward, and pushing open the door.

To find the dark-haired woman with her arms wrapped around Noah. She was kissing him in a frenzy, dotting kisses all over his face and then she held his face in her hands.

"My baby. They've made you look even more handsome. You looked so good out there."

I knew what he'd said to me about Mya being the one who made him a vampire and that there'd never been a romance, but I saw a bond between them that hurt my head and heart so bad I felt like I'd been spiked through my own. I staggered back and away before he saw me and returned to our own dressing room.

"Where'd you disappear off to?" Donna asked.

"Just needed a quick walk. I'm feeling nervous." It was only a half-lie.

"Well, no more disappearing now, because we don't want to have to invoke my mediumship skills again to locate you." She laughed.

Donna had been unable to turn up any more information on either Dan or Jack and had just dropped the matter as if she'd spent the other evening colouring in a picture and then scrunched it up and thrown it in the bin. I didn't know how she could be okay being possessed by a dead person's spirit one day and then act like it had never happened the next. She was a peculiar one was our Donna. After her outburst the other day, I was trying to make sure I listened to her and didn't overlook her because of her being small. She'd been right to call me out on it and I actually felt a little ashamed of my behaviour.

That was why I'd decided that she should provide the main backing vocals tonight and be a bit more visible on stage.

We sang Britney's *Womanizer* and I put all my internalised anger into the song to such a point that to my utter amazement we received a standing ovation.

"Fucking hell, Stacey, where did that come from?" Estelle tapped me on the shoulder. "Even I'm turned on and I'm dead inside according to my husband." She turned to the others. "If she keeps this up, we're winning this thing."

I saw that Donna's expression looked sullen. "There's credit due to Donna too," I said. "I think her backing vocals made me sound better than I was."

"Yeah, I think so too. I think I added a harmonic element that made your performance seem to zing," Donna claimed.

Ultimately, I didn't give a shit. I was really beginning to wonder why I was even there. The more this competition progressed, the less it seemed about being connected with my dreams and the more it seemed to be about settling a score with an ex.

There was no doubt that I loved singing. I loved my friends and coven sisters, and singing in the band had given me the same sense of belonging I'd had when I sang with Noah. But was that it? Was the family/friend/support part of it the main reason I did it? If someone said to me right now, 'Go solo and we'll give you a recording contract', would I? Did I want it as a career? Did I really want to win this competition and go on tour?

Fuck me. I didn't.

Looking around at my bandmates, I felt like I'd let them all down. Because I knew that I would do my best to win this competition for them, and then I was going to leave the band.

Stacey Williams wanted more. I wanted to be someone's everything. Not a lead singer. Not an ex. When I found someone who put me first above everything, I knew I'd follow that person to the ends of the earth.

Because all I'd ever been searching for was love.

Ten years earlier

"For God's sake, Stacey, get out from under my feet, and stop making that noise," my mum yelled at me for the billionth time that day. She'd been telling me all my life I'd been a mistake, and as soon as I was old enough to look after myself, she went out with her mates and largely ignored me. Oh, she made sure there was always a pizza or a microwave curry in the fridge, and left me money for buying clothes, but she'd had me at fifteen, didn't talk to her parents—my grandparents—and said it was her time now.

I grabbed my schoolbag and set off to school early. I bought toast and a drink at breakfast club and then walked around the halls looking at the noticeboard, wasting time until the bell went. I didn't really have any friends. People knew I was from the Scarsdale Estate and so pretended I didn't exist because only the poor or those with mental illness lived there. Social housing prejudice at its finest.

I spotted the notice.

Choir
Singers required for school plays. Rehearsals Monday and Fridays 4pm, more sessions nearer to performance dates.

It was perfect. I could sing without my mum harping on, and it kept me out of the way.

I'd been there about three months when Noah joined. I spotted him sitting at the back in the corner. He looked as lonely as I felt so I went over to him.

"Hi, I'm Stacey."

He stared up at me and my heart thudded a little because up close I saw how gorgeous his eyes were, with his long, dark lashes. "Noah," he replied.

"You don't look all that excited to be here." I sat beside him, and he didn't tell me to move which led me to think he was okay with it.

"Truth? I'm here because my enemies won't come here for me. It's not worth it, and hopefully they'll have got bored and left before I get out."

"So you don't actually want to be in the choir?" I said, disappointed.

"Oh I love music, and I'm happy enough to be here, although I didn't really need another excuse for them to call me gay or a pansy, but Mrs Hellier seems to think it'll help me with my 'issues'."

Mrs Hellier was the school pastoral counsellor.

"If it's any consolation, I'm here because my mother doesn't want me at home. I don't have any friends either. Not because I'm bullied, but because people like to pretend I don't exist."

Noah turned to me. "I don't know how anyone could not notice you. You're really pretty." Then he blushed. But that was the day I became friends with Noah Granger and a week later he asked if I wanted to be his girlfriend. The rejection from others meant we'd found each other.

And that was why Noah should have known more than anyone how his actions would affect me, when he rejected me later.

The results show wasn't until ten pm the following evening, so as tears threatened to overflow my lower lashes, I faked a yawn and turned to my friends.

"I'm totally beat, so I'm going to make tracks, okay? I'll see you all tomorrow."

I caught the Tube back to my house and sat with the curtains open while I stared at the moonlight. I was alone, but I felt a sense of peace I'd not had in a long time as I enjoyed my own company and own home. And as I sat on my sofa looking out, I realised where I was yet again going wrong. I wanted someone to love me.

Yet, I didn't love myself.

That was where I needed to start. To find out what made Stacey Williams happy inside. And work out what came after the end of this competition.

Getting out my candles, I created a spell of optimism, and for a few minutes it seemed to hang in the air like diamond dust. I slept better that night than I had in years.

Chapter 19

Noah

We came off stage on a natural high. There was just no feeling like it... well other than the time I'd sunk deep into Stacey after that concert, but I tried not to let my mind dwell on that. Our plans had been to shower, change, and go watch the rest of our competition, but it soon became apparent that I wasn't going to get to do that any time soon when the door pushed open and Mya walked in, accompanied by her husband, Death, a man who made Aaron the security guy look like a comedian.

Mya flung herself at me. "Surprise!"

"I'll say this is a surprise," I stated. "You didn't even give out a tiny tweak on the mind meld." I hugged her and she beamed at me.

"It wouldn't have been much of a surprise if I did that, would it?" She turned to everyone else. "You were all phenomenal out there. You'd better win. I've taken a bet on you."

"I hope you got it in early, because we're on evens at the moment," Roman informed her.

"Oh, sweetpea. I haven't bet like that. I've told a tormented soul he can have ten minutes with his ex if he doesn't win."

Roman backed away from Mya with haste, made his excuses and went to the showers.

"Hey, De—" I began to say, but Mya's husband scowled at me, reminding me that it probably wasn't a good idea to announce his name in public.

"De-nny," I said instead.

Mya burst into laughter. "Denny. Denny-wenny. Might call you that instead of Big D."

I pulled a grimace at Death. Yup my sire was wed to the Grim Reaper himself. "Sorry!"

He shrugged. "I'm used to her by now."

Rex walked over and held out his hand for Denny to shake, but Mya jumped over and slapped it down to his side.

"Don't do that. You'll feel like death," she told him.

Rex looked at me, quirked a brow, and made his excuses, saying he needed water.

Death's attention shot to the doorway. "There's a soul here. I'm confused though. It's unhappy and happy at the same time."

"Denny, darling. Can you shut up?" Mya scolded him. "I'm here to see my son, not to work."

Zak raised a brow. "If you were my sire, I'd have definite mummy issues".

Death stepped forward, "Pardon?"

"Nothing. Time for me to go shower." Zak departed with haste.

There was only Rex left in the room now, standing over at the drinks trolley. Rex had never felt threatened in Mya's company, not that they'd seen each other often. But vampires and shifters had a history, sometimes good, sometimes bad. A shifter would never show fear in front of a vamp and vice versa unless they really were in the shit.

"You know Denny and I have very busy careers, but I'll make sure I get to every live round where possible," Mya stated, "and I will definitely be at the final if you get through. I'm so proud of you. Your mum would be too."

"Oh sorry, did she pass? I can try to ask for permission for you to visit the Home of the Wayward as a one off. I can't promise though," Death said.

My brow creased. "No, she just moved to Australia. Met the love of her life. Lives off grid without any television. Surfs a lot and sends me the odd letter."

"Oh."

"I've told you that before. You men never listen," Mya scolded.

I'd been so happy for my mum when she'd met Matt. I'd insisted she went and lived her best life. She'd done everything she could for me. I didn't want her to think she had to sacrifice anything more. Knowing she was happy made me happy. That was all I could ask for. My mother knew I was a vampire as I'd had to explain why I wasn't aging. She hadn't bought my excuse of a good face cream as she assured me she'd tried them all and 'None fucking worked, so you're lying, son'.

She'd then met Mya who had assured her she would take on a motherly role, being that she'd sired me anyway. It had all been bizarre and Mya had called me son ever since, which given she looked about three years older than me had garnered us some weird looks at times.

"My baby. They've made you look even more handsome. You looked so good out there." Mya started hugging me again and dotting me with kisses which she thought mums did. She held my face in her hands.

Then she dropped her hands and sniffed the air.

"So, are you and Stacey still on the outs?" she asked.

"Yep, you know that ship sailed a long time ago," I replied.

"Really? Only I just smelled her approach. Her blood is so damn sweet, but then it went away, so I'm guessing she changed her mind. Has her band been on yet?"

I groaned. My guess was that if Stacey had headed this way, she'd taken one look at Mya and turned on her heel.

"Seven Sisters are closing the show," I told her.

"Great, we'll stay and watch."

Death groaned. "I can only hope someone in the audience dies to get me out of here."

"But you love music," I queried.

"Music, yes. The hours taken to film a TV programme... let's just say Hell puts individuals in such scenarios as part of their torture rituals."

"Quit whining. Parents are supposed to be supportive." Mya turned towards me. "Okay, we'll leave you to shower. Catch you later." She gave me another hug.

Death gave me one of his smiles and a small wave. Even all these years later his rictus grin was enough to have a person running for the hills. But he tried, bless him, and that's what counted.

"Is it me, or does the audience seem particularly enraptured by every appearance Harley makes?" Zak asked me from the wings.

"They've all been told how to act, haven't they? They said on the live shows they'd let them be a bit more natural, but they all look like brainwashed zombies."

We looked at them when Harley was on stage, mouths open, especially the guys. The guys whose wives would think they had an amazing hubby because he'd helped their dreams come true by going to the Hex Factor live shows with them, when really, they were looking at Harley and the female judges and depositing material for the spank bank.

"You've got to admit, she's a great presenter. Not to knock Dan—he was good too—but she's better off when she's not sharing the stage."

Zak stumbled forward and then looked behind him.

"What's up with you? Had too much beer?" I asked.

"Someone just pushed me. I felt their hand on my back."

I turned and looked at the space around us. "Think you need to hit the sack, mate, because you're already dreaming."

He was about to protest, but then Seven Sisters came on stage. As Stacey not only captivated the audience but received a standing ovation from the crowd and the judges, we became otherwise occupied.

"Fuck, your ex might just be a thorn in our side in winning this competition. Do you reckon they're using their powers and bewitching everyone?" Roman asked.

"No, she wouldn't do that."

"It's clear we need to up our game, and I'd thought I was faultless, so actually you lot need to up your game," Zak chastised us. "We didn't get a standing ovation. You lot aren't working hard enough."

A security guy pulled back the curtain to where we were standing.

"You've got two reporters at the door to your dressing room. Got time to talk to them?"

"Do they want to talk to Seven Sisters or any of the other bands too?" Zak asked.

"Didn't say so. Just showed a press badge and asked for you." Security guy looked bored. It was nearly time to wrap things up and no doubt he was looking forward to going home.

"We're on our way," I told him, and we left the wings and went back to the dressing room.

What we found at our door didn't look much like press. It looked a lot more like two twenty-somethings, one of whom, a woman with pink hair, was so drunk she could barely stand. The drunk one took one look at Zak and blurted out, "Fuck me. I really do think I died."

I saw the other woman elbow her in the side.

Zak looked bored. "I'm off. You can sort out whatever this

is," he whispered in my ear. Then he turned on the charm for the women, saying it was good to meet them, but he had an urgent appointment, and off he went. Twat.

The pink-haired one's drunk eyes followed him the whole way down and she let out a regretful sigh.

"Let's get you on your feet and some coffee down you," I said, looking from one woman to the other. "And don't pretend to be press. I know you aren't."

I did have to hold in a snigger and eyeroll when the pink-haired one asked, "How?"

"I can read both your minds," I said honestly. "You couldn't be more open if you had a shop sign hung around your neck."

"It's you," the brunette huffed, side-eyeing her friend. "Being drunk gave the game away."

Inviting them into our dressing room, I asked their real names and discovered the brunette was Freya and 'pink' was called Erica.

Erica was still legless, but then her eyes widened, and she announced: "It's true I'm not a press person. I'm the president of your fan club."

"Fan club?" I smirked.

"Yes." Erica was becoming more exuberant as she warmed to her own idea which she was clearly thinking up as she went along. "Whether you win or not, I believe you are on the brink of stardom, and I want to run your official fan club. What say you?"

Rex shot forward, his hair flying around his face. "Hell, yeah. I even know what we can call our fans."

"Oh God, don't encourage him," Roman groaned.

"The Subs," Rex said proudly. "Do you get it? Short for subscribers to our club, but meaning submissive, doing what we want them to."

Freya's hand shot up. "I want to be the first official Sub."

He winked at her. "Done. So, coffee, and then you can take some notes about the band; how we started up etc. Sound good?" His voice had gone extra husky.

Freya took the notepad and pen from Erica. "While my bestie sobers up, I can start by getting to know you. Is there somewhere more comfortable we could go?"

Freya's mind was a cacophony of cuss words when both Rex and Roman suggested going to the canteen and it looked like she would actually have to write down some facts about the band. Seemed like I was staying with Erica and sobering her up.

♪

"Will my friend currently be part of a threesome?" was the first thing Erica asked when more in control of her faculties.

I laughed. "No. She's quite safe in the canteen. You'll have just made their day by saying you're making a fan club. Don't worry, I'll let them down gently. Sorry that Zak left when I know you came to see him."

"Was I that obvious?" Erica said, her mouth turning down at the corners.

I didn't want to say I could read her mind again, so I smiled gently. "A little."

"Huh. Yeah, he was so interested, he left in a split-second."

I patted her arm. "Zak has a great amount on his plate, not least of which is we're trying to win this competition. I definitely wouldn't pin your hopes on him. He's not a settling down kind of guy. Or a one-woman kind of guy." I hoped she wouldn't start crying, but she was on a one-way ticket to brokenheartsville if she pursued Zak.

"Is Stacey really with Dray? Because I think you two look good together."

I'd not expected that one. She bloody could be press; the woman had a natural flair for asking you questions you felt you wanted to answer. "Matchmaker, are you?"

"You must be joking. I can't get myself a date, never mind anyone else. Nope, if you still like Stacey you're on your own there. I just think you seem nicer than Dray."

I smirked. "But you don't actually know me. What if I'm a vampire or something and not as nice as you think?"

She guffawed with laughter. "I like you, you're stupid." Clapping her hand over her mouth, she gasped. "Sorry, I mean, you're funny, not stupid as in a fool. You make me laugh. I don't laugh much. My life's pretty boring, so I'm so pleased I'm now running your fan club." She patted down her pockets. "Oh, but Freya went off with my pad and pen so I can't write down anything you tell me."

"It's fine. You don't have to run our fan club. I'll tell the others. Thanks for supporting us, and hopefully, you now realise that alcohol is not your friend."

She blushed a little. "I shouldn't let myself get pulled into Freya's hairbrained ideas, but hey, I got to meet you all. And I really am a huge fan and would definitely, truly, like to run your fan club. You'll need one. You're going to be huge. I just know it."

Oh, what the hell. "Give me your phone number and email address and we'll be in touch. You can totally run our fan club if you want. You can ask us anything via emails and then we'll leave how you run things up to you. That's if you wake up in the morning still wanting to be our fan club president and it's not the alcohol talking."

"I don't usually drink," she confessed.

"Funnily enough, I kind of worked that out." I stood up and escorted her to the door. "Let's go find your friend in the canteen."

She nodded.

"I really do think you and Stacey seem better suited than her and Dray," she said, as her friend stood up in the canteen and they got ready to leave.

"You stick to creating the fan club, and I'll run my love life, or lack of it." I gave her a hug.

"Bye. It was nice to meet you. Thanks for being so kind and not kicking us out," Erica said.

Bless her. Erica seemed a really nice girl. I hoped she wasn't taking on this fan club thing just to try to get near Zak. Her soul seemed far too good for him. He'd ruin her. But... she was a grown woman, and I clearly had no clue about love, so it wasn't my problem.

We said goodbye to the women and made our way home.

Back at the show the following evening, we found we'd made it through to the following week's live rounds. So had Seven Sisters and Flame-Grilled Steak.

Chapter 20

Stacey

For someone who seemingly had the world at her feet if the stories in the press were anything to go by, I was pretty damn miserable. I'd enjoyed my time alone, but now I was back here waiting for the results to be announced and the amount of people and noise surrounding me was overwhelming.

Most of the chatter was coming from my bandmates as Donna almost had them in a frenzy with her excited chatter about how we could win this. She was full of ideas about what we could do next, and I noticed Carmela smiled at her without it reaching her eyes. We did what Carmela told us, end of. She'd been okay with the changes we'd suggested last time, but as she cast her eyes upon Donna once more, I got the impression that the already small Donna was going to get cut down soon.

I only wished I had the same enthusiasm.

We walked out onto the stage for the bit where there was the overexaggerated announcement of who had and hadn't made it to the next round. For the first week we were being whittled from twenty acts to seventeen acts and then two acts a week would leave for the next seven weeks, leaving three acts in the final.

We made it through to the next week. I was happy for the band, but I still had this unsettled feeling inside. After making my excuses to be on my own for a second night in a row, I went home where I took some time trying to work out what was making me feel this way. Okay, I'd realised I needed to focus on myself a little, but that couldn't be it. I had this edgy feeling, and thinking about it, I'd had it since Donna had done her contacting of the dead.

I needed answers. She'd supposedly had Jack Brooks talking through her. I wanted to know if Noah had killed him. He'd acted like he was unaware that Jack had taken my virginity, but he'd been around at that time. He could have been following me.

Taking out my grimoire, I laid it open on a blank page. After crushing sage on it, I dusted the sage off into my wastepaper bin and then I threw down some black soot on the white paper. I recited my spell.

> *"Goddess, I have cleared the page.*
> *And now I've made a mess.*
> *Please come forward to my aid,*
> *And form in an address."*

I carried on. "Please tell me the address for Noah Granger, my ex-boyfriend." The soot re-arranged itself, forming a London address, and then the soot soaked into the page, leaving a black written imprint. I thanked the goddess, noted the address, and ordered an Uber.

It was clear Noah wasn't expecting to see me. Thinking about it, he hadn't been forced to be home, but luckily, he was. He rubbed his eyes. "Sorry, Stace. I wasn't expecting you, was I...?" He looked tired. A rare look on a vampire.

"No, you weren't. I wasn't expecting to be here either. Can I come in?" I waited a few seconds.

Noah nodded his head. "Yeah, course you can. Sorry, I just need a minute to wake up. I'd nodded off on the sofa. All this rehearsing is making me need a bit more sleep than usual. Come through and make yourself at home while I go throw some water on my face, and then I'll put the kettle on." He paused. "Unless you want something stronger?"

"A coffee would be good. Thanks."

I walked inside. Noah's place wasn't a million miles away from my own studio apartment. We'd both gone for no-frills, 'places to rest your head' décor, and I wondered if it meant that like me, he'd not found anywhere he felt he could call home yet.

After asking how I drank my coffee, he brought two mugs in and placed them on top of a music magazine lying on the coffee table in front of the sofa. I'd taken a seat on the sofa and so Noah sat in the nearby chair.

"Okay, so let's cut to the chase now. Why are you here, Stace?"

I took a deep breath. "Did you murder Jack Brooks?"

"That's why you came here?" Noah jumped up and started pacing, scrubbing a hand through his hair. As he turned to me, a tic pulsed in his cheek. "You think I'm capable of that?" He walked over to his window, pulling back the curtains and staring out into the night sky.

"You had yourself turned into a vampire. I don't know what you're capable of," I said truthfully.

Noah sucked in his top lip for a moment. "No, I didn't kill Jack Brooks. That's the truth, but you can choose to believe it or not, seeing as you don't know what I'm capable of." He threw my words back in my face. "And I know he's missing, but are you saying they've found a body?"

"No." I looked up at him. "Please sit down, Noah. I need to

talk about this with someone, and you'll understand, being supernatural."

Slowly, he wandered back over, but this time he sat beside me on the sofa. "What's going on?"

I sighed. "My friend and bandmate Donna decided to do some mediumship and she claimed to be possessed by Jack. He'd become furious and said it was my fault he was dead. Then she was sick, and he 'left'." I air quoted left.

"And do you trust this Donna? Know that she wasn't winding you up in some way?"

"Yes, I'd trust her with my life. We've been friends for a long time. She's a coven sister. She's just guilty of being a little impulsive. But that's what was said, and with your history, I'd always wondered…"

"If I'd returned and drained him in a revenge plot for everything he'd done to me?" Noah stated.

"Well, yes."

"Stacey, Jack was a dickhead who made my life a misery. A bully. But the worst thing he did to me was name-call me and give me a kicking. Not things that in my book equate with me taking his life. It crossed my mind to give him a good kicking back at first, given I was a hell of a lot stronger, but I couldn't be bothered. Once I'd been turned, I had no interest in losers like Jack Brooks, who made themselves feel better by picking on others."

"And loser girlfriends," the words were out before I could stop them.

"No," Noah said vehemently. "I'll keep saying this over and over again until the day someone puts a stake through my heart. I let you go because I was a danger to you. Have you any idea how your sweet, virginal blood sang to me? As a newly turned vampire I would have fucked you raw and then drained you dry, Stacey. I'm not lying. You were in complete and utter danger from me. I had to feed myself on bottles of blood to the point of wanting to be sick in case I caught a passing glimpse of you. Rex was my main wingman, because as a shifter he could hold me down if it looked like I might bolt towards you."

"But you hardly ever looked my way."

"Stace, I didn't need to. I could smell you from miles away. I daren't look because if I had, I was afraid that Rex wouldn't have been able to hold me down. You weren't a witch then, or maybe, you'd just started hanging around them, I don't know; but you certainly wouldn't have been any match for me. It's been hard enough trying to exist without you in my life. But it's been a hell of a lot better than being responsible for your death, because make no mistake, I. Would. Have. Killed. You."

"I-it's been hard trying to exist...?" I repeated what I was sure he'd just said.

"Very hard. In more ways than one." His eyes hooded as he stared at me hungrily. "You'd better leave now, Stacey, if I've satisfied what you came here for." There was no mistaking the implication in his tone or his expression.

"You have, but now I have another question," I told him.

He sighed. "Yes?"

"Do you still want to fuck me raw?" I asked.

His answer was that his eyes flashed red, his fangs descended, and he pulled me into his arms and through to his bedroom at a speed that made me dizzy.

His bedroom was shades of grey, shadowed by the half-closed curtains at the window. He threw me down onto the top of his duvet and I bounced slightly. Scooting up the top of the bed and resting my back against the pillows, I looked up as Noah stood against the end of the bed.

"You'll have to promise me you're not going to just slip out in the middle of the night this time, Stacey."

"Why? I have a home. Why would I not go to it afterwards?" I retorted.

"Because you belong in my arms and if you can't stay there forever, at least stay there this one night."

I nodded. My body was overridden with lust, and I'd worry about the fallout once I'd had a few orgasms.

Noah stripped off his clothes and my mouth went so dry I had to lick around my lips. He was lean but sculpted, his arms threaded with corded muscle. A dark trail of hair ran down from his belly button to his groin where his hard cock rose in a greeting. He grasped his length and pumped it a few times. I grasped the bottom of my sweater ready to lift it up, and then he was there, kneeling astride me, helping me.

His gaze grazed over me hungrily as he feasted on the sight of me in just my red lacy bra and panties. Pulling down a cup, his tongue flicked over my already hard nipple and then he nipped softly. I looked down to see if he'd drawn blood—he was a vampire with a cracking set of incisors after all—but no. He gave the same attention to my other nipple and then he ripped the fabric of my bra in half.

"Noah! I could have magicked it off. Now you've ripped it."

He grinned, his eyes flashing with mischief. "I always wanted to do that. You can magic yourself a replacement pair, because..." He ripped my panties clean off me. Then he moved down between my legs, and I stopped giving a crap about my undies being torn.

I didn't want to think about where he'd practised this stuff to such a professional level. It had been three years since we'd fucked and he'd got even better, damn him. But then I was no virgin either. We both had pasts.

Shut up, Stacey. You're shagging Noah and your brain is going on and on when this amazing lover is between your legs.

Fair point, I told myself and concentrated on what he was doing again.

That talented tongue delved in and out of me and tickled at my nub until it teased me to the point of no return. As I began to convulse against his mouth, I grabbed Noah's hair and rode his face until my body sagged with satisfaction. I felt like I'd had a truckload of Valium or something I was that chilled out. And then Noah bit the top of my thigh. My blood fizzed and whirled as it responded to his vampire touch. His venom captivated my cells, leading them into a dance where I felt like they almost did a conga all the way into Noah's mouth. My core clenched and I raised my thighs as he sucked on me.

Breaking off, Noah moved so he was above me and he knelt between my thighs guiding his cock to where my soaking wet pussy was waiting.

As Noah pushed inside me, I gasped in sheer and utter pleasure and wrapped my legs around him.

"God, you feel so fucking good, Stace," he groaned as he moved in and out of me.

All I could do was moan my clear agreement.

Noah grabbed my breast and tweaked a nipple as he continued to thrust, and then he moved his hand to between us, flicking my clit while he changed to lazy strokes. I opened my eyes because I could sense his gaze on me.

"What?"

"You're just so fucking beautiful," he said. "And so fucking *mine*."

And as if he knew I'd protest against his words, he chose that moment to bite my neck and slam against me in a hard thrust. Then I was spinning and lost in a vortex of ecstasy as my mind, body, and soul exploded in satisfaction.

Panting against Noah, I slowly came back down to earth. He licked at my neck, and I knew from our last encounter that he was sealing the bite wounds.

"Say nothing if you can't say anything good." He smirked, looking down at me.

"That was amazing," I told him. "I'm definitely staying the night."

And I did. I slept in between bouts of bedroom antics and when I finally fell into a deep sleep at around four am, I knew nothing more until Noah woke me.

At midday.

"Shit!" I shot up and immediately went dizzy.

I scowled at Noah. "Is that because you bit me? Did you take too much?"

All I got in return was a bemused smirk. "No, Stacey. I hardly took a drop. It's because we screwed all night and you've just shot up quick."

"Oh."

"I wouldn't drain you."

"Such a romantic statement."

He tilted his head at me. "Do you want me to be romantic? I can be."

I rubbed at my eyes. "All I know right now is I want a cup of coffee. As for anything else, I seriously have no idea. I wasn't expecting this to happen."

"So you're not ready for my 'What does this mean' question?"

"God, you're a needy bitch." I laughed.

I couldn't really magic myself a new pair of undies, so I just had to put my top, sweater, and jeans back on. "Am I okay to grab a shower?" I asked.

"Sure. I'll be fixing that coffee. Is toast okay? I don't keep a lot in with not needing to eat."

"Yeah, that's fine."

I took my time in the shower thinking about what had happened between us. It didn't help that our bodies had melded perfectly together. But the fact remained that nothing had changed between us. He still put the band first and I was actually dating another guy. Okay, I'd not slept with Dray, but still, this hadn't been a cool thing to do. I wasn't that kind of woman who strung a guy along or kept things open. I know Dray flirted with other women, but that didn't mean that I should change my own stance on things.

Sitting at his kitchen island on a tall stool, Noah passed me a coffee. "I don't need to read your mind, you know," he told me. "Your truths are written all over your face."

I took a sip, scalding my tongue. "Could you put me a splash of cold in? I'm so thirsty."

"Me too." Noah winked.

My breasts and core perked up in response. Luckily, my brain was in situ this morning and leading the way forward.

"Noah..."

"I know. Nothing's changed," he replied, and then he looked up at me sharply.

"What if I did, Stacey? What if I quit right now, and left it all behind?"

"Pardon?" I was hearing things.

"What if I went back to the guys now and quit? Would you give us a chance?"

I wanted to say yes. I really did. But it was the wrong time and the wrong place again for us. I'd seen him on stage. It was in his blood. He would not be happy at a life without music. And I wasn't ready to give myself over to anyone right now. I needed to find my own path. Find out what I wanted to do after the competition.

"Oh," was all he said.

"I'm not saying we can never happen, Noah. But I don't want this right now. Us. It's not the right time for me." I got up off my stool. "Thanks for the coffee."

He nodded and then I walked out of the door, calling for an Uber to take me home from the street outside his place.

I felt like I'd just made a huge mistake. But was it sleeping with Noah, or walking away from him?

Chapter 21

Noah

I threw myself into rehearsing for the live performances because it took my mind off Stacey. When I saw her, she'd smile at me like you would a friend, but she continued to hang around with Drayton. Looked like she'd made her choice. Why had she left me with hope, saying never say never? It twisted me up worse than being in the vicinity of kebab sticks.

"Look at this." Zak beckoned me over to look at his phone. "There's a piece in today's *Daily Mirror* about one of those women that said they were press. Apparently, she has set up a fan club with a newsletter and it's got fifteen thousand subscribers in two days."

I took the phone off him and sure enough there was a picture of Erica holding up a press photograph of us.

"Bill says he's getting his PA onto it and that he'll make sure that Erica lets us see what she's posting before she posts it, and in return he'll cover her costs and send her merch, tickets, etc. We might have to answer some inane questions he says, but it's all PR."

"She seemed a really nice woman," I said.

"Bloody naïve, she was, thinking she could hoodwink us into believing she was press."

"They got backstage and all the way to our dressing room," I reminded him.

"Yeah, well, security leaves a lot to be desired here, let's face it. I mean the fucking presenter disappeared."

"I wonder what did happen to him?" I pondered out loud.

"I dunno. Maybe Harley being a better presenter got to him and he's crying in a corner somewhere?"

Then Zak screamed, "Ow," and smacked at his arm.

"What?"

"Something nipped me hard. Or maybe it was a sting. It was bloody weird."

"Maybe Dan's dead and it was his ghost punishing you for your stinging comments. Get it? Stinging," I joked. "Anyway, it wasn't that long ago we were crying in corners, Zachariah. Remember where you came from."

"God, do you have to remind me? Though I believe I'm between a rock and a hard place, and by that, I mean I used to have rocks thrown at me at school, and now I'm constantly having to be hard."

"Look, you have a reprieve from Don and then after the competition we'll have a think about your next options."

"There won't be any. I need to face facts. I made a deal with a demon and I'm going to have more access to souls than ever."

"The thing with demons is they get greedy and they like deals. We just have to find something that tempts him more than you. But right now, let's concentrate on rehearsing, okay?"

"Yes, Boss," he said, but he didn't look convinced.

The next few weeks were a constant merry-go-round of rehearsing, eating, and sleeping. Then the semi-finals approached. There were four bands left: us; Seven Sisters; Flame-Grilled Steak; and RokUrWorld, a human act with a singer, a cello player, and a synth player. They were all male and worked an EMO style. Being

Irish and looking like they should be the lead in teen movies meant that they'd received a solid vote week after week from their country and from teenage girls.

My life had become nothing more than music, as once again I pushed my feelings about Stacey down somewhere deep inside myself and threw everything into the band. If I walked into the canteen and saw her with Dray, I'd nod at them as if I didn't give a toss and then ignore them and concentrate on my friends. I kept my desires satisfied by working my way through the female staff on the show. I was feeding off their blood and then Zak was appearing in some of their dreams at night to take a piece of their souls.

For this reason, there were rumours of a virus going around the catering staff and runners. As they were almost all female, no one had noticed that the male staff population were largely unaffected. Yup, sometimes one had flirted with Stacey, and being pathetic, I'd bit them and made them too tired to flirt any more. I wasn't proud of my behaviour, but well, bite me.

We had two tracks to perform for the show and Bill was taking a keen interest now in our performances. He'd made us change one song this week which put additional pressure on us to learn our altered performance quickly.

The pressure could be witnessed now as the atmosphere in the canteen during breaks was no longer frivolous. There was an underlying tension, and it was as if there was a rope being pulled tighter and tighter, ready to snap at any point.

And people were acting weirder.

Harley stood in the queue for food behind Dray, who stood behind Stacey. I was standing behind Harley.

Dray turned around to Harley beaming widely, while rubbing his right arse cheek.

"Hey, hey, hey, Harley Davies. Keep your hands to yourself, cos my missus might get mad."

Harley looked at him like he was deranged. "What are you talking about?"

"You felt my arse several times. Wanna ride me, Harley?"

"No, I don't, and I didn't feel any part of you, and especially not your bum. That would be sexual harassment; a bit like what you're doing now asking me if I want to ride you. I suggest you quit this conversation unless you want throwing out of the competition."

Drayton stood up to his full height and growled. "Hey, lady. You clearly touched me. Let's not accuse me of something I'm not doing. I'm with this chick." He pointed to Stacey, who was looking around at the audience we now had from the rest of the canteen. Dray's inner bear was coming out as his voice boomed a deep bass that carried around the place.

"Harley didn't touch you, Drayton. I'd have seen it."

His head shot around fast, so he was glaring at me. "Really, dude? Because every time I look, your eyes seem to be on my missus."

"Drayton, lower your voice," Stacey hissed under her breath. She moved so she was next to Harley and rolled her eyes in Harley's direction.

Harley turned to me. "Thanks, because I really didn't touch him. He's far too alpha for my liking."

"No problem," I said, but my mind was starting to think about the weird shit happening lately. Zak being pushed forward, Marianne's weird outburst, Zak's feeling of being pinched, and now this. Something was going on, but what? With a missing presenter and these weird occurrences, we needed to keep our wits about us, because something wasn't quite right.

Chapter 22

Erica

From: TheSubsofTheParanormals@gmail.com
Date: 15 November 2022
Subject: THEY MADE THE FINAL!!! (Of course they did).

From the ONLY OFFICIAL fan group of The Paranormals.

OMG did you see this week's live show? Of course, you did, you're a Sub!!! That rendition of Wildest Dreams! Like Carmela said they certainly put the wild into their performance. Did you growl too?!!!

But it's next week now that we need to get prepared for. Get your dialling fingers at the ready so we can have our Paranormals crowned as Britain's Best New Band. (I'm already having to fan myself).

Also, don't forget to send any questions you have for the band to me, so I can go meet them and put your questions to them.

Aren't I the luckiest woman in the world? Please don't hate me, someone has to get you the lowdown on our rock gods.

Until next week (eeek).

Erica xoxo

Chapter 23

THE DAILY NEWS

LOVE FEUD AS THE PARANORMALS, SEVEN SISTERS, AND FLAME-GRILLED STEAK BATTLE IT OUT FOR THE TITLE OF BRITAIN'S BEST NEW BAND.

16 November 2022

Saturday night's final looks like being the mother of all showdowns as guitarist Noah Granger from The Paranormals faces ex-girlfriend Stacey Williams of Seven Sisters and her rumoured new lover Drayton Beyer from Flame-Grilled Steak.

If rumours of a bust-up in the canteen this week between the three are true, then maybe the competition isn't just about the record deal but also about winning Stacey's heart?

The bets are on The Paranormals winning the show, but the true winner seems to be presenter Harley Davies, who has just signed a million-pound deal to be the face of ITV. This follows her success fronting the show this year alone after previous co-presenter Dan Trent went missing shortly after the first show of the new series.

Chapter 24

Dan

For God's sake. Harley was impenetrable. My hate for her grew stronger every day, and I, in turn, became stronger. I could take over Marianne of all people. Probably because she'd always been a hole to sink into if her rumoured antics in the swinging sixties were anything to go by.

Other than that, it was parlour tricks. Amusing ones, but still not enough for me to possess Harley. If I'd had a substantial body, it was at that point I would have smacked myself up the head.

Why was I trying to possess Harley?

I could aim for the top. I could possess the boss himself, Bill Traynor. He acted like he was the big guy, but in actual fact his minions did everything for him. Without everyone around him feeding his ego he was nothing.

I laughed even though no one could hear it.

Chapter 25

Stacey

It was the final rehearsals and Carmela was working us hard. The band were getting fed up. All apart from Donna. She'd placed herself into deputy position and was like a cheerleader captain.

Tempers flared at the first refreshment break of the day when Kiki spoke up. "I'm starting to think that I don't actually want to be part of a touring band," she said, wringing her hands. "I don't want to upset anyone, but I'd rather tell you how I'm feeling now, rather than before we might win. I'm actually missing my husband."

"You mean you want us to quit? Now, as we've reached the final?" Donna spat out.

"No. Not at all. I just mean that if you win, I don't want to, well, erm, carry on. I'm just going to go home. You don't need to be seven sisters. Most bands only have four in them."

"Four sisters. Yeah, that's witchy sounding," Donna huffed.

"You're bitchy sounding right now." Kiki's defences rose.

"Hey, hey," I said, trying to calm things down. "Let's just focus on the final. We might not even win, so you're arguing about a record deal and tour we might not get anyway."

"But what if we do?" Donna folded her arms across her chest.

"Then we can strip down to whoever wants to be in the band and negotiate."

She huffed. "Don't be ridiculous. Bill would just drop us and sign the runners up." She stormed off.

Kiki's eyes were glassy. I put my hand over hers. "Kiki, I have mixed feelings too."

"And me," Shonna added. "I think I'd rather sit home reading than have to learn all these dances all the time. It gets a bit repetitive."

"Does anyone else think Donna's turned into a demanding diva?" Meryl queried.

A couple of the others agreed, and I sighed internally. My band was at war and no one's heart seemed to be in winning anymore, apart from Donna's.

"Look, we can't get this far and then give up. I see why she's so pissed off. We've been all for it and then right at the final hurdle we're all falling down. We are Seven Sisters and we can win this competition." I roused the others. "Just think of the opportunities winning could bring. It doesn't necessarily have to be a tour. Maybe we could get some sponsorship for designer clothes and things. Let's just carry on for now."

Kiki and Shonna didn't look convinced.

"I promise you that I have your back if you decide it goes no further than the end of this competition."

They nodded.

"Right, let me go and calm Donna down," I told them. "Then we can get back to rehearsing."

I found Donna sitting outside in the main hall. She looked like she was waiting to see the headteacher, all agitated and fidgety. I sat on a plastic chair beside her.

"What's going on, Donna?"

"I feel like I'm finally being seen by people, you know, and now they want to take that away from me."

"Oh, Donna." I pulled her towards me, my arm around her. "You can't make other people do your bidding just to make yourself feel better."

She shrugged off my hold. "It's okay for you. Mrs I'm-between-two-guys-and-I-get-all-the-press-coverage. There's more to this band than you, but you wouldn't know it. I'm fed up of being invisible, Stacey. I want to be seen."

"What's got into you lately? You're all nasty and it's just not like you." I stood up. I didn't need to be insulted when I was trying to help someone. "Carry on and there will be no band to sing tonight. You're scaring them off," I warned. She ignored me and so I left her and went back to rehearsals. She didn't return for the rest of that day and then the following day she acted like it had never happened.

It was a sign of the price of fame and how it could go to people's heads. I was becoming increasingly onside with Kiki and Shonna's point of view. I liked the clubs—playing smaller, more intimate venues—and the idea of staying at that level appealed. But it was probably too late now. Like Donna said, I was becoming a household name thanks to the imaginary war the press were dreaming up across their pages.

There was no fight for my heart.

And that would become clear at the final.

When the guys went all out to win for themselves.

The day following Donna's outburst we had a spectator watching our rehearsals. Dray was sitting on a stool in the corner of the studio after finishing up with his own band. His eyes watched our every move. If I'd had a true interest in him, I'd be seriously pissed off that his attention wandered so much to the others, but my feelings didn't go beyond me liking him and enjoying his company. I knew I'd have ended our 'dating' by now if it wasn't for not wanting any awkwardness around the place.

"God, you know how to move, ladies," he announced. "That routine is hot as fuck. I'm feeling a bit nervous now about my band competing against yours."

"If it wasn't for the fact that I can't see you rock gods performing a Jennifer Lopez style dance routine, you'd have been barred from watching," I warned him.

"The very thought." He laughed. It looked good on him. Made his eyes twinkle and his cheeks pink up. But my brain had a hard time adjusting to him not being Noah Granger. *For God's sake, brain.* I was getting increasingly angry at myself. *Just forget him. Forget. Him.*

Of course, as we left the rehearsal space, Noah chose that moment to come walking down the corridor, accompanied by Zak.

"Rivals, see you at showtime." Zak tipped the baseball cap he was wearing.

Noah just narrowed his gaze in Dray's direction. It pissed me off to see his reaction when he hadn't wanted me, so I grabbed Dray's hand. "Shall we grab some beers and burgers at the bar? We have to eat, right?"

"If that's the only thing you're offering up for eating today, a burger it is," Dray growled, pulling me closer to him.

I turned to see Noah's reaction, but he'd gone. Then I got angry at myself for checking in the first place.

I enjoyed my beer and burger. Dray was good company. It was just you never had his attention exclusively. He checked over the barmaid, the other female customers, and no doubt his senses would be on high alert with the audience tonight. He couldn't help it. As shifters, Flame-Grilled Steak all knew their mates were out there somewhere. Dray could offer no woman his heart because it was meant for that mate. But the fact I wasn't his mate wouldn't stop Dray trying to get me horizontal as soon as possible. A topic he seemed to bring up approximately every three minutes.

"Once this competition is over, I just want you to know that I'm gonna be hankering after some of your mighty fine arse, preferably bouncing up and down on my knee, before I spin you around and have you pogo-ing on my cock."

I couldn't help but chuckle. These words somehow came out of his mouth endearingly, even though they were brash and coarse.

"What a romantic," I quipped.

"Can't promise you romance, but I can promise you a good time." He winked.

"Shut up and finish your burger," I told him. Because I knew he told me the truth, and I didn't want to face up to reality right now.

Chapter 26

Noah

"I'm gasping for refreshments and fresh towels," Rex huffed looking from Zak to me. "Can't you two go play a little further afield? We need these people to make sure the show runs smoothly."

"Show's almost over, my friend. And after tonight, Don is going to have me bedding everyone in sight, so if there's anyone you have your eye on or feel a calling to, you'd better give me a heads up," Zak replied.

"Huh, fabulous." Rex threw a drumstick across the room.

"You're just jealous because you have to wait for 'the one'. Your mate. How very boring having to stick to one person for life," Zak teased him.

"Yeah, but until I meet them, I can practice my prowess. That's if there's anyone left after you greedy fuckers have finished." Another drumstick sailed after the first.

"First past the post, my friend."

"Harley's single. I read online that her career comes first but she's not ruling out love," Roman piped up.

"The only person Harley's in love with is herself," Zak answered. "I went full on incubus on her arse and she barely gave me a second glance. She gave the mirrors and windows she passed a lot more attention."

"Is someone a little bitter that there's one woman he's failed to seduce?" I tormented.

"Are you sure she's not a witch?" Zak asked me.

"How should I know?" I became defensive. I couldn't help myself. "Just because my ex was one doesn't mean I have a homing signal for all of their kind."

"You could just ask Stacey."

"Of course I could," I replied sarcastically. "Hey, Stacey, I know we didn't part on the best of terms when I chose the chance of a rock career over you, but could you tell me if Harley is a witch, only we're wondering why she isn't boning Zak?"

"I didn't say you were an expert on witches. I was just pondering whether Harley was one out loud."

"Because she hasn't fallen for your seduction techniques?" I scoffed.

"Yes. I'm an incubus. All human women are supposed to fall at my feet, so that would suggest that she is somehow, something else."

"You're something else," I told him. He stuck his middle finger up at me in response.

It did however get me thinking, because there was still the weird stuff happening that I couldn't explain. Could Harley actually be the cause of it all?

"You're mighty defensive when it comes to talk of Stacey. Has something happened?" Rex asked.

"No," I protested, and as soon as I did, I knew my answer had been a little too quick.

"Noah Granger, you lying bastard. Spill."

Fuck my life, shifters were so damn nosy. They could scent secrets as much as prey.

"We may have spent the night together a few weeks ago," I confessed.

"You devious fucker." Zak stood with his hands on his hips. "So, what happened? And I don't mean between the sheets. Might you two actually sort out your issues?"

"No. Because she'll never forgive me for putting the band before her."

"So do something that puts her before the band," Roman suggested.

Rex and Zak spun their heads towards him as if he'd lost his mind.

"He'd have to quit, dickhead," Zak stated.

I didn't feel like getting into this right now.

"Guys, let's get rehearsing. We've a final to win." I picked up my guitar, and despite receiving a heavy sigh from Roman, we went on to do our final practice of the day.

Before we knew it, the final was here. We had to sing three songs. Two covers and then one we'd written and done the music for ourselves.

Harley went on stage. She announced the judges who made their grand entrance and took their seats and then the show was underway. The show was live, but on a delay so they could edit where needed, mainly in case someone said something they shouldn't, like Marianne had previously.

"First up tonight is Bill's remaining act The Paranormals." A deafening roar came from the audience. "What have they chosen as their first song of the evening?" she asked him.

Bill leaned over to the microphone. "Well, Harley, let's face it. Every performance from these guys has been incredible. I mean, just look at them." He gestured with his hand. "They already look like they are playing a sell-out gig, not that they're just in the final of a competition. But for our first song we decided they'd sing Bruno Mars, *Marry you*."

And then we were on stage. The audience screamed their approval, so loud that you couldn't hear the opening bars. Our song was the perfect choice because there wouldn't be a female or male watching who wouldn't be imagining Zak Jones singing directly to them. My eyes flitted out over the audience, and I saw Erica enraptured, bless her. Bill had sent her tickets for the final. Her friend Freya was craning her head towards the back. Yep, she definitely liked our Rex. Shame he was destined for a mate, and if she was it, Rex would already have felt it. This was how it would be now. Meeting women who thought they had a chance with us, when most of the time they wouldn't. As much as being in this competition would bring good things, it would bring an equal amount of trouble. My mind went back to Stacey and how Erica had said we looked good together. We were good together. Goddamn it. They said the path of true love never ran smooth. Our path was littered with obstacles.

As soon as we'd finished, every member of the audience was on their feet. A complete standing ovation.

Harley walked back out onto the stage and beckoned for us to stand at the side of her.

"Okay, guys, that's your first performance of the evening and I think the audience liked it." There were more screams. "Now let's see what the judges thought, starting with your mentor, Bill." Harley gestured to him.

Bill looked smug as the camera returned to him.

"Bill, what an opening to the show. You must be ecstatic right now."

Bill looked directly into the camera, holding up his hand. "What can I say? I told you when I first met these guys, they were the ones to watch, and lads, you just owned the stage."

Next, the camera panned to Carmela. She flicked her fringe, pushed out her hand with her painted talons and roared. "I'd marry you, for sure. Wow. What a smoking performance." She fanned herself, while making sure to squeeze her outfit so her boobs popped out more. From there it was Maxwell, the only one who didn't have an act in the final, who said, "You made it your own. It was sensational." Finally, Marianne told us, "The girls at home will love you. You deserve a place in the final performance a million percent."

The audience were still screaming. I looked at my bandmates and every one of their faces held a huge grin. I knew then, that continuing with the competition had been the right thing to do. For them, at least.

Harley turned to us. "I think the judges liked your performance, don't you?" She beamed her large 'teeth-gleaming under the lights' grin.

"It's always fantastic to hear great comments from the judges and we couldn't ask for a better audience," Zak said, blowing a kiss and getting the audience in a frenzy again when Harley had only just got them to quieten down.

She looked out at the audience, smiled, and asked for quiet again. "So, before the audience all explode again, is there anything anyone else would like to add?"

"Just to pick up the phone and vote for us," I said.

That was it. The audience were once again deafeningly loud, and you could hardly hear Harley as we left the stage.

"Did you see that?" Zak was bouncing off the walls. "Oh my god, the audience were insane. I think we might actually win this thing."

"Steady on, Zak." I was excited myself, but I didn't want us heading for a huge disappointment. "There are two other really good bands against us."

"Ugh, I can tell you're a vampire, because you suck the life out of anyone's joy." He clapped my back. "We're in the final, my friend. For fuck's sake, enjoy it, and please stop looking like it's the end of days."

"Yes, Noah, enjoy yourself," a familiar voice came from the doorway, and I spun around to find Mya standing there.

"How did you get past secur—" I stopped when I realised the answer. Compulsion.

"Sorry, I'm late. I watched your first act on my phone on the way, but I'm here now."

"Where's Mr Chirpy?" Zak snarked.

"De-nny is around. He'll say hi later," Mya said. "Okay, well good luck, boys, and I'll catch you after the show."

She disappeared at superspeed, and we watched as Seven Sisters took to the stage.

The beginning notes of *Since u Been Gone* by Kelly Clarkson started up. Mmm, I couldn't help but think this was entirely targeted in my direction, and also would help the band as the viewers speculated that it was part of the feud between us. Stacey's vocals were amazing as always, but something seemed off. She didn't seem her usual self. In fact, the band themselves as a whole had a weird vibe.

They still however did a fabulous performance and got great praise from the judges, with the exception of Bill, who played up to his nasty reputation by saying he felt it wasn't the right song choice.

When Harley asked the band what they thought, Donna took the mic off her and told him that he obviously needed a hearing aid.

I saw the shock in Stacey's face at her bandmate's outburst.

Bill shrugged it all off as a joke and Seven Sisters left the stage.

🎸

I'd never really thought of Flame-Grilled Steak as our main competition. Dray and his band were talented, but they didn't hold a candle to Seven Sisters or us. But you should never underestimate the underdogs, especially when they're competitive shifters.

They swaggered onto the stage and began singing their chosen track, The Rolling Stones *(I Can't Get No) Satisfaction*. They'd performed most of the song when suddenly the band placed down their instruments. The audience went quiet, looking at each other wondering what was going on. Marianne, whose band it was, stared smugly at the other judges as their expressions of 'what's happening' struck their faces, even though we knew that nothing that went on stage hadn't been totally agreed beforehand.

And then Flame-Grilled steak began to dance. They took off their shirts, turned and shook their arses, and ran their hands down their body like they were in Magic Mike and the crowd went insane.

Stacey was standing a few people away from me and I turned and looked at her. Her cheeks were puce, and she shook with anger. "Betrayed again. Yet another man puts his music before me. The absolute bastard." She stomped off, one of the other band members trailing after her. Dray would be lucky if that was the only cursing she did after his performance.

With one song down each, there was still everything to play for. But rather than be focusing on our next performance, all I could think about was Stacey.

There was a live performance from Carmela up next, so while I had the opportunity, I decided I'd go and check on my ex.

But it wasn't to be.

"Right, lads." Bill came walking towards us. The guy had a presence and seemed to bring a sense of power in with him, but he didn't smell of magic. It just seemed to be a genuine charisma. "That stunt Marianne pulled. I knew it was coming, but honestly, I thought they'd look ridiculous. Didn't expect it to be such a success, so what are we going to do to get this back on track and you winning this thing?"

Rex opened his mouth, no doubt to make a suggestion, but Bill was talking rhetorically. "I'll tell you what. You're going to sing *Stay* by Shakespear's Sister as if it's the last song you'll ever sing to your terminally ill wife on her death bed. I want collapsing on your knees and tears streaming down your cheeks, Zak. Then the others come crowd round you. Let the audience think there's been some past lost love and the song has reminded you of it. Okay?"

"Will it get me women falling at my feet?" Zak asked.

"They'll be queuing, mate."

"Done. Prepare to send it for consideration for a BAFTA." He shook Bill's hand and we got quickly changed. Then we were back and they were calling our name to take to the stage.

Chapter 27

Stacey

"I'm going to kill him." I was pacing backstage. "They stole our signature moves. He watched us at the rehearsal, and he pinched our idea, transferred what we were going to do with the final song into their first song.

"So now what do we do?" Meryl asked.

"We carry on as planned, but we take our dance out. Instead, this is what we'll do." I explained my plan. "I'm going to quickly run it past Carmela."

I noticed Donna was keeping quiet. I'd planned on calling her out on her ridiculous outburst until Drayton had pulled that stunt. Now there just wasn't time and I had to hope she kept her mouth shut from now on except for singing.

We made our way back to the stage where The Paranormals had just walked back on. I watched from the shadows. Zak Jones worked the audience like he was a snake charmer, and they were a pit full of adders, but my eyes kept straying to the guy on bass guitar. The first time I let my eyes wander, his gaze snapped to mine, and I realised my guard was down. Fuck. I quickly shut my mind down, locking it in a vault he had no access to. His eyes seemed to dull, and he returned to giving his all to his performance.

They were singing an emotive song, and the audience were mesmerised. Marianne was wiping her eyes. Once again, The Paranormals had pulled ahead of us, with a performance that went beyond an act in a final of a talent competition. Part of me just felt like walking away.

But the other part of me now wanted us to at least wipe out Flame-Grilled Steak from the competition. So we needed to sing our hearts out.

"Come on. Let's make sure that the next performance is Flame-Grilled Steak's final performance."

"Yes, let's," Donna added, and she held up a hand to high five us all.

We sang Pat Benatar's *Love Is A Battlefield* next. We rocked the audience, and you could tell our performance was electric because we were all sharing secret smiles as the crowd got up and danced along. We kept the small dance we had for this one, all of us doing a solo dance move in turn.

We had great feedback from the judges, and I had to hope it had been enough. Because now Flame-Grilled Steak were coming back out and I had no idea what they were going to do.

Seemed like most of Flame-Grilled Steak had no idea too...

I stood backstage near the monitors and near The Paranormals and waited for Dray to walk on.

"What the actual fuck?" Zak stated.

Their drummer shrugged his shoulders as they walked past. "We don't know what's going on. He's adamant this is what he's doing. We're fucked."

Dray pranced onto the stage with my fishnet tights on his legs. He'd hacked through them, and they were half hung down because of course otherwise he wouldn't have got them anywhere near his bulky frame. He'd put make-up on to look like mine and a purple wig he'd obviously got from wardrobe. He'd cut his jeans into jean shorts with half his arse hanging out at the back.

Half of the audience were stunned, the other half in hysterics.

The production crew ran around panicking. "We can't let him go on stage like that."

But no one could stop one determined lead singer, not when he was a giant bear of a man. He took to the stage, cued the music and began to sing Rod Stewart's *Da Ya Think I'm Sexy*... in my higher notes. He sounded like a strangled cat.

"What the actual fuck is happening? Someone tell me." My mouth hung open.

"He wanted to copy us," Donna stated matter of factly. "I gave him a little help."

She said some words of magic and we watched as Dray first looked confused and then down at himself. The crew obviously then managed to get him to listen to instructions in his earpiece as he bolted off stage. Their lead guitarist took over the microphone.

"My apologies. Drayton has been taken ill, which just goes to show that even the most alpha looking of males can at times be vulnerable with their mental health. If these issues affect you, please consult your doctor. Now, if it's okay with everyone, can we start again? I can do the vocals."

They got a thumbs up from the crew and then they sang their song, but the lead guitarist didn't hold the same allure as their lead singer. It was good, but it wasn't final good.

I turned to Donna. "I'm not sure that we can in all good faith join in a final when we cheated our way to it."

"Stacey, what did Dray do? You take this 'do no harm' shit too far. We all have an element of bad in us, it's natural. We don't sign up to practice our craft and then become Mother fucking Teresa. I'm going to get a drink. I'll be back for the results." Once more Donna walked away from us. She was really starting to piss me off.

"What's with her?" I asked Shonna.

"Fucked if I know," she replied.

The judges had been supportive with their feedback of Flame-Grilled Steak's performance and gave their best wishes to Dray. Marianne no longer looked so smug. On a final show, judges were never too mean, so they'd not been critical of the stand-in lead's performance.

Harley spoke to the camera announcing that the rest of the final would take place after the evening news, and that was it. We had a short break in proceedings before we'd find out who won Britain's Best New Band.

I turned to walk back to my dressing room, but a tall, pale man blocked my way. Noah passed me a bottle of water.

I took it. "Thanks."

"Nice touch with Dray. I gather you're no longer seeing him." His eyes bored into mine.

"I didn't do it actually. I'm going to go check the guy is okay now, and in answer to your question we were never anything serious. He was good company. Sometimes you need a friend."

"Stacey, I—"

A crew member interrupted us. "They need some shots of you all backstage for the after-show on ITV2."

That was the excuse I needed. I ran ahead of the crew and away from Noah and whatever he wanted to say, because now was not the time, not when either of us might be about to win a lifechanging competition where our lives once more would move in different directions.

The three of our bands stood side by side on the stage with our mentors as Harley got ready to announce who had made it through to the final two acts.

"I can now announce, the first band through to the final round is..." She paused for what seemed like several years. "The Paranormals."

The audience shrieked and I watched as Noah and his band jumped up and down hugging each other. After he'd gathered himself, his eyes sought mine. I looked away.

Harley got ready to stop one bands journey towards a recording contract. "Okay, if we can have silence now please. The second act through to the final round is..."

Please. Please. Please. Please. Please.

"Seven Sisters."

My bandmates squealed. My own reaction was more one of relief, but I couldn't help but be carried by the happiness of my band, and joy filled my body.

I could feel Noah's gaze on me again. *For heaven's sake, stop,* I mentally begged him, letting my guard down so he could hear my thoughts.

"Flame-Grilled Steak, come gather around me, boys. It's time to take a look at your best bits," Harley stated and the rest of us piled off stage.

🎸

"Stacey," Noah's voice shouted out from behind.

I spun around. "Noah, for God's sake. We're about to sing our final songs, can you leave me alone?"

"I don't want to leave you alone, Stacey. I love you."

He... *what?*

I should have been ecstatic to hear those words. Instead, he'd pissed me right off.

"Now? Now you announce you love me? Just before you

might win the record deal with the bandmates you ditched me for?"

"You said you wanted me to choose. I'm sorry for everything that went on before." He grabbed my hand. "I choose you, Stacey. I'll walk away right now. I'll get on that stage and tell everyone, the crowd and the audience of millions, that I'm walking away from the band and walking towards the love of my life."

I snatched my hand back. "I'm not having this conversation right now. Don't be stupid and get ready to sing. I want to beat you."

His eyes bored into mine and he spoke softly. "What for? Why did you enter this competition? You wanted to face me, beat me, and why? I'll tell you why. Because you wanted me to realise what I'd been missing. I can see that, Stacey. I've known since I walked away and I'm here, in front of you. You don't have to beat me."

"Yes, she does." Donna stepped forward. "Because regardless of her intentions for entering, she has six bandmates who are in this with her. You might want to remember your own."

Zak stepped forward from behind Noah. He shrugged his shoulders. "We don't actually give a toss. Clear to see our guy loves your girl. He's a great guitarist, but we could get another one. I'm sure the one from Flame-Grilled Steak would jump right now."

"I think I'm saying 'thanks'." Noah gave Zak a withering gaze.

"I wish I could have one woman for the rest of my life, instead of thousands," Zak added, sighing. Then he pulled a grimace. "Did you hear what I just said?" He pushed Donna on the shoulder. "You put a spell on me or something?"

"Touch me again, I'll put my fist in your balls," she snarked.

"Oooh you like it rough?" Zak's eyes twinkled with mischief.

The production manager came forward. "It's time to sing."

Noah looked at me.

"We'll talk *after* the competition, Noah. I want to know who'd win."

He smiled. "That's not a fuck off. I'll take it."

I smirked and walked away.

I wanted to jump for joy but I kept it cool. Noah loved me! He'd have walked away from it all and he loved me!

Chapter 28

Noah

This was it, the final of the competition, and... I couldn't give a toss if we won. I thought I had a chance with Stacey.

"Oooooph." I clutched my balls, seeing stars.

Looking up once my vision cleared, I stared straight into the eyes of... Roman??? Jesus, he was the last person I expected to knee me in the nuts.

"You might get your girl. It's all your dreams come true. Fantastic. Guess what my dream is? Winning this competition. So get your focus on going out there and playing that guitar like your life depends on it, because it does. Screw up and I'll fucking kill you."

"Whoa. Listen to goat-boy go. Oooooph." Zak had suffered a similar fate.

Roman turned to Rex, head tilted.

"I ain't got nothing to say except let's do this. I'd like to keep my balls bruise free thanks."

"Let's win this thing!" Roman yelled.

We all high-fived.

It was down to fate now. The competition, my love life. Time to go enjoy our time on stage and see where it took us.

Harley came out on stage. "Our first act in the final is The Paranormals."

We walked out and sang our song. We gave it everything we had.

Then Seven Sisters came out and did the same.

It was all down to the public now, and who they wanted as Britain's Best New Band.

This was it. We were on stage to find out who had won. I looked out into the audience. I could see Erica and Freya. I could see Mya and Death. I could see an audience full of screaming supporters.

If my heart beat it would have been thumping now.

My eyes begged me to look at Stacey, but I wouldn't. Not until the announcement. Not until I either rushed to congratulate her or told her I'd leave again. That I chose her.

Harley asked for the audience to be quiet.

"Before we announce the winners, we'd just like to take a few moments to remind you of Dan Trent, who should have been here with me sharing the stage this evening. We haven't given up hope on you, Dan. Please if you're out there watching. Get in touch."

"Like you give a shit, you fame hungry whore," shot out of Bill's mouth.

The audience gasped. Harley froze and Bill laughed like a madman. Getting up from his seat, he walked over and up to Harley's side. He snatched the microphone from her and stood in the centre of the stage.

"This is my show. I'll announce the winner." He listened to his earpiece.

"The winner of tonight's final is..."

The music started up, but now both of our bands were looking at each other, mouthing 'What's happening?'.

"Oh no," Donna shouted.

"What?" Stacey snapped.

"It's... Dan. I think it's Dan. In Bill's body. He would say that. He would say fame hungry whore. Somehow, I must have let him in."

"Me," Bill/Dan announced. "The winner is me. Who cares about the bands? I'm going home to sit by a pool with multiple prostitutes and a mountain of crack, both arse and the white stuff."

The crowd went insane, booing and trying to get at the stage.

And then Death came up with Mya in tow.

"We aren't filming anymore, are we?" I shouted at the others. "Please tell me supernatural identities are not being revealed live on ITV."

"No, they cut us off straight after Bill called me a whore," Harley stated and then Bill/Dan grabbed her by the throat.

"If I'm dead then why should you live?" he whined.

Mya swept forward and pulled his hand away. Stacey dashed towards a spluttering Harley, and then Donna rushed over. "Can someone help me? I accidentally unleashed him. It's the spirit of Dan Trent."

Mya looked shocked. Her eyes widened and she grabbed hold of 'Bill's' throat.

"Is that true? Is that you, Dan? I thought I warned you before. I should have known you'd be a nuisance." She turned to Death. "Take him."

Death walked forward and placed a hand on 'Bill's' forehead.

He uttered words in no language I knew, and then said. "Daniel Trent, leave this body now. You will be sent straight to the Home of Wayward Souls."

"Do not pass Go," Zak yelled before guffawing.

I elbowed him in the ribs.

"Ouch. God, it had to be said. It was too good an opportunity to miss," he complained.

We knew Dan had gone when Bill's face turned pale and he collapsed. Unfortunately, Dan had one last parting shot.

He'd turned to where Stacey was comforting Harley and he'd pushed them. Harley managed to right herself, but Stacey stumbled and fell clean off the stage.

Vampiric speed had never been so welcomed. I got to her within a foot of the floor and threw her up onto the stage. She'd have bruises, but she'd survive.

I wasn't sure I would. Some of the surging angry crowd had tried ripping up floorboards and a sharp upturned piece of wood was about to go through me. I felt it push through my chest and I waited to combust to dust.

Chapter 29

Stacey

I rolled across the stage floor, smarting as my bony bits hit, but then I flew up, my only thoughts of Noah being okay.

However, as I looked over the stage all I could see was a group of people, one of them Mya who was shouting, "Noah, oh fuck, Noah."

Harley grabbed me. "He's okay. I don't know if I am though because I'm seeing some weird shit this evening and I'm wondering if I've been slipped something."

"No, it's real," I told her, and I ran down to where I realised Noah lay on the ground. A piece of wood had gone through his chest and must have just missed his heart. Mya was carefully extracting it, and as it finally came out with a resounding pop that made me feel sick, the gap closed and healed up.

"Oh thank God. My son, I thought you were going to leave me." She began to cry, which was disconcerting as red tears tracked down her cheeks.

Death joined her. "We need to go, Mya. We have to deal with Dan."

She looked up at him, her fangs bared. "I hate you."

Death just shrugged. "You're the Queen of the Wayward, so tough titty."

"Let me have a moment alone with my son," she commanded. Everyone stepped back including me. "And you, Stacey. This concerns you."

※

With everyone rushing around trying to deal with the aftermath of the final going haywire, I sat alongside Noah and Mya on the floor at the front of the stage.

"So Dan *was* killed," Noah said. "Shit, wonder what happened there?"

"I drained him," Mya said, looking at her fingernails as if she hadn't just confessed to murder.

She looked up and caught mine and Noah's wide-eyed expressions. "Oh, his time was up. Death told me. He accidentally said it while we were watching the auditions. Told me he'd seen his name on the board. Was gonna get hit by a bus. Anyway, I secretly came to the earlier auditions to keep an eye on you two, and I saw him threaten Harley. Said if she didn't leave, he would... well, it wasn't nice stuff he threatened to do with her. His aura was all off, he smelled bad. He'd have done something evil. So I offed him a week early."

Noah sighed. "Mya, did you by any chance have anything to do with the disappearance of Jack Brooks?"

"What?" I half-shouted.

Mya just shrugged. "He was another one. When they're truly evil I can smell them; they're like really bad diarrhoea after sprouts. I couldn't stop Stacey giving away her virginity, she did that freely, but he was going to attack her after." She looked at me. "He was going to hurt you, and then go on to hurt others before taking the cowards way out when caught, so I did the world a favour."

"Mya, you can't just go around draining people," I said.

"I'm a vampire queen, sweetpea, that's exactly what I can do." She patted my hair. "Bless."

Rising to her feet, she knocked dust off the back of her dress. "Right, me and Death need to get moving. I'm hoping you two can finally stop wasting time, although you're going become a vampire and live with him forever now. I've seen the entry where your human life ends in The Book of the Dead."

"MYA," Death shouted. "The book is confidential. How many more times?"

"Oops, I'm in trouble again. Hopefully I'll get punished." She winked, kissed our cheeks, went to Death's side and then they were gone.

We realised the hysteria surrounding us.

"I need to do my bit," Noah said, and he whizzed to the stage.

I guessed what he was going to do, and sure enough, he held the audience, staff, and judges in a huge compulsion, clearing their minds off anything that had happened.

The power of suggestion meant that everyone believed an overwhelmed Bill had suffered a breakdown on live TV. A production member then added that a substitute programme had hastily been added to the schedule.

The production team gathered the members of the two bands together and Bill himself came to find us. He looked a lot better, though shellshocked.

"Look, darlings, I'm not sure what happened this evening, but it's clear I've obviously been working myself into the ground. Anyhow, the results came in at a dead heat. It's never been known. With that in mind you'll both be joining my team. Someone will be in touch, okay?"

I looked across at Noah. "Seven Sisters would have won if there was one more voter."

He looked back at me. "Come on, Stace, give it up. It's a dead heat. We drew. Can we finally call a truce?"

I took a deep breath. Now I needed to decide what my future held. Were music and Noah a part of it?

Chapter 30

Mya

On my way out of the building with Death I'd passed Bill. "Just a minute, sweetie. I need a quick word with him."

Death sighed heavily but stood still and folded his arms over his chest.

I got the medics standing with Bill to move away with a kind word in their ears (aka the power of suggestion) and then I looked deep into Bill's eyes.

"You will cancel the phone vote and refund every penny, and you will believe regardless of the results that it was a dead heat."

He nodded.

No one would ever know who actually won the competition.

No one. Not even me.

Are you annoyed? Now you know what my mood was like when someone turned me into a vampire and made me Queen of the Wayward.

Fucking infuriating, isn't it?

Chapter 31

Noah

Bill walked away, the production crew left us, and our two bands sat dumbstruck. It was an expression we'd worn on more than one occasion that evening.

Harley walked in with a bottle of champagne in each hand and passed one to Roman, and one to Donna.

I'd just asked Stacey what was happening now, but as Roman popped the cork and my bandmates started jumping around, I once again realised that this wasn't the time either. Maybe there'd never be a right time. Donna dragged Stacey by the hand, and they popped the cork of their bottle. Then champagne was being shaken and poured over all of us and we began to realise we'd won a fucking recording contract.

"Let's move this party somewhere better," Donna said.

"I know just the place," Zak answered.

And with that we all set off for Sheol.

***

I watched from the edge of the dance floor as Stacey moved her hips to the beat of the music. She raised her hands and swayed, while around her, her bandmates made similar moves. But I wasn't interested in them.

The Paranormals had celebrated our future with shots, and as a bevy of females began to keep approaching us, we realised that life was about to change. Don had sent Aaron down to make sure no one harmed his incubus. Zak was going to be a busy boy.

Aaron walked over to me, and no one was more surprised than me when he spoke.

"You need to stop staring at her and go get her. Don't take no for an answer. You're a vampire. A predator. Why are you not claiming her as your own?"

"I don't know, Aaron," I admitted honestly. "When it comes to Stacey, I'm weak."

"We're all weak when it comes to love," he said. "Even demons."

He looked over at Zak, who was charming the ladies, but who wore a tormented expression around his eyes.

I realised that Aaron was telling me something.

"Us demons learn certain information at each level, but as I'm working for the big, bad boss, I'm privy to more information than I should know. If he finds out I've told you, I'll be incinerated, but I have a son Zak's age, and I can't imagine him being bound to a life like Zak's." He took a deep breath. "When he finds true love, his contract ends. His soul will be returned."

I gasped.

"But you can't tell him that. To tell him would be to torment him. He'd be unlikely to find it if too focused. And more than that, it would mean a disqualification. He wouldn't be able to end his contract with Don."

"But I can try to help him look for love, albeit discreetly?"

"As long as you don't tell him the truth."

I patted Aaron on the arm. "Thank you, Aaron. Thank you so much."

Aaron nodded his head and began to walk away, and then he turned back around. "She's looked over here at least six times while we've been talking. If you let her leave this time, it will be the end of this. I can see it in her eyes."

I remembered what Zak had said about being able to find another bass guitarist if needed. I realised that was fine with me.

Oh I'd be crushed for a while. Music had been my dream, but Stacey... Stacey was reality, and right now, it was time to do what I did best.

Stalk and claim my prey.

I waited for Stacey to walk down the corridor towards the ladies bathrooms and then I swiftly grabbed her and pulled her into a dark alcove of the club at lightning speed. The scream was only just appearing at her lips when she realised who'd done it and where we were.

"For God's sake, Noah. I'm going to need my hairdresser on speed dial at this rate to cover my grey."

"I'm done, Stacey," I told her.

"What?" Her eyes looked panicked.

"With the band. With The Paranormals. I'm done with the band."

"Oh." She let out an exhale.

"Shit, you thought I meant with you."

"Duh," she said, punching me in the chest.

My stomach flipped as I realised she'd have been upset if we were over.

"I'm far from done with you, Stacey Williams. I haven't even started what I intend to do with you."

"Oh yeah? Like what?" She raised a brow.

"I'm going to kiss you, love you, fuck you, make love to you, and marry you, Stacey. That's if you forgive me for the mistakes of my youth. I promise you'll never come second in my life ever again."

"I'll consider this on one condition." Stacey folded her arms across her chest.

"Okay, what is it?"

"You take the recording contract and see where your music takes you."

I shook my head. "No, Stacey…"

She raised a hand and put her fingers across my lips. "Noah, I asked you to choose, and you did. You chose me. You would put me before everything. That's all I've ever thought I wanted, but actually it's selfish. I couldn't live with myself knowing I stopped your dreams. We'd not survive that."

I smirked.

"Yeah, okay, you're dead anyway and I'm apparently going to become a vampire, so neither of us is surviving, but you get my gist."

"I do."

"I've realised there are things I need to do for myself. I quite fancy being a theatre actress down the line. Therefore, I've decided that I'm going to tour with whoever of the Seven Sisters wants to and see what opportunities it brings. I spoke to Harley, and she says it's going to be a joint tour with two headline acts."

"Looks like we're stuck with each other for a while then." My smile broke across my face, and I swear it almost cracked my jaw it was so wide.

"Yep, sure looks that way." Stacey smiled back. "Now what did you say you were going to do with me again?"

"I think I started with kiss you," I said, and I leaned forward and claimed her mouth with my own.

Chapter 32

Erica

**From: TheSubsofTheParanormals@gmail.com
Subject: EXCLUSIVE – EXCLUSIVE – EXCLUSIVE – OMG THEY GOT MARRIED!
Date: 20 May 2023**

From the ONLY OFFICIAL fan group of The Paranormals.

OMFG Subs!

They only went and did it in secret!

Noah Granger and Stacey Williams are now man and wife! Photos are being released to the press, but here's one they sent especially for the Subs along with this sweet message.

Subs,

We couldn't wait any longer and didn't need a fancy ceremony. All we need is each other.
Now we're Mr & Mrs Granger and couldn't be happier.
We look forward to seeing you on tour soon. Don't forget to grab your tickets as from September, Stacey will be leaving The Seven to star in the West End as Velma in Chicago.
There's no time for a honeymoon, but we're okay with that. We're enjoying singing our music to you all.
Thanks for all your support. You're the best!
Noah & Stacey (Mr & Mrs Granger) xo

I have it on good authority that Donna Matthews will be taking over the lead. I have to say when I first heard a few of Seven Sisters weren't going ahead with the tour, I was worried as you know, but then three of Flame-Grilled Steak joined them and now I think The Seven are amazing.

I asked Charlie from FGS how Dray was doing and apparently, he met his 'one' in hospital and he's home and living happy ever after so that's good news isn't it?

Anyway, I'll leave you to celebrate the exciting news and I'll be in touch with you soon, when I'll have an exclusive interview with our lead singer. Yes, Zak Jones will be talking to me. Is this real life? Where I get up close and personal with The Paranormals?

Happy sigh.

Erica xoxo

I proofread the piece and then I pressed send to the thousands of subscribers. It grew day by day. The Seven did well, but The Paranormals were becoming superstars.

They were so busy that now I dealt with their PA, Vikki.

I began to write my list of questions for Zak. I'd send them to Vikki and she'd send me the answers back. It was just like backstage on Britain's Best New Band. To the Subs, it looked like I was living my dreams, speaking to the hottest band of the moment regularly, but in reality, I was nowhere near them.

And I so wanted to be near Zak Jones. Preferably underneath him.

I sighed as I clicked onto the showbiz pages where I looked at him with woman after woman after woman.

Seemed some things just weren't meant to be.

🎸

I met Freya. We'd decided to have a meal at the Rock Hard Bistro where Stacey used to work. Their food was amazing, and the atmosphere was great.

We'd just taken our seats when a woman came rushing over to us, followed by an older lady.

"Ebony, can we not have this every time you visit?" the older woman yelled.

The woman grabbed my arm. I flinched, but then she said. "You must follow your heart. Don't give up on your dreams of love."

Her perfectly enunciated words, said in a cut-glass accent that sounded like the tinkle of piano keys, took away the shock of her having grabbed my arm.

The older woman pulled her away and apologised.

I said it was fine. And it really was.

Because my heart belonged to Zak Jones, and now I would go follow him.

THE END

Can Zak find true love and end his demonic contract? Find out in ROCK 'N' SOULS.

Read Mya's story in SUCK MY LIFE.

If you enjoyed HEX FACTOR please consider leaving a review.

To keep up with latest release news and receive an exclusive subscriber only ebook DATING SUCKS:
A Supernatural Dating Agency prequel short story, sign up here: geni.us/andiemlongparanormal

Playlist

Taylor Swift, *Wildest Dreams*
Britney Spears, *Toxic*
Britney Spears, *Womanizer*
Kelly Clarkson, *Since u Been Gone*
Rolling Stones, *(I Can't Get No) Satisfaction*
Bruno Mars, *Marry You*
Pat Benatar, *Love Is A Battlefield*
Rod Stewart, *Da Ya Think I'm Sexy*

ROCK 'N' SOULS

*To **Duran Duran**, and most especially the major obsessive crush of my youth, **John Taylor**.*

I hope you liked the giant homemade birthday card I sent you when you were twenty-four via your fan club...

Prologue

Erica

**From: TheSubsofTheParanormals@gmail.com
Subject: EXCLUSIVE – EXCLUSIVE – EXCLUSIVE – OMG THEY GOT MARRIED!
Date: 20 May 2023**

From the ONLY OFFICIAL fan group of The Paranormals.

OMFG Subs!
They only went and did it in secret!
Noah Granger and Stacey Williams are now man and wife!
Photos are being released to the press, but here's one they sent especially for the Subs along with this sweet message.

Subs,

We couldn't wait any longer and didn't need a fancy ceremony. All we need is each other.

Now we're Mr & Mrs Granger and couldn't be happier.

We look forward to seeing you on tour soon. Don't forget

to grab your tickets as from September, Stacey will be leaving The Seven to star in the West End as Velma in Chicago.

There's no time for a honeymoon, but we're okay with that. We're enjoying singing our music to you all.

Thanks for all your support. You're the best!
Noah & Stacey (Mr & Mrs Granger) xo

I have it on good authority that Donna Matthews will be taking over the lead. I have to say when I first heard a few of Seven Sisters weren't going ahead with the tour, I was worried as you know, but then three of Flame-Grilled Steak joined them and now I think The Seven are amazing.

I asked Charlie from FGS how Dray was doing and apparently, he met his 'one' in hospital and he's home and living happy ever after so that's good news isn't it?

Anyway, I'll leave you to celebrate the exciting news and I'll be in touch with you soon, when I'll have an exclusive interview with our lead singer. Yes, Zak Jones will be talking to me. Is this real life? Where I get up close and personal with The Paranormals?

Happy sigh.

Erica xoxo

I began to write my list of interview questions for Zak Jones, lead singer of the hottest band on the planet right now, The Paranormals. Six months ago, they'd been the joint winners of a TV talent show called Britain's Best New Band.

I'd met the guys at the live rounds of the show, and well, long story that I'll get to, but I ended up running their fan club. It was an honour. Plus, also, I thought it might get me nearer to my crush—Zak.

But I'd underestimated how busy they'd get. Now I sent my questions to their PA, Vikki, and she'd send me the answers back. It was like the show they'd won—not all it seemed. Just as reality shows set things up to look better than they were, to the Subs (what we called the subscribers), it looked like I was living my dreams, speaking to the hottest band of the moment regularly, while in reality, I was nowhere near them.

And I so wanted to be near Zak Jones. Preferably underneath him.

I sighed as I clicked onto the showbiz pages on my laptop where I looked at him with woman after woman after woman.

The last time I'd caught sight of him had been at the final itself, when I'd gone there with my best friend Freya, but we hadn't been able to talk to them. As soon as they'd won, they'd been steered into press conferences where despite my best efforts to join in, security had told me I wasn't official press.

I'd made sure I had an official press badge now. Vikki had sorted that out for me.

The band had gone stellar after winning the competition and they and The Seven (the other joint winners) had been recording albums and touring the world in the six months that had passed since that night back in November of last year.

But where lead singer Noah was now happily married and loved up with Stacey from The Seven; my own crush, Zak, was bedding as many females as he could. It should have put me off him, but instead, my crazy, soppy heart just told me it was because he'd not fallen in love with his soulmate yet, which was of course *me*.

Sighing, I switched off my computer, and got ready to go have a meal out with Freya—one involving lots of wine.

We'd decided to have a meal at the Rock Hard Bistro where Stacey Granger used to work before she found fame. Their food was amazing, and the atmosphere was great.

Freya took one look at my face as I walked inside the entrance and rolled her eyes. "Oh God. I'd ask who died, but this has been your perpetual face of late. It's a Saturday night, babe. Time to get some drinks and then I'll be your wingwoman and help get you some dick."

"Freya! That was too loud," I chuntered.

"If I don't say it loudly, how will any of the men here know you're up for riding their cock?" she replied.

I was in two minds of whether or not to feign a headache and go right back home, but the food smelled too good to leave.

We'd just taken our seats when a woman came rushing over to us, followed by an older lady.

"Ebony, can we not have this every time you visit?" the older woman yelled, just as the younger one grabbed my arm.

I flinched and looked to Freya for help, but then the woman said, "You must follow your heart. Don't give up on your dreams of love."

Her perfectly enunciated words, said in a cut glass accent that sounded like the tinkle of piano keys, took away the shock of her invading my personal space.

The older woman pulled her away. "I'm so sorry. We'll leave you to enjoy your meal, and it's on me, okay? I'll tell the waiter to send me your bill."

"No, no. It's absolutely fine." The woman had been well out of order, but she'd told me what my ears wanted to hear.

Because my heart belonged to Zak Jones, and now I would go follow him. Whatever I needed to do to get up close and personal to that man I would now do. The woman had made me determined. Had given me a sign of encouragement.

He needed to realise I existed.

It was time for me to make another move. To not give up this time like I did six months ago.

"Well, that was weird," Freya said. "A posho acting like a fortune teller."

"Freya."

"Yeah?"

"I'm not going for any of the guys here tonight."

She huffed. "Erica, I know your last few dates have not gone to plan, but you have to keep trying."

I held a hand up. "I am. I've decided. I'm going for Zak Jones. We're doing this. I will get near to him, and he will realise I exist."

Freya's grin grew wide. "You mean we're going to meet the band again? I'm going to get to see Sexy Rexy again?" Freya had the hots for Rex Colton, The Paranormals' drummer.

"Yes. I'm going to demand face-to-face contact. I run their official fan club. There should be perks."

"Yes, like our nipples when we see the boys."

"Just so I'm making myself clear. I need your help in landing myself at least one night in the sack with Zak Jones, and if possible, the rest of my life."

Freya nodded her head enthusiastically. "Absolutely, and if it just so happens that to do so I am forced to shag Rex Colton, as your very best friend I would take one for the team. One very big one I hope."

"You're such a martyr."

"Waiter!" Freya yelled. She winked at me. "We need more wine and to make some plans, because so far, has NOT been so good."

Part One

BEFORE THE PARANORMALS JOINTLY WON
BRITAIN'S BEST NEW BAND.

Chapter 1

Erica

September 2022 – watching televised episode of the first judges auditions of Britain's Best New Band (filmed July 2022).

I tended to get a bit obsessed with things. Okay, not a bit, a lot. Like I'd binge watch a show, take *Queer Eye* for example, and then I'd get their autobiographies, and Antoni's cookbook even though I struggled to butter a slice of bread. I'd follow them on Instagram, follow them on TikTok. You get the picture. Then I'd be onto the next programme, the next obsession. Basically, I needed to get a life and I was spending far too much time on my own at home.

I blamed my best friend, Freya. She was in love and so my social life had taken a tumble. It wasn't that she'd abandoned me for her boyfriend. More that I couldn't face listening to how wonderful he was and having to witness her lovesick face. Yes, that made me a cow. I was happy for her, but I was twenty-one years old, worked in a supermarket, and lived with my mum in a council house in Clapham with no love life whatsoever. I couldn't even have a battery-operated boyfriend because my mother still insisted on cleaning my room.

Anyway, this was why, when I should be out living it up on a

Saturday night, I was instead lying on my bed in my bedroom, TV on, watching Britain's Best New Band, with only a packet of crisps for company. We were at the live auditions stage where they performed for the judges, (note my use of the word 'we' because of my mental overinvolvement) and my heart was in my mouth as the next band came onto the screen. Dan and Harley, the presenters, always chatted backstage with whoever was going on stage next and I'd never wanted to be Harley Davies so much in my damn life. Lucky, lucky bitch.

"Hi, guys, so you're The Para-not-normals. How did you four get together?" she asked them.

A dark-haired guy spoke. "We met at college and practised in our spare time. We've played a few gigs, but this is the competition we've always wanted to be in."

"Well, the judges are waiting for you. Good luck." Harley smiled, and the guys sauntered onto the stage.

Seriously, I had never in my life seen such fit blokes. Every one of them was a hunk. Nearly always in a band you had at least one who looked like, as my mum would say, 'they'd had a hard paper round', but no. They looked in need of an image overhaul, but I'd watched this show before and knew that they liked to make entrants look worse because they all got a makeover before the live competition weeks started. I could clearly see that I was going to be licking the television screen if this lot got through. Especially the lead singer. He just had this aura about him. It seemed otherworldly, like he almost glowed out of the screen. I know, I was getting far too overexcited, but seriously, it was like he called to me. Fuck, I really did need to get a dildo because I was clearly heading for the edge. My mother needed a bingo night so she could shout 'house' while I shouted in the house. With numbers for mum and the letter 'O' for me, I could almost talk myself into believing my masturbation would be educational. Here's the current math, my current 'O' was numerical, as in zero = fuck all.

"Okay," Bill Traynor, the main guy from the auditions said, dragging me back from my imagination. "So who are you guys?"

The lead singer began to speak, and I was lost once more. "I'm Zak. This is Rex, Roman, and Noah. We're the Para-not-normals and we're going to sing *Paradise City* for you."

"Okay," Bill said. "When you're ready."

The band began to sing, but within thirty seconds, Bill put a hand up and stopped them.

"Noooooooo," I yelled, my grab packet of *Doritos* flying off my lap as I sprang up off the bed and to my feet. He could not stop my guys. No way!

"Do you have something else? I don't think that song is the right one for you," Bill said looking frustrated.

"For God's sake, Bill," I ranted. "This better be a wind up."

My phone beeped and I sat back on the bed and looked at the message that had come through.

Mum: Can you keep it down? If you've that much energy maybe you could wash the dishes?

And this was why I needed to move out. I couldn't even enjoy myself watching television outside of my covers, never mind enjoy myself under them.

The band had moved onto *Wildest Dreams* by Taylor Swift, and I watched enraptured as they sang their hearts out, the guys giving backing vocals to Zak. Then Dan and Harley came back on stage, the band standing between them, and Dan asked for the judges' response to the audition.

Talent scout Maxwell Johnson spoke first. "I think you have potential. It's a yes from me."

I took a slow breath out. Come on!

Then it was Marianne Moore's turn. I didn't know her, but Mum had said she had been really famous in the 1960's. "You remind me of The Rolling Stones in their early days when we used to hang around together. Great times. It's a yes from me."

Carmela Toto was up next. I didn't like her much. She'd been in a girl band, but always seemed to want the spotlight on herself. "I like you. You have a great energy. Yes, from me," she told them. And just like that I liked her again because she saved my band. Although if she went anywhere near Zak, I'd make a voodoo doll of her using one of my niece's Barbies. Poppy had so many, she'd not miss one, and I'd bought her most of them anyway. I could set fire to it. A Barbie-cue.

Finally, it was Bill's turn. "I like you guys. There's something about you, but I'm not sure..."

"Don't be fucking stupid, Bill," I shouted.

The audience began to protest and chanted, "Yes, yes, yes." I joined in.

Bill looked back at the audience and his face contorted as he considered his verdict. "I think with a little image styling and some expert advice you could have something. One thing though. Your name. I'm not into it. I'd prefer just The Paranormals. Get you looking like you're too fantastic to simply be human. I think we could have a little fun with that."

The band looked on tenterhooks and I realised I was sitting on my hands.

"What do you say? Ready for an image and name change?"

They said yes.

I yelled, "Yeeeeeeeesssssssss."

"Then that's four yeses. You're through to the next round. Congratulations, guys," Bill announced.

And my mother sent me another text.

Mum: The neighbours will think you've got a bloke round. FFS can you Please. Keep. The. Noise. Down. Before they report us to the council, and we end up homeless.

. . .

An advert came on as the show finished and the voice said. "Win tickets to be in the audience of Britain's Best New Band," and before I knew it, my phone was in my hand, and I was dialling the number.

Something told me that I needed to see this band for real.

I decided after calling, that my obsessional behaviour had hit an all-time high.

And then on Monday morning I got a text.

Congratulations! You are a winner of two tickets for the live rounds of Britain's Best New Band. Please reply to this message with your name and email address.

Oh my god! I could barely tap the keys on my phone as I answered. *Please don't go wrong.* I needed those tickets like I needed the air to breathe.

Shortly afterwards, I got a text confirming that tickets were on their way to my email address.

I rang Freya.

"Freya, next Saturday night, I need you. We're off down to the London Landmark," I spilled out excitedly.

"Uhm, why?"

Freya needed to get on board with my level of enthusiasm. This would not do.

"I just won two tickets to the first live round of Britain's Best New Band."

She shrieked and nearly took my ear off. "OMG, we have to get backstage. I need to be up close and personal with that Rex dude. He is so HOT."

"I thought you were loved up with John?" I queried. My eyebrow was arched although she couldn't see it.

"John is amazing, but I want to lick the sweat directly off Rex's skin."

Wow, it seemed my friend was also a tad overexcited about a member of The Paranormals. Good job it wasn't my man, because we always said ho's before bros, and I'd have felt bereaved.

Your behaviour gets more worrying by the day, my inner voice chided.

"Erm, okay then. Well, I have to be getting to work, so talk soon."

"Yes, very soon. We need to plan outfits. We have to look killer, but also undercover. Maybe black, so we can sneak around," Freya stated.

I ended the call wondering if I should have just taken my mum.

Chapter 2

Zak

July 2022 - Britain's Best New Band auditions.

God, I was knackered. We'd been rehearsing hard all week and had just sung for the actual judges. The producers had made us go through hair and make-up for a 'make under' before doing so. Now the judges' audition was a wrap and we were through to the next round. I should have been ecstatic, except I still needed to go out and make contact with a fuck ton of women so I could appear in their dreams tonight and make *them* ecstatic.

Did that sound heavenly?

It was not. It was a curse straight from the seventh dimension of hell—Abaddon to be precise. The bastard had tricked me when I was a virginal eighteen-year-old who'd thought he was going to die that way. Drunken Zak went into a bar, not knowing it masked the 'Destroyer's' dwelling, and came out minus his soul after promising some of all those he slept withs because he'd been told there would be a LOT. And that wasn't a lie, as my quota got larger to the point where sex was now often a chore to meet my soul targets rather than my orgasm.

And you couldn't sleep well, when bedtime was when you

had to work. I was doing the day with the band, the evening with the flirting, and the night shift with soul searching, and I didn't mean figuring out the meaning of my life. I was too fucking exhausted for all that.

"I'm going to check out the competition until they call us for make-up," our bass guitarist, Noah said. None of us were that dumb. By competition, he meant his ex, Stacey.

"I'm going to check out Harley," I informed my bandmates and off I went in search of her. Harley Davies was the co-presenter of the show. She was gorgeous, with blonde, long-bobbed hair I imagined would shake a little as her head bobbed later as she sucked my cock. And those lips were made for encasing my manhood. I adjusted my trousers. Things were getting tight back there.

Harley's personality shone out of her like the sunlight. I reckoned if I could get her to sleep with me, her soul would be worth ten other women's. That's how it went. On the rarest of occasions, you found one so good and pure that it was like a 100-watt soul against the usual 15-watt.

Harley and her co-presenter Dan were hanging around backstage. They were filming segments interviewing acts that would be slotted in between the live performances when the shows aired. I spotted them as I walked through the auditorium, and I walked closer. From a distance it just appeared like they were having an everyday conversation, but as I neared, I could hear the venom in Dan's voice.

"This is my gig. I hosted this show perfectly fine by myself before and I don't see why they would have brought you in this year, if not to push me out."

"That's not the case, Dan," Harley pleaded with him. "They want to appeal more to a male viewership and so they brought me in too. At least you're rated on your talent as a presenter. I'm rated on what outfits I wear!"

"We're not talking about you; we're talking about me. You need to resign. It's the right thing to do. Quit."

I'd heard enough. "I think you should give the lady some space, mate," I drawled, walking over to them.

Dan turned to me and scowled. "Why, what are you going to do?" He raised a brow. "Touch me and your career's over before it's started."

"I'm going to tell security and then what will that do for your presenting career?" I told him. "They might just kick you out, so Harley gets the stage all to herself."

He bristled at that. "Think about what I said," he snarled at Harley as a parting shot and then he stomped off.

Harley smiled at me. There it was again, that white, beaming light. "Thanks so much. I was okay though. He's just a very bitter and angry man."

"He's jealous as fuck and he had no right to talk to you like that. And for what it's worth, I think you're a fantastic presenter. Yes, you're pretty, but you're good at what you do."

"You think so? Thank you," she said, holding a hand to her chest. And what a chest it was. She was hiding a cracking rack under that sweater. I wanted to release them, like unlocking a cage of puppies at breakfast time.

"Right, I'd better go and get make-up to freshen me up and get ready to deal with Dan again." She started to walk away from me.

I startled at that.

Women did not walk away from me. Ever. Not when I turned on my incubus charm. They hung onto my every word like I hung the moon and some of them drooled, and not only from their mouth.

Was it the new crimped hair they'd forced me to have? My inner incubus charm should override such things...

"Erm," I said.

She turned back around. "Sorry, did you want something else?"

"Oh, er, no," I answered, and she walked away.

Well, that was bloody weird.

And now it meant I had to go find some other women to sleep with tonight, because it didn't look likely I was going to be able to plug in the 100-watt bulb after all.

I climbed onto Louise's bed, and sitting at the side of her, I whispered her name. This was all taking place in Louise's mind in her dream state, but to her it was real, and I was in her hotel room. She'd been in the audience watching the show, and lucky for me, her friend hadn't felt well and had caught an early train home.

"You came back," she said.

"I sure did, baby." I climbed across and sat astride her thighs leaning over to kiss her.

"You're squashing me. I can hardly breathe."

"Sorry, Lou. Maybe we should switch around and get you on top?"

"Yes," she gasped. "Yes."

I flipped her so I was laid down and she was astride my hips. Her blonde hair cascaded over one side, mussed by sleep. I lifted up the edge of her bright pink slip.

"Landing strip. My favourite." I ran my hand down her stomach and trailed my fingers along the line until I met her clit and her wet heat. I stroked her clit with my thumb and Lou's head rolled back as she sighed. "Oh, Zak, yes. Is this really happening or am I dreaming?"

"Take off the clothes," I instructed. She lifted the silk slip up and over her head and discarded it. I watched as it hit the floor.

My hands clasped her breasts, stroking them and playing with her nipples, making her hard. That was enough foreplay, I had a job to do.

I lined myself up against her wet entrance and pushed up as she bore down, her pussy enveloping me, managing all my length with ease. This wasn't Lou's first rodeo.

"Ahhhh," she moaned as she rocked up and down on my cock. "Oh yeah. Just like that. Oh yeah."

I continued to play with her clit as I rocked my hips back and forth. My hands were now on her waist steadying her as she took me on a wild ride.

I could feel my balls tighten and knew I was about to come. I increased the pressure on her clit to help take her over.

"Oh, I'm coming, oooh..."

I slammed my hips up, my cock being milked by her greedy pussy as I emptied myself inside her. Then I felt it, the euphoria as I filled up with part of her soul.

She collapsed against the bed. A minute or so passed and then she said, "God, I don't feel so good."

"Oh dear. Maybe you're coming down with what your friend's got? I'm sure you'll be okay in a couple of days. Maybe take a sick day today, yeah?" I told her.

She nodded and closed her eyes, falling to sleep, and I left her dream.

She'd probably have to stay an extra night in her hotel room, but I had another part of a soul towards my target.

And now I needed to try to get some sleep myself.

Chapter 3

Erica

September 2022

Well. I was not impressed. NOT. IMPRESSED.

We were in the audience for the first live audition, and I didn't know what I'd expected but it wasn't for an emcee to come on stage and get us to perform like circus monkeys.

'Can you stand and cheer?'

'Can you pretend the judges just came out and you are so bloody excited for them to take their seats?'

They made us cheer and scream. They made us yell certain things out. It was all just so FAKE.

"What's with your face?" Freya said, thoroughly in her element.

"I came here to watch The Paranormals. I didn't know I'd be in the audience for hours before I even saw a single band member."

"Then let's get backstage." She wiggled her eyebrows.

"Oh yeah, let's just walk backstage, say we're what, press, and then go mingle with all the band?" I said sarcastically.

"Exactly." Freya took out two lanyards.

My eyes widened. "Erm, Frey. What are they?"

Her eyes twinkled with mischief. "Fake backstage passes. I've been watching YouTube and some dingbat did a behind the scenes and showed her pass. I know people. They made me two fake ones. As long as they don't look too closely, we're good."

"You know people?"

She sighed. "My brother designed it for me. You know he's brilliant on Photoshop. Charged me fifty quid for them, little bastard. Can't complain if it gets me to Rex though."

My jaw dropped, "And if they do look too closely, what are we? Arrested?"

Freya folded her arms across her chest and started to look huffy. "Do you, or do you not, want to take a chance on seeing Zak Jones up close and personal? Because here in our seats they are a mile away and all you're going to see is them looking like ants on stage. I'd rather be kicked out or arrested. Anyway, we won't be because they're excellent copies."

I took a deep breath. The final didn't start for at least another hour. "Let me get a couple of quick shots down me at the bar first and then let's do it."

"Good girl." Freya squeezed my hand and squealed. "Oh, I hope we get to talk to them."

I felt a little bit sick. What was I doing?

Taking a chance on seeing Zak. Who knows, if he meets you, he might fall madly in love with you.

"Bar," I repeated.

I might have gone slightly over the top by drinking four shots of vodka in quick succession, but fifteen minutes later, I stood feeling a bit dizzy by Freya's side as we held up our passes and GOT. IN. BACKSTAGE. I was swaying a little, gobsmacked by the guy waving us through. He'd barely looked at the passes. Freya dragged my arm, and I heard her mutter to the guy, "She's just got over the flu, excuse her." He muttered something back about it going around backstage amongst all the females.

The next thing I knew we were wandering down dark corridors. People were flying about everywhere. Lots had walkie-talkies. It was so dark. I saw monitors that showed the stage and the audience, tons of people looking at them. The noise was unbelievable. I'd envisaged that backstage everyone would be relaxing in a bar or green room, a stage manager telling people what to do and the usual make-up and wardrobe people. But there were hundreds here. I pulled a notepad and pen out of my bag.

"What are you doing?" Freya whispered.

"I'm going to write down everything we see and experience." I began to get excited. "I'm going to start a blog, and maybe we can keep doing this? Getting behind the scenes at shows with our fake passes?"

"Sssh, you pissed as a fart idiot. But you've given me an idea." Grabbing my hand, Freya dragged me past what seemed like a million people who were all too busy to watch what we were doing. Suddenly, the darkness disappeared as we approached the doorway of a well-lit corridor.

"We're here to just get a few words from the bands," Freya said, holding up a pass that said PRESS. Where the fuck had that one come from?

And then we were through, walking down the corridor and as I let her hold my hand and guide my inebriated body, I realised that soon I was going to see them. My heroes.

"Have I died, Freya?"

She stopped dead and turned to look at me.

"What?"

"Am I dead and this lit path is my way to heaven?"

"You've only had four vodkas." Freya stopped and looked closely at my face. "How much have you eaten today?"

"I couldn't eat. I was far too excited."

"Fuck my life. Just keep quiet, okay? I'll do the talking."

"Okay."

I followed behind her until we approached a door on which was a sign saying DRESSING ROOM: THE PARANORMALS.

It nearly burst several blood vessels for me not to scream like the fangirl I was, but Freya's mutinous glare told me if I made one false move, she was leaving me and going solo on this adventure.

"Can I help you?" a security guy said, opening the door, and I thought this is it. We got all the way to the room where my crush hangs out, and now I'm going to be thrown in jail and never get to meet him.

Freya held up the press badge again while I concentrated on just holding myself up. "The Paranormals agreed to meet us here for a few words. Are they around?"

"They're just backstage. Wait there and I'll go fetch them for you," he said and then he went wandering off.

"Fuck me, it worked. Rex Colton will be here in the flesh at any moment," Freya squealed.

I tried to share her enthusiasm, but I didn't know which one of her to share it with. I could currently see three of her.

I missed a bit of time somehow because when I next opened my eyes I was staring up into the pale green eyes of Zak. Oh my fucking god. He was here. Or was he? Was this a dream? I had just opened my eyes after all. I could still be half asleep.

"Fuck me. I really do think I died," I announced.

Freya, who was now by my side attempting to hold me up, elbowed me in the side.

Zak looked at Noah and whispered something. Hopefully about how he was in love with me and was about to take me out of here and to his bed. He turned back to me, and I got lost in his eyes. He opened his mouth. Oh my, Zak was about to talk to me.

"Ladies, sorry I can't stay, but I have another engagement. I'll leave you in the good care of my friends though. Have a lovely evening." He smiled, and I fell into the abyss of his beams, and then he walked away.

My eyes followed him the whole way down the corridor, and I let out a regretful sigh.

"Let's get you on your feet and some coffee down you," Noah

said, looking from me to Freya. "And don't pretend to be press. I know you aren't."

"How?" I asked him.

"I can read both your minds. You couldn't be more open if you had a shop sign hung around your neck."

"It's you," Freya huffed, giving me side eye. "Being drunk gave the game away."

Noah invited us into his dressing room. I let my gaze sweep around and wondered if I could find out which hairbrush Zak had used and steal it. The trouble was that my body was still not cooperating so I could barely step away from the walls. I needed to be able to be around Zak Jones. This could not be my future, where he walked away from me. Then I got an idea.

"It's true I'm not a press person. I'm the president of your fan club," I announced with a large dose of over-enthusiasm.

"Fan club?" Noah smiled.

"Yes." Fuck, why had I not thought of this before? "Whether you win or not I believe you are on the brink of stardom and I want to run your official fan club. What say you?"

At this point Rex shot forward, making me jump. "Hell, yeah. I even know what we can call our fans."

"Oh God, don't encourage him," Roman groaned, still standing at the back of the group.

"The Subs," Rex said proudly. "Do you get it? Short for subscribers to our club, but meaning submissive, doing what we want them to."

Freya's hand shot up. "I want to be the first official Sub."

He winked at her. "Done. So, coffee, and then you can take some notes about the band, how we started up etc. Sound good?"

Freya took my notepad and pen, and she gave me the look she gave me when she was telling me not to fuck things up. I tried to concentrate. "While my bestie sobers up, I can start by getting to know you. Is there somewhere more comfortable we could go?"

"Yes," Rex said. "You can come to the canteen with Roman and I and ask us anything you want to know."

I watched as my best friend smiled in Roman's direction, and even inebriated, I knew that smile was masking her true feelings about the third wheel accompanying her and her crush.

"Will my friend currently be part of a threesome?"

Noah had given me several mugs of black coffee. That and time meant I was starting to sober up a little. Jeez, I was alone with Noah Granger, bass guitarist of The Paranormals. If only it could have been Zak, but still, I was in their dressing room and talking to one of the band!

Noah laughed. "No. She's quite safe in the canteen. You'll have made their day by saying you're making a fan club. Don't worry, I'll let them down gently. Sorry that Zak left when I know you came to see him."

"Was I that obvious?" I asked, my mouth turning down at the corners.

"A little."

"Huh. Yeah, he was so interested, he left in a split-second."

Noah patted my arm. "Zak has a great amount on his plate, not least of which is we're trying to win this competition. I definitely wouldn't pin your hopes on him. He's not a settling down kind of guy. Or a one-woman kind of guy."

My heart felt broken and my stomach like it was full of concrete. Here was the truth from his friend. Zak wouldn't be interested in me. I decided to change the subject while I was with Noah. Seeing how I'd told him I was making a fan club, I'd be nosy and ask him about the rumours circulating about him and his ex.

"Is Stacey really with Dray? Because I think you two look good together."

His mouth dropped open for a moment and then he arched a brow. "Matchmaker, are you?"

"You must be joking. I can't get myself a date, never mind

anyone else. Nope, if you still like Stacey you're on your own there. I just think you seem nicer than Dray."

He smirked. "But you don't actually know me. What if I'm a vampire or something and not as nice as you think?"

I guffawed with laughter. "I like you, you're silly."

Oh my fucking god, what did I just say to this man? This is why I shouldn't be let out in public. What was I thinking coming to talk to the band? I should have stayed at home, talking to the television where I couldn't embarrass myself. "Sorry, I mean, you're funny. You make me laugh. I don't laugh much. My life's pretty boring, so I'm so pleased I'm now running your fan club."

Now where was my notepad and pen? I patted down my pockets. "Oh, but Freya went off with my pad and pen so I can't write down anything you tell me."

"It's fine. You don't have to run our fan club. I'll tell the others. Thanks for supporting us and hopefully you now realise that alcohol is not your friend."

I felt my cheeks heat. "I shouldn't let myself get pulled into Freya's hairbrained ideas, but hey, I got to meet you all. And I really am a huge fan and would definitely, truly, like to run your fan club. You'll need one. You're going to be huge. I just know it."

Noah nodded and smiled. "Give me your phone number and email address and we'll be in touch. You can totally run our fan club if you want. You can ask us anything via emails and then we'll leave it up to you how you run things. That's if you still wake up in the morning wanting to run things and it's not the alcohol talking."

Was this really happening? Noah had told me I could run their fan club? Constant contact with the band. I wanted to jump up and down and squeal, but instead, I sat on my hands.

"I don't usually drink," I confessed.

"Funnily enough, I kind of worked that out." He stood up and beckoned for me to follow him out of the room. "Let's go find your friend in the canteen."

I nodded.

"I really do think you and Stacey seem better suited than her and Dray," I said, as Freya stood up in the canteen and headed towards me.

"You stick to creating the fan club, and I'll run my love life, or lack of it." He gave me a hug.

"Bye. It was nice to meet you. Thanks for being so kind and not kicking us out," I told him.

"No problem. You took my mind off some things for a while so it's all good."

I wondered if it was Stacey on his mind.

Freya put her arm through mine, and after visiting the ladies —because I was about to wet myself after the copious amounts of liquid I'd consumed—we made our way out of the building and into the fresh air.

"Let's go and get a drink and talk about what just happened," Freya suggested. "Like over and over again." She let out a satisfied moan. "I touched Rex's arm, Erica. It was so hairy and just lush. So soft." She swooned a little.

"I can't drink. I only just sobered up," I protested.

"Okay, let's go get a McDonalds then. We'll be able to hear better to chat anyway."

My stomach growled.

"Yes, let's," I agreed.

I tore into my double cheeseburger like I'd never eaten before, clearly having the I've-drunk-too-much munchies.

"I can't believe I just spent my evening with Rex Carlton," Freya said dreamily.

"In a canteen with Roman Idiri and having to take notes." I took the notepad from my bag and had a look at what she'd written down to find only doodles of love hearts with hers and Rex's name on them.

I slammed it on the table. "Really, Freya? No information on them whatsoever?"

She sipped her coke through the straw before breaking off. "I'd have liked to have written down his inside leg measurements, the size of his cock, and his address and contact details, but being in a canteen meant the nearest I got to a sausage was seeing bangers and mash on the menu."

She put her drink down. "Anyway, what were you up to with Noah Granger for all that time, shut in a private dressing room? Have you jumped onto Team Noah, or actually jumped Noah?"

I huffed. "No. Noah made me lots of coffee and helped me sober up. He's clearly in love with Stacey, poor guy. He warned me off Zak. Told me he's basically after anything in a skirt." I looked down, "and here I am wearing trousers."

"Erica, you are now running their fan club. You're going to be able to get clear access to the dude. So, we can make sure next time you have a skirt and no panties. All is not lost."

"Except my panties apparently."

We giggled, and I felt better. It was true. This would not be the last time I met my crush. Not now I was a main player in their future career. I celebrated with two more double cheeseburgers.

Chapter 4

Erica

From: TheSubsofTheParanormals@gmail.com
Subject: THEY MADE THE FINAL!!! (Of course they did).
Date: 15 November 2022

From the ONLY OFFICIAL fan group of The Paranormals.

OMG did you see this week's live show? Of course you did, you're a Sub!!! That rendition of Wildest Dreams! Like Carmela said they certainly put the wild into their performance. Did you growl too?!!!

But it's next week now that we need to get ready for. Get your dialling fingers at the ready so we can have our Paranormals crowned as Britain's Best New Band. (I'm already having to fan myself).

Also, don't forget to send any questions you have for the band to me, so I can go meet them and put your questions to them.

Aren't I the luckiest woman in the world? Please don't hate me, someone has to get you the lowdown on our rock gods.

Until next week (eeek).

Erica xoxo

I typed the kisses and hugs with a flourish. This was really happening. I'd been in touch with Bill Traynor's personal assistant and she'd set me up with everything I needed to launch my fan club and sent me two tickets to the final! I was going to get to meet Zak again and this time I'd make sure I looked amazing.

Bill was the main man on the show and his PA had explained that the band had a contract with him to handle their PR, but should they win they would get their own team. For now though, Alana was my contact.

I had to admit to being disappointed at not having the band members' personal emails or phone numbers. Then again, I'd have probably drunk-dialled Zak, so maybe for now it was for the best. I just had to hope that when the final came, it wasn't the only thing that did, and that I managed to get horizontal under Mr Jones.

"Erica! You're going to be late for work," my mum's voice shouted up the stairs.

I sighed and putting the laptop on the desk in my room, I headed for the shower. Twenty-one years old and still living at home, being treated like a fourteen-year-old by my mother. But then again, my obsession with The Paranormals bordered on a teen crush, so what did I expect? Yes, I had a couple of photos of the band on my walls now, sue me.

I wandered down to the kitchen and my mum handed me a slice of toast. "Your coffee is on the table. I'm off. I'll see you tonight. Chicken dinner for tea, okay?"

"Yeah, great." I kissed her on the cheek. "Have a good day."

Once I heard the door bang, I took my drink and toast

through to the living room where I wasn't supposed to eat because my mum hated crumbs going down the edge of the sofa. I needed to set off soon but for now I'd have a little daydream about Zak and the final before real life—AKA my supermarket job—beckoned.

I thought about the few boyfriends I'd had up until now. There'd been no one serious. My mum said I was too picky, but I just thought maybe it was me and I attracted the idiots. My longest relationship had been for three months, but Gary had been in love with his reflection, not me. He'd started going to the gym and that had been the end of us, because the nearest I got to sport was on the name of my deodorant. At least he'd probably found his happy ever after there, AKA the gym's floor-to-ceiling mirrors.

Finishing my coffee, I grabbed my belongings and walked to the local supermarket where I worked.

I didn't mind working on the checkout. You got to know people who lived in the area. Passing the time of day with people made the day go faster. Mrs Merrill who came in every morning for a paper for her husband was one of the first to my till.

"Morning, Erica dear."

"Morning, Mrs Merrill. How are you today?"

"I'm great, apart from my left hip's giving me a bit of grief as usual. Now, that young man you like is on the front of the paper again."

I already knew and had read in detail all the day's newspaper reports about Zak's antics and the rest of the bands' news. Alana had arranged for me to be sent a daily press email and then I also pored over all the papers and magazines before I started my shift. Zak had apparently been involved in a threesome, and the women were both reporting that he was so amazing they were dreaming about him and having sleep orgasms. I wanted Zak-related sleep orgasms.

"I know. He's a bit of a naughty one," I settled for as a reply, rather than sharing my thoughts on sleep orgasms.

"Well." She leaned in conspiratorially. "If I was fifty years younger, I'd queue up for a go."

I laughed. "I have tickets for the final."

"Ooh, with you doing that fan thing?"

"Yep."

"I don't know how you work all that machinery. My granddaughter has set up my phone for me. I said I only wanted to do phone calls, but she taught me texts, and then she got me to do a TikTok with her. I had to wave my arms about. I think teenagers are bored. Anyway, she left the app on my phone and let me tell you, I did not know how many gorgeous men over the age of thirty lived in the world and they are all showing their pecs and swinging their hips on TikTok. Made this seventy-nine-year-old woman here feel like she has a new reason to carry on living."

She did a bit of a dance. I wondered if Mrs Merrill was having TikTok hot men sleep orgasms and then I wanted to puke out my own thoughts.

"Oh, it's only really sending emails. But I'm hoping I'll get close to the band at the final and get some good gossip and info for the fans."

"You go enjoy yourself, girl, and if you get chance for a ride with that one." She nodded at the paper. "Just make sure he wraps it up because it's been everywhere."

With that she paid for her items and made her way out of the shop.

*

The day passed quickly enough, and before I knew it, I was back home and sitting at the table with Mum eating my chicken dinner.

"How was your day?" Mum asked as usual.

"Fine, thanks."

"Didn't meet any hot men then at work today?"

"Do I ever?"

"Someone will come along for you, pet. You're still only young. Have you thought about saving up and travelling the world? Doing a gap year type thing? It wasn't done in my day, and I wished it had been. I might have avoided meeting your father... although I'll never regret having you and your sister," she quickly added.

The last we'd heard my father was living in Spain with his third wife. Mainly because he'd decided it was for the best to cut off all contact with us. Whatever. I didn't have time for a man who couldn't make the time for me. I had an older sister, a niece, loving grandparents, and aunties and uncles. I got by.

"I'd love to go travelling, but oh look, I earn minimum wage and can barely afford to pay my phone contract." I sighed.

Mum patted my hand. "I just don't think this is the life you're destined for, darling. It's a pit stop. Something will come along, or someone. I just know it."

It was the pits, not a pit stop. I wished I could share my mum's enthusiasm for life. It mainly came from her work as a receptionist for a life coach. She quite often came home imparting words of wisdom she'd overheard.

But she needed to work harder on the manifesting side if I was to travel the world.

Chapter 5

Zak

"Well, well, Zachariah, you've even managed to wipe the supposed threesome between Stacey, Dray, and Noah off the front pages." Roman threw a newspaper at me.

"You sound jealous, my friend. Is that because you had to settle for just one chick last night?" I yawned. Even though Don had agreed to give me a reduced target for the month, due to rehearsing and press junkets, I was still living on the edge of my energy sources. And after the final, he'd upped my quota. I honestly didn't know what I was going to do going forward.

Noah was going to help me try to find a way out of my predicament, or should that be pre*dick*ament? We just had to find a way to trick a demon, one whose nickname was The Destroyer. Yeah, I didn't have a lot of faith in that happening.

"So you really had a threesome?"

"Yeah, I took them back to their hotel room, but it didn't happen like they think. I did my incubus mojo so they fell asleep, made my way home and then I appeared in their dreams."

"Yes, they've spoken about their sleep orgasms in great detail."

"They have?" I took another look at the paper. "Ha. I'm becoming the ultimate sex rock god in the press."

I slumped down onto our dressing room sofa.

"If only they could see you in real life." Roman raised a brow.

"Grab us a strong black coffee would you, mate?"

I must have dozed off because the next thing I knew, I could feel something smacking me in the face. I opened my eyes to find a dick slapping my cheek and I reared back in alarm screaming.

Rex fell about laughing while tucking himself back into his jeans. "Told you that'd wake him up."

I made retching noises. "You had your dick in my face, you sick fuck. What was that all about?"

Rex held up his phone. "We've been trying to wake you up for the last forty-three minutes. Drastic measures were called for. Worked, didn't it?"

"I'll be lucky if I manage to do anything but hurl for the rest of the day. My eyeballs are burning." I blinked rapidly as if that would make the image leave.

"You're just jealous cos you've been reminded my dick's bigger than yours. Now get up. We've a final to rehearse for."

"Here's your microphone." One of the runners passed me my mic. I wasn't concentrating. I'd gone tired again and as my hand grasped something hairy, I flung it to the floor, screaming like a nine-year-old girl.

Everyone around me burst into high-pitched laughter and I saw that the bastards had set me up by wrapping a microphone in a hairy wig. It was just too reminiscent of the dick in the face I'd suffered earlier.

I took a deep breath. "I can safely say I'm fully awake now. Let's get practicing." At some point I would have my revenge with these fuckers. When I could find the time and energy that was.

Before I knew it, the day of the final was here, and it was the last day of my reduced workload. The date had been in my mind more than Christmas: 21 November. A day of mixed emotions where I was excited and nervous about the final, and then apprehensive about what came next: me lots of times and a whole new future for the band.

"I'm gasping for refreshments and fresh towels," Rex huffed, looking from Zak to me. "Can't you two go play a little further afield? We need these people to make sure the show runs smoothly."

Noah and I had been using the show staff as our own personal food banks. Noah had taken blood donations and I'd taken a little bit of soul. The staff had assumed there was a virus going around so it had made life a little easier for us both.

"Show's almost over, my friend. And after tonight, Don is going to have me bedding everyone in sight, so if there's anyone you have your eye on or feel a calling to, you'd better give me a heads up," I replied.

"Huh, fabulous." Rex threw a drumstick across the room.

"You're just jealous because you have to wait for 'the one'. Your mate. How very boring having to stick to one person for life," I teased him.

"Yeah, but until I meet them, I can practice my prowess. That's if there's anyone left after you greedy fuckers have finished." Another drumstick sailed after the first.

"First past the post, my friend."

"Harley's single. I read online that her career comes first, but she's not ruling out love," Roman piped up.

I felt the hackles on my back rise.

"The only person Harley's in love with is herself. I went full on incubus on her arse, and she barely gave me a second glance. She gave the mirrors and windows she passed a lot more attention."

"Is someone a little bitter that there's one woman he's failed to seduce?" Noah tried to get a rise out of me, but my mind was wandering to all the encounters I'd had with Harley during the competition. And since her co-presenter had gone missing, my something-not-right radar was beeping.

"Are you sure she's not a witch?" I asked Noah.

"How should I know? Just because my ex was one doesn't mean I have a homing signal for all of their kind."

"You could just ask Stacey," I suggested.

"Of course I could. Hey, Stacey, I know we didn't part on the best terms when I chose the chance of a rock career over you, but could you tell me if Harley is a witch, only we're wondering why she isn't boning Zak?"

"I didn't say you were an expert on witches. I was just pondering whether Harley was one out loud," I huffed.

"Because she hasn't fallen for your seduction techniques?" Noah scoffed.

My eyes narrowed in his direction. "Yes. I'm an incubus. All human women are supposed to fall at my feet, so that would suggest that she is somehow, something else."

"You're something else," he stated.

I gave him the middle finger.

The conversation moved on to Noah spilling his secret of a night of passion with Stacey. Those two just needed to get their act together and soon.

My mind kept wandering back to Harley. I was going to keep a close eye on her and I'd tell myself that it was because her co-presenter was missing and Harley got to take the spotlight, and not for the fact that she didn't appear to be attracted to me.

I would find out what was going on with her, if it was the last thing I did.

Harley Davies needed to fall for my charms, and by charms I meant my sex bits and by fall I meant right onto my dick.

We had jointly won the competition with Seven Sisters. The night had been the strangest experience ever, and from a guy who'd made a deal with a demon that was saying something.

There had been two 'possessions' that turned out to be via the went-missing-and-now- appeared-to-be-a-ghost Dan, Harley's envious co-presenter who couldn't let his quest for fame lie. This had been followed by a visit from Death himself, and then my vampire best mate had narrowly escaped a dusting. But Noah had gone on to get the girl and we'd all gone on to party.

Now here we were in *Sheol*, the nightclub that masked the seventh dimension of Hell. My deal with my boss was about to benefit him further and as a myriad of women moved closer to me, I could see that I wasn't going to have any problem with willing participants. It was just a question of time management.

Aaron, Don's assistant, came to find me. He looked like he should be in *Men in Black* and his face was always oh so serious.

"Hey, Aaron, my man. There's plenty of spare pussy here tonight. Want me to get one to drop to your knees?"

"No, thank you, Zak. My wife would replace my sphincter," he said, monotone.

I looked at him with my head tilted. "Do you mean rip you a new arsehole?"

"That's what I said."

"Can I help you?" I shouted over the music.

"Oh yes. Abaddon will allow you a lie in tomorrow morning because he presumes you'll be extremely busy tonight, but you need to come back here to meet him at one pm sharp to discuss moving onto the new arrangement you made with him."

"One pm. Got ya. Is that everything?"

"Yes, oh, just to remind you that if you ever appear in my wife's dreams, I will replace your sphincter." He walked off.

I went back to partying because tonight for me was for celebrating being the lead singer of a band with a recording contract and a top manager. I'd have plenty of sex tonight, but because I wanted to, not because I had to, and I wouldn't appear in their dreams. It was time for Zak to give the newspapers something new to report.

An orgy. Let the celebrations begin in Ernest.

And, no, that wasn't a spelling mistake. Ernest was a waiter with a fantastic mouth.

Chapter 6

Erica

We were sitting in the audience at the final of Britain's Best New Band. Not only that, but I looked hot if I said so myself. I was wearing a black dress that hugged my curves and had redone my purple hair dye, so it looked fresh.

Freya was sweltering in a mohair jumper which she'd decided might make Rex more attracted to her. As the minutes went on in the packed auditorium, her cheeks went redder and her hair limper and wetter. I wasn't sure she was going to achieve her aims.

This time around, the atmosphere was naturally electric. We didn't need the emcee there to get us warmed up this time. Everyone was whooping and hollering anyway.

"Do you want a drink?" Freya asked. "Only I'm getting dehydrated."

Well, duh. Creating your own portable sauna would do that.

"You need to lose the jumper, Freya. Put it back on when we get nearer to Rex."

She thumped me.

"Ow. What's that for?"

"Why the hell didn't you tell me that in the first place? I had no need to sit here almost dying. Now, do you want a beer?"

I held a hand up. "No alcohol for me tonight, thank you. I want to know exactly what I'm doing with Zak Jones."

My soberness made it all the more peculiar when the competition was over and I found myself standing near the band knowing that The Paranormals and Seven Sisters had drawn on votes and therefore had both won the competition. I only had a vague recollection of the actual evening and no idea how I'd got near the stage. *Huh?*

Freya looked down at herself, saw how near to Rex she was, and she quickly put her jumper back on. But it was fruitless as the band were taken away to do their press calls.

"Quickly, get out your press badge," she said.

"I don't have one. Did you not bring the fake one?" I asked.

"No. Why would I need to bring a fake when you're their fan club president? You must be able to get in. Come on, let's go ask over there." She dragged me over to where a security guy was looking at badges.

It was the same guy we'd met outside the dressing room before. Bingo! He knew us.

"Hey, Security Guy," I said, following it up with a beaming smile, and then I made to walk past him.

He held out an arm to stop me.

"Sorry, Miss, it's press only."

"Yeah, we are. Don't you remember?" Freya queried.

"Oh, I remember," he said, standing taller so his pecs flexed under his shirt. "Especially when I was given a warning about not checking ID properly and almost lost my job."

Our faces fell.

"I'm so very sorry about that, but it's okay now. I'm actually the president of their fan club and so I can go through," I explained.

"Yeah, and I'm the president of the United States of America.

It's not working this time, Miss." He looked behind us. "There are real press queuing up behind you now. If you could move, so I don't actually lose my job this time..."

We stepped away as it was clear we weren't getting anywhere near the band this way.

Instead, we waited nearby so we could see where they were going next.

Two hours later, next turned out to be a nightclub called Sheol. By this time, I'd decided I may as well have a glass of wine, given my evening was still a bit vague. I'd guessed the coke Freya had bought me must have had a sneaky vodka in it and that she was just not admitting the truth. She said she felt the same way strangely, but she *had* been drinking so I wasn't taking much notice of her thoughts on the matter.

I tried and tried to get near the band, to get near Zak, but it was no use. Other women were trying to get to him too, and they were far meaner than I was. After my fifth hard elbow in my gut, I told Freya I was giving up.

As she'd not gotten anywhere near Rex either, she nodded.

"Come on. There's no need for us to be in this zoo. We have your access to them through the fan club. We'll get there another day."

With that we made our way home. It had been a great night experiencing the live final. I just couldn't help feeling disappointed at not experiencing Zak's manhood.

But we didn't get access to them through my fan club either. Because immediately after their joint win, there was Paranormals pandemonium, and all my fan club queries went via their new personal PA, Vikki.

The band went on a worldwide tour and the last places on the tour would be in the UK. Zak wasn't even in the same country as me any longer.

I gave up. I still ran the fanclub, still adored the band, but my feelings for that were just like crushing on a movie actor. Not really a chance in hell of it ever becoming anything real.

And I never did get a Zak orgasm dream.

My mundane life carried on until the night I went to the Rock Hard café with Freya and found a new determination to get my man.

Part Two

AFTER THE PARANORMALS JOINTLY WON
BRITAIN'S BEST NEW BAND.

Chapter 7

Zak

Thursday 1 June 2023

The radio alarm blasted out and I hit it with such force it flew across the room and smacked into the wall.

"Oh, Zak. What are we going to do with you?" a deep, monotone voice rumbled around my bedroom. I groaned, rubbing at my eyes, and dragged myself into a sitting position, leaning against my pillows.

"You don't even give me a chance to wake up properly now?" I reached out to my bedside table for a glass of water but saw a scotch I'd not finished drinking before I'd crashed out. I picked that up instead and let the burn hit my throat. I coughed, cleared my throat, and then stared at the man sitting in a chair in the corner of my hotel room.

"You're one short. The boss isn't happy."

"Look, I did my best. He must have seen that. One stupid bitch got cold feet. I didn't have time to find another, things got busy with the band."

"He's not going to accept the band as an excuse," Aaron replied.

"Well, my quota is too fucking high. I love sex, but sixty

women a month? I do need to sleep, you know? Not be partying all night long. We're touring. I need to renegotiate the terms of my agreement again."

"I'll organise a meeting for you. I'm sure the boss will be pleased to see you. It's been a while."

It had been a while. It had been over six months of touring different countries and having to send my souls by a demon-run courier service, or was that every courier service?

"It's been seven freaking years since I made this deal. A lot has changed since then. I'm not some pathetic teenage boy anymore who couldn't find their way to an animal sanctuary never mind find some real pussy. Now I'm the lead singer of *the* band of the moment. I'm needed on stage, not in the bedroom."

"You do remember you were the pathetic teenage boy who made the deal, right? And your success with the band is probably a by-product of the charisma you were trained in to score with the pussy?"

I glared at Aaron. "I was taken advantage of, and you know it. I never thought I'd say this, but I am sick of women."

Aaron stood up, unfolding his long, thick muscled legs. He stretched revealing his tight abs as they strained against his shirt. I hated that demons could travel through portals and therefore crash hotel rooms uninvited. "I'm sure the boss would be happy for you to switch over."

"That's not what I meant. When a hole's a goal it doesn't matter whose it is, I'm still gonna be knackered."

"Okay, I'll go set up this meeting, but in the meantime, you might want to have another nap. You still look beat. There's got to be some part of the world where it's still yesterday, right?"

"I'm wiped, Aaron."

He shrugged. "All the more reason to nap, and I know you say you're sick of women, but maybe you just need to find a steady one for your normal life, to balance out the chaos in your dream life?"

"Yeah, sure. Hi, honey, I'm home after getting the numbers of six women I'm going to screw in their dreams tonight."

Sighing, I rubbed at my eyes. When I moved away my hands he was gone. I needed to do something about my current deal; this couldn't go on.

After napping again, I was still exhausted. But unless my meeting with the boss was arranged quickly, tonight I'd be starting all over again on this brand-new month. I know that the cliché about rock stars was that they fucked the groupies all the time, but my behaviour was starting to cause friction. The other band members were complaining my head wasn't in the game. They knew my deal, but still, I needed to do my share of the band stuff.

I threw myself through the shower and then opened my laptop. I'd get some of these emails answered and then at least, Vikki, the bands PA, would be off my case. I phoned down to room service for coffee and food and logged in to my mail.

There was a message from Erica, the woman who ran our fan club, that had been forwarded to me by Vikki. Erica wrote articles as if we'd really met. We had met once, briefly, when she and her friend had pretended to be reporters. I remembered she had purple hair, but that was all. I'd taken one look at the needy fan girls, seen Erica was drunk, and for once I'd run for the hills. I looked at the list of interview questions she'd sent through and one in particular caught my eye.

Erica: So leading on from that, you won an award in *Girl Power* magazine as the most 'Sex-dreamed about male'. How does that feel, knowing that women all around the world are dreaming about doing naughty things to you?

. . .

I began to type my answer, smiling to myself as I wrote the truth but shrouded it in carefully constructed words.

Zak: Oh it fills me right up. Makes me feel energised to hear that!

I snorted. Then I wondered what Erica's reaction would be if she discovered that the band she loved so much consisted of a vampire, an incubus, a wolf shifter, and a satyr.

In two weeks' time we would be back home, in London, where we had five gigs in seven days. Following that, we were back in the recording studio, but we would have some actual days off in between. Noah had negotiated that as he wanted to spend as much time with Stacey as he could before she started her stint in the West End.

For a while, things would still be ridiculously busy.

I looked down at the rest of Erica's questions. At the top of her email, she'd asked Vikki if there was any chance she could come to see us in person while we were back in London. She was so enthusiastic, bless her. I answered them and forwarded the answers back to Vikki, along with a covering email.

To: Vikkipa@theparanormals.com
From: Zakpersonal@theparanormals.com
Date: 1 June 2023
Subject: Fan club answers and an idea

Why don't we put Erica and her friend up in the hotel for a week, with backstage passes for them for the gigs? She could do a feature for the fans and ask some questions face-to-face. I think she'd like that, and it would be a thank you for her hard work over the last months.

Z.

Also, her friend Freya had got on Rex's nerves being like a fly round horse shit and I still needed to pay him back for when he whacked me in the face with his cock.

I pressed send and got ready for that night's show.

Once more, we took to the stage and took in the sea of faces before us before the lights dimmed down. It was a feeling that was indescribable, but most definitely almost equated to being filled with part of a soul.

It would have been so easy to get carried away by it all, but I wasn't living the dream. As soon as my work commitments finished, my other ones started. I'd wished on more than one occasion for a way to drain the auditoriums and concert halls of souls in one fell swoop, but that wasn't a possibility. Orgies were the most I could do in one go. I'd managed ten souls one night and I'd been so exhausted we'd had to cancel a show, so I'd never repeated it.

I began to sing our latest release and the audience held up candles like they were in worship to us, which they kind of were, because to them we *were* gods. Rock gods.

When my body hits the bed, I feel like I can feel you.
Like you're here with me, when you're only in my dreams.
Feel your hands on me
Trailing down my skin
Feel your touch on me
Feeling you within

But it can't be the truth
It must be your sweet lies
As I wake alone
And face up to the skies
Hoping and praying
That on this, another day,
You'll be here with me.
And this time... you'll stay.

We wrote the songs between us, but this one was one of mine. It had been written after a night of self-pity and two bottles of scotch but had become a massive hit.

The first time Noah's wife Stacey had heard it, she'd asked me if I'd wanted to talk, but I'd just said, 'What about?' She'd called me a fucktard, and then Noah had shaken his head and said, 'My day of reckoning couldn't come soon enough', whatever that meant.

As the song came to a close, the fans roared their approval, and I basked in the atmosphere. It was possibly the only time I felt any peace.

Returning to my hotel room after an hour of greeting fans in the dressing room, I found Aaron sat on the chair in my room.

"Please tell me you're here because you've trained as a masseuse, and you want to give me a back rub?"

"If I trained as a masseuse my back rubs would be only for my wife."

"Or she'd replace your sphincter. Yeah, I get it. So why are you here?"

"Abaddon has made a space in his diary for you this evening. Are you ready to go?"

"No, but do I have a choice?"

"Of course... not."

I stood up. "Come on then. Do the zappy thing."

Aaron drew enchantments in the air until a portal of fire opened and then he dragged us both through it.

And within the blink of an eye, I was standing in Don's office.

"Take a seat, Zak." Abaddon smiled. As he did, a large black beetle fell out of his mouth. He picked it up and crunched it clean in half, chewing one half and then the other. Green liquid ran down his lip.

"I really must stop rushing dinner and make sure I chew properly," he said before burping. "See, it's bad for my digestion."

Don turned to Aaron. "Can you get me a wet wipe for my mouth, and don't forget to check it's for sensitive skin."

"Yes, sir." Aaron left the room.

"Okay, Zak." Abaddon leaned forward and steepled his chin in his hands, elbows on his desk. "Now, let's talk about the fact that last month you were one soul less."

"It was the touring."

I leapt back as Abaddon turned into his natural, ulcer-festooned, red, slug-like self for a moment and a stench of days old sweaty socks came forth while sparks flew out all around me. Then he returned to his Brendon Urie looking outer persona.

I looked at my clothes which were now covered in holes from burn marks as if I'd had two hundred cigarette butts through my outfit.

"Might start a new trend on the High Street." Don shrugged, staring at my attire. "Anyway, we will not be making any excuses for you being one short, just as I couldn't make any excuses with the demon above me in the hierarchy. Do you know what my punishment was because of you, Zak?"

I trembled a little. I'd not considered Abaddon would get in trouble for my failure to meet my monthly target. Which was stupid, because of course he would. This was the demon realm.

"N-no."

"Astoroth cursed me to supermarket own brand tea bags for an entire day. No PG Tips. For twenty-four hours. My own brand of Hell."

If Abaddon had said being tea-bagged was his punishment, I'd have understood his horror, but no PG tips? I wanted a companion in the room. Someone I could do a mind-link with that said, 'Is this guy for real?', but no such luck. Aaron still hadn't yet returned, and we didn't have a mind-link anyway.

"And for that, you shall be punished. For the soul you failed to deliver you shall bring me nine more this month. Your target is now sixty-nine." He snorted.

"Sixty-nine? That's three or four a day." I gasped.

Abaddon looked at his watch. "Yes, and the first day of the month is almost over. If you fail me this month, Zak, I will trap you in a room with your captured soul and believe me while it calls back to your body it is very, very painful. I should dine on that pain."

"I'll do it. I'll do sixty-nine," I said, just as Aaron walked back in.

"Shall I leave again?" He put the wipes on the desk. "Now I see why you needed the wipes. I thought it was for the green gunk."

Don threw the packet at Aaron's head. "Get me a cup of tea, fool," he shouted, and then he roared. "No, don't. I can't take that shit. This is so not fairrrrr." His voice was so loud that the room vibrated, he went slug-like again, and I ended up diving under the table.

When all returned to normal, Aaron bobbed down and offered me a hand. "Before he gets ideas about you being down there," he whispered. My mind went back to tea-bagging and I shot out pronto.

Chapter 8

Erica

From: TheSubsofTheParanormals@gmail.com
Date: 1 June 2023
Subject: **EXCLUSIVE – EXCLUSIVE – EXCLUSIVE – INTERVIEW WITH ZAK JONES!**

From the ONLY OFFICIAL fan group of The Paranormals. Our monthly exclusive with a band member. Which rumours are true? What's the latest news? Read it here first!

Yeah, I know. You're all green with envy, right? I'm here with Zak Jones, our esteemed lead singer. Picture the scene: we're in his hotel suite. I'm sure it's the size of a small island. I'm on one end of a red couch and Zak is at the other, his legs tucked beneath him. He's ordered us coffee and pastries and now I have his full, undivided attention. So here we go...

Erica: Okay, firstly, we'd like to know about the tour. Is it true that you're back in the studio after the

London gigs, recording new songs and staying around the capital for a while?

Zak: Yes. We'll be back in the studio recording our next album. And I can exclusively reveal that the album will be called *Foursome*.

Erica: So is there anything in particular you're wanting to see up close and personal in London, given you've been away for months?

Zak: Yeah, British chicks. *laughs* Only joking. We're looking forward to catching up with family and friends.

Erica: Okay, onto the gossip next. I know this is your private life and you might not want to answer, but the fans would be annoyed if I didn't at least ask... *blushes*

Zak: Go on...

Erica: *deep breath for courage* Is it true what was reported in the press, that you had an orgy? You and ten women?

Zak: Well, I wouldn't like to boast but... they were all underwear models. How was I supposed to choose?

Erica: *rolls eyes*

Zak: I saw that.

Erica: So leading on from that, you won an award in *Girl Power* magazine as the most 'Sex-dreamed about male'. How does that feel, knowing that women all around the world are dreaming about doing naughty things to you?

Zak: Oh it fills me right up. Makes me feel energised to hear that.

. . .

Erica: I heard Rex bought a house with woodland in Poplar Heights because there are rumours he owns a wolf? Do you own anything outrageous? Things that us regular people can't afford.

Zak: I buy the usual: fast cars and designer clothes. Haven't found a place to call home yet. I do like Poplar Heights though. Rex's place is amazing. I'm not telling you if there's a wolf there though, you'll have to ask him when you next interview him.

Erica: Can the Subs have an exclusive on which track of *Hidden in Plain Sight* is the next release?

Zak: Oh, I'm not sure I'm going to let you have that information.

Erica: Pretty please?

Zak: Okay, seeing as it's you, the next track to be released is *Forbidden*.

Erica: Oh yeeeaaasss. That is my favourite track off the whole album.

Zak: As I love making women happy, my work here is done.

Erica: Yes, you're a busy man, so I'd better let you go. Thanks for talking to your fans again and giving us all the gossip and exclusives.

Zak: Anytime, you know that.

I read the interview through and then I pressed send. Then I put The Paranormals next single on Spotify and turned on my wireless speaker. I sat back and listened to the words.

Never did I think this could happen.
Never thought I'd feel this way.

Your love is forbidden.
But I just want to make you stay.

I know you'll never be mine
They say we went too far this time
It wasn't meant to be this way
But you're forbidden, you're forbidden

Now they're coming for us
Going to take you away
Going to take you away
But I'll fight, I'll fight
They say we're wrong, but it feels so right

I'd not had any response from Vikki about asking to go to the London gig, so I sent her another message. I couldn't afford to miss the opportunity to see Zak.

To: Vikkipa@theparanormals.com
From: Erica@theSubsofTheParanormals.com
Date: 1 June 2023
Subject: Tickets for London?

Hey, Vikki.
Sorry to bother you, but I was wondering if the band had said I could have tickets for the London shows and do my next interview in actual person?
Erica.

I didn't expect to hear back to be honest, in which case the next thing Freya and I were going to do was to pay her brother a premium for more fake passes. We were not giving up. There were five chances to get to see our heroes and we'd do whatever it took.

A notification of a new email appeared in my inbox and I had to read the message five times before I believed my eyes.

To: Erica@theSubsofTheParanormals.com
From: Vikkipa@theparanormals.com
Date: 1 June 2023
Subject: Tickets for London?

Hey, Erica.
God, sorry, I totally forgot (I'm just so busy). Zak and the rest of the guys are inviting you to spend the week with them. Access all areas (except their personal spaces). You and a friend can come. They will pay for you to stay in the hotel they're in for the week and you can put together a ton of promo for the fans!
Sound good?
You'll need security passes and to sign confidentiality agreements etc, but for now just send me a yes or no.
Vikki.

I leapt out of my chair. "Yes, yes, yes!" I punched the air. And then I went straight back to my seat and typed a reply accepting the invitation before I phoned Freya to tell her the news.

Freya's response was similar to mine. Lots of squealing and shouting. She almost caused me to go deaf in my right ear.

"Okay. Right, I must dash. Things to do."

"Like what?" I asked. We didn't have to go until Saturday.

"I need to go dump John. He's been boring me for months now as you know."

"You said he was a nice guy."

"Yeah, he is. Nice and boring. I want to be a free agent when I go to that hotel for a week. I have morals, and cheating is not something I agree with."

"Poor John."

"We weren't going anywhere. This would have happened soon anyway. I was just going to wait past my birthday and get my pressies."

"And you say you have morals?"

"Erica?"

"Yeah?"

"We're going to spend a week with The Paranormals. Going to be in the same hotel and everything."

We squealed again.

Chapter 9

Noah

Friday 2 June 2023

We were having a band meeting in the boardroom of The Broadleaf Hotel. Even though we could have stayed at home for the London shows, it made more sense for us and security to stay in a hotel near the concert venue for the week. The first gig was tomorrow, and we'd been here since last night. We'd all just crashed in our rooms after the flight back from Canada where we'd just finished playing.

It was just us four and our PA, Vikki, this morning.

Zak was fidgety and I made a mental note to ask him afterwards about what was going on with him. I was worried about him.

"So, I invited Erica and Freya to spend the week with us," he announced.

The rest of us apart from Vikki sat with our mouths open, before Rex found his voice, or rather his growl.

"You did *what?*"

Zak shrugged his shoulders. "Erica sent me questions and I thought about how long she's run our fan club for and that she could get some good proper stuff while we tour. They won't be in the way much. Seemed a nice thing to do."

"Zak, are you having a breakdown because you thought of somebody else for a change instead of yourself?" I queried.

"I don't quite know *what* happened, except I was feeling sorry for myself and some of it must have spilled out." He pouted.

"I'll have that bloody Freya following me around like a permanently hungry cub," Rex snarled. "Did you not think to ask the band before you made a decision that affected us all?" He shook his head. "What am I saying? Of course, you didn't. You just thought about yourself."

"No, I didn't," Zak protested. "I thought about poor Erica, sitting at home pretending she gets to see us in real life when she doesn't, and I thought this time I can make her dreams come true and she *can* see us in real life."

Rex's mouth dropped open again.

"Do you think we need to call a doctor?" Roman asked.

It was indeed something very new, Zak actually looking outside of, well, Zak, but I decided to actively encourage it. I knew from speaking to Aaron that for Zak to break his deal with Don, he had to fall in true love. Only I wasn't allowed to tell him that. Therefore, the more females he encountered, the more this could happen. He'd not made any connection with Vikki, mainly because Rex had threatened to kneecap him if he ruined our PA, but true love would have conquered all anyway and it hadn't. Erica and Freya meant two more women around and two more possibilities of him breaking that curse. And he needed to, given Don had set him a ridiculously high target for the month.

Zak's extra-curricular duties put a strain on the band as we ended up putting more admin on our own shoulders as Zak just didn't have the time. It wasn't ideal and I needed to get as many females one-on-one with Zak as I could.

"I'm thinking while we're here we could do a meet and greet," I suggested to Vikki, warming up to the idea. "The four of us, in separate rooms, and people go in one by one and sit and chat for five mins, grab a photo and then leave."

"Why wouldn't we sit together?" Roman looked puzzled.

"It'd run better like a production line. Otherwise, they'll want a pic with all of us together and that would take longer."

"So?"

"So we're doing it this way and that's that." I fixed Roman with a look and he eye-rolled.

"You're all fucking cracking up. Solo meet and greets with a *band*, and the fan club president and Rex's fangirl on site. I'm getting out of here before you infect me."

"Before you go. I sent out some VIP invites for the first show. Harley Davies is coming and said she can't wait to catch up with you," Vikki said.

"I knew she'd not be able to resist the opportunity to come hang round me." Zak smirked, looking more his usual self.

"Actually, she said she couldn't wait to catch up with Roman, not you."

Roman's eyes widened.

"She did?"

Vikki nodded.

Zak scowled. "There's something wrong with that woman."

"We've had this conversation several times. You thought she was responsible for Dan going missing and that wasn't the case, was it? Just because she doesn't fancy you doesn't mean there's anything wrong with her," I told him.

"Yes, it does."

I sighed. "Vikki doesn't fancy you."

"I did actually, but I knew it was just him being an incubi, so Stacey performed a spell so it wouldn't work. She does them on all her friends."

"That's it!!" Zak leapt up. "Stacey and Harley are friends. She'll have had the spell put on her."

He looked a lot happier, so I didn't argue with him. It could well be the case and if it shut him up, I would let him believe it.

Roman was in a dreamworld.

"You okay there, Rome?"

"Er, what? Yeah, fine. Are we ready to rehearse now?"

"Yeah, come on. I'm pumped and ready to rock and roll," Zak sing-songed.

I called an end to the meeting, and we went to the venue.

Back in my hotel room after the rehearsals, I watched closely as my sexy wife climbed into bed beside me.

"How was your day?" she asked, pulling the covers up and sitting propped up against the headboard.

"Rehearsals went well. Zak—for reasons none of us can compute—has asked Erica, the fan club woman, and her friend to spend the week with us. They're arriving in the morning. Pretty please, if you see them around can you and the other girls extend a hand of friendship to them, because I imagine they're going to be like fishes out of water amongst all the roadies.

"I'll come meet them when they arrive. I'll tell Vikki. I won't be able to stay long, but I'll do a quick tour and introduction and then they can hang out and watch the final rehearsals. But ultimately, let Zak know that he invited them and so he has overall responsibility for them."

"Yeah, I will. I'm hoping one of them will be his true love. I also organized a weird solo meet and greet that will put hundreds more women in his path."

Stacey trailed her fingertips down my face. "You're such a romantic, Noah. I love that you want to help him find true love."

"There's nothing romantic about it. I want him with a broken curse so he can help out more, then I have more time with you." I waggled my brows.

And then we were done talking. We were newlyweds after all.

Chapter 10

Erica

Work were fine about me taking annual leave at short notice, and Freya didn't have any problems getting leave either. As for my mum, she looked far too happy about the fact she was getting a week without me.

Saturday morning, with cases packed, Freya arrived outside in a taxi. As I climbed inside, we shared a secret smile.

The cabbie looked at us through the rear-view mirror. "Where are you off to then, ladies?"

"The Broadleaf Hotel, please."

"Ooh, any special occasion?"

"Just meeting some friends," I said. "But no real plans yet for how we'll be spending our time."

"Living by the seat of your pants. I like it," the cabbie replied, and then he pulled away from the kerb and we were on our way.

I don't know how, but we managed to keep relatively calm in the taxi. However, the minute the taxi driver had left us with the hotel concierge who took our cases into the hotel, we squealed and hugged each other.

"This is it, babes. The start of our adventure." Freya grinned. "But I know I'm here because of your connection to the band, so I promise I won't do anything to jeopardise that, no matter how much I want to sneak into Rex's hotel room at night."

"Thanks, Frey. I had to admit to wondering if you might actually get us thrown out on the first day from stealing a keycard and hiding in his bed."

"I'd be lying if I said I hadn't considered it, but I want to win his heart."

"Aww, you romantic, you." I clutched her hand.

"Although if I can only sleep with him that will be perfectly acceptable."

"Come on." I dragged her in the direction of where the concierge had disappeared. "Let's get in there and check-in."

A tall woman with long, curly, dark hair, dressed in a cream trouser suit with a red blouse walked towards us as we came in.

"Erica?" she queried.

"Yes, how did you know?" I asked.

The woman pointed at my head. "I was told you had purple hair. Though you are the third person I've asked today. I'm Vikki." She held out her hand and I shook it.

"Hi, Vikki. This is my best friend Freya who is helping me this week."

Freya also shook Vikki's hand.

"Let's get you booked in at the reception desk and then I've arranged for us to meet Stacey Granger in the bar. She was going to come meet you, but I said we needed to get you checked-in and given your security stuff first."

"I'm going to have a drink with Stacey Granger?" I half squealed.

"You are such a fangirl." Freya laughed.

"Duh, that's why I'm here, idiot." I eye-rolled my best friend.

"I have no idea how she's going to behave when she comes face to face with Zak again," Freya whisper-shouted to Vikki.

"I was going to ask which one you both liked best. So it's Zak for you, and..."

"Rex."

"Rex for you. Well, they are both single..."

"What about you? Which one do you like best?" I asked.

Vikki leaned in. "None. Stacey put me off them all."

"Phew. I was worried with you having access to them at all times." Yes, I had actually said those words out loud.

"She means access to the band, not to their penises," Freya helpfully explained.

"It's going to be so much fun having you two around this week." Vikki laughed. "I can't wait for you to see the room we've got for you."

And with that she walked us up to the reception and grabbed some keys.

"Jesus fucking Christ," Freya shouted as we stepped into our suite. There were floor-to-ceiling windows, a bar, living area, small dining area with a kitchenette, and two king-size beds. The bathroom was huge, with a large walk-in shower and jacuzzi bath, and it had a steam room and sauna.

A welcome basket on the table held champagne, strawberries, chocolate, posh crisps, and a bottle each of white, red, and rosé wine.

There were also spa passes.

"Anything else you need just give me a call on this number," Vikki said, passing us each a card. "You have pre-arranged meals booked; so breakfast, lunch, and your evening meal can be taken in the restaurant or in your room at any time and you can charge any sundries within reason."

She went into her bag.

"Here are your passes for the O2 Arena, and your passes for around the hotel as we have meeting rooms etc here. This is a card with the number if you need a driver. Please only use our official drivers as otherwise you might be kidnapped by groupies or hounded by the press."

"You're joking, right?" Freya queried.

Vikki shook her head. "Nope. It happened to me a couple of months back, although that was in the US who have the craziest fans I've ever seen. But the band are superstars now. You have to make sure you are safe at all times. So official drivers if you go to and from the hotel to the concert arena and vice versa, or if you go anywhere else for that matter. You aren't prisoners and if you want to skip a concert or eat out you may do so, but obviously we won't fund that."

"I can't believe you're funding all this," I said.

"It's all Zak. I don't know what you did, but you've turned out to be a good influence on him. Keep up the good work." She patted my shoulder.

I was? I was a good influence on Zak? At any moment I was going to wake up and find I'd banged my head on the coffee table. I'd told my mum the rug curled up time and time again.

"Okay, I'll leave you for thirty minutes to have a look around the suite and get settled, then come down and meet us in the bar." She looked at her watch. "See you at eleven, okay?"

"Absolutely. We'll see you then." I beamed, and I walked Vikki over to the door.

The minute the door closed, I turned towards Freya.

For a moment we just looked at each other incredulous, like we were waiting for someone to pop out and say we'd been pranked.

But no one did.

Then we ran towards each other, hugged and span around.

"Shit, shit, shit, shit, shit. We're in a five-star hotel for a week. Everything paid for. Spa passes. Alcohol. Food. And we're with the band. Getting those fake passes to get us backstage at the live auditions was the best thing I ever did because it all led to this."

"Who says crime doesn't pay?" I giggled.

"Let's open the champagne and have a little tipple before we go downstairs, shall we? We have thirty minutes before we need to be down there."

I agreed. It was indeed a time of celebration. Plus, it might make me less nervous about meeting Stacey.

Freya picked up the champagne and popped the cork effortlessly and then she tried to catch the overflow from the bottle in her mouth. I held two glasses underneath and she poured us a glass each.

We clinked.

"To our week with the band," Freya toasted.

"To our week with the band," I repeated.

We flopped back onto the comfy sofa with the glass in one hand and a strawberry in the other.

"Is this really happening?" I asked my friend.

"Yep, and we haven't even seen the band yet. I'm not sure my heart can cope with all this excitement."

I turned to face her. "I know the chances of it happening are remote, but can you just imagine if I did end up with Zak or you with Rex, or both of us did? This would probably be part of our normal life. How far removed would that be from working in a supermarket or a jewellery store?"

"I'd be able to buy the jewellery instead of sell it!" Freya daydreamed.

Soon it was five minutes to eleven.

"Come on then. Let's meet Stacey, and then..." Freya did a drumroll. "We can go and see the band."

My stomach flipped over. I was going to be near my crush, very, very soon.

Walking into the bar and having Stacey Granger stand up to greet us as Vikki waved us over was a surreal experience. I had only seen her from a distance or on the television.

Vikki did the introductions and then a waiter came over and took our drinks order.

"How's your room?" Stacey asked.

"It's the best room I've ever been in, like in my entire life," Freya answered. "I want to meet the band so much, but another part of me just wants to stay in the room all the time."

Stacey laughed. "It is like that at first. Then can you believe it, but it actually gets boring and you crave a normal comfy bed."

I was sure my face gave away the fact I thought she was nuts, but Freya's certainly did.

"You've got bored of the luxury?"

She nodded. "Yup. I'm at the point now where I'm tired of keeping packing up my stuff. I want to go home to the same place every night, to cook my own food like beans on toast. Of course, I'm sure we'll not have the simplest of lifestyles given we need security around us now, but just some normalcy would be good."

"I get you," I said. "I absolutely loathe packing and you're having to do it every few days."

"And none of the stuff around me is actually mine. It's not my sofa, or my bed. There's no bookcase with all my books. Some nights I just want to pick my feet in peace."

We all burst out laughing. I loved Stacey already. She was so down to earth.

"Will I be able to ask you some questions about your wedding later in the week, Stacey?" I asked tentatively. "N-nothing too nosy. Just a few details that yours and Noah's fans will love."

"Sure."

We chatted a little longer while we had our coffees. Vikki and Stacey explained about how the tour was arranged and described the staff that formed part of the crew.

"So, shall we go over to the arena?" Stacey asked. "I need to make a start on rehearsals and I'm sure you'll be ready to say hi to the band."

It took me a while to find my words because a big lump had

emerged in my throat. I nodded my head while Freya said yes. Eventually, I squawked out a, "Yes, please."

A driver met us just outside the hotel and within ten minutes we were entering the car park of the arena.

Yet time seemed to be going in slow motion because I was about to meet Zak Jones, and hopefully for more than one minute this time. Yet he was still so far away.

We passed through layers of security and down corridors. The security was a lot tighter than it had been at the competition, which wasn't difficult really, but then a lot of the staff who worked on Britain's Best New Band had been struck down by a virus which can't have helped things.

Stacey said goodbye to us and went off to meet the rest of her band and the remainder of us walked through a set of double doors.

And then I could hear him. Singing *Forbidden*. He was at the other side of the vast arena, but his voice echoed around the space, and I imagined how it would be later when I got to see him like this for real.

"Never did I think this could happen.
Never thought I'd feel this way."

Goosebumps skittered up my spine as his soulful voice sounded out. We strode quickly, eating up space to approach the front rows. My eyes were fixed on getting to Zak. So much so that although I'd noticed there were people ahead of us, I'd not realised there were around twenty other women there at the front of the stage.

My heart sank in my chest the closer we got towards them, as some of the women were gorgeous and dressed to kill.

"These women won competitions to come and meet the band, along with a VIP pass for the concert, so they'll be around today too, but they won't have access all areas like you two," Vikki explained.

She didn't make me feel any better with her explanation as the only area I wanted to access was Zak's body and these women were possibly going to get as near to him as I was.

"Do you know, I hear about competitions to meet bands in the press, but I never actually thought about the logistics of it. Did all these people also have security checks?" Freya asked.

"Absolutely, and background checks before they even came here. You can't be too careful these days."

They'd done a background check on me before letting me set up the fan club officially, no doubt to check I wasn't a batshit crazy stalker.

We approached the group of women. Two dressed in navy-blue trouser suits with lanyards stepped towards Vikki.

"This is Leigh, and this is Harriet. Both are part of the tour team. Leigh is one of the PR team and Harriet security."

"Hi." I waved and got a wave back. It was clear they knew we were coming.

"Right, I'm going to take these two backstage," Vikki announced.

One of the tallest women in the group stepped out and looked me up and down. "They're going backstage? What competition did they win? I thought we got to go backstage too?"

"You do, tonight after the show. But Erica is staff. She runs The Paranormals' fan club."

All the other nineteen or so bodies turned around to look at me. "Oh my god," one squealed. "It's Erica. Can I have your autograph?"

Around half of the group of women gathered around me like

I was famous, taking out their phones and asking for a photo of us together, while the other half looked like they wanted to gut me for having access to their men. Harriet had to get the snap happy ones to form an orderly line. One by one they had their photos taken with me.

"I am so, so jelly of you being able to see the band all the time. It must be amazing," one asked.

"Yes, yes, I'm very lucky to be able to do what I do," I lied.

Eventually, the photos were taken, and Vikki told the crowd that we needed to leave, and they could catch up with me later. The bitchy ones had got bored with me long ago and had turned to the front to watch the band.

Even though I knew it was Zak up there singing, it still didn't seem real. It wasn't until we went through a door that led backstage and Vikki walked onto that stage and asked if the guys had five minutes to meet us that I realised this was all truly happening.

"I can't believe you had to sign autographs for some of their fans." Freya giggled. "I'm gonna fangirl you later. I didn't realise I was in such esteemed company."

"Shut up." I elbowed her in the ribs.

And then the band were walking towards us. Noah was through the door first. He smiled at us both. "I'm not gonna hug you because I'm all sweaty, but it's good to see you again. Welcome to the tour."

"Thanks," I replied. I looked at the side of me for Freya, but she wasn't there. Then I saw her in the doorway hung around Rex's neck while he slowly extricated her from his body. He promptly carried her over and plonked her back down at my side. "Hi, Erica."

"Hey, Rex."

A bemused Roman had followed Rex through the door. One of the staff passed him a towel and a bottle of Jack Daniels which he took a huge glug of. How did it not burn his throat out?

And then he was there. Zak Jones swaggered in from the

stage. He ran a hand through his blonde strands and those green eyes fixed on mine as he took the offered towel and wiped his face and neck on it. I made a note of where it landed because I was so stealing that towel.

He opened his mouth and I waited with bated breath for his first words to me.

"Well, hey, who do we have here then?" he asked.

Chapter 11

Erica

My blood ran cold. What had Zak just said? This man had organised this. He'd invited me here. In my mind I'd told myself that he'd felt guilty from running off so quickly when we'd first met, and he wanted to apologise.

But no, he had absolutely no idea who I was.

I heard Noah take a huge exhale.

"Zak, this is Erica and her friend Freya. You remember? The woman who runs our fan club who you invited to spend the week with us?"

"Ohhhh. My apologies. Of course, I recognise you now." He looked from under his lashes, all coy and guilty. "I am so sorry. Rehearsing takes me out of reality, and I have a hard time coming back." He grabbed Freya's hand and raised a brow. "So, let me guess. You're Erica?"

I waited for Freya to snatch her hand back and correct him, but when I looked, she was kind of staring back into his eyes. Now what was happening? Freya liked Rex, not Zak. Please don't tell me she was changing her mind.

Then Rex flicked Zak's ear, *hard*.

"That's Freya. This is Erica," he said, pointing to me. "It's good to see you again, Erica. Thanks for all you do. I know our fans love being the Subs, and you give us a way to address the crap the press comes out with on a daily basis."

"It's no problem at all," I replied, a big cheesy grin breaking out across my face.

I felt a sharp pain in my right foot and when I sought the source of my discomfort, Freya was crushing my toes with her shoe. Her interest in Zak seemed to have waned and now she appeared narked I was smiling at Rex. We'd be having words when we got out of here.

All was forgotten though when Zak reached for my hand. I was lost as he stared into my eyes. "Sorry, Erica. I seem to have had some kind of brain trauma today. It's so wonderful to see you again. Thank you for all you do running our fan club and I hope you enjoy spending the week here watching the band and how everything is put together."

There was something about this guy. He had a kind of aura that just drew you in. Like when they said people had charm, or the X-factor. Zak Jones had something about him that drew me in like a bluebottle to an open living room window.

But then it was as if someone had severed the connection between us as he spoke to the band about grabbing lunch. He left me standing there, remembering that at first, he hadn't known who I was.

"We're going to grab a burger in the canteen. Want to come?" Noah asked.

I just nodded my head while Freya excitedly said yes.

The canteen was full of crew members, and we walked over to get seats at a long table where Stacey and the rest of her band, The Seven, sat. Stacey told her band who we were and then a waitress came over to ask everyone what they wanted to eat and drink. No queuing for food for the bands.

Tobias, the drummer from The Seven was sitting to my left and he moved his chair to face me a little more.

"Tell me, what do I have to do to get you to run my fan club?" He winked, moving a piece of curly brown hair out of his eyes.

"I'm afraid I don't have time to take on any more bands," I told him. I felt guilty though because they'd jointly won the competition.

"That's a shame. I think to make amends you should have dinner with me one night," he replied.

My eyes almost bugged out of my head. Tobias was a good-looking guy with a really nice pair of arms. I'd noticed while watching him banging his drums. It was just... he wasn't Zak.

Tobias smiled. "Okay, I realise that was a little fast. Just... get to know us too, okay? And then later on in the week if you fancy that dinner, how about you let me know?"

"Okay." I nodded.

Once all the food and drink had arrived, Donna, another one of The Seven, tapped the top of her glass and called for order.

"Bands. Here's to an amazing first night and an amazing week in our hometown."

Everyone stamped their feet on the floor and then yelled, "Amazing." It would seem there was a little good luck, pre-show ritual for me to note down.

I tucked into my food and listened to everyone around me. There was such comfortable banter, the band members often teasing each other, or asking which family members were turning up to watch them perform. It hadn't occurred to me that their family and friends would be attending.

"Who have you got coming tonight?" I asked Noah. I had Freya at my left-hand side and Noah was sitting next to her. "Just my friend, Mya. My mum lives abroad."

"Harley's looking forward to catching up with everyone," Stacey said.

"Harley Davies?" Freya queried.

"Yeah. She'll be at tonight's show."

"Wow. And we will be in the VIP section with everyone?" Freya double checked.

"Yep, you sure will." Stacey looked pensive for a few moments. "You know. This is all still really new to us all, and we're not used to it. We've fallen into the routines of touring and it's so busy that I guess you just get on with it. But when I stop, like now... when I hear you two talking about it like, wowing about being here and meeting Harley, it's strange because I don't feel any different to the woman who was gigging a few months back."

"Newsflash! You are different, Stacey," I told her. "You're an absolute superstar. The press can't get enough of you, even more so since you married Noah."

"She's definitely different," Donna added. "Since Noah turned her into—"

"Mrs Granger," Stacey said loudly. "Yes, since Noah turned me into Mrs Granger."

"So, Erica, what kind of thing will you be researching for your fan club?" Donna asked. "Like a proper behind the scenes, or gossip and scandal?"

"Behind the scenes," I replied. "It would be great if I could get any exclusives of course, but I'm not here for scandal."

"Even though you could sell the story and make shitloads of cash?"

"I've signed an NDA. There will be no selling of stories and I wouldn't do that anyway. I'm not like that," I said firmly.

"Of course you're not," Stacey replied, delivering Donna a portion of side-eye.

Donna seemed oblivious to Stacey's stare. "It's a shame you aren't doing The Seven as well. I could tell you my exclusive about when I was possessed with the spirit of Dan Trent at the final."

There was silence at the table as the bandmates all looked at each other and then at Donna.

"Ow!" Donna complained, jumping a little, before quickly adding, "Just joking." The table chatter cautiously started up again.

"She's a frikking weird one," Freya whispered to me.

"Right?" I whispered back.

Throughout lunch my gaze had wandered over to Zak, but he'd never once looked my way. In fact, at one point I noticed he'd fallen asleep at the table.

Stacey and Freya both went to the loos together like women do, and Noah moved into Stacey's seat. I looked up at him. "Erica, please don't take what I'm about to ask you the wrong way, but did you only come here for the fan club?"

I sighed. "Is it that obvious? I still like Zak. I can't help it. But I did come for the fan club stuff... as well."

"Oh dear." Noah's head tilted to one side. "I told you about Zak before. He's complicated."

I couldn't meet Noah's gaze and instead cast my gaze downward. "I know he sleeps with stacks of women, but I just feel he hasn't met the right one yet." I sounded pathetic even to my own ears.

"I agree with you. He hasn't. But Zak has another job he has to do outside of the band. That and his work with us takes all his effort."

"Another job? Why does he need another job?" I'd not come across any rumour of another job in all the info I'd dug up on Zak. This was news to me.

"It's complicated but he had a previous contract in a service industry, and he still has to meet the terms of his contract."

"And how long is this contract?"

"Not sure, but for the foreseeable future. Now please don't speak of this outside of us two, not even to Freya."

"Oh. Okay. Sure, I won't. Thanks for warning me about him again, Noah, but the thing is... and I know this is going to sound silly... but a woman told me to follow my heart and not give up on my dreams of love, and I think that means Zak."

Noah's eyes widened.

"I know I sound crazy. Sorry, I shouldn't have said that out loud."

"No, that's not it. It's just... a similar thing happened to Stacey in the restaurant where she works." He shouted over to her. "Come here, Stace, and listen to this."

I repeated my story to Stacey, and she looked at Noah. "It's the same woman. Mine was almost three years ago now, but she told me it was my destiny to enter Britain's Best New Band."

"That's so weird," I said.

"She's probably a crazy stalker," Freya added. "I mean fortune tellers aren't legit, are they? People can't really tell your future."

"Freya doesn't believe in anything 'other' like ghosts or psychics," I said.

"And you do?"

I nodded. "I've never seen anything, but I do think there's more to life than what we see."

"You're right. I'm a witch," Donna shouted across the table. "So's Stacey and the other two women in the band."

"Oh, erm, right..." I looked from Donna to Stacey for a further explanation as I was beginning to wonder if Donna was having a side of hallucinogenic with her lunch.

"We don't ride broomsticks. We just respect our goddess and the earth," Stacey attempted to explain.

"Yeah, but you're not going around turning people into frogs, are you, like in story books," Freya reasoned.

"No. No, we're not. Anyway, back to your story, Erica. So you believe following your dreams will lead to love?"

"I kind of *hope* it does, more than I actually believe it."

"She thinks it means Zak," Noah explained.

At that point the person sitting next to Rex got up. Freya moved at lightning speed to sit next to him, leaving me with Noah and Stacey.

"It wouldn't hurt to spend time with Zak this week and see where it goes," Stacey encouraged.

"You think I should try? He didn't even know who I was when I turned up earlier."

"Then you need to make sure he knows exactly who you are, Erica. Don't let him get away with it." Stacey lowered her voice. "Zak can get almost any woman he wants. The thing that drives him mad is when he can't. Maybe you just need to keep his interest by playing hard to get."

"He has to realise I exist before I can play hard to get," I whined.

"Oh, I'll help you with all that." Stacey sounded extremely determined.

"Are you seriously saying that I should try to make a move on Zak Jones?" I double-checked.

"I entered Britain's Best New Band and my destiny was definitely there. I think you should try. And maybe it's not Zak. Maybe it's someone else."

I thought about Tobias.

"Okay, I'm going to follow my heart like the woman said."

Noah put a hand on Stacey's arm. "You know that thing you did with the female band members. Can you do that with Freya and Erica?"

"What?" I asked, and then I noticed that Zak was awake, and Freya was hanging onto his every word once more.

"Oh, it's just a few hair care tips. Everyday styling can be drying for the hair," Stacey answered.

Something felt off. Why would Noah ask Stacey to advise us about hair care? But Stacey had been nothing but kind since we'd arrived, so I pushed the conversation to the back of my mind and pushed getting Zak's attention to the front.

I made my excuses, left my seat, and walked over to Freya's side. "Freya, will you come to the ladies with me?"

Freya blinked and looked at where she was sitting, and then turned towards Rex who was deep in conversation with Roman and another woman from the band.

"H-how did I...?"

Zak yawned and stood up. "I'm off back to rehearse, guys. See you in a bit."

Everyone began to move at that point and make their way out of the room. Stacey walked past and mumbled some words that made no sense. It actually sounded like an... incantation. "Pardon?" I said to her.

"Ignore me. I'm just mumbling under my breath about how much my shoes are hurting my feet. Catch you later. Feel free to watch more rehearsals, but if I were you, I'd go get ready for the show, and the after-party."

"After-party?" Freya's eyes lit up.

"Yes, and there's always a free bar."

Freya looked at me. "It might be a good idea to get back and get ready, don't you think?"

I nodded. I had a lead singer to impress.

"Let's go."

Visiting the ladies' bathroom on the way, I challenged my friend. "Frey, twice today I caught you flirting with Zak. What was that all about?"

She pulled her nose up and scrunched her face in a grimace. "No, I didn't. What are you talking about?"

"You did it when we first met them today and then again at lunch. You were looking at him like you were one step from shoving your tongue down his throat."

"Have you had a lot to drink today because from where I'm standing it looks like you're hallucinating," she snapped.

"I know what I saw," I snapped back.

"Erica." Freya walked towards me and grabbed my arm. "You're my best friend and you are in love with Zak Jones. I wouldn't do that to you. I like Rex, not Zak. Okay?"

"Okay," I said, but as we walked out of the bathroom, for the first time I was doubting my best friend, and I didn't like it.

Chapter 12

Zak

More rehearsing, the gig itself, and then an after-party. At the after-party I'd secure a couple of phone numbers and then I'd go to sleep and add to my tally. We had some VIPs today and so I could tap a couple of those, and then tomorrow was the meet and greet in the afternoon. It meant that this week should be fine for hitting some numbers. I needed coffee set up through an IV though to survive.

Noah came up to the side of me. "Stop hitting on Freya," he bit out.

"No, continue hitting on her," Rex growled back.

I raised my hands in a gesture of surrender. "I'm going to disappoint one of you."

"Erica and Freya are friends of the band and are therefore not to have their souls drained," Noah yelled, his eyes flashing red. Wow, that happened rarely, so the guy really was pissed off. Even Rex took a step back and usually he could hand Noah his arse.

"But if he does it means she leaves me alone," Rex said.

"For a start, what is so bad about Freya?" Noah asked Rex.

He shrugged. "She's a nice enough woman, but I can't screw her and dump her because she's Erica's mate, and there's no future because she's not my mate."

"Okay, but you're just going to have to let her down gently, because Zak will no longer be doing his voodoo moves on her," Noah told him.

"I still have fifty-nine pieces of soul to collect. Even Mrs Danvers is looking like a possible candidate," I huffed. Mrs Danvers was the eighty-nine-year-old helper at the concert hall who volunteered, and everyone loved.

"Don't discount her, she's probably still a right little raver." Rex winked.

Noah shuddered and pulled a face. "Pleaaasseee, stop."

"No Freya, and I've not been anywhere near Erica so there you go," I told him, hoping he'd leave me alone.

Rex walked on in front, but Noah held back. "Why? Why have you not been near Erica?"

Fuck. Looked like I needed to confess all.

"I may actually like her, ever so slightly. Just in case, I'm avoiding her at all costs," I admitted, speaking as quietly as I could.

Rearing back, Noah shook his head as if his hearing was deficient, when as a vampire he should know he heard me right. "Can you say that again?"

I looked around us, making sure we were alone. "Keep your voice down. I'm only telling you as you're my best friend."

"Okay."

"When I first met Erica, something weird happened. I looked at her and my stomach flipped a bit, so I got the hell out of there because I felt strange. Then when I got her questions and decided to invite her here, I was kind of wanting to test if it happened again."

I looked at Noah, who looked like a stiff waxwork. I pushed him and he came to. "I was not expecting you to say that, mate. Gimme a minute, I'm stunned." He continued to say, 'Fucking hell' under his breath a few times. Ignoring him, I carried on talking because now I'd started confessing, it looked like I couldn't stop. My gob was like a runaway train when the only tracks I wanted in my life were ones I was laying down to music.

"Anyway, when she arrived, I felt a bit weird again when I saw her. I pretended I didn't remember her as I figured she'd be annoyed and stay away from me."

"Is that why you've been flirting with Freya? To keep Erica at arm's length?"

"Yes," I sighed.

He smacked me around the head. "You're such a dickhead."

"Ow. What did you do that for?"

"For a start, you could cause problems between Freya and Erica."

"Why?"

Noah ran a hand over his face with a sigh. "Because Erica has a crush on you, dummy."

Shaking my head, panic hit me. "What? Oh no, oh hell to the no. I thought as much with the way she looked at me when I first met her. I could feel her eyes on me when she was near. No, no, no. I need to put her off." I was feeling weird again. My stomach flipping. If I'd had a heart that beat, I'd bet I'd have palpitations. I was falling apart in front of Noah's eyes and my best mate was still chatting on and hadn't even noticed.

"Why in the hell would you put her off? Are you having a brain aneurysm or something? You like her, she likes you. What's the fucking problem?"

I finally felt like I wasn't going to puke. No thanks to my mate. "It's the *fucking* problem. How can I have a girlfriend when I have to satisfy sixty-nine other women in a month? I'm sure most girlfriends like their partners to be faithful, but me, I have to flirt relentlessly all day and all night and then go fuck people in their dreams. That does not make me the ideal boyfriend, does it?"

Noah sighed. "I suppose not, but you could get to know her. Who knows, one day you might not be cursed anymore." That sentence came accompanied by a look of sadness and resignation.

I shook my head. "It's better that I keep my distance, because that's not the life I've ended up with and I have to accept that." *Stupid twatting demons.*

"You need to keep hope there." Noah patted me on the back. "You just never know what's around the corner."

As we rounded the corner, the twenty VIPs were there, every one a potential new soul.

"Fate itself couldn't be clearer. Give up on me, Noah. I know you got your hearts and flowers eventually, but I'm a lost cause."

I walked up to the women. "Hello there, VIPs. I'm Zak. Why don't you all introduce yourselves?"

Noah gave me a look of reproach as he walked away from me, but I ignored him. I knew and was accepting my life. Until I came up with a way to offer Abaddon a better deal than me, this was my lot in life.

After securing all twenty of their phone numbers but adding a little dot to the corner of the ones that seemed more 'pure' and therefore better quality, I retired back to my room. I ordered a fresh pot of coffee, and some vodka and red bulls. Hard drugs were easily accessible to the band, but none of us went there, tempting though it felt at times on my part at least. I didn't want to get past a point of no return.

Lying on the sofa in my room, I enjoyed a rare moment of utter peace, with no-one else around. But the truth was I felt lonely. I was hardly ever alone—usually surrounded by my bandmates, crew, or women—yet when I did get some time to myself it reminded me of how sad my life was outside of the busy world I inhabited.

Noah getting married hadn't helped. I was so pleased for him. His and Stacey's road to happiness had been littered with speed humps, craters, and a few collisions, but now they were finally settled and loved up, and I was jealous. I couldn't help it. They shone in each other's company, their souls on fire. Mine wouldn't do that because I didn't have one. All because I fell for a deal with a demon.

A knock came to the door, and I walked over to it looking through the spyhole. I opened the door quickly.

My parents and younger brother were outside.

"Surprise," they all yelled.

"Oh my god. I thought you said you couldn't make it?" They all lived in Devon, had moved a few years ago, and I'd been crushed when Mum had said their holiday home was full and they couldn't get away.

"We were just messing with you. We wouldn't miss it for the world," my mum said, pulling me into her embrace. I sank into her arms. It felt so good. My parents were amazing people who'd offered me support all through my life, especially through my school years where I'd been picked on for puberty giving me a ton of spots and extra-greasy hair.

I hugged my dad next and then turned to my brother, Richie. He was fifteen—ten years younger than me—but where I'd looked like I'd been covered in sweetcorn at his age, Richie was six foot and clear skinned. He'd yet to fill out though and so only looked his age.

"I'm not hugging you, man. I might catch a disease," he said.

"Richie!" Mum admonished.

"Seriously, a crab might crawl out of his trousers and onto me or something." He pulled a face.

"I don't have crabs or any other sexually transmitted diseases," I informed him, much to my parents' horror.

"Er, could we change the conversation?" Dad said. "Maybe you could order us some tea and coffee, and some sandwiches? We haven't had a chance to eat yet."

"Of course. What would you like, Richie?"

"Coke, and a burger and chips please."

I sorted out their food order while they hung up their coats and visited my loo to freshen up. After, we all went to sit in the living room area of my suite.

"How've you been?" Mum asked.

"Not much has happened since we last spoke." We'd chatted when I'd first arrived back in London.

"You've not met a nice young woman here yet? I thought with how many female staff there would be that you might."

"Mum, he'll just be giving them all his D. It's what he's famous for," Richie helpfully piped up.

"You jealous, bro? Your balls dropped yet?"

Mum huffed. "Do you think we could actually have some decorum here?"

"With two sons?" Dad looked at her and raised a brow. "Not a chance."

Mum shuffled on her seat, and she tucked a few errant hairs from her blonde sleek bob behind her ear. "I am hoping that once you've grown bored of sowing your wild oats, you'll settle down and give me some grandbabies."

"Huh, there are probably some already cooking out there," Richie piped up again.

"I keep it wrapped and I'm not hitting it as often as you think, brother," I said, which was part-truth given that most of my antics took place in women's dreams.

"That's not what the papers say."

"You should know better than to believe what the trashy tabloids report."

"Exactly. I've told him that. One last Sunday had an 'exclusive' that Noah and Stacey had ordered bottles of blood of all things as part of their dressing room demands. I mean as if," Mum scoffed.

"So where are you staying?" I asked them, quickly changing the subject away from my friends' foodstuffs.

"We're at the Premier Inn near Euston, darling."

"Mum, I could have booked you something much better." Always with the deals and offers was my mum. I guess when you were used to having very little in the past it was hard to change the habits of years of scrimping and scraping for us.

"I know, sweetheart, but it's like I said when you offered us the big house... it's just not me."

Dad sighed, "Unfortunately."

She patted his arm. "Dougie, why would we want to live in a mansion with our every whim attended to when we can run our little guest accommodation near the beach that keeps us happy and occupied?"

"Why indeed?" he said, rolling his eyes at me.

Dad would never get a quiet life with Mum. She liked to stay active, and while he might crave an easier life, he'd no doubt be bored quickly with the reality of having everything done for him. Then again, Mum fussed around him so much that most things were done for him. He was Mr Fix Things. She always had a task for him to keep his 'brain agile'.

I realised that Richie had a small travel suitcase with him. "What's that for?" I asked. He opened it up to reveal it was empty.

"Can you fill it with signed merch that I can sell? Got quite a few people interested and that's just from school. I'll get set up on *eBay* and make a mint."

"No. No, I cannot. Plus, I told Mum you can have anything you need with her and Dad's agreement."

He narrowed his eyes in her direction. "You did not tell me this, Mother."

"You're not being spoiled just because your brother is doing well for himself at the moment. You need to learn how to earn your own money, so you get a sense of self."

"That's why I'm trying to set up my own online business," he said, exasperated.

They were driving me crackers as they bantered in my room, and I was loving every minute of it. Normality and a reminder of times when I didn't have to suck the soul out of sixty-nine women a month.

"Tell him, Zak," Mum said.

"Tell him what?"

"How you are grounded today because of how I brought you up."

"Listen to Mum. She's amazing and always right," I told Richie. "Also, if you're ever offered unlimited sex in a night club by a guy, don't fall for it."

"I'm straight, bro," Richie protested.

"It was with women."

"Oh, a pimp. I ain't paying anyone to have sex with me," Richie said.

I left it at that.

Chapter 13

Erica

Even though we'd just eaten burgers and fries, somehow, we found room for some of the handmade chocolates left on the table. Freya poured us both another glass of champagne. This time we took them through to our bedroom where we both relaxed on our massive beds.

"This is the life," Freya sighed. "It almost makes up for the fact that Rex isn't the slightest bit interested in me."

Freya was too far away, and also, she'd put the box of chocolates on her bed, so I walked over with my glass of champers and a pillow and made her move up. It wasn't like there was no room. I laid at the side of her.

"Zak's not the slightest bit interested in me either. Let's face it, we're just two more faces in a sea of females. They have a never-ending supply. Somehow, we have to be different. Now, Stacey's told me that Zak is so used to getting anyone he wants that if I show I'm resisting him I might pique his interest. Though I did ask how he'd know I was resisting if he didn't realise I existed in the first place."

Freya chewed on her bottom lip for a moment.

"Hmm, maybe do what I've done with Rex and basically throw yourself at him. Then he'll either take you up on it and you're winning, or he'll get fed up, like Rex, and try to get you to leave him alone. I need to do what Stacey says and ignore Rex. I'll flirt with someone else."

I stared at her.

"Not with Zak. I don't want Zak for heaven's sake. There's Roman and then there's Carl, Tobias, and Splinter from The Seven."

"We need to find out why his nickname is splinter," I said.

"I hope it's not because he has a tiny cock. That would make one less."

"Can you not go for Tobias either because he asked me out to dinner," I confessed.

Freya's mouth dropped open. "When did this happen? Why did you not tell me? Oooh, did you say yes?"

"No. It was about five seconds after I'd sat next to him. He said to let him know if I wanted to go out later in the week."

Freya sprung forward, looking much more animated. I wasn't sure if it was getting behind this 'treat them mean' idea or due to the champagne she'd knocked back quickly. "You can use him to make Zak jealous."

I shook my head. "No, I wouldn't do that. It's not nice. But if Zak fails to show interest in me then I'm going to accept. Tobias is nice. I'd be stupid not to go."

"We are stupid though, aren't we, babe? We have our hearts set on famous rock stars. Are we dreaming, Erica? Are we aiming too high?"

I shrugged my shoulders. "Look, we didn't expect to meet them. I didn't expect to run their fan club. We didn't expect to spend a week with them. Let's have no expectations and hope everything works out."

"Okay." Freya nodded. "No expectations, but we need to look scorchingly hot at all times and I need to play hard to get. So, tonight at the after-party you have to get up close and personal with Zak, and I must ignore Rex altogether. Deal?"

I shook her hand. "Deal."

I hadn't brought any clothes with me that in any way would serve to be seductive, so we headed out to central London to try to find a new outfit each. Having a driver take us there, and a member of security watching us from a distance, made us feel like we were famous. I was just pleased the security man was happy to wait outside the waiting room. For a moment, I'd panicked that the guy would follow us in.

Freya had me way out of my comfort zone trying on a silver wrap dress with a black belt. "Are you sure I don't just look like a chicken ready for the oven?" I asked her.

"Are you kidding me? You look like a star. Look when the light catches it, it turns all different colours, and it clings to every curve in all the right places. You look amazing. You need black and purple nails, black shoes, a purple and silver bag. Oh, and a black hair clip, and you'll be sorted."

"Okay, you try yours on then now," I ordered. We were sharing a large changing room for two.

Freya put on the black jumpsuit she'd chosen. Plain, and not at all figure-hugging. She still looked cute, but it wasn't an attention seeking outfit.

"Do I look like I don't care, but in an 'I'm still sexy' way?"

"Absolutely."

"Fantastic. Let's get some shoes and accessories and go back and get ready, because..." she looked at her watch, "...in three hours' time we'll be in the VIP section watching the bands."

"This has already been one of the best days of my life, and not only is it not over yet, but there are another six days with the bands to go." I squeezed Freya's arm.

"How will we ever return to our normal, dull arse lives?" Freya sighed.

It was a question I wasn't willing to think about because it was too sad to contemplate.

Our seats were on the front row.

The.

Front.

Row.

Vikki guided us down and explained that the first four rows were celebrities, and dotted in between them and on the row behind them were security dressed as normal concertgoers. I spotted Harley, and Carmela from Britain's Best New Band. There were also a few people from the latest series of *Love Island*, a new male singer recently signed by Bill Traynor—the bands' manager—and some soap opera stars and other TV presenters.

We soaked up the atmosphere of the bustling and busy auditorium and then the lights went down and The Seven came on stage. They all appeared one by one as if by magic, seeming explosions making band members appear. A box was brought on stage and twirled around, showing it was open and empty, and then when it spun around again Donna was in it. She stepped out to gasps and applause. Next, an empty cage came down from the ceiling. Donna and the other two female band members made a show of covering the cage with a black cover and then they pulled it away, and Stacey was inside. Everyone—including Freya and me—screamed. The cage doors opened out and Stacey stepped to the front of the stage. The band took their places and started their set.

They were spellbinding. We'd seen them play in the competition and I'd seen some clips of them live on YouTube, but no one could have prepared me for hearing Stacey's mountain of a voice now she'd done months of touring. I knew she was leaving soon, and I also knew that she would be a West End star. She just owned the stage. They may have been a band, (and there had been rumours Donna was jealous of the attention Stacey got), but Stacey outshone them all. They were quite simply Stacey's backing band, whether they liked it or not. Maybe once she'd left, they could form a more equal group, but Stacey Granger would be a hard act to follow.

The time flew, and when the band finally said goodbye and a tannoyed voice announced that there was an interval before The Paranormals took to the stage, I realised that I'd forgotten about everyone else around me apart from Freya. We'd shared some smiles and 'wows' throughout The Seven's appearance, but other than that we'd been entranced.

We quickly moved to use some bathrooms earmarked for the VIPs and got back to our seats as early as we could as we didn't want to miss a single second of our band.

"This is it, Erica. We're finally going to see a whole show of The Paranormals. Hear new material. Take note of the new songs so you can tell the fans about some of them," Freya almost squealed. She looked around. "Do you think we'll actually get to meet some of these celebrities to talk to, or do you think they'll keep their distance from us plebeians?"

"I have absolutely no idea, but we aren't plebeians. What did Elizabeth Hurley call people like us? Civilians? That sounds a damn sight better than plebs."

"Well, I might be a 'civilian', but I'm here in the front row, and many, *many* people are jealous sick of me right now." Freya grinned.

"We are so lucky, and hopefully later on we'll get lucky." I winked.

"Oooh, get you. Is that because you're all dressed up and raring to go?"

"It must be the adrenaline. This must be what the band get like. That's probably why Zak sleeps with so many women. Gets high on the concert rush and has to satisfy his desires."

The five-minute warning came on for people to return to the auditorium. Ten minutes later, the lights dimmed and The Paranormals were on the stage.

The stage was dark and then a spotlight appeared as Rex stalked on twirling his drumsticks. The crowd were deafening. It was triple the reaction of what The Seven had got. Or was that just Freya being hysterical at the side of me? Another spotlight and Noah walked on with his bass guitar, waving to the audience. Another, and Roman strutted out with his lead guitar. My heart thudded with anticipation as the crowd shouted, "Zak, Zak. Zak. Zak. Zak."

Then he emerged slowly out from the floor as we screamed and screamed and screamed. He leapt forward grasping his microphone and he shouted. "London, baby. Are you ready to rock?"

The screams were of a resounding yes and he began singing.

I could feel the music thudding up from the floor into my body. Zak's voice, up close and personal, sang straight to my panties. Now I knew why people whipped them off and threw them at concerts. In fact...

"What are you doing?" Freya complained as I jostled her a few times.

"I'm taking my knickers off. I'm going to throw them at Zak."

"Whaaaat? You crazy fucker. What's got into you?"

"What's not got into me, that I want in me more like?" I shouted.

I refused to throw them until the man himself was looking at me. But songs passed and he'd not looked my way once. I was on the front row, goddamn it. How could he not have met my gaze at least once?

"Let me climb on your shoulder so I can throw my panties," I said to my best friend.

"Yeah, not gonna happen," she said. "You'd break my neck."

"I'll do it." A man who I presumed was a security guy from the other side of Freya offered.

"Really?"

He nodded.

"Thank you. Thank you so much," I said, and before I could change my mind, I hutched myself up and climbed on his shoulders.

Things happened then in a succession of the unexpected. Firstly, as the cold air hit my arse, I realised that while I held my panties in my hand, I'd forgotten they weren't on my body. Now my minge was resting on the back of the security guy's head and his hands were firmly on the bare cheeks of my arse. I now realised why he'd been so eager to assist me.

Next, Zak's eyes did fix on mine, mainly because instead of throwing my panties, I was slapping the guy's head and yelling for him to put me back down.

I stopped yelling and threw my panties, just as the screens at the side of the band flashed around the arena and put my bare arse cheeks on display for the entire O2. A cheer went up as my pants landed over Zak's microphone. Recovering himself, he took them off and stuffed them in his pocket.

"Steady there, girl. Save your energy for later." He winked, playing up to the part of lothario.

I knew full well that he wouldn't be saving his energy for me because my antics looked as sexy as a granny strip-o-gram. Meanwhile, Freya was just staring at me agog. "Help me," I mouthed.

She shook the security guy. "She's thrown the panties. Can you put her down now?" she demanded.

"Sure," I heard him say and then he lifted me off.

Over... his... front.

Meaning that Zak, and any other band members who might have been looking—I didn't know as I couldn't take my eyes off Zak's—were treated to a full frontal. Thank the Lord, I'd had a wax recently. Also thank the Lord, and every other deity that existed, that the screens were not on my front bottom.

Zak forgot his lines. He stood there for a couple of minutes absolutely speechless until I was lowered back down and then he picked back up from where he'd left off.

My face was no doubt as purple as my handbag. My so-called best friend's was. She could barely breathe. Bent over, clutching her stomach, she kept trying to apologise for laughing, before laughing again.

Mr Security Guy leaned over and whispered to Freya when she'd finally recovered herself. I heard her telling him that he had no chance as my heart belonged to Zak.

"What did he say?"

"He said to tell you that your sitting on his neck was the most erotic experience of his life. That he never plans to wash it, and he wondered what you were doing after the after-show or any other evening so you could sit on other parts of him."

"I may as well just kill myself," I told her.

"Are you joking?" she said. "You wanted Zak's attention, and fuck me, did you get it. If he's not interested in you now after he's just seen your pussy, then I don't know what else you can do, mate."

"I can never look him in the face again."

"Not sure he'll be interested in looking at your face anyway." She started laughing again. In fact, they were massive guffaws. I ignored her and focused on the concert and the music, although I wasn't able to enjoy it as much now that I daren't look at Zak again for fear he might actually look back.

Chapter 14

Zak

There I'd been in my element, singing to my home crowd—and avoiding looking at Erica—when all of a sudden I saw someone clambering onto another person's shoulders, and the flash of purple in my peripheral vision alerted me to the fact it was Erica herself.

At first, I'd been bemused seeing the panties in her hand, as although I knew Erica very little, she'd not come across as the kind of person who'd throw panties on stage. I'd thought she was more reserved than that. Either she'd been drinking all afternoon —because I knew from when I'd first met her that she couldn't handle alcohol well—or she was a racy little number after all, just like those black lacy panties in her hand. It was when her face turned to one of horror and she began hitting the guy holding her in the head that I wondered what had gone wrong. He wasn't doing anything except holding her securely on his shoulders. Then her panties soared in the air, and they landed right on my microphone. Fuck me, the sexiest woman in the auditorium had thrown her knickers at me. The only thing hotter would be if they'd just been next to her pussy. That was the moment I caught sight of the screens to the side and saw her bare arse with the guy's hands on it, and I realised why she was hitting him in the head. Until that point, even when the pants had landed over the mic, I'd carried on singing. I'd made a joke and tucked the panties into my pocket. But as realisation hit me that they *had* just come off her body, and the guy lifted her off and I got a direct view of her sweet pussy... well...

For the first time *ever*, I forgot the words to the song. Picking the song back up and keeping my eyes firmly *off* Erica, I looked at my bandmates. Noah was looking at me confused, Rex was smirking, and Roman looked at me with wide eyes.

In my ear I heard the tour manager tell us. "We are skipping the song we were doing next. We'll put a different one in tomorrow night's show, but tonight we'll just be one track short. It'll be fine."

Given it was a cover of Queen's *Fat Bottomed Girls*, I could see why it was a wise choice to avoid it.

I managed to get my focus back fully on the concert and kept my eyes well away from the front rows. The band played two encores and then the first gig was under our belt, and it was time to let loose a little at the after-party. We walked off to the dressing room to get showered and changed. All of us were pumped and buzzing and we hugged, high-fived, and jumped around because it had been a total high.

Once in the dressing room where it was just the four of us, Rex started. "Are you going to give Erica her pants back tonight then?"

Noah looked at him with a double take, his head swinging from Rex to me. "What? How do you have her pants? What did I miss?"

"Did you not see Erica flash her backside to the whole crowd, and her panties hanging over Zak's microphone?" Rex queried, a crease between his brows.

"No. I spent most of my time focused on my wife." The penny dropped. "Oh, so that's why they pulled the song from the list," he said.

"It was worse than that," Roman said, swigging from his bottle. "We all got a look at her lady parts. I wouldn't be surprised if she hasn't gone home. I'm amazed she stayed to watch the rest of the concert."

"She did?" I asked. I had to admit, I also thought she'd have probably run out embarrassed.

Roman nodded.

"Poor Erica," Noah said. "She must be mortified. When we see her, we must act like nothing happened, okay? No jokes about this at all."

We all agreed and then we got ready for the party, although Roman was always ready for a party anyway. I was surprised his hand hadn't fused in a 'carrying a bottle' shape. He might be the largely silent type, but he was no shy boy and I wondered what he planned to do given Harley had shown interest in him.

The after-party was taking place in one of the banqueting suites, and we were greeted by Bill, our manager, the minute we walked through the door.

"Here are my favourite people in the whole world." He clapped us all on the back, and we went through the part where we met anyone Bill introduced us to with enthusiasm. It was 'schmoozing time'. You never knew who would give us a sponsorship deal or a front cover of a coveted glossy magazine. As lead singer, I always had more of the schmoozing to do, but I'd had plenty of practice with being an incubus, so it wasn't a great hardship.

I could see in my peripheral vision that there were lots of women hanging around, waiting for the band to be free. Stacey was also hanging around and I pitied anyone who ever tried to make a move on Noah, and not just because she was a witch and vampire hybrid.

As soon as we were free of our responsibilities and Bill had moved on, the women moved in. They gathered around like annoying midges who tried to get in your face, their simpering or trying to be seductive voices were like the annoying buzz.

"Hey, Zak."

"You were incredible tonight."

"Your voice is like an angel."

"Can I get you a drink?"

And the best and most said by far: *"Do you wanna escape these crowds and go somewhere more private?"*

Tonight, this line came from a tall, willowy predator. She was wearing leopard print and had red nails and red lips. Say no more.

"No, honey, because as tempting as that is, we kinda have to be at our own after-party," I replied. I was just beginning to get annoyed given there were so many hands on my butt and cupping my junk that I couldn't bat them away fast enough, when a purple-haired beauty came into view. Erica strode right up to me. Now I could see her wearing her dress properly I noted how it clung in all the right places and suddenly I forgot about every other woman in the room. What was it with this chick?

"Oh, Jesus. It's the streaker from the show," said Predator, putting her arm through mine. "Let me protect you."

Erica came closer and flicked her hair. "Excuse me," she said to Predator, tapping her on the shoulder. "I need some alone time with my boyfriend now."

Boyfriend?

BOYFRIEND?

What the fuck was she...? OH!

As Erica's ploy became clear to me, I extricated myself from Predator's grasp.

"You'll have to excuse me, but that streaker is actually my *girlfriend*, and when she demands my attention, I have to give it." I winked lustfully at Erica. "That was very naughty what you did out at the concert. It threw me off my game, Angel."

Erica wiggled her eyebrows. "Sorry, babe. I can't control myself when I'm near you. If I could have my panties back though?"

"Come on. Let's go to the bathroom, and I'll help you put them back on... maybe..."

Erica nodded and I walked away from the women and towards the bathrooms wondering what on earth was going to happen next.

※

I got security to clear everyone out for us for a while. There were other bathrooms a few minutes' walk away and guests could go there instead.

Once we were through the main doors, and inside, I placed my hand in my pocket and took out her panties. "There you go."

"Thanks," she said, back to being a little shy. Walking away from me, she went into the bathroom and put them back on. While she did, I checked that no one but security was outside of the door.

"Keep people out of earshot," I ordered, and then I closed the door behind me.

There was a small seating area near the sinks and hand dryers, and I sat there while I waited for Erica to come back out. I could hear Erica talking. Had she phoned someone from the bathroom?

I listened more closely.

"You stupid woman. Could you embarrass yourself any more tonight? First you show off your private parts, then you push your way into his space and declare you're his girlfriend. No wonder he ran off as soon as he returned your knickers."

"Erm." I cleared my throat. "I've not run off."

There was a groan from the loo. "But I heard the door close."

"I was just checking with security."

Next came a loud sigh. "Do you want to leave now then and escape the madwoman sitting in the toilet stall talking to herself?"

"Nope. I want the madwoman to come out so I can thank her for rescuing me from the groupies."

After half a minute, the door opened, and Erica walked out. She was so pretty, and I didn't think she even had a clue. I patted the seat next to me. "I don't bite. That's more Noah's thing."

I forgot for a moment that she had no clue of our paranormal status until she looked at me a bit strangely.

"Sorry, too much information there."

Erica slowly sat next to me.

"So... thanks again for the interruption."

"S'okay." She shrugged. "I was nearby, and I could tell by your expression that you were starting to get annoyed. I saw them all groping you. It's not what women should be like. I thought I'd give you an option for getting away. It wasn't like I could embarrass myself any further this evening."

"It was much appreciated, and okay, you didn't plan to flash yourself on screen, but I can't say it was an unpleasant view. There are no complaints from me."

She blushed. "I run your fan club and now I'll have to resign because I'll be a laughingstock."

"Erica, all that flashed on that screen was your arse. No one saw who it belonged to apart from the rest of the VIPs in the front section and none of them will say anything. Most have done a lot more than flash their bottom."

"So I can keep running the fan club?" she asked meekly.

"Of course you can keep running the fan club." I moved closer to her and put my arm around her while she had a little weep. It was so pleasant, and I closed my eyes while I enjoyed the warmth from her body. I considered just how nice it would be if I really could have a girlfriend in my life.

"C-could you get me a t-tissue?"

I broke the embrace and went to the sink and grabbed her a handful of tissues.

She accepted them and blew her nose, sounding like a baby elephant. It was adorable.

After that, she walked over to the sink and splashed her face, blotting with more tissue afterwards and then she went in her bag and fixed her make-up. I watched her every move.

"Thanks for helping. I'm ready to go back out now," she said. "People will be wondering where the lead singer is."

"Can we have five more minutes?" I surprised myself by asking. "Just so I can psych myself up to go back out there."

"Sure." She hesitated. "What's it like having all these women around you, really?" she asked, looking down at me before sitting back next to me. "And this question is from me, not on behalf of the fan club."

"Exhausting," I replied truthfully. "They try to pull out pieces of my hair to keep, they molest me, they try to rip my clothes. And I have to grin and bear it mainly, because it's a small part of what's otherwise the most incredible experience. I'm just going to have to up security and get them to intervene quicker, maybe."

"I guess it sends out mixed signals though when you sleep with so many."

"Yeah, I guess."

"Do the management make you do it? Sleep with so many women? Because you don't actually seem all that ecstatic about it when I talk to you. Is it in your contract?"

"It's complicated. It's not in the band's contract no. But I have my reasons."

For a moment we sat in silence and then Erica gasped. "Oh fuck. I get it now. Noah said you had an extra job you couldn't get out of in the service industry. Zak, are you a male gigolo?"

Her face looked like she'd had a brain freeze from a slushie.

"Nope, I sold my soul to a demon, and I have to pay him in the partial souls of women. I'm an incubus."

"Oh ha bloody ha. Fine. If you don't want to answer the question you don't have to. I admit it must be a difficult subject and now I can see why you always look so tired. How long do you have to continue this? Are they blackmailing you?"

"It's a contract. I signed it and it's binding. I'm looking for a way to get out of it, but nothing's revealed itself yet," I said truthfully.

"Shit."

"Yup."

"Well, if you ever want to talk, Zak. I'm here. For the next six days anyway. Maybe I can help you find a loophole?"

"Yeah, maybe. Thanks, Erica, and thank you for all you do for the fan club. Sorry I was a bit of a dick to you today. I just get grumpy because of being so tired."

"I saw you asleep at the dining table. Make sure you're taking plenty of vitamins and practicing very safe sex, okay?" She ran a hand through her hair. "I thought this evening couldn't get any weirder but I'm now feeling sympathy for a man who has to bed lots of women."

"It sounds amazing, but it means I can't settle down with just one. Not while I'm under contract."

Erica nodded sadly.

"Things will work out eventually, I'm sure. Now come on, we've been in here long enough." I ruffled her hair, and then I leaned in and kissed her. I just couldn't resist. As our mouths met, it was everything I'd thought it would be. She melted at my touch as we moved our lips together like a perfect musical arrangement. I broke off the kiss and she looked at me heavy-lidded and lust-fuelled.

"Now you look freshly mussed up like we've been up to no good in here," I said.

"You kissed me," she stated.

"I needed to smudge your lipstick and I forgot I could have just used my fingers," I lied.

"Okay," she said, still looking stunned and now holding her fingers against her lips.

"I'm off to mingle, little E. That's what I'm gonna call you now around the Subs."

"Uh-huh." Her mouth opened and closed like a fish, and it was so cute I wanted to kiss her all over again, but I couldn't.

And she'd think my nickname meant little Erica, but it didn't. It meant little elephant, because that noise she'd made had been just too cute.

As I replayed that thought in my mind, I realised I was in serious trouble. Because I was falling in love with a woman I couldn't be with.

Chapter 15

Erica

Holy fucking hell fire. When I'd first come into the after-party, I'd been sure people were looking at me and staring. Freya had told me I had to get a couple of vodka shots down me and brazen it out. After she'd told me of some of the antics of the VIPs I was in the room with, I'd felt much better. Some people present had done full frontal nudes, others had sex tapes out there, and the Love Islanders had shagged on TV. It made my antics pale in comparison.

It had been the two shots and my newfound confidence that had made me step forward when I'd seen Zak getting molested by the group of women. That and jealousy that their hands were on *my* man.

I replayed the swoonworthy kiss I'd just received in my mind's eye. I was sure that somewhere fireworks had exploded, the sun had shone brighter than ever, babies gurgled, and puppies made cute barking noises as his lips had moved against mine. I'd even got tongue!

And now I knew his secret. He was a male prostitute. Poor Zak. I wondered what in his past had made him go down that route. There was no judgement from me. It couldn't have been an easy decision. No wonder the guy was always falling asleep.

Plus, he had to do it in secret somehow, because if that got out in the press...

I needed to let him know that any time he needed a fake girlfriend I was more than willing.

"No, Erica. You're supposed to be playing hard to get," I told myself, just as my best friend walked in.

"What the hell happened in here with you and Zak?" She was fit to burst. "It felt like forever waiting for you outside."

I got her up to speed in detail and then I sat touching my lips some more.

"I love him," I declared.

"Oh good grief, what a smitten kitten."

"He called me 'little E'. I have a pet name and everything."

"I'm not going to get any sense out of you for the rest of the evening, am I? And I came to also tell you that we're now standing with Stacey, Harley, and a Love Islander called Tawney."

"Whaaaat? I love Tawney. She was the one with all the great slogans who didn't put up with any shit. But she didn't get coupled up in the end. The guy was horrible to her."

"Yeah, she's been telling us how he's been begging for them to get back together, now he's back working as an electrician, and she has deals worth millions with clothing and make-up brands."

That was when my brain caught up and told me that even though I'd just had the most amazing moment with Zak, that he would now be back in the room doing God knows what, and I had just this one week to make the most of all opportunities.

"For goodness' sake, Freya, why are we in the ladies' bathrooms if we can hang around with celebs?" I mock scolded. Getting to my feet, I began walking in the direction of the door.

Freya pulled my dress up and I grabbed it and pulled it back down.

"What on earth are you doing? I already showed my arse, now you have me flashing my pants."

"I wanted to check you did indeed have them back on, or whether you were lying, and your butt was covered in love bites."

That was a thought I was keeping for later back in my room, when I went to sleep thinking about Zak. But, Jesus, even now I couldn't 'enjoy myself' because I was sharing a room with Freya. I really, really, really needed my own place and fast!

"Hi. Sorry about exposing myself to you all earlier," I said to Harley and Stacey, and then I told Tawney how I'd been one of her biggest fans. I told you I had obsessions. I'd bought half of her clothing range because it had great slogan t-shirts and hoodies saying stuff like, 'I don't run but you can jog on'.

I kept my eyes on Zak. He was working the crowd. Now and then he'd look my way and give me a smile and Freya would have to pinch my arm to get me to return to the real world.

"Why does Zak look at you with narrowed eyes?" Freya asked Harley. "Is there gossip there?"

I froze. *Please don't let Zak have been romantically involved with Harley*, I prayed inside. Harley was beyond beautiful with a personality that shone. I couldn't compete.

"Oh, take no notice. He tried his patter on me, and it didn't work. He's too smooth for me," Harley said. "It clearly annoys him that I didn't fall at his feet."

I felt a heavy sensation in my gut like someone had put a mud pie in there. He'd flirted with Harley. I mean of course he had, look at the woman! I'd half a mind to flirt with her myself and I didn't do women, but still. If she'd have said yes, would they be an item now?

It brought me back down to earth. Zak Jones, superstar, was not destined for a supermarket assistant. He'd fall in love with some showbiz star or a top model. I needed to accept my reality.

Not much later than that, I made my excuses to Freya, and assuring her that she could stay, I left.

I woke up to find Zak sitting at the side of me on my bed.

I shot up. "What are you doing here? How did you get in?" At the same time, I was desperately trying to flatten my hair down because I could feel with my fingers that it was total bedhead.

"I'm not here. You're asleep and dreaming. Although why I'm here is a very good question because I should not be," he said strangely.

I sighed. "Of course, I'm asleep. As if Zak Jones would come to my room."

"Little E, of course I'd come to your room. You're gorgeous. But I can't do relationships. I told you that. Like I said, I shouldn't be here, but I've just spent all night wanting to kiss you again. I couldn't stay away."

I realised that it was possible I was going to have a Zak Jones Sex Dream. Yipppppeeee.

It was then I remembered I shared a hotel bedroom with Freya. My eyes darted to her bed, but it was empty. Thank God. I did not need her in my sex dream. That would have been weird.

"What are you thinking, little E?"

"That I'm glad Freya isn't in my sex dream."

He choked on his own saliva.

"Sex dream?"

This was indeed the weirdest of dreams, like being awake asleep. Maybe I should avoid vodka. It didn't seem to suit me.

"Like in the press. All the women, all the time, saying you ravish them in their sleep. Every night I go to sleep, and I don't get ravished, and now, hurrah, our kiss must have woken my brain up, because here you are in my dreams. Finally."

I looked down my duvet at my comfy pjs. "Why could I not have dreamed up a sexy chemise and a figure like a supermodel's?"

Zak came closer. "Well, I'm glad you didn't, because I prefer you. Now scoot over."

Alert. Alert. Zak Jones is climbing into your bed. This is not a drill. A drilling hopefully, but not a drill.

I moved up, my body stiffening as I went way out of my comfort zone. Zak pulled me towards him, so his forehead rested on mine. "Hey, you," he said.

"Hi," I squeaked back.

And then he kissed me again and my body relaxed in his arms. We kissed for hours, and Zak trailed his hands in my hair and down my body but kept to over the top of my clothes.

I huffed.

"What's up?"

"I'm not naked. This dream needs to get a move on."

Zak laughed against my mouth. "What's the rush? Just enjoy the feel of my lips on yours. I'm enjoying yours on mine."

"But I want those orgasms I heard of."

He shook his head. "Not tonight, little E, but what about us spooning?"

He turned me around and cuddled behind me and the next thing I knew it was morning and I woke up, where I found, of course, there was no Zak.

"Stupid fucking brain." I hit myself in the forehead. "You're supposed to have shagged him. Gaaaaahh." I turned to my friend's bed. Just like in my dream she wasn't there. Fuck, where was she?

I didn't have to ponder for long as I went into the living area to find Freya sprawled across the sofa still fully dressed from last night, though her shoes and handbag had been discarded on her way to the sofa. Her cheek was smushed into one of the large cushions and small snores came out of her mouth. I walked over to the kitchenette and began to fix some coffee because I was ready for one, and my friend looked like she'd be ready for about six.

My dream wouldn't leave me. One of those that was so vivid you felt like it actually happened. Sighing, I wondered what Zak actually did do last night and whether it was some of his 'clients'.

The guy deserved happiness, not to be living the dream of rock stardom but being dragged back into a sordid past.

"Oh my head," Freya groaned as she woke. "I drank waaay too much last night." She held her hand out for the coffee I was passing towards her. "Thank you. Oh fuck, Erica, I snogged Tawney for a bet. For once, Rex was interested, but only if he could watch. I like him, but no way was my mouth going on lady bits. Seeing yours yesterday was a stark reminder of how straight I am."

"Sod off."

"You made the right choice coming back when you did. There was only more drinking, nothing of any excitement. Oh, Zak left not long after you."

Yeah, I'd bet he'd had to go and work.

"I dreamed about him, and do you know what I dreamed?" I carried on before she could speak. "That he kissed me and then we spooned. All these women in the press are 'Oh I had forty-three orgasms',"—I was exaggerating but I didn't care—"and in my dreams Zak says, 'Oh let me get on your back' and he didn't even press his cock into me." I slumped onto the sofa next to Freya. "I'm having words with my brain. Sex dreams next time."

"You should be trying for the real thing in real life. The guy kissed you last night. Not in your dreams, in your reality."

"Yeah, he also told me he's not a one-woman guy, so there you go."

Freya looked at me with sympathy. "He said that?"

I nodded. "Yup."

"Huh, well you know what to do now, don't you?"

"Nope."

"Arrange to have dinner with Tobias. If Zak's not interested, Tobias certainly is."

It was food for thought, but I had to make sure if I accepted Tobias' offer of a date it was because I was genuinely interested in having dinner with him and not in some great 'fuck you' to Zak.

"So, what's on today's agenda?" Freya asked.

"Oh, shoot, Vikki texted me last night. I forgot. Let me get my phone." I scrambled off the sofa and headed for my bedroom.

I strolled back. "The band are doing press interviews early this afternoon, after a morning off. I'm not interested in that, are you?" Freya shook her head. "Then later tonight, it's the meet and greet with the fans and they've asked if we can help. You'll be with Rex, and I'll be with Zak." We both grinned.

"Vikki is a superstar." Freya beamed.

"So how about we relax in our lovely suite while we wake up properly? We could order some breakfast. After, we could hit the spa?"

"That sounds like perfection," Freya agreed. "And we can plot our evenings with our men."

I didn't have the heart to tell her she'd just be introducing Rex to other women and taking photos while the other women fawned all over their fave drummer. I could only hope Freya didn't beat them away with his drumsticks.

Chapter 16

Zak

We were having a 'breakfast' this morning with the celebrities who had stayed for the concert last night, along with Bill and some other execs. I was currently sitting up in my bed cursing at myself for the fact I'd visited Erica in her dreams.

I'd tried my best not to, but I couldn't resist. And worse, when I had then gone on to visit the women whose souls I needed to partake in, I'd sunk into their depths imagining it was Erica.

I was fucked. Literally and metaphorically.

Even worse, when I eventually made my way down to the breakfast, I cast my eyes around, and on not seeing Erica there, I felt crushed in disappointment. I cornered Vikki.

"The fan club girls not here?"

"No. They're having a morning off."

I did my best to hide my disappointment.

I sat down next to Roman. Harley was sitting opposite him. "Morning, Zak," she sing-songed. The woman was too happy. Far too happy and shiny. Something was up with her. No one was perky all the bloody time. She indicated to the side of her where a younger, dark-haired girl sat. "This is my younger sister, Bonnie. She's seventeen."

"So old enough." Bonnie winked.

"Oh hahahahahaha. She's just joking." Harley glared at her sister and received an eye-roll in return.

"I prefer Drake and Dua Lipa, but Harley brought me here," the little ray of sunshine added.

"Yeah, I'd have left you at home," I told her. "Could have given someone else a chance who wanted to be here."

"That's what I said, but she insisted," Bonnie sighed.

"I wanted to spend some time with my sister. Sorry that I care," Harley said, her shininess finally dimming a little.

"Half-sister," Bonnie added.

"Why do you do that? You mean just as much to me as you would if we didn't have different dads."

"You're the lucky one. Yours is in heaven," Bonnie huffed. 'Whereas my deadbeat dickhead dad still turns up anytime he wants a shag or money off Mum, which is most weeks." She looked at me. "And then all we hear is, 'Oh if only Remy were here'."

Roman spoke up. "I'm sorry that your father died, Harley, and I'm sorry that yours is still alive, Bonnie."

"Thanks, Roman," Bonnie said, and a strange thing happened. She smiled at him. When she did, Harley also smiled at him.

"So, Bonnie. I know you think we suck, but tonight we have a meet and greet with fans. Do you and your sister want to help out in my room? You can make sure they stick to their times, and I bet you're amazing at taking pics. You younger ones are so good with tech."

It was like Bonnie re-animated from her corpse like state. "Ooh, can we, Harley? That sounds interesting. I can see how pathetic women get around famous people."

"Sure," Harley replied. "Thanks, Roman."

"Thanks, Roman," I mimicked, receiving a look of hurt from

Harley and one of 'I'm going to stab you in your sleep' from Bonnie.

"Sorry. I didn't sleep well and I'm really grumpy, and you're so... lively and awake."

"Look, Zak," Harley said. "I'm sorry that I didn't fall for your charm, but there's no need to be such a jerk with me all the time. I can't be the only woman to have told you no."

"No, you are," Roman explained. "And that's why he's a jerk about it. He'll get over it though, won't you, Zak?"

From the look on Roman's face that was an order, not a request.

"Yeah. I'm sorry, Harley. Obviously, my ego was wounded, but my apologies for me being a jerk." I was saying it to her face, but I still figured there was something about this woman I'd yet to work out, and I would. Especially if she had her sights set on my friend. Roman was a sensitive soul and I wouldn't let her hurt him.

Vikki walked over to us and Roman looked up at her. "Harley and Bonnie are helping me tonight, so I don't need you to find me anyone now."

"Oh great. That's everyone sorted then," she said.

"Oh, you got me a helper too?" I asked.

Vikki smirked. "Yes. Noah has Stacey, Roman has organized himself, Rex has Freya, and you have Erica."

I was spending the evening with Erica, and however many other women turned up during the hours of six pm and ten pm. But still, Erica.

Smiling, I looked at Vikki and then I felt the stares of those around me.

Roman nudged my arm. "Bro, do you have a crush?"

"Fuck you. I was thinking of the women I shagged last night that's all. Just got distracted for a sec. Thanks, Vik. Erica will do at a push, as long as she's not going to interrupt me and ask me loads of fan girl questions all the time. Make sure she knows she's there to help."

"Okay, sweetie. I'll make sure to tell her not to pay you too much attention." She smiled sweetly with a raised brow.

"I can see why you'd piss people off, Harls," Bonnie said, bringing my attention back to the table. "You are super perky and smiley all the time. It is weird."

"You're grouchy all the time."

"I'm a teenager. I'm supposed to be grouchy."

Roman raised his wrist, twirling it this way and that and grimaced.

"You all right, mate?"

"It's just aching a bit. Nothing to worry about."

"Ooh let me try to heal it. I'm really good at getting the heat to my hands," Harley offered while leaping up.

"Fuck's sake. Here she goes." Bonnie looked at me. "More of her weirdness."

Harley rubbed her hands together, closed her eyes and asked for God and the angels to lend her their healing powers. Then when she was satisfied, she asked for Roman's wrist. She held the underneath with her left hand and placed her right one a few inches away and then concentrated.

"Can you feel the heat?" she asked.

"Yeah, probably in his dick," I said, and Bonnie laughed.

Harley ignored me. She was too busy concentrating on healing my friend.

"I can absolutely feel that," Roman said. "I swear the ache is going."

After five minutes, Harley gently placed his arm back down. She thanked God and the angels and shook out her hands.

"I'm shaking out the toxicity," she explained.

My brows creased as I looked at Roman who was now wiggling his hand and thanking Harley profusely because it was all better.

"Placebo, pal," I whispered to him. "Like she can commune with angels."

And then like an actual lightning bolt struck me, it all fell into place. Her father was in 'Heaven', she was always so happy and seemed to shine, and she'd just healed my friend. Why had I not realised before?

I'd put a rather large bet on a human mummy and an angelic daddy rather than a dead one. Was Harley a Nephilim?

"Harley, are you a Ne—"

"New Look shopper because there's a large store nearby. Maybe Bonnie'd like to go?" Roman interrupted. Then he looked at me and surreptitiously shook his head.

Had he known all along?

"Yes. Oh please, Harley. Can we go and get something new to wear tonight?" Bonnie was indeed like a changed teen. Offer them a spending spree and they'd postpone their next teen tantrum.

"Absolutely. We'll see you later, guys. Thanks for breakfast."

We watched them leave and the minute they were out of the door I turned to Roman, lifting a brow.

"I guessed she was from the angelic realm a while ago, but I didn't work out until now that she's a Nephilim. But she clearly doesn't know herself, so you can't say anything. Okay?"

"Are you going to tell her sometime? She so obviously has a crush on you. Are you going to ask her out?"

Roman sighed. "Zak. I'm a satyr. In my real body I have horns and hooves. Harley is half angel and doesn't know that yet. Not only that but I'm busy with the band and she's about to go to America filming for a month. So no, I won't be asking her out anytime soon."

"But she's hanging around here to spend time with you." I was actually kind of feeling quite sorry for her now I'd worked out what her weird shit entailed.

"I told her I liked her last night, but that I felt we were both too busy right now. We pressed pause. Just friends for the time being."

My deluded friend. He'd given Harley hope that she was

clinging onto, but if he wasn't careful, she'd go to the states and meet someone else.

"You need to work out your issues about your horns and hooves. It's who you are. Don't kick about in the forest so long that you miss out on love, mate, because I can only wish for the love of one woman."

He sighed and tapped the table. "I fucking hate it when you of all people make sense."

"Thanks."

He laughed. "Look the time is not now. I have family stuff. You'll notice none of them have come to see me, right?"

"Erm."

"Your family came. Mya appeared at the after party last night, and Rex's folks and siblings were there. But none of mine. You didn't notice?"

"Forgot my own were in the audience to be honest."

"And that's the Zak I know and love. Come on, drink up your coffee, we've press to charm. I'm going for a piss."

He left me to finish my hot beverage. I worried about him for a minute and then my mind turned to kissing and spooning Erica. As I closed my eyes at the table to daydream further, I slipped straight into Erica's mind. *She was asleep?* But it was eleven am. I took in the surroundings of where she was. When I entered a person's dreams, their true surroundings would always appear. She was lying on a double bed, but it wasn't the one from her room. Was that a waterbed? She must be in the spa. It made sense why she'd fallen back to sleep. I was just about to slip back out of her dreams and leave her there when she spoke.

"Zak, you're back."

Oh balls.

Chapter 17

Erica

This was the life, I sighed. We'd only recently arrived at the spa, had gone straight into the sauna, and now we were enjoying a lie down on a waterbed. The bed was toasty warm with a comfy pillow and the most gorgeous blanket. I'd laid there, pulled the blanket over me, and told Freya to leave me be for a while. This must be what being in the womb was like. When I eventually moved out, I needed one of all of these things.

The next thing I knew, Zak was sitting at the side of the bed, but weirdly, he'd not made it move. Oh, I was clearly dreaming again.

"Zak, you're back." I smiled happily.

He looked around at Freya and the other patrons lying on nearby beds and looked uncomfortable.

"Zak. It's just my dream. People aren't really here," I told him. Then I wondered why I was explaining it was just a dream to another part of my dream. "I'm going to kiss you, as this is my dream and what I say goes," I warned him.

Sitting up and leaning forward, I smushed my mouth to his. He let out a large sigh, but then took ownership of the kiss, pushing me back against the pillow, his tongue darting inside my mouth.

"Fuck me, Zak," I demanded, only to feel a large blow to the head.

I shot up, opened my eyes, and realised Zak wasn't there. But my best friend was, and she had her pillow in her hand.

"Did you just hit me with that pillow?" I asked, looking around and realizing that other nearby patrons weren't looking at me but did have smirks on their faces.

"I thought it was a good idea seeing as you just yelled out, 'Fuck me, Zak' to the entire spa while writhing around on the waterbed."

My cheeks heated. "Shit. Can we go to the steam room, please? ASAP?"

"I think you need to go to a Red Room, and not only because of the colour of your cheeks. You need some action, either with Zak, or with Tobias, because otherwise I'm locking your bedroom door and sleeping on the sofa."

I got off the waterbed sulkily. "It's not fair. The dreams are so real. I'm going to see him tonight and wonder why he's not trying to get me into bed."

"He kissed you yesterday, he might try and get you into bed," Freya asserted.

"No, he won't. He'll be too busy flirting with all the other women."

"If he does, you go out with Tobias. You hear me?"

"Yes, Miss." I saluted.

I managed to spend the rest of the time in the spa awake. Mainly, because Freya prodded me in the arm every five minutes making sure of it. We finished off with mani-pedis and blow-dries, and they let us go back up to our room in robes via a back lift which meant we didn't need to pull our old clothes back over our heads. We ordered afternoon tea, and then once again it was time to get ready. Only this time we'd be sort of one-on-one with our idols; well, along with all their meet and greets.

"After this, do you fancy going clubbing back to that Sheol place we went to when it was too busy with all The Paranormals fans?" Freya asked.

"Won't we be too tired?" I queried. I was still sleepy from the spa, and quite tempted to have as many naps as possible in case Zak came back.

"Okay, how about I ask Rex and you ask Zak, and if they don't want to go, we don't go, but if they do..."

A chance to dance up close and personal with my crush? Hell yeah. "We can but try." I shrugged my shoulders.

I dressed in a pair of faded light-blue skinny jeans and a Paranormals t-shirt with their slogan, *A foursome is awesome,* under *The Paranormals* emblem. Freya wore a black t-shirt with rips through the stomach area—so she showed off a ton of naked flesh—along with some low-slung straight jeans.

"Ready?" she asked me.

"Oh so ready." I laughed. She put her arm through mine and we went down in the lift to the rooms assigned for the meet and greet.

🎸

Vikki was there waiting for us and came over smiling. "Hi there, you two. Had fun today?"

"Yeah, we went to the spa."

"Erica nearly had too much fun," Freya said. I elbowed her hard to shut up.

"Good. Good. Okay, so you are in room one." She handed a clipboard to Freya. "And you're room two." Another clipboard came to me. Then we were given a pen each. "You have a security person in each room stationed near the doorway. They'll keep the queues in line. You let one person forward at a time. They get five minutes maximum including having their photo taken, so let them chat a couple of minutes then do the picture and then you call up the next person and make the previous one move their arses. If they refuse, you beckon security. Got it?"

"Got it," we both answered.

"Cool. Go have fun with the guys." Vikki winked and we grinned in return. She was fast becoming one of my most favourite people was Vikki.

As we walked down the corridors to approach the doors to the rooms, we were given the evilest of looks by the people in the queues. Every one of them no doubt wondering why we got to walk ahead and wondering what our lanyards said. There were a few remarks that let me know some people knew who I was, but most fans just looked murderous.

Freya flicked her hair. "I'm enjoying this moment," she said wickedly. As I reached my door, she winked at me with a, "Catch ya later." I pushed open the door and met the security guy who checked my lanyard and ushered me in, and there he was. Zak.

He walked towards me, and my heart almost leapt out of my chest.

"Hey there, helper girl." He smiled.

"Oh, that's my name today, is it?"

"Only for the next four hours, little E."

"So where do you want me?" I asked.

His nostrils flared slightly. "So not a fair question to ask me, helper girl. I'm going to have to say at the front of my table. There's some swag, signed photos, and badges to hand out. The water on the desk is for me and you, but there are a few spares in case anyone feels faint." He wiggled his walkie-talkie. "And if anyone is completely overcome by me, I have access to paramedics."

That was likely to be me if I didn't get my breathing under control in a moment. But as Vikki knocked on the door and walked in saying, "One minute to showtime," all of a sudden I was too busy to think about anything but the meet and greet. Oh, except one thing...

"Zak... me and Freya are going to Sheol tonight? Do you and any of the band want to come?"

"Sheol? Why Sheol?" Zak didn't look happy.

"Oh, do you not like it there? Only you had the party there and it was too busy for us to get much of a look. All the reviews are great, and we fancied some dancing."

"We'll come. Definitely. All of us. After this, yes?"

"Really? You'll come?" Wow, I hadn't expected him to agree so quickly.

"Yep."

Yeeaaasssss. All I needed now was for him to get out of this goddamn contract and there might be a chance little Erica could actually date Zak Jones. Somehow, I needed to find out more about who he worked for.

But the doors opened, and I had to put it out of my mind for now.

The first few people to come up were so sweet and reminded me of the fans I encountered most through running the fan club. They were in awe of the band, took a minute before being able to speak, hung onto Zak's every word, then thanked me over and over for taking photos of him with them before taking their swag and going on their way.

Unfortunately, there were other fans, and it started to remind me of the music reality show auditions where you got to laugh at the strange ones.

An older lady walked up. She looked in her seventies and had walked over slowly pushing a shopping cart. Her white curls were tight, and clearly freshly permed, and loose powder was evident on her cheeks.

"Hello there, sweetheart. What's your name?" Zak asked, taking her hand.

Her face turned from a loved-up glow to one of sour milk. "You know what my name is, honey. I'm your wife."

He casually tried to drop his hand, but she was holding on for dear life.

"I haven't had the pleasure." I stepped forward and held my hand out. "I'm Erica who runs the fan club. You must be one of the subscribers if you're his wife?"

She dropped his hand to shake mine. "Sheila Jones, and yes, I was one of the first to sign up." She began to pull up her skirt and my eyes went wide. On her bare thigh was a tattoo. A love heart with an arrow through and 'Zak and Sheila' written on it.

"How long have you been married?" I asked, knowing we were in danger of going past five minutes, but having fun at Zak's expense.

"We got hitched just after he won the show. He came to my house and that was it. One minute my eyes were closed, the next we were married."

"So like a dream?" I pointed out.

"It really happened," she said, her eyes narrowing, but then she didn't look so sure.

"Shall I take a photo of you with Zak?" I suggested and she nodded and passed me her phone.

She looked up at Zak. "Sorry, love. I think I dreamed we were married. I get confused sometimes. It's my age. I'm under a doctor."

"Looks like the honeymoon's over," I whispered at Zak. I took a few photos and then I passed her phone back to her.

"Seems you've got a few messages there." I helped her open them and they were from her daughter wondering where she was. Zak radioed for someone to come assist her and Sheila went off with a kindly looking female.

"It seems you have quite the reputation for entering women's dreams," I joked.

"I swear I didn't visit hers," he said.

I pulled a face. "Yeah, because of course you actually go in other peoples. You need a rest, my friend, you're cracking up."

"Tell me about it," he answered.

The worst people at the meet and greet were of course the women dressed to kill who wanted to get in Zak's pants. They refused my offer of taking the photo, getting Zak to move in closer to them so they could take a selfie, and then did anything from pass him their phone number, to putting their pants in his pocket, or suggesting he take a break and visit the bathroom with them. I would have preferred it if he'd told them all to take a running jump because the love of his life was standing right in front of them, but instead he flirted back and did accept a lot of phone numbers. It made me wonder if he had to get his own clients as a gigolo. Then I even thought about paying for him and wondered what he charged.

At that point it dawned on me that I'd hit an all-time desperate low.

Chapter 18

Zak

I'd made the most of the opportunity to meet thirty-six women. Not all of them were suitable candidates for soul retrieval such as my confused 'wife', but I'd secured a good twenty numbers, which meant I should get down my quota a little more. The final show was on Friday evening, and so that night following the end of tour party, I could visit a ton of women and sleep all weekend. After that we were in the studio, but hopefully I'd be able to negotiate some free time with the lads so I could do another glut.

A crazy idea came into my head then. If I managed to get my souls done within a few days each week—Like really piled them up—then maybe I could date Erica on a couple of other days? I'd need a few big sleeps, but...

I sighed. Who was I kidding? There was no time for monster sleeps, not with our band schedule, and as if a woman would be okay dating me while believing that on other nights I was whoring myself around.

As much as it pained me, I was going to have to be cruel to be kind with Erica and let her go. I'd seen Tobias from The Seven look at her on more than one occasion, so I knew other men were interested. He couldn't have her. He was a shifter and unless he declared she was his mate, there was no way I was allowing him to use her for sex.

Said the man who slept with thousands of women, in and out of their dreams.

"How'd it go?" Rex said as he came up to me. I saw the other doors open and Roman and Noah began wandering over in our direction.

"Yeah, went okay. Only one real crazy, but she was an old lady, so not too bad. Can't bite when they have no teeth."

"The only crazy in my room was Freya. Every time someone flirted with me, she bared her teeth. Anyone would have thought she was a wolf shifter, not me. I'm glad I can escape her now. Fancy a nightcap in my room?"

"Erm, about that." I looked at the rest of the band shifty-eyed. "We might be going to Sheol now to party."

"Say what? I'm tuckered and ready for laying on my sofa with a bottle of scotch," Roman complained.

"Erica said she and Freya were going to Sheol. I can't risk Don getting his hands on her. So where they go, we go," I insisted.

"You should have just made her a better offer. She'd have stayed at the hotel then," Roman whined some more.

"Goat boy, I like this woman, catch up. I'm not screwing her like one of my quota. I'm going to the club to make sure she's okay. You lot don't want to come, fine. I'll go on my own."

"Yeah, cos you're amazing at handling Don." Rex sighed.

"Good, I'm glad we're all agreed. I'll sort transport," I told them all.

Noah called Stacey. "Hey, sweetheart. Change of plans, we're off to Sheol with the band, Erica, and Freya. Yeah, you can ask Harley if you like."

Roman chuntered something that sounded like a sarcastic, "Oh yippee."

And that was it. We were going to Sheol.

No one would know from looking at the place that six floors down on the seventh level was the seventh dimension of Hell. The office and lair of Abaddon, destroyer, and collector of souls. He traded the ones he got whole and fed off the ones I collected for him.

As he had eyes all over the club, mainly via security cameras, I had no doubt that I'd be spotted soon, but while I could get away with it, I was determined to enjoy myself and hit the dance floor. And although not thirty minutes earlier I'd said I needed to somehow let Erica go, I decided it could wait until tomorrow, or even more kindly, I convinced myself, I could wait until her and Freya were going back home after their week with us.

Erica had got changed into a short black dress that dipped at the front in a V. It didn't show much of her cleavage, but even the hint of what was underneath made my cock twitch. I looked at Freya's top, a black one with rips she was wearing with leather trousers. "Is that your work?" I chided Rex. "Got a bit careless with the claws?"

"You're hilarious." He shoved me in the arm. "She wore that in the room and kept getting 'itches' that meant she showed me as much of the bare flesh underneath as possible."

"And your response was?"

"I asked her if she needed an antihistamine."

"Cruel, wolf. Cruel."

Freya looked over and winked in his direction.

"She needs spraying with a hosepipe or something. Nothing puts her off."

"So make her dreams come true and then tell her there's no future in it."

"And you said I was cruel."

"I'm going to have to let Erica go." I sighed.

Noah spoke. I hadn't even known he was there.

"I'm sorry, Zak. You really like this woman then? We'll find a way, I'm sure. Do you think your feelings are grow—"

"Evening, gentlemen." We turned to see Aaron.

Noah sighed. "The fun police have arrived."

"Drinks are on the house, courtesy of the Boss. He says to let you know it's an unexpected pleasure that you're here tonight and he'll probably see you later," Aaron told me.

"Your boss is here?" a female voice piped up, and all I could think was, 'Oh shit'. I turned around to see Erica staring at me. "I guess that makes sense. Owning a club. Good cover for the business. Probably runs a drug cartel from here too, right?"

The others stepped away as I moved nearer to Erica. "No. They just meant my ex-boss. I used to bartend here."

"Really?" Erica said, "Wow. I thought I'd researched all your past, but I never knew that." Her lips had thinned slightly. "At least if the bar's busy later, I can ask you to nip behind and fix me a drink."

There was a challenge there and I knew it. She didn't believe me. I was so sick of my life and so sick of the lies, but I was part-demon, and it came with the territory. It's just that the human part of me felt guilty as hell.

"Shall we all go dance?" I shouted, to desperately change the subject.

As we all piled on the floor, what had been just boring generic club music suddenly switched up and *Coño* by Puri featuring Jason Derulo came on. The sexy swing-your-hips tune meant that Erica and Freya were suddenly raising their hands above their hands and gyrating their bodies in time, and I had to use everything within me, every last ounce of strength, to stop myself from picking Erica up, wrapping her legs around my waist and fucking her in the middle of the dance floor. Instead, I left the floor, went to the bar, and asked for a double scotch on the rocks which I poured straight down my throat.

Aaron appeared at my side. "The Boss wants to see you." He

nodded over to the lift. Sighing, I got off the bar stool where I'd been planning on staying the rest of the night and headed down to Don's office.

I walked in to see him, and he stood behind his desk. "Come closer, Zak. Let me see you a little better." His voice sounded like insects skittering up a ceramic tile.

"Everything okay, Boss?"

"You tell me, Zak," he said, a finger on his chin scratching absentmindedly. "Only I can see two females on the dance floor who keep looking your way. Yet you actually moved away from them instead of towards them."

"Oh that's two people connected with the band. Special guests. I can't go there," I told him.

He emitted a wicked, slow laugh. "Oh, Zak, my sweet, innocent boy." He walked near me and looked like he was going to put his arm around me but then he grabbed a handful of my fringe.

"Owwww." Tears sprang to my eyes.

"You can go anywhere, Zak. And you will go anywhere and everywhere. I want their souls, especially the purple-haired one. I like purple and her soul shines brighter than her friend's." He took a deep exhale. "I'll tell you what. Because I'm so generous I'll just take that one, and you can leave the other. What do you think, Zakky?" He pulled me closer, once again by my hair.

"Yes, okay. Okay," I said. "I'll do it." Fuck knew what I was actually going to do, but I just needed him to get off my fringe while I still had a scalp.

"Excellent. Good chatting with you, and of course, if you don't do it, I'll find out who they both are, and I'll have them both sucked dry by someone else. You get me?"

"Y-yes."

"Good boy." He petted me on the top of my head. "Right, off you go. Enjoy yourself. Free bar for my favourite band."

Nodding gently because my head still sodding well hurt, I walked back to the lift wondering what on earth I was going to do. If I didn't take some of Erica's soul, he was going to destroy her and Freya. I'd not wanted to do things this way, hadn't wanted to take advantage of Erica in her dreams, but it was the only way right now I could protect her.

But I couldn't help feeling she was going to be my addiction and having her in dreams wouldn't be enough.

Chapter 19

Erica

"Rex isn't interested in me, Erica. It's sad, but I'm going to back off now," Freya said while swaying on a bar stool.

"I'm sorry, bestie," I replied, putting an arm around her.

"S'okay." She tapped her glass down on the bar and asked for another vodka and coke. I winked at the barman. She'd been getting coke only for the last three drinks and had yet to notice. No way was I dealing with Freya vomit tonight.

"There are other men in the sea, Erica. Let's change your fan club and like farm animals instead."

Where the fuck was she going with this conversation?

"Do you mean fish in the sea?"

"That's what I said. But we need farmers, not rock stars. Single, hot farmers."

"You want to fork up pig shit and live on government subsidies?"

"Pffffffffffttt. An heir to a stately home then?"

"Either one-hundred-and-three years old and still frisky, or lives in one room of it because the rest has woodworm and leaks."

"You're making me sad, Erica. Where are all the lovely men?"

"There are lovely men all around us, Frey. We just need to let some others in and get to know them. We'll go and hang with

The Seven tomorrow, yeah? Get to know them better. Let's face it, we came on an invitation as me running The Paranormals Fan Club. They didn't swipe right for us."

"Fucking sucks."

"I know. It's not what we hoped, but there is still the rest of the week." I turned to find my friend asleep with her head on the bar.

I blew out a breath. This evening hadn't turned out how I'd hoped at all. Zak had seemed okay at first and then he'd gone all strange when I'd asked if his boss was here. Like fuck had Zak ever been a bartender. Someone from his fandom would have remembered him doing it.

When I'd danced, he'd shot off the floor like he was doing a one hundred metre sprint, and he'd ignored me for the rest of the night. I hadn't ignored him, however, so I saw when the security guy had whispered in his ear, and he'd disappeared through the back of the club.

I would find out about his boss because something had to change. He couldn't go on like this. The band needed him, and his boss needed to let him go. Surely, he could be bought off? Zak was stinking rich now. Although if this man ran a club and a brothel, he was probably rich too.

"Can I have a vodka and coke?" I asked the bartender. "With vodka in it this time. In fact, make it a double."

Once I was suitably mellow and my best friend more awake, I helped her to her feet, and I let Stacey know that we were heading home. She called for a driver and wished us a good night, then we made our way back to the hotel.

Freya was still largely out of it and one of the security detail helped to carry her up to our suite, depositing her in our room. When he'd left, I helped get her shoes off, and covered her over with the duvet. I sat on the other bed until I was sure she was okay and sleeping. A couple of hours had passed, but I was no nearer to going to sleep myself. Sighing, I left the bedroom and walked into the living area where I opened the mini bar and took out a bottle of vodka. Might as well have a pity party for one. Adding Kettle Chips to the mix, I brought them to the coffee table and laid on the sofa pulling a blanket over me. I put on the TV and searched until I found an old episode of *Tattoo Fixers*. I wondered if Sheila would be a good candidate for the show, now she realised she wasn't married to Zak?

Out of crisps and a few glasses into the vodka, I must have fallen asleep because I startled suddenly.

I opened an eye, convinced I'd heard someone say my name. When I couldn't see anything, I shut it again.

"Erica," a whisper-hiss.

I opened both eyes this time and sat myself up. Zak was sitting in a chair next to the sofa.

"Oh for God's sake. Not this again. Look, dreams, either screw him properly, all romantic and something to go to the papers about, or just throw him out of the room." I sat there, waiting for my body to do one of them. It didn't.

"Shooo," I told Zak.

"No," he replied.

"Great. Dream Zak is a stubborn arsehole. What are you doing just sitting there, you useless lump? Fuck me or fuck off," I ordered him.

Standing up, he walked over to me and sat right at my side.

"Erica?"

"Yeah?"

"I'm not fucking off so that means I'm going to do something else. But I agree, it needs to be a little more romantic, so could I take a moment to do a few things?"

"Okay," I squeaked, because for once it seemed my dreams were going to come true. If I woke up before anything good happened, I was going to hit myself in the head repeatedly with the half-drunk vodka bottle.

I was already in a room with subdued lighting, but Zak turned off all the lights leaving the room lit only by what came through the windows from the hotel lighting outside.

He placed a chair under the bedroom door so that if she woke up, Freya would not be able to get out, which I thought was an intelligent move on Dream Zak's part, because I'd forgotten she existed.

Returning to my side, he sat next to me and took my hand. "Erica, I can't do this without being entirely honest with you, so here goes. I'm not a gigolo, I'm an incubus. That means I appear in women's dreams where I give them the most amazing time in bed, and then I steal some of their soul. It usually makes them very sleepy afterwards, so if we do this, you'll probably sleep all day tomorrow."

I blinked at him about a thousand times. This dream was so fucked up. I really needed to lay off the vodka.

"You're taking this very well." Zak looked pleased.

"Gigolo. Incubus. Either way you're going to have your wicked way with me tonight, right?" I double checked that my dreams weren't going off on some weird tangent again where he would fly out of the window on a broomstick or something.

"If I have your permission," he said.

"Hell, yeah," I agreed quickly.

"Well, I'm more of a seventh-dimension person myself, but great," Zak answered and then he leaned over and kissed me.

Talking was done.

Kissing and touching had commenced.

My dreams were actually coming true.

Zak leaned me back against the sofa arm and the cushions, then he trailed a hand over my shoulder, edging the material off so it slid to one side. The V of my dress exposed the top of my breasts encased in their black silky bra.

Breaking off our kiss, Zak's mouth moved to my neck. He trailed soft kisses all the way down, going over my collarbone making me shiver, then moved further down my chest to the swell of my breast. His hands trailed and he moaned.

"Let's get you out of this dress and me out of these clothes."

I wasn't sure why dream me had to go through the rigmarole

of taking everything off. At one point I even got my zip caught in my hair, but as long as I didn't wake up before the grand finale, I'd suffer through whatever else my imagination cooked up.

And it had cooked up a gigantic cock for Mr Zak Jones. Well, hello there, cockmonster.

As it dawned on me that dream me could be confident and take some initiative, I grasped him in my hand and started to stroke up and down his girth.

"Oh, Erica, fuck, that's so good."

"You've seen nothing yet." I moved so he was sitting on the sofa, and I kneeled before him and took him in my mouth. His hands threaded in my hair, and weirdly, my scalp still felt sensitive from the zip. My dreams had a lot of detail to them. I sucked him hard, and I hummed slightly which I'd heard did great things. Zak seemed happy enough. As his pace got more frenetic, he softly stopped me and pulled out of me.

"I want to come inside you."

Another great thing about sex dreams. No need for contraception! I let Zak push me back against the sofa and he positioned himself on top of me. His fingers trailed over my body, caressing my breasts and tweaking my nipples. Then lower, lower until they teased my damp places and drove me into a frenzy of need. My hips rose higher.

"Zak, I need—"

He kissed my mouth. "I know. I got you."

Grabbing his cockmonster in his hand he adjusted himself until he was situated and then he pushed inside me. I swear Big Ben chimed for me like it had just struck twelve at New Year's and the fireworks went off around the London Eye.

"Oh my god. Oh my god. Oh my god." I'd have been shouting were it not for Zak's mouth eating up my words with his lips against mine while he moved in and out of me.

For the next hour he moved me into different positions and took me over and over again. I had more orgasms in this one evening than I'd ever had in total with any of my previous lovers.

As we lay sated in each other's arms, he cuddled me close and said, "I'll find a way that we can be together properly, Erica. So that we can do this for real."

I nodded and said, "I'd like that." Then happy in his arms I closed my eyes.

"Aaaaaaarrrggghhhh."

I jumped a foot in the air as I shot up from the sofa and stared at my best friend who was staring at me slack jawed. How had she got out of her room? Zak had put the chair up to it.

My face fell. Oh, it was just a dream.

Then I remembered it and I smiled a huge face-splitting grin.

"What the hell is the matter with you?" Freya yelled. "Get some clothes on. Why are you lying stark bollock naked on the sofa we both have to sit on?"

I looked down at myself and indeed I didn't have a stitch of clothing on. "I can explain. I had a sex dream about Zak. It was amazzzzing."

"Ew. Ew. Ew. Ew. Ew. You got naked and what, writhed all over the sofa like that? I'm not sitting on the sofa again, and for God's sake *get some clothes on.*"

I reached for my dress and pulled it back on. "I'm going to get a shower and relive my dreams, because Zak and I did it over and over."

"I'm going to ring housekeeping and say I spilled orange juice all over the sofa and can they clean it."

"But you haven't."

"I will have. There's some in the fridge. Once I've done that, I'm going to go get a Costa and a chocolate pastry and then I'm going to spy on the band from a distance. I want to see if absence makes the heart grow fonder with Rex, but I also want to make sure he's not flirting with anyone else."

"So you're going to stalk him?"

"Pretty much. I have my mobile, so call me when you've finished masturbating, and leave the rest of the hotel furniture alone. Will I need to order a new shower head?"

I shrugged. "I'll let you know."

The shower had all mod cons, but then I remembered the jacuzzi bath and decided to have a relax and daydream in that instead. I felt amazing and not tired at all. So much for dream Zak saying he was taking my soul and I'd sleep for days. I could do something for days, but it wasn't sleep.

CHAPTER 20

ZAK

I felt seriously guilty. Seducing Erica had been everything I'd wanted, but I wanted it in the real world, not to be blackmailed into it by my demon boss.

Rehearsing with Rex and Roman, as Noah hadn't made it to the room yet, my constant sighing finally got the better of Rex's temper.

"Can you shut the fuck up? Soon they're going to set you up as a renewable energy source with all the heavy breathing."

"Don't ask me what's wrong, just bollock me," I whined.

"There's always something wrong with you. It's usually a bad hair day. You're a needy little bitch." He growled. "I'll tell you something, you wouldn't last a day with the females from my pack. My temperament plus female hormones... you'd be a goner."

"Then it's a good job I don't want one of your pack then, isn't it?"

Roman walked over. "You lovesick, bro?"

"Not exactly. I'm... what would be a better term? Cock sick. It wants a normal relationship."

"So your cock's weeping but not with pre-cum?" Rex tittered. "You're cocksure, but cock unsure. You're—"

"About to sign an even bigger contract with Don, if he'll seal up your mouth."

"Tell us all about it," Roman said, to a withering glare from Rex.

"I like Erica. But I saw Don last night and he said if I didn't sleep with her in her dreams and steal some of her soul for him, then he'd hurt her and Freya."

"So you took one for the team?"

"I took several. I really like her but how do I tell her I'm an incubus? That she'd have to share me with all those other women?"

"Mate, you can't actually know the answer to that question unless you speak to her. A fuck off is better than the great unknown."

Sighing, I chewed on my bottom lip. "Maybe I'll talk to her. At the end of the week though. I don't want to spoil her experience."

"Okay, can we get on now?" Rex asked, and as Noah joined us not much later, we practised working on a new song for the album we'd be recording soon. And I decided that when I left, I'd work on another song, one to empty my mind of guilt and mixed emotions.

Chapter 21

Erica

I was covered in bubbles from the Jacuzzi jets and feeling like a celebrity myself living the high life, when the bathroom door burst open.

"Thank God for bubbles or you'd be getting another view of my naked body!" I squealed.

"Never mind about that. I just heard the most ridiculous conversation when I was hanging around outside the band's door. If I hadn't seen Noah heading down the corridor, I'd have got more information, but... oh Jesus, it just makes no sense... unless, oh of course," she took a moment to hold her waist, shouting, "stitch."

"Okay, crazy lady. Take a seat on the loo and tell me what you're on about... in English this time, instead of mumbojumbo."

Thudding down onto the loo seat, Freya turned to me. "It's okay. I think what I overheard must be a new part of their stage performance. They're building the paranormal element in. Panic over. Thought I'd gone completely insane for a moment."

"You've spoiled my bath so please humour me by telling me what you actually overheard."

"Funny thing is actually... he mentioned us and that can't be part of the act."

"*Freya!* For fuck's sake."

"Okay, okay. So I heard Zak say he liked you but he had to sleep with you in his dreams to take some of your soul, or some guy called Don would hurt us both. And he was sad because his cock wanted to just sleep with one woman, not tons. Something on those lines. That's crazy, right? My ears must need syringing."

It was good now that Freya was muttering on and on and on as my heart had stopped beating and my brain had frozen in shock at her words.

Dreams.

Taking souls.

Last night.

Now *I* must be having some kind of brain fart.

Freya was still talking. "They said he was an... oh what was that word? An incubus. That's it."

I managed to compose myself enough to speak. "Freya, have you eaten yet today?"

"Erm, no actually. I couldn't face it after my hangover."

"Yeah, well, you've just walked out of your bedroom and come out with a pile of crap about the band, so you're in some kind of still asleep, but slightly awake dream state," I lied.

"What?"

"Freya, you're going on about hanging around near the band and you've not left the suite yet. You just got up. I told you I was going in the bath, and you went back to bed."

"Did I?" She was looking so confused, bless her, but it was nothing to what was running through my mind.

"Did you party a little too hard last night? Take a little something?"

"I may have had a joint."

"Eat. Go back to bed. Then you'll realise how ridiculous you sound saying Zak is an incubus trying to take my soul."

"Yeah, I think you're right. Sorry, Erica. I think I need to calm party girl Freya down. Tonight, I'll stick to coke, and I do mean the fizzy drink. Okay, try to forget I was here and enjoy the rest of your bath."

She backed out of the room, and I dunked my head the whole way under the water. I even let a jet thud into my head in the hopes that when I came back up, I'd have different thoughts.

Because the ones I had now were telling me that I needed to look up incubi, though I already knew that they were male demons who appeared in women's dreams and sucked out their soul. But he said I'd sleep all day and I hadn't. I was wide awake.

As I sat there a while longer, I just didn't know what to do. This idea was preposterous. I got out of the bath and went to our room to get ready. Freya was back under the covers asleep. I left a note on her bed, and I set off downstairs, arranging for a driver.

There was only one place I could get answers as to what Zak really was and that was at Sheol. If I called in there on the pretence of looking for bar work, I could ask a few questions about Zak. It was the best idea I could come up with, so grabbing my bag—which included my attack alarm for safety—I made my way across London.

As I sat in the back of the car considering the fact that I was potentially putting myself in front of someone who might have threatened to hurt me and Freya, I did start to reconsider my position. But, come on, if that was true, then Zak was an incubus and last night's dreams had been him coming to raid my soul instead of coming for enjoyment.

I'd always been a nosy bitch anyway. This guy held information about my biggest obsession, information I didn't know, and that made me take risks. Freya always said I was too uptight and played too safe. I'd needed vodkas to get near the band when I'd first met them after all. The new improved Erica was brave and stood up for what she wanted.

And I'd had the most fabulous shagfest ever last night, so if it all went wrong, I could die happy.

I sniggered to myself. As if. It would go like this. Ask about a job, get an application form or a no. Ask if it was true Zak had been a bartender there. Leave.

"We're here," the driver said. "Shall I wait nearby?"

"Yes please, if you can find anywhere. I doubt I'll be long. If I'm going to be longer, I'll call you, okay?"

He nodded, got out of the car to help me out, and then I was walking into the club.

Pushing the door open, inside I could see the lights were subtle and the place empty. I could hear a vacuum cleaner being pushed around in the distance and a man was polishing the countertop of the bar.

"Can I help you?" he shouted out.

"Hey." I waved. "I was wondering if you had any jobs?"

"Not here," the man said hurriedly. "So off you go."

Rude.

"Can you just tell me, did Zak Jones work the bar here?"

"Oh Lord, you're another of those groupies. Piss off out of here. Right now, lady."

A voice came from the back of the bar.

"Who do we have here, Grayson?"

"Too late," he mumbled under his breath.

A tall guy with dark hair walked towards me. He looked like the singer who'd done the duet with Taylor Swift with all the pastel colours in it. He was stunning to look at.

He held out a hand. "Hello there...?"

I held out my own. "Erica. Erica Daniels."

"And what brings you into my club today, Erica?"

His club? This was Zak's boss?

"I came in asking about a job," I said, at the same time Grayson announced I was a groupie.

"Why don't we have a drink, and we can chat more?" the boss

suggested. "I can tell you anything you want to know about Zachariah. I've known him since he was eighteen years old."

"You have? Did he bartend here?" I asked.

"No. I met him here though. He came into the club one night, and I offered him a job."

"Which was?"

He tilted his head to look at me. "How well do you know Zak? Really?"

"I run The Paranormals fan club," I confessed.

"Ahhhh, oh why didn't you say so when you came in?" He turned to Grayson. "Get us both a drink will you and bring them over to our table. Tea for me, and what would you like, Miss Daniels?"

"I'd love a coffee please and call me Erica."

Any nerves I'd had were gone now he'd welcomed me as the fan club girl.

"I'm Don. I own the club. And if you really want a job we can chat, but I'm guessing you actually want to talk about young Zak?"

"Am I that transparent?"

"Don't play poker anytime soon, hey?"

I laughed and he laughed back, his brown eyes twinkling.

Don actually seemed really nice. I took out my phone. "Just letting the driver know I'm staying for a coffee, and I'll call him later."

He nodded his head. "Good thinking."

Phone call done, I followed Don over to the seating area at the other side of the dance floor and sat on the comfy banquette seating opposite him. "This is a great place. I love the atmosphere," I told him.

"Thanks. I enjoy owning the club. My business empire can be a little stressful, but being around the club helps me unwind."

"You run more than just the club?"

"Yes. I buy and sell stock, and the items I sell are hard to obtain, so sometimes it can be stressful. The bosses higher than me can be really mean."

"That sucks."

"Yeah. I'd rather be giving than receiving." He burst out laughing.

I had no idea what he meant, so I just smiled and hoped it covered it.

"Okay, so what job does Zak do for you?" I asked him. "Because I know it's making him unhappy and increasingly exhausted."

Don picked up his freshly made tea and drank the whole thing down. I was wondering how he'd not burned out the inside of his mouth while he answered me, so it took a moment for me to realise what he said.

"He's part of stock acquisition."

"Ohhhhh. So he has to what? Find this rare thing you deal in? I guess that's difficult work and that's why he's tired. Wouldn't you be better with someone who's not in a rock band?"

"I am looking to replace him. What job do you do for a living, Erica? Are you seeking a more *satisfying* role by any chance?"

Gosh, was he really thinking of offering me work, and not behind the bar?

"I work in a supermarket, and it's handy because it's near home, but it doesn't give me a huge sense of satisfaction, not unless I manage to find something in the stock room that a customer desperately needed for making their dinner."

"Working for me, satisfaction is guaranteed." Don's words were so confident and assured.

"What is it I'd have to search for?"

"Before I tell you, let me just tell you my deal. That is, to put it simply, in order to let Zak free of all his obligations to me, you just have to agree to do his job for a day. Does that sound tempting?"

I could get Zak out of his agreement, by signing up for a day?

My mind argued with me. *What if Zak is truly a demon and the man in front of you is an even larger one?*

Don't be ridiculous.

He told you in your dreams, and then Freya confirmed it.

Demons aren't real. The Paranormals is the band name, and your obsession has tipped over into a fantasy realm.

There was only one way I could think of to see if someone was a demon, I reckoned. Piss them off.

I reckoned a demon would be beyond vain.

Was I really going to do this? If he was human, my new job prospects would be down the toilet faster than a half-dead goldfish.

"Did anyone ever tell you, that you are really fucking ugly?" I announced, and as every bottle behind the bar broke into a zillion pieces and Don's eyes flashed red, I realised I'd not just poked the beast, I'd rogered it hard and I'd done it without protection.

As I thanked God for the life I'd enjoyed, and prayed to be saved, the door flew in, wooden splinters flying everywhere.

I screamed and hid under the table as Don turned into this freaky red slug with twig like arms. A smell like I'd never come across even when customers who'd run out of deodorant and shower gel entered the supermarket poured from his pores.

Feet stamped over in our direction, and I prayed it was help, but that no one got hurt. As I dared to open my eyes, I saw a large, clawed hand reach for me, and I screamed.

Chapter 22

Zak

When Freya hurtled into the room, Rex sighed a little too loudly.

"It's fine. You can take the look of boredom and irritation off your face. I'm not here for you," Freya sassed. "I'll admit I liked you best and I did try to see if you were interested, but not only is it clear you aren't, I've realised that your beauty is on the outside and inside you're a complete turd."

I sniggered.

"If I wanted a shit, I'd take a laxative, and at the side of being around you, the pain and unpleasantness of sitting on a toilet for hours would be ultimately more pleasurable than sitting with you for even a minute."

"What can we do for you, Freya?" Noah interjected.

"I just came to see if anyone could help me. Erica left me a note that she'd gone to Sheol, but I can't get any answer from her mobile and the driver said he left her there having a coffee with the boss."

"Oh, Christ," I yelled.

I leaped to the door, my bandmates hot on my heels and I radioed for urgent assistance.

"Why was she going to Sheol?" I shouted in Freya's direction.

"I'm not sure. My morning has been really strange."

"Define strange."

"I had a weird dream."

"Tell me."

"I dreamed I stood outside this door and heard that you were an incubus. I told Erica. I think. But she said I'd been dreaming, even though it felt real."

Oh fuck. Oh fuck. Oh fuck.

All I could hope was that we got there in time. Because to say Erica was in danger would be the understatement of the century.

In times of need you needed paranormal mates. My wolf shifter friend kicked the club door clean off its hinges without needing an extra breath and we dived inside.

The club was being torn up around us like a mini tornado was inside and I knew that whatever she'd done, Erica had fucked off Abaddon big style if he was living up to his nickname of destroyer. His true self sat at the table, and I saw his arm reach out for her throat.

"Get away from Erica," I yelled. "You can't hurt her. I love her."

A scream like a thousand nails down a blackboard sounded around the room and everyone fell to their knees with their hands over their ears. I watched as Don turned into a gloop and dripped through the floor until he was no longer there.

Freya ran over to her friend, and they sat there hugging each other and shaking.

Noah came to my side. "You only have to say the word. I can wipe their memories."

I shook my head. "Not yet. Not unless she can't deal with who I am."

"And what do you think you are?" said another voice, a monotone one. Aaron stepped out from the shadows.

"A fucking incubus. Did a flying bottle hit your head?"

Aaron looked at me bemused. "Oh, my dear Zak. You don't even realise what just happened. You shouted that you loved her. You broke the curse. You're not immortal anymore. You're a real boy now. Your soul is back."

"It... it is?"

Aaron smiled at me. "No one is allowed to share how an incubus gets their soul back. If you ever tell one, you will lose yours again."

"I won't tell a soul, because I don't ever want to be near another soul." I wanted to leap for joy, but first I needed to see if my woman was okay. Oh it felt good to say that. My woman. To hold in my arms for real, to seduce for real.

The woman herself stood up and stared at me.

"You l-love me?" she asked.

"I do. I really fucking love you," I replied, as Freya stepped back and I pulled Erica into my arms. "My soul came back, Erica. I'm human again."

"Wh-what about my soul, because you took some, right?" she asked, her top lip wobbling. I just wanted to reach down and take it between my teeth to soothe her.

But bloody Aaron was here again. "He didn't get any of your soul because you're his soul mate. Even without his, his body couldn't do anything to harm yours."

"That's the most romantic thing I ever heard," she whispered.

"You all need to get out of here," Aaron warned. "Because when Don recovers, he's going to be one very angry demon.

"Will he come for revenge?" I asked.

"He's a demon." Aaron rolled his eyes at me.

"Shit."

But without delay, we got everyone out of there and back to the hotel.

We took Erica and Freya back to my suite and we all sat around while we gave the women a lot of sweet tea and answered their questions about our supernatural abilities.

"If you think you'll not be able to deal with it, just say the word and I can clear your mind," Noah explained.

"This is a mind fuck. I feel like one of those colour-blind people who gets those expensive glasses and can't stop looking around as everything they see is different to what they thought." Freya was still shaking her head after a few hours. "So you're a wolf, and you're like a goat, and you're a bat."

"I'm not a bat. I'm either a human, or I'm a vampire. Never a bat. That's a myth. I can move really quickly though."

"Not with Stacey you can't. Took you years," I snorted.

"You're the NOT again now," he said bitchily.

"Oh yeah." I pretended to look glum.

"What do you mean?" Erica asked.

"When we first auditioned..." I didn't need to carry on, this was our fan club leader. "Oh the name you had to change. The ParaNOTnormals."

"Yeah, I was the NOT when we first formed. Until I took my virgin self into Sheol and lost my soul. Now I'm the NOT again."

"You're the CAN, not the not." Erica smiled at me. "Think of what you can do now, that you couldn't before."

She was in my arms before she could say another word.

"Everyone out," I shouted. "We'll see you just before the concert."

They all left moaning and groaning, although I knew they were pleased really.

And then it was me and Erica moaning and groaning and it was everything I'd thought it would be and more.

One day I'd marry this girl, but for now, I figured she'd had enough shocks for one day without me proposing.

Chapter 23

Zak

"Hellllooo, London," I shouted to the crowd on our final night. I looked out over them all and thought about how happy I was and what a difference a week made.

I could tell my soul was back because I felt different inside and not only because I was in love. There was just no feeling of emptiness there anymore. Smiling at my bandmates, we gave the crowd the concert of their... current reality, but it was awesome. I was done with dreams!

As we came back on to do our final encore, I spoke to the crowd. "This is a new song, and it's dedicated to my girlfriend, Erica."

Not everyone in the crowd was pleased I was singing a song to my loved one, but most cheered and that was what counted. We knew we'd have to take the rough with the smooth.

I began, "This song is called A One-way Ticket to Love."

"Been on the road awhile
Driving fast cars
for no satisfaction.
But the journey changed.

A new road to travel
A one-way ticket to love.

There's mileage on my clock.
I'm slowing right down.
The view is amazing.
The journey changed.
A new destination.
A one-way ticket to love.

When I first met you
The boot was full
With heavy souls
They weighed me down
But I came around
Flung them right back out
And made room in my car
For you.

Come travel with me.
Wherever it leads.
You're my forever.
Take this journey with me
A new destination
And a one-way ticket to love.

When I first met you

ROCK 'N' SOULS

The boot was full
With heavy souls
They weighed me down
But I came around
Flung them right back out
And made room in my car
For you.

No more heavy souls.
Just future goals.
In our one-way ticket for looooovvveee."

The crowd were on their feet and the spotlight shone on my girl standing in the wings. I beckoned her out and everyone cheered as I took her in my arms and kissed her.

"I love you, forever and ever, Erica," I told her.

"I love you right back, Zak Jones." She grinned.

And then I forgot about the audience as I picked my woman up and carried her off the stage.

※

"No, no, no, no, no." Rex stood in my way. "I know what you want to do, but we have the wrap up party for the tour. We have gifts to give the crew and everything."

I put Erica down. "Sorry, babe."

"That's okay. I quite like delayed gratification." She took off her pants and put them in my pocket, then toddled off without a word.

"I know it's hard, and I mean that in every connotation," Noah said, clapping me on the shoulder. "Newlyweds remember? Oh, and also, never, EVER give me shit about how long it took me and Stace to get together when your own romance has gone from nought to a hundred in a few days."

"When you know, you know." I sighed happily.

The party was good fun, and it was great to give our huge appreciation to all the many staff who had helped us.

Erica and I stood with Stacey and Noah, and the next thing I knew, his sire Mya was by his side. These bloody vampires moved quick.

"Hi, again!" She beamed, clutching Noah to her bosom. "How are you, my son? I am super proud. You were amazing out there once more."

"Death not with you tonight?" I asked her. Erica turned to me, her brows furrowed.

"Her husband," I explained.

"I made him stay in charge of the wayward souls tonight. We're a little overrun right now because there was a fire at an illegal bare-knuckle boxing building. Some were willing to let the men fight to their death, but others are a little more of a grey area."

"And I'm guessing not bad to look at?" I grinned at Mya.

"Gonna take me a while to process this lot." She grinned back. "Anyway, how are you? Noah told me about the whole get your own soul back gig and falling in love." She did a swoon face. "Sometimes me and my guy are like that. It's just when he starts the whole 'how his day went' conversation it can be a little depressing..."

"Erica and I are fab, but apparently Don won't be happy until he has my soul again," I told her.

"Abaddon?" Mya checked.

"Yeah, fucking demons off is not the best thing you can do, and falling in love is high on his list of misdemeanours. The destroyer says he will destroy our love."

"Back in a tick, sweets," Mya said, and then she was gone with only our hair swirling as an indication she was there.

We carried on drinking and celebrating until she returned.

"All sorted," she announced with a smirk.

"What is?" I asked.

"Don. He'll leave you two alone. Call it my happy getting together gift."

"How the hell did you manage that?" Erica asked. "Oh and thank you."

Mya flicked her long, dark hair. "Well, first of all when I got there he was scolding his security guy about making a weak cup of PG Tips and wasting a valuable teabag. So I told him that if he got in the path of true love, I would buy out the makers of PG Tips and make sure he never got another cup of their tea." She giggled, tapping at her cheeks. "You ought to have seen his face! Oh, and then I gave him Dan Trent's soul."

"Dan Trent. Presenter Dan Trent?"

"You're going to have to explain all this to me later, babe," Erica whispered.

"Yes." Mya nodded enthusiastically. "We took him to my home of wayward souls remember, but, unfortunately, he proved beyond redemption. I tried to work to improve him, but he was just thoroughly evil and ugly, so I took him to Don. I'll get in a little trouble from Satan, but nothing I can't handle with the sweetener of a few serial killers we have upcoming. Don can dine on Dan's awful soul for years, so I had it written in blood for you to be left alone." She went in her pocket and drew out a sopping red handkerchief. "Shall I keep it safe? I have a secure facility."

"Where she stays," Roman whispered, having joined us.

Mya turned to him. "Did you forget I have vampire hearing, sweetie? I can always offer Don you and change your hooves into cloven ones?"

"Sorry, Mya. I was just jesting."

She trailed a talon down his face. "I know, sweetie, me too."

"Hey, Freya's on her way in," Erica said. Freya had hit it off with Splinter, the bass guitarist from The Seven and had gone to dinner with him.

They came over, both smiling.

"Hey all," Freya said.

"Have you had a good time?" Erica asked her bestie.

"A great time." She beamed, looking at her date.

"It could have been better," Splinter stated.

As Freya's face fell, he scooped her into his arms. "This would have made it better," he said, and he planted his lips on hers.

The PDA got PG18 as she melted into his kiss, and they began grinding against each other. Then all of a sudden Splinter wasn't there anymore. He was crouched on all fours at the other side of the room.

"Mine," Rex growled, now at the side of Freya. "My mate."

"Holy fucking shitballs. Looks like Rex's have finally dropped," I announced.

THE END

Is Rex too late to get his mate?

Find out in WE WOLF ROCK YOU

Read Mya's story in SUCK MY LIFE.

To keep up with latest release news and receive an exclusive subscriber only ebook DATING SUCKS: A Supernatural Dating Agency prequel short story, sign up here: geni.us/andiemlongparanormal

Playlist

Queen, *Fat-Bottomed Girls*
Puri featuring Jason Derulo, *Coño*
Natasha Bedingfield, *Soulmate*
Kali Uchis, *In My Dreams*
DaBaby, Roddy Ricch, *Rockstar*
Kylie Minogue, *Love at First Sight*
Harry Styles, *Watermelon Sugar High*
The Weekend, *Blinding Lights*
Bobby Darin, *Dream Lover*
Taylor Swift, *London Boy*
Imagine Dragons, *Demons*
Justin Timberlake, *Rock Your Body*

WE WOLF
ROCK YOU

*For naughty **Harry Styles** and **watermelons**.*

Your honorary membership of the Poplar Heights Wolf Shifter Pack awaits you Harry ;)

Chapter 1

Freya

Splinter's mouth met my own in a scorching kiss and I melted into his embrace, the party going on around me disappearing. A hot man who actually showed me some attention. It had made a change this week that was for sure. I could feel his hard cock pressing up against me, and forgetting myself for a moment, I pushed back against him.

And then I was kissing fresh air, as the fact I was in a full room came back to me. I looked around at my best mate, Erica, and she pointed to a few metres away—where Splinter was crouched on all fours snarling. Oh, surely not? We all wanted an animal in bed, but out of it? Was he a bloody shifter too?

But the biggest growl came from the man whose attention I'd been trying to get all week. The one who had shown zero interest in me to the point of rudeness, and who I'd just a couple of days ago told I was no longer going to bother with.

The Paranormals' drummer, Rex Colton.

"Mine," Rex growled. "My mate."

"Holy fucking shitballs. Looks like Rex's have finally dropped," Erica's new boyfriend, lead singer, Zak announced.

Rex stalked towards me, his eyes predatory, and he reached

out and pulled me into his arms. As I raised my knee to give him a clear message of what I thought of his actions, he yelled out in pain. I'd not even hit my target yet, but Splinter had. He had Rex's junk in his hand and was twisting hard.

I was pulled to one side by Zak as Noah and Mya pulled the men apart. They were struggling, but members of security joined in until finally, the guys stood facing off.

"She's mine. My mate," Rex growled at Splinter.

"Since when?" Splinter asked.

"Since you kissed her."

"Oh, sorry, pal. I'd not heard you say that. I just thought you were being one of those 'don't want her but no one else can have her' kind of arseholes. Only I know all about how you've been treating her. She told me." Splinter looked at me, releasing an appreciative sigh. "Freya's a beautiful woman and she deserves someone who will treat her with respect. If you're mated, then you need to sort your fucking self out."

"He is not my mate," I announced, glad that only those in the know about paranormal creatures were within earshot. "Because NEWSFLASH, I'm not a fucking shifter."

"Neither was Renesmee in Twilight, but Jacob imprinted with her," Erica said none too helpfully.

I pointed at Rex. "He has seen me on many occasions. If I was his mate, he'd have known it before now. He needs to go see his furry friends and find out what the fuck is going on with him, because he's clearly confusing asshattery with fated mates."

"That's true," Zak said to Rex. "Don't you usually instantly know your mate?"

"She's my mate. I just must have a delayed response." Rex was still grinding his words out as if they were pieces of hare in his mouth he was trying to chew while another wolf tried to get the carcass off him.

"Listen up, you mutt," I shouted over to him. "You had your chance and you made me feel like an idiot. You totally affected my self-esteem and had me heading towards Loserville. The week we were spending with you is over, and so is my time with you. So fuck off and good riddance."

I turned to my best friend. "Can I talk to you for a minute, outside?"

"Sure. In fact, let's go back up to our room for a bit, shall we? Get a break from all this intensity."

As I walked out of the room, I heard Rex emit a painful howl.

Yeah, well, I'd felt like doing that myself at some points this week, so rather than feel sympathy I just thought 'good' and I hoped it hurt like toothache.

Once back in our hotel suite, I walked over to the windows that looked out over the city and sighed. Staying in this suite with every meal provided and every comfort afforded had been truly special, but the week was over and real life beckoned. We were supposed to depart by noon tomorrow, but I was done.

"Talk to me." Erica patted the sofa next to her. "What's going through your mind? Because days ago you wanted to climb Rex like a tree, and now you're acting like someone shit on his branches."

I paced around the room. "He didn't want me. Then I date someone else and all of a sudden, I'm his mate? That's huge, isn't it? To be a mate. Like forever and ever, amen. I don't think so. I'm not being the mate of an arsehole who didn't want me, so he needs to go unmate himself. As I've seen from my date this evening, there are plenty more shifters in the woods. Plus, I'll take a human boy thank you very much. I've no intention of birthing something with claws."

"It was all very strange. They're supposed to mate with their own pack, aren't they?"

I sighed. "I have no idea. All I know is that I want to go home, Erica."

"Oh, Frey. It's our last night."

"It is, and I want you to spend it with Zak, bestie. You only just got together and I really, really want to be in my own house —alone. We've spent all week around so many people and it has been the most incredible experience to have shared with you, but I want to pack my stuff now and get the hell out of here."

Erica had known me long enough to know when my mind was made up.

"Come on then. I'll help you pack and make sure you get out of here safely. You must call me the moment you're home though."

"Yes, Mum," I said, and she rolled her eyes at me.

"I almost got destroyed by a demon this week. You'll forgive me for being a little safety sensitive."

My bestie had experienced quite the week. She ran The Paranormals fan club, and we'd been invited by Zak to spend the week with them as VIPs. She'd ended up as Zak's own VIP, but not before having to face Abaddon, the demon who ran the seventh dimension of Hell.

"I'll let you know when I'm home, and then I won't be contacting you until Monday, because I'm spending all weekend in bed, and I have a feeling you'll be doing the same... only I'll be sleeping." I winked at her.

Bless her, her eyes lit up. I'd been like that when I'd first got together with my ex, John. But it hadn't lasted, to the point where I'd split up with him just before we came here. I had no regrets about that. All my regrets centred around the fact I'd wasted so much time throwing myself at Rex like a fly near a yellow-coloured sticky pad in a greenhouse.

No more. I was going home, and I'd throw myself into work —which my boss would no doubt tell me would make a nice change—and I'd be on the lookout for a new man to fancy.

I packed up my stuff, and wheeling my case to the door, I gave my bestie a massive hug. "I'll speak to you next week, Erica, because talking with Zak's cock in your mouth will be difficult for you."

I shook my head in amused dismay when she just smiled. Time to leave my loved-up bestie to it.

Vikki, the Paranormals' PA, had said we could have a driver take us back home, so I contacted them and waited until I received a text telling me the car was there before making my way down in the lift to the lobby. I took in my surroundings one final time: the luxurious lobby of the five-star Broadleaf Hotel with its deep red carpets, gold accents, and staff who couldn't do enough for you. It had been a week to remember, seeing how a tour was put together and what went on behind the scenes, but I was ready for my own bed and some space.

The concierge took my case, and I followed him out of the doors. He placed it in the boot of the car while the driver opened the rear door for me to climb inside. How would I ever cope with public transport again? As the door closed and the driver got behind the wheel, I looked up at the front of the hotel.

Where Rex's face was smushed up against the floor-to-ceiling window next to the revolving door, his hands pressed against the glass. I saw him bang against it. Behind him, I could see Noah trying to hold him, but then Rex was gone and in the revolving doors. However, he'd forgotten about vampire speed. Noah spun the door, so it went too fast for Rex to get out.

The driver pulled out and we were on our way.

And I reflected that Rex's sudden about-face regarding the two of us had sent me dizzy, so it was only fair really that now he would be too.

🎸

I lived in a small, two-bedroomed terraced house in Forest Gate. The only reason I could afford it was because my parents were so keen to get me out of their house, they'd agreed to pay half my rent. It was very basic, but it was mine, and I felt happy as the driver pulled up outside my front door.

With one last car door opened for me and my case brought

up to my doorstep, I bid farewell with a hearty thanks and a handshake to the driver, and then I unlocked my front door and pushed it open.

It was so quiet. Mail piled up behind the door, and I kicked it away so I could get inside. Once through, I opened a couple of windows to let some fresh air in—well, as fresh as London air got—and I filled the kettle and switched it on. I'd taken a handful of UHT milk cartons from the hotel, even though while there they'd actually provided fresh. It would do until I got to the shops tomorrow. Drink made, I walked upstairs to my small but adequate bedroom, and I flopped down onto my mattress after putting my drink on my bedside table. I sent Erica a quick text to let her know I was home.

What a week!

What a night!

There were paranormals living amongst us. I would be suspicious of any hairy or pale-skinned person forevermore.

I decided that once I'd drunk my tea, I'd put on my laptop and look up werewolves, to check out what it meant to be one before I finally tried to get to sleep. I did wonder if sleep would be an impossibility tonight given everything floating around my mind. It wouldn't hurt to have information on my side, seeing as a wild animal was trying to mate with me. I mean what if they lost control and ripped your skin off as well as your clothes? I should know if there were any sprays you could buy to make them back off. You could get stuff for the garden to keep cats and dogs off. I needed a 'Wolf-off' spray. I'd check out Amazon just in case.

Then I found myself wondering what happened if a wolf shifter and a human female did get together and I got cross with myself for letting my thoughts go there.

Rex had lost his chance. He'd been unbelievably cold and dismissive of me.

Now he could have a taste of his own medicine.

I hoped it tasted really fucking disgusting and gave him side effects.

Chapter 2

Rex

I heard a beast growl, and I realised it was *my* beast. He was looking at Freya kissing another shifter and he was not fucking happy. Not fucking happy at all.

MINNNEEEEEEEEEEE.

As Freya left the room with Erica, it felt like my heart went with her; like it would shatter into a million pieces. I felt her loss the moment she was too far away for my inner wolf to smell her, and I howled.

And then I made a different howl as once again someone grabbed my balls and twisted.

"Fucking hell. I'll never have cubs if people keep doing this," I said looking into the red eyes of my fanged friend, Noah.

"Are you back with us, my friend?" he half asked, half hissed.

"Yes," I sighed. "But I feel all funny inside."

Zak tilted his head, looking at me. "Is your tummy flip-flopping?"

"Yeah, that and my heart feels all pangy."

"Ah, well my heart doesn't beat so I haven't had any pangs, but it's love, my friend. You're in love."

I considered his words. Which was another miracle along with my having mated because Zak's words were usually a complete crock of crap.

"Dear God. I think you might be right." I held a hand against my chest. "Could you get me a bottle of scotch, Zak, please?"

One was thrust into my hand from another direction, and I turned around to see Roman. He shrugged his shoulders. "I always have a spare on me, don't I?"

I quickly took the lid off and swallowed a huge amount of the honey-coloured liquid. It warmed me through, and I finally started to calm a little.

"It's a good job we have the jabs to stop you turning, or I think you and Splinter would have had fur flying around the place."

"That's why my butt cheek hurts," I stated.

"My pleasure, Zak said. "Though my days of giving someone one in the arse other than Erica are done now I'm a one-woman man."

And there he was. The Zak we knew and loved.

Noah slapped me on the back. "Come on. Let's get out of here and go sit in the suite with you for a while, talk things through."

"Fine by me. Erica's gonna be a while with Freya no doubt, so I've nothing else on my agenda."

"Zak, if you don't stop the idiocy coming out of your mouth, I'm going to get Stacey to seal it shut with a spell."

"Oh please do it anyway." Roman clapped his hands together in prayer.

Noah rolled his own eyes heavenward. "Give me strength."

Once we were in my suite, I ordered more alcohol and some snacks, and we all sat in my vast living area.

"So, what are you going to do about Freya being your mate?" Noah asked.

"I have to woo her, of course. Follow the rules and make her mine." I thought he already knew all this, but it seemed he'd not been listening when I'd told him of the werewolf way in the past.

"But she's a human and it all happened late. I think you should ring your dad and ask him for advice. Maybe your mate-ometer broke and needs fixing," Roman suggested.

I pondered his words. It was true that I'd been told you knew your mate at first sight. It was also true it was supposed to be another shifter of your kind so that you could continue the pack. What if my DNA was somehow screwed up and I just needed an injection or some medication to clear me of my new attachment to Freya? A reboot to wipe her from my system.

"I'll call him right now," I said, and I brought up their house number on my mobile and dialled.

A panicked voice came down the line: my mother's. "Rex, what is it, darling? What's happening? Are you okay? Not hurt?"

My head looked around the room for a clock. Oh God. I'd called at half past midnight on a Saturday morning.

"Sorry, Mum. Forgot the time again."

She let out a deep exhale. "But you're in London, so you're on the same time as we are," she pointed out. "Just give me a moment so my heart rate might approach normal again, now I know you're not being held at gunpoint."

"Mum, I need to ask you something. It is urgent. That's why I called."

"Oh, Rex. I think I know what you're going to say. Your dad did wonder, with all the photos of Jon Bon Jovi in his heyday you had on your walls when you were younger. Love is love, darling. I'm happy for you. When do we get to meet him, or have we already? Is it one of the band? Zak? Is it Zak?"

"MOTHER." I stopped her before my mind could be any further polluted with thoughts of Zak being my intended.

"Sorry, I'm spoiling your announcement yet again. I just get so excited thinking about you loved up."

"Earlier today. I felt it. The call of the mate."

I heard a weird noise.

"Mum. Are you clapping?"

"Carry on, darling. Your dad's awake now. I'm putting you on speakerphone. It's Rex," I heard her whisper. "He's mated. I don't know. That's why I've woken you up. Now listen."

"You hit me in the face," I heard Dad say to Mum.

"I was just waking you up."

"Course you were. It's nothing to do with me eating your last box of Jaffa Cakes then?"

"Hello, son calling," I yelled out.

"Go ahead, son, I'm listening," Dad told me.

"I need to talk to you about mating," I said. I was greeted with a silence.

"As in, when you meet your mate," I clarified.

"Oh thank God," he replied.

"So, I met a woman earlier this week, and... nothing. I felt no attraction to her. Well, that's not strictly true, she was fit, but she was following me around like a lovesick puppy. Anyway, tonight she's with another guy and BOOM, my wolf cries that she's mine. But she's a human. Am I broken? Can you get me a doctor's appointment to get me fixed?"

"There'll be no doctor's appointments to get you fixed until you've had at least one set of cubs," my mum announced. "I'm not hearing a problem. What are you talking about?"

I scrubbed a hand through my hair. Much more of these two and I'd be pulling it out in clumps.

"Mum, I didn't fall for her at first sight. We're supposed to know straightaway."

"Don't be so stupid, Rex. Where did you get that nonsense from?"

That was it. I got a handful of my own hair and tugged until tears came to my eyes. It was the only way to keep me sane.

"You and Aunty Rose. You're always going on about when you met Dad and Uncle Clay."

"Well, that's because we talk shit to the other one, trying to make out our love is the strongest."

"What?"

"The first time I saw your father he was in wolf form, and he was taking a dump in the woods. I'm not going to tell people that was how we met, am I? No, I say it was love at first sight and I just knew he was my mate. We actually both pinged at a dance two weeks later when there was a heatwave and we both went skinny dipping. But if anyone asks, he saw me across—"

I finished for her. "—the room at the dance and you couldn't take your eyes off each other as you both just knew."

"Is that what you tell people?" Dad said. "I just liked your tits."

"Ditto, honey. Although when you lost the cub fat, and they became pecs I liked it a lot more."

"Are you telling me this is perfectly normal? That I liked the woman after I'd seen her several times?"

"Yes, son," Dad piped up. "You said yourself that she was acting like a lovesick puppy. That's why you didn't react to her then. Wolves like to be dominant. They don't want a woman throwing themselves at them until they've courted them and won them over. Then they can act like lovesick puppies."

There was another weird noise.

"That was your mother snorting if you were wondering. The lovesick stage tends to be on and off after many years together. Usually, you have a spike of attentiveness from them near Christmas, birthdays, and when they're horny."

My ears were going to bleed.

"What about the fact my mate is human?"

"We mate with humans frequently as female births are much rarer than male ones. She must be a very healthy specimen. The humans chosen by us are usually very fertile, so expect her to get with cub easily. This is so exciting. When can we meet her?"

"You can't. Because she's not mated back. We aren't together yet."

"Then why are you on the phone to us, son? Go get your woman for goodness' sake," Dad shouted.

"Oh, honey. I do love it when you're all forceful."

"We've gotta go, son. Good luck." Dad ended the call. Obviously, Mum was now horny.

I'd forgotten I'd had the whole call on speakerphone. My friends sat around with their mouths dropped open, looking like they needed urgent therapy.

I opened yet another bottle of whisky and poured out shots.

"Let's get wasted," I announced.

It wasn't long afterwards that a knock came to the door, and Noah opened it to find Erica there. I looked behind her, but of course there was no Freya. I would have to try to talk to her in the morning before she vacated her room.

"How did it go, babe?" Zak almost ran over to his new girlfriend.

"Okay, I guess. Freya decided to go home tonight. She's just on her way downstairs now."

"She's what?" I yelled, and before any of them could stop me I was out of the room and heading for the stairwell.

But I was thwarted by vampiric speed yet again as I found myself pulled away from the rotating doors and pushed up against the window, watching as Freya was helped into the back of the car.

"You've no right to keep me here like this," I tried to say, but my mouth was squashed into the window so all I heard was, 'Wovnowitetocpmfeheeeeliths'.

"Let her go. It's the middle of the night. Go talk to her

tomorrow when you've both had some sleep," Noah pleaded. I let the fight go out of me and he let me slowly turn around. The guy needed to feed, his skin had paled more than usual, which meant...

I escaped him and managed to get myself into the revolving door, and then the bastard sped it up. It whizzed round and I was like a hamster on a wheel, except this hamster had been drinking whisky all night. By the time Noah pulled me back out, I hit the floor so hard I saw stars. Then I realised I was actually seeing them. I was facing the window and the night sky, and the entrance to the hotel no longer had Freya in a car in front of it.

"Nooooooooo," I said again, but this time I didn't know if it was my inner wolf howling, or the fact I felt like hurling.

"Now can we finally go to bed?" Noah said loudly.

"I told you that the whole Stacey marriage was a cover up and those two were an item," I heard a woman say as she walked past.

"Do you promise I can go see her tomorrow and that you will help me to win my girl?" I begged.

"I promise."

"Come to think of it, why am I asking you? I don't want to win her in eight years' time. I'll ask Zak." I stopped. "Did I just say that out loud?" I checked with Noah.

"Yup. You are going to ask Zak for dating advice. I can't fucking wait. Breakfast tomorrow?" Noah laughed all the way back to our floor.

CHAPTER 3

FREYA

Drink finished, I brought my laptop to my bed and switched it on. Of course, I'd not used it all week, so the bastard forced me to endure a Windows update before finally letting me access the internet. As I first browsed, all I found were mythological sites about werewolves and other paranormal creatures, and every site seemed to say something different. I was getting tired now and increasingly frustrated. Then I found a link to a membership site called *Supernaturals Uncovered*. There was a sign-up where you could get seven days free, so, feeling I had nothing to lose, I signed up. They'd promised not to sell on my details or spam me. In fact, the site looked very professional.

There was an 'about me' page so I clicked onto that first to see the kind of person who was maintaining the site. If he said anything whacko, I was out of there.

Welcome to Supernaturals Uncovered.

I'm Frankie Love. I was formerly a physician in the NHS, but then personal circumstances meant I needed a change of role. I fell into researching supernatural creatures during a period of illness and I've never looked back.

I try where possible to keep the site up to date, but if you spot an error or have an update please drop me an email.

Even if you are just enjoying the seven days free, I do ask you to consider a monthly membership or a donation via my Patreon account so that I can continue to manage and host this database. Please do not share this information with anyone outside of this resource, but rather ask them to sign up themselves to access it.

I live in Withernsea with my wife Lucy.

I typed wolf shifter into the search bar and clicked on the relevant page to find out general information about them. Then I sat back against my headboard and read what Frankie had put.

GENERAL WOLF SHIFTER INFORMATION
(Not to be reproduced. Copyright F. Love, 2018)

Werewolf (werwulf, man-wolf, lycanthrope)

The ability to shift into a wolf from human form.

The rumour that you can become a werewolf from a scratch is untrue folklore. In reality, you have to either be born a were, or in the instance of a mate, bitten during the mating ritual under a full moon.

Weres are vulnerable to silver and can be killed by being shot by a silver bullet to the heart.

Weres can shift at any night through choice, but on the night of a full moon will always change. This is when mating rituals occur.

It is not true that wolves rampage at this time with a lack of control over their animal selves.

Mates primarily come through the pack; however due to a lack of female offspring (8 out of 10 were births result in male children), mates are often selected from outside of the pack. Weres mate for life.

A male werewolf is expected to take a mate no later than at the age of thirty years and can be ostracised from the pack if still single by then.

Bitten? Bitten during the mating ritual under a full moon? When was the next fucking full moon? Jesus, summer had started, and it looked like I was going to have to dress up in fencing gear or something until Rex was 'fixed'. I Googled. God, I loved Google, it told you everything. There was a 'Buck Moon' on the 5 July at 12:44 am. Today was the 9th June so there was just over three weeks before Rex went full on Wolfmeister. I relaxed a bit at that. At least I had some time to figure things out before, well God knows what, because I needed to read the whole section about wolves.

I decided that tomorrow I would sign up for a full membership which gave you the ability to save information across into a personal folder on the site and ask any questions. Right now, I was absolutely shattered and needed some sleep.

After I'd put my laptop away and got down under the covers, my mind tormented me before I finally drifted off. Because I'd spent ages wanting to bed Rex and now he wanted me, part of me was shouting, 'So go let him ravage you, you idiot', while the main part of me, the stubborn part, thought 'too late, mate'. Plus, what if he ONLY now wanted me due to some error in his biology? And I feared ravaged might be the word if I banged him and I ended up in tiny pieces.

No, until I knew more, I would keep my distance from Rex Colton.

Opening my eyes, I reached over to the side of my bed to call reception and ask them to bring fresh coffee and some pastries. After tapping the side with my hand several times and realising the only thing to hand was a light covering of dust on my bedside table, reality sunk in. I was no longer in the five-star Broadleaf Hotel. I was home, and breakfast was still in the shops. I flopped back against my pillows and lifted my legs in turn, kicking them against the mattress.

Damn, stupid Rex Colton. I could have had one more morning of being served breakfast like a princess if it wasn't for him. Now, I would have to get dressed and go to the store like any other 'civilian'. I reached for my phone and checked for messages, but of course there weren't any. Erica would be too busy shagging, and no one else was expecting me back until later today.

My agenda was a shower, a supermarket shop, and then more time on the database looking at shifters.

Dragging myself out of bed, I walked into my bathroom and turned on the shower. It ran its usual slow, lukewarm self and I sighed again heavily. I'd been ruined by luxury. Ruined.

Rex lives in a mansion so large it has its own wood; my mind helpfully reminded me. I gasped when I remembered the press saying there was a rumour he owned a pet wolf, and I realised he didn't own it, he *was* the wolf. Water went in my mouth and made me splutter like a sixty-cigarettes-a-day chain smoker. Then I heard a huge crashing sound, and scared for my life, I crouched down small in the shower cubicle while I waited for a clue of what was happening. A bomb? Car crashed nearby? Clumsiest burglar in London?

I screamed as my bathroom door flew open and I hid my head down near my knees and prayed the attacker would somehow not see me or would accept a knackered iPhone 6 as being the only half-decent thing I had worth taking.

"Don't hurt me. Don't hurt me," I yelled into my legs.

"Freya," a familiar but unwelcome voice said. "I'm not here to hurt you. I'm here to save you."

Lifting my head up, I craned it around. At the moment, all my intruder could see was the curve of my arse and my back and that's how it needed to stay.

"Rex, you've just given me a heart attack. What are you saving me from? There's no chance of me drowning with the trickle that comes out of this thing." I looked at the shower that was still running.

"I heard you choking. No way can you die, my mate. Not now I've found you."

"How the hell did you hear me cough? Where were you?" I spat out.

"On your patio hidden behind the conifer. Most people bitch about leylandii as growing too quickly and getting out of hand, but it offered me the perfect refuge while I came to check on you this morning."

Closing my eyes, I thought about my current predicament. I was naked in the shower with Rex Colton. My crush was in the bathroom declaring he was my mate again. I could either ask him to pass me a bath sheet or stand up and show him the goods.

You don't know what that might commit you to, seeing as you haven't fully researched shifters yet, my stupid, sensible brain piped up.

Great, my brain had decided to have its annual good common-sense day today. I'd celebrate with a cold shower, which I'd got now all the warm water had run out.

"Could you pass me a towel please, Rex, and then after you've arranged for someone to fix my property you can take me for breakfast somewhere really fancy, okay?"

"You're agreeing to come out on a date, and I haven't even asked yet. That's amazing," Rex said. "Gallantry is all that was needed. Huh and Zak just said I needed to show you my massive dick. Fool."

"PASS ME A TOWEL."

"Oh, yes, of course." He took one off the back of the door and placed it over the top of the shower cubicle. "I shall be making some calls about repairs and things while you get ready for breakfast."

With that, he left the room, though my bathroom door didn't close quite as well as it had previously.

For a few moments I just stood up in the shower and let the cold water run over me. I needed to try to get over the shock of thinking someone had broken into my house. Then I turned the shower off, stepped out of the cubicle and towelled myself down before getting a new bath sheet from the unit under the sink and wrapping that around me.

I managed to get the bathroom door open after three pulls on it that made me feel like I was doing a tug-of-war with Rex and a few of his shifter mates, and then padded across the landing to my room.

My phone had a message on it. No surprise there then.

Erica: Keep an eye out for Rex. He did a runner this morning.

I started to type a reply, but then I decided that if I told her he was here, the band or their security would collect him before I got my luxury breakfast. Sod that.

Freya: Oh God. I will do.

Dots appeared on screen, showing she was typing a message back.

Erica: He will probably turn up at yours so shall I send some security round?

Freya: No. I'm going out anyway. I need to do some shopping. If he turns up, I'll call you straightaway.

Erica: How are you this morning?

Freya: Bummed I'm not in five-star accommodation. You?

Erica: Being bummed in five-star accommodation.

Freya: TMI!!!!!?????!!!!

There was a delay.

Erica: That was Zak. I needed a wee. Now I need a PIN number for my phone!

Freya: Bahahahaha. What are your plans now, other than being shagged senseless?

Erica: Well, it was to come home, hand in my notice at the supermarket, and start looking for a place of my own, as from Monday you're looking at an official member of The Paranormals PR Team.

Freya: OMG that's amazing!

Erica: I know, right? And from next week they're all in the recording studio, so I'll be staying in the surrounding accommodation for the time being.

Freya: You lucky sod.

Erica: It won't be the same without you. I wish you could be here. Think of a job you could do for the band!

Freya: A few days ago, I'd have said a hand job or a blow job for Rex, but now he can kiss my arse. Scrap that, he probably would take it as an invitation right now. Anyway, when you've worn your vagina out, come meet me for coffee or something, okay? I'm back at work tomorrow given that stupid jewellery stores in shopping centres open on weekends. Let me know when you're free.

Erica: I will do. Look out for Rex.

A knock came at my bedroom door.

Freya: I will, and in the meantime, I'm reading up on shifters. Anyway, I'd better go. Speak soon xo

Erica: xo

There was a further knock.

"Yes?"

"Freya, I'm just popping out for a few things I need. I've arranged for someone to come and repair the doors, but they'll be about an hour. I'm going to pop for some food and we'll eat here, okay? If you're still hungry after we can always go out later."

"Fine."

While Rex was gone, I finished getting dried and changed and then I logged back into my computer and continued to read about shifters.

THE MATING OF WERE SHIFTERS - FACTS AND RULES
(Not to be reproduced. Copyright F. Love, 2018)

To ask a wolf on a date is stating your interest in becoming their mate.

To attend the date and eat with a wolf is part one of courtship. Part two is to find out if you are physically compatible through the act of sexual intercourse. Part three is to complete the mating process under the full moon and be bitten by the wolf at which time non-pack members become both wolf (if not already) and pack.

Most wolves determine their mate by a scent. This scent is so intoxicating it can lead to periods of overwhelm until mates become accustomed to it.

Should a female show interest in more than one wolf then they must let the female decide. Alternatively, they can take out the other wolf.

To cook for a potential mate is a demonstration of the fact you will care for that woman and her future cubs.

. . .

He was trying to trick me! The twat was trying to cook me a meal. But... it said you could have sex just to find out if you were physically compatible. Hmm, that was food for thought. I carried on looking at the information. I'd no intention of asking him on a date, so I was safe on that score, although I had said he could take me for breakfast so did that count? I continued reading.

If a wolf asks you out for a meal as a potential mate you must realise that this is a binding sign of you being interested in courtship if you accept.

Fuck my life! So I daren't go out for lunch now either. This just all sucked. I needed to think of a way around things because I deserved luxury today after the shocks I'd endured. I put my computer down and made my way downstairs.

Chapter 4

Rex

It had taken me a while to escape the clutches of my 'security guard' Roman, but escape him I did. They'd all stayed with me for far longer than I desired, especially after my room dash, but eventually Noah and Zak's dicks got the better of them and they went back to their respective partners, leaving me with Roman.

We'd already had our fair share of whisky, but Roman was a party boy... so I kept the music flowing. Some good old-fashioned rock anthems like Def Leppard's *Pour Some Sugar on Me*, and Alice Cooper's *Schools Out*. And while the music rocked, I kept Roman topped up, until he was in a stupor, his head bowed as he snored softly, his back against the sofa.

I needed him to be comfortable and not disturbed. Roman's natural habitat as a satyr was woodland so I looked around the room. We'd been sent some congratulatory flowers and also the hotel's interior design person had filled the place with plants.

Taking a cushion from the sofa, I put that on the floor and

then I carefully moved Roman into a position lying on his side, his back against the sofa, and his head on the cushion. The music had moved onto Whitesnake's *Is this Love?* and I started to feel a pang. Oh no. I needed to put something different on. The playlist clicked over to Thunder's *Love Walked In*. What was this sorcery? It was making my chest ache with longing. I took a large swig from the whisky bottle to give me the strength to carry on and picked up the first plant.

I did feel a tiny bit guilty for ruining the display, but hey, I was a rock god, we were supposed to trash rooms, weren't we? I pulled the parlour palm out and threw the dirt over Roman's body and then laid the plant in front of him. It was a five-foot specimen so did a good job of being woodland-style. I did the same with two more plants, scattering the loose soil around him and putting one at his head and one at his feet and then I put the flowers from the large bouquet over his body.

That was Roman sorted, but now what? I looked at my watch. It was four am. I was tired and needed some sleep. I knew that my satyr friend would sleep for hours upon hours in his deeply inebriated state, and decided I would risk closing my own eyes for a couple of hours. The perfect idea came to me. I moved the sofa which was sat on high legs until it covered Roman. It meant I had to make sure he moved onto his back okay, but with me laid on the sofa above him, if he did wake up, I could run from the room before he even managed to get out. The perfect plan.

Climbing onto the sofa, I set my Apple watch's alarm to wake me at seven am and closed my eyes.

When my alarm beeped a few hours later, Roman was still fast asleep, so I quickly got ready and made my way out of the room. The moment I opened the door, Harriet, one of our security team stood up to get in my way.

"There's been an accident," I yelled. "Please help Roman."

As her eyes widened and she got on her radio for assistance while running into our room, I ran in the other direction. Out down the stairs and out of the hotel. I'd like to say I followed the scent of my mate all the way to her house, but the actual truth was that I'd got Zak to spill the deets on the area she lived in last night while we were drinking. Once in the vicinity, I would be able to scent her to her door.

I could have run, but I hailed a cab instead. If she was awake, I didn't want to be a sweaty mess on her doorstep; that wouldn't make a good impression.

Forest Gate seemed a nice place. I'd never been here before. I took in my surroundings as I followed my nose to Freya's place. I went via a cafe and got myself a coffee and a couple of bacon sarnies for while I did my stakeout. That name made me crave an actual steak. Looked like I needed to hunt soon or order a take-out steak-out. There was a passageway at the side of Freya's house, and I slipped down there and round to her back yard. There was the tiniest postage stamp sized grassed area at the back, with one of those leylandii conifers in it that had grown to a ridiculous size, but it did mean you couldn't be seen from the back-to-back neighbour's property. I sat down next to it as I could detect no movement or smell in the air that would indicate Freya was awake yet. That and the fact that all week she'd not managed to appear until mid-morning at the earliest. I may have taken note, even if she had got on my nerves before my mate gene kicked in.

Now, as I sat eating my sandwiches and drinking my coffee, I felt mean and almost broken-hearted that I'd treated my mate this way. I had to make it up to her starting immediately.

I remembered I'd turned my phone off, and so I grabbed it from my pocket and switched it back on. Voicemails and messages came immediately. Unlucky for them I had tracking turned off. They weren't finding me unless I wanted them to.

I dialled into my messages.

. . .

"Rex. It's Noah. Look, my friend. You need to come back so we can get an expert in and deal with this mating thing properly. You running away all the time is not the answer and now we've another problem because Roman is having to see a therapist this morning because of you."

Huh, was it my fault he had a drinking problem? Erm, no, it was the satyr way.

Noah continued. "I don't think you realised, but you covered him in earth, laid flowers on him, and pulled the sofa over him. He thought he'd been buried alive, Rex. It's only the fact that you'd panicked Harriet that meant she and Steve could pull the sofa off him quickly, but he's been in a state ever since. He won't even drink right now. That's how bad it is. You need to come back because you caused this mess, so you should help him recover from it. What on earth were you doing anyway? I suggest you drink less for sure."

I didn't hear the rest of his message. I was too busy lying on the ground behind the conifer and laughing. Proper belly laughs that hurt my stomach. As I sat up, I realised how much I'd needed that giggle. I'd make it up to my friend, just not now. I replayed the message and this time held in my laughter until after it had all played. All Noah had said at the end was for me to please at least text to let him know I was okay. No chance. I didn't know how good vamp hearing was, maybe he could detect the text coming down the phone or something. He was a lovely but conniving sod. It was a shame cos I wanted to text Roman with **did you rest in peace?**

Eventually, I saw Freya's bathroom window open, and I smiled, realising that she was up. I decided to give her a chance to come around and get ready. That was until I heard her begin to choke.

My mate was potentially dying.

I kicked through the door at the rear of her property with all my might and thundered up the stairs to find she was perfectly all right. Well, she had been until I'd broken in. Oops.

So now, I was in a local supermarket buying bacon, eggs, and anything else I could think of including some flowers. Freya hadn't seemed very impressed that I'd set out to rescue her. In fact, she'd shouted at me. She had however asked me to take her out for breakfast, which in my book was almost asking me on a date, right? It was another thing I needed clarification on. After finally making my way back to Freya's house, she opened the door to me, and told me to follow her into the kitchen and take a seat. She looked different. Her brown hair was in a ponytail, and she was dressed in a casual t-shirt and jeans. Unusually, there wasn't even a smidgen of make-up on her face. She was Freya unplugged and I loved it. She also smelled heavenly: of mate and toiletries.

"Do you think you could sit back down?" Freya sighed, and I realised I'd got up and was sniffing her hair.

"Sorry. This mate thing is very strange to me and I'm trying to behave, but it's my inbuilt nature."

She cocked a hip. "I get that, and I know it's going to take time to figure things out, but before we talk about any of that, your wolf rules give me a headache. Is it right that if I ask you to come out for food, or you make me food, we're basically boyfriend and girlfriend?"

"I'm not entirely sure myself," I replied truthfully. "If I cook for you, it means I'm showing you I can take care of you and any future babies, but unless we go out on a proper date, I think we're okay."

"Hmmm, but then you might say that anyway to trick me."

"Freya," I started, exasperated, "it's taking every ounce of strength I have not to drag you to bed, fuck you senseless, and get ready to bite you on the full moon and make you mine. But I want you to want me too; so no, I will not trick you into being my mate. Because you are anyway. You just need to accept it." I sighed. "I don't know what your issue with it is to be honest. You were all over me last week."

"And there is my issue, because *you* didn't want to know." Freya scowled. "Now your weird mojo has kicked in and you want me. But what if it's some chemical imbalance and when it's corrected you're all 'Oh no, I changed my mind, you're a clinger, back off'."

I paused, hanging my head in shame for a moment, before I looked back at her and spoke softly. Well, as softly as a wolf could speak. "I'm sorry. I realise I wasn't very nice to you, but Freya, we could have only been a shag, as wolves are destined for mates. The band would have killed me if I'd fucked you, given you're Erica's friend, and then dumped you."

"But I wanted to fuck, and I was more than prepared for being dumped. I just wanted a night with Rex Colton, you dipshit."

"Oh."

Freya started to go through the bag of shopping I'd brought. "If I cook this food and we eat it, there's no dating going on, right? We'll not be engaged or anything?"

"You're safe to make me a full English breakfast." I might have already eaten bacon sandwiches, but I was a wolf with a very hearty appetite.

While she was cooking, the workmen I'd contacted to repair her doors had turned up. I made sure to ask that they gave me a spare key for the door I'd kicked in. You know, just in case.

And so eating our lunch was accompanied by a man showing his arse crack as he bent down to fix hinges on her new door. It was okay for Freya; she had her back to him. The guy's arse was almost as hairy as me in wolf form.

"What job do you do?" I asked her in polite conversation. I should get to know my mate better after all.

She finished her mouthful of food before replying. "I'm a sales assistant in a jewellery store. I love it. I get to help people find their perfect piece. It could be engagement rings; wedding rings; or they've been left some money by a loved one who's passed, and they want a piece to remember them by. It's very sociable, as you need to get to know the client to make sure they get the right jewellery. That way they'll return. They know you're not trying to rip them off just to get a sale."

"You earn commission?"

"We have sales targets on the jewellery sales that can lead to prizes for salesperson of the month, that's in store and branch wide. Some people have won holidays."

I could see how much she loved her job from her expression as she talked about it. "When are you due back?"

"Tomorrow at ten. It's in a shopping centre and opens seven days a week. I do five shifts: four weekdays and one of the weekend days." She wiped her mouth with a piece of kitchen towel. "What about you? What did you do while waiting for fame and fortune?"

"I was a nightclub bouncer. It worked with my build, and meant I met plenty of chicks."

"You're such a mutt." She got up and refilled the kettle before switching it back on. I picked up the piece of discarded kitchen towel, sniffed it, and put it in my pocket. I wondered if I could steal her pillowcase without her realising. Doubtful. Damn.

Once she'd returned to the table, I carried on trying to get to know her. "Now I know you love your job? What else?" I guessed adding 'me yet?' was a tad premature.

"Huh, I love it in terms of it's not the worst place to spend time, but if I could afford to not go there I wouldn't."

"What would you do instead?"

"Erm, go shopping?"

I laughed. "You'd soon get bored of all that."

Freya sighed. "You mean you're bored of being rich already? It's not been that long."

"Oh no, I'm not bored yet. I have my house and I've still plenty I want to do to the place. Being on the road gets to be wearing as the band are in each other's pockets and every tour stop starts to look the same, but we're living the dream and I'm grateful. It'll be good to spend some time at home though while we get some new tracks recorded."

"But you'll be in the studio mainly, won't you?"

"Yes, but it's on my property." I grinned.

She paused, her drink halfway to her mouth.

"You have a recording studio at your home?"

I nodded. "It's in a separate building at the side of my house. I've eighteen bedrooms in the house which means if the band want to stay over any night they can."

"*Eighteen* bedrooms?"

"I have a large family who come to stay at times. And, of course, there's the wood surrounding the place. It's a great home. I'm looking forward to spending more time there."

"And yet, instead you're here." Freya glared at me. "So what are we going to do about that? Because you can't stay here. I need to go shopping and you need to let the band know where you are. I told my best friend I'd not seen you, but I'll have to tell her the truth soon because she'll be worrying about you."

"Can you come back with me and stay at mine?" I pleaded.

"No, I can't, Rex. I have a home, and a job, and responsibilities. You need to go now."

I insisted we swap phone numbers for in case I needed to hear her voice.

"The thing is..." I paused. "I kind of crave your smell, so I'm not sure how I can leave you." I thought about the pillowcase. "I know it seems weird, but can I take your pillowcase with me? That might help."

"*No.* Don't be ridiculous."

"I'll pay you a grand for it," I declared.

"A thousand pounds for my pillowcase?"

"For the pillow and pillowcase."

Freya stood up.

"What are you doing?"

"I'm getting you a black sack to put it in."

As she retrieved a black sack from a kitchen drawer, I stood and took it from her hand. "I'll get it. I need to use your bathroom before I leave."

She looked like a kid handing over a toy they're nagging for in a supermarket as she passed it to me.

I visited the bathroom and then went into her bedroom where I smelled the pillow and sighing with delight, I put it in the sack. Hopefully, it would do the trick. Spotting her hairbrush, I pulled out the hair from it and added that to the bag.

Finally, after a minute, I dragged myself out of the room that smelled of my mate.

"Thanks for the hospitality," I said as I walked back into the kitchen. "The repairs look like they're almost completed, and they'll send me the bill." I headed towards the back door. "I can't promise I won't come back if the call to see my mate is strong, but hopefully this pillow will help." I gave her my best, sad, wolf-eyed look. "I'll get Vikki to send the money to your account." I waved the bag.

Freya shook her head. "I don't want your money. If it can help you then take it. I also didn't want to be free of you," she said sadly. "I just wanted you to want me for me, and not because of a biological call, but you didn't, Rex. You weren't interested."

I nodded because I could understand where she was coming from even if walking away from her felt like my heart was being shattered by lasers.

"Bye, Freya."

"Bye, Rex."

I went out of her house, thankful that the maintenance team had watertight confidentiality agreements, though to be honest reporters would think they were delusional in any case if they tried to say I was a werewolf.

Making my way down the street, I called for a driver to take me home and then I sent Noah a text to tell him I was on my way back and that I'd see them all in the morning for breakfast before we started our first day in the studio.

He called me within minutes.

"Where have you been?"

"Around. Just trying to get my head on straight."

"Nice try, but Freya just texted Erica who texted Stacey to say you've been there all day."

"Bloody women."

"I called your parents and they'll be at yours Tuesday tea-time to see if they can help. They couldn't come before then."

"You called my parents?"

"Well, duh, I thought you might be there. I called a lot of people."

"What did they say, other than they'd visit Tuesday?"

"Your mum said not to worry and that it couldn't possibly be any worse to sort out than when you got your dick stuck in a tangled slinky."

My fucking mother.

"We'll see you tomorrow and you'd better make sure you have a good apology ready for Roman, who is still shaking."

I ended the call and sniggered. Roman needed to grow a pair.

My phone rang immediately and thinking it would be Noah who'd remembered something else, I answered without looking.

"Yeah, what else do you want to nag me about?" I asked.

"Where the fuck is my laundry, dickhead? All my clothes I wore this week that were in my suitcase. Where. Is. It. All?"

I looked at the bag in my hand. My folding skills were impressive; plus, her clothing had been deliberately tiny.

"I don't know what you're talking about, babes." I laughed heartily. "But I know I'm gonna spend the night with my head where it should be. In your panties."

I ended the call just as her pitch rose to a level my ears couldn't take.

Chapter 5

Freya

I'd actually regretted letting him walk out of my door for a moment. Then I'd said goodbye to the maintenance guy and gone upstairs to get my suitcase, thinking I'd put a wash load on before I went food shopping. Except what I found was a case empty of any of my clothing. All my best stuff that I'd worn last week in the hopes of impressing Rex bloody Colton was now in his possession. I guessed I should be grateful he wasn't planning on doing a Drayton in any of it (a bear shifter singer who'd been hexed into wearing women's clothes on stage in the Britain's Best New Band final in revenge, courtesy of Donna from The Seven).

Still, I'd given him permission to take my pillow and pillowcase, not my bloody used knickers, the absolute pervert. I sighed at myself as I felt my current pair dampen. Shameless hussy getting turned on at the thought of Rex sniffing my panties. *Stop thoughts. Stop. We are not turned on, we are annoyed.*

Making my way downstairs, I walked over to my noticeboard and copied down the shopping list onto a piece of paper adding new pants to it. It wasn't the only thing I'd be adding to my basket. A few bottles of wine would be going on too.

Finally, I was ready. Leaving by my front door, I began to make my way on foot to the supermarket. I was ready for some fresh air and the walk would do me good. I'd get a taxi back with all the shopping because the amount of wine I intended to buy would be too heavy for me to carry on its own, never mind the rest of my shopping. I'd only just reached the end of my path when a blonde-haired teenager who lived two doors down ran up to me.

"Hey, lady."

I realised she was talking to me. At twenty-one, to be called a lady was a total insult. She was all of about fourteen and to her I was clearly ancient. But her eyes were narrowed in my direction, and the scowl on her face warned me that she did indeed mean me.

"Can I help you?" I asked.

"Did I see Rex Colton leave your house earlier?" she ground out.

"Nope."

"I fucking well did. I'd know him anywhere. He's mine, bitch. You need to back off."

Suddenly, I didn't feel safe on my own doorstep because psycho teenage hormone girl was looking like she was going to slit my throat.

I sighed and looked at her with my best sympathetic gaze. "I have a brother who looks exactly like Rex from the back. He keeps being followed everywhere. Rest assured, if I ever meet Rex, I'll tell him that he's yours, okay?"

She hesitated. "Does your brother not look like him from the front?"

"Not in the slightest. He looks like Justin Bieber with warts and masses of nose hair."

"Shame," she mumbled as she walked off.

Crisis averted. That man was causing me a lot of bother.

I survived my trip to the supermarket without any further psychotic fan stalking. Once home and unpacked, I sat down with a now opened bottle of wine, a large pack of Kettle chips, and erm... five newspapers and eight magazines. They all had the band in them. Oh okay, they all had Rex in them, and I wanted to keep up to date. I needed to know where he was and what he was doing, you know, just so that I could keep tabs on him seeing as he was so attracted to me right now.

I drank half a glass of wine in one go. Why the fuck hadn't I shagged him? Idiot.

I had no idea what time it was. The clock seemed to say four or five-ish, maybe six, but I couldn't see it properly. I was in my living room playing Harry Styles' *Watermelon Sugar* on repeat imagining Rex eating me like a ripe melon.

I'd called Erica as soon as Rex had left and confessed that he'd been here all along. She hadn't been impressed, telling me I'd caused them all a stack of worry. But then she'd started laughing as Zak tickled her and all of a sudden it hadn't been so important. With an 'Oh well, as long as he's safe' she'd buggered off.

It wasn't fair. She was getting shagged mercilessly and I was daydreaming in my living room with a bottle of wine, wondering why I hadn't bought a watermelon.

The next thing I knew I'd drunk-dialled Rex.

"Are you still mad about the fact I have your panties?" he drawled down the line.

"Yesssssh," I slurred. "You should have ashked."

"Have you been drinking by any chance?" I could hear the amusement in his voice.

"I may have had a couple of drinksh."

"So was that it? You just wanted to let me know you're still cross?"

"Yesh. I'm cross because you didn't shag me when you had

the chansh, fuckwit. And because I had to buy new pantsh, and wine, and newshpapers and magasheens. AND," I heard my own voice get louder and higher but I couldn't control it. My gob was an escaped snowball running down a snowy hill becoming bigger and more out of control. "I do not have a fucking w-w-watermelon."

"Ohh-kay, and that's a problem, is it?"

"Yesh, because I am danshing, and I need a watermelon and some shhugar and I have the shhugar but no watermelon."

"Do you want me to bring you a watermelon?"

"NO. You do not come here, because a) you're too late and b) sh-psychotic teenage neighbour thinksh you're my brother with a wart-face, and c) what wash I shaying?"

"You were saying that you were going to get ready for bed now after having a few coffees, because even though it's only a quarter to six in the afternoon, you've had a busy week and it's time for a rest."

"Yesh, that's why I called. I'm going to sleep now, and you, you, are a fuckwit. Good night."

I hung up and went to put the kettle on.

Sometime later, I knew not how much longer because I'd zoned out at the kitchen table, there was a knock on the back door, and I opened it to find my best friend standing there.

"Erica," I screamed.

"Shit the bed, you really are off your tits," she exclaimed, walking inside.

"What are you doing here? Are you really here? Is thish for real?" I threw my arms around her. "Oh you are real, yaayy. I mished my best friend."

"Ow, ow, ow, ow, ow. Freya, you're squeezing me a little too hard."

Letting my arms drop, I stood a bit further back from her.

"Okay, sit down at the table while I make you some strong, black coffee, and let me turn the bloody music down before the noise police turn up."

"It's Harry Shtyles. No one will complain about Harry Shtylsh." I happy sighed at being with my bestie. "I don't shuppose you brought a watermelon with you?"

🎸

The next thing I knew, I woke up on the sofa. As I cracked open an eye, my head slammed with pain. "Fuck," I squealed.

"I'll get you some painkillers and some water," came a voice from across the room and I just made out my best friend rising from my armchair.

"Erica?" I queried. "What happened? Did I get mugged by psycho teen?" I felt at my head for lumps.

She walked over to me and knelt down near my head. "No, you got hammered. I found two bottles of wine empty and a third halfway down. Now it's hammering your head."

"Oh," I said, and I pulled a face as I ran my teeth around my mouth. "Ugh, this is vile. Vile." I tried to sit up, but my body was part stuck to my leather sofa. "What the actual fuck is going on here?" I muttered. "I can't cope with this right now, along with my head."

"All I know is you stood up in the kitchen while I was making your coffee, and you poured sugar down yourself followed by dripping water down your body and attempting some kind of dance. You complained endlessly about having no watermelon and having to compromise. You are stuck because you kind of made your own syrup glue."

I recalled the dancing from earlier vaguely when I'd been simply enjoying myself and not pissed as a fart. "Does Zak know Harry Styles? Maybe I could approach the man about contributing to cleaning my home?"

"Now you're awake, let's get your painkillers down you, and then you can have a shower while I make a fresh pot of coffee, okay?"

"Okay?" I bit my lip. "I'm sorry I took you away from Zak."

"Zak and I are dating. We aren't joined at the hip. Yes, we're a bit heady and wanting sex every five seconds, but I can make time to come help my bestie when she's having a drunken crisis."

"How did you know to come anyway?" I realised I didn't know when she'd got here or how she'd known I was drunk.

"You called Rex."

My face drained of all blood. "Oh no. Please no. Promise me I didn't tell him I wanted to be his mate after all."

Erica laughed. "No, apparently you told him he was a fuckwit."

"Phew."

"Anyway, go and get showered and then I can help you get cleaned up in here. There's sugar everywhere."

And that's exactly what my best friend did. She helped me feel slightly more human, made me some toast and a hell of a lot of coffee, and then we cleaned up the living room and kitchen while I vowed to never drink so much again. I insisted she left at eleven pm and I took myself off to bed to read all the newspapers and magazines I'd bought. At around three am, I finally fell back to sleep until my phone alarm bleeped at nine am reminding me that I was back at work.

The store opened at eleven on a Sunday, but first we had to get the new stock unpacked and give the store a little clean and polish because it needed to be pristine. Customers expected quality and the utmost professionalism at *Sparkles*.

Thank goodness therefore for make-up which had stopped me looking like the undead. When I'd woken, I could have been an extra for *The Walking Dead*. I should have sent Rex a photo, that would have had him un-mated from me within the time it took for him to scream in shock. But instead, I looked well put together on the outside even if the inside of me was still a little bit queasy. I was wearing some of the jewellery I'd bought from the store. We had to showcase the store's brands and for that we got a hefty discount.

"Well, well, well. The superstar returns," Joelle, one of the other assistants and a complete bitch snarled out. "What's it like realising that despite your friend knowing the band, you're still so very, very, *ordinary*."

God, I hated her. I hated her dark, almost jet-black hair, her stupid botoxed face, and veneered teeth. She made out like she was loaded when all she had was a credit card and a number of 'sugar daddies' that she managed to keep hanging while they hoped to get in her pants. She did however have the gift of the gab to the extent that every single month she beat me to Salesperson of the Month. I had never won it despite my best efforts. Maybe this month I could do it and wipe the smug look off her face. It was still relatively early in the month, so I had a chance.

"Hi, Joelle. I think you've got a pubic hair stuck between your teeth," I lied, but as she paled and hot-footed it to the bathroom, it looked like one of her 'daddies' had called in his debt after all.

As the morning passed and we got busy, my hangover finally began to abate, and I started to relax. I'd made a few sales and Joelle's constant glaring at me did nothing but spur me on further.

I was feeling fragile but determined when into the store walked John, my ex.

I deflated like a leaking helium balloon and as I said hello to him in a squeaky voice, I sounded like I'd been inhaling it.

"Hey, Freya," he said, smiling at me. It disturbed me because ex-boyfriends you'd dumped just over a week ago were not supposed to smile at you. They were supposed to be really pissed off at you or deeply depressed.

"Hi, John. Is there something I can do for you?"

He nodded. "Yes, I'd like to buy an engagement ring please."

"P-pardon?" I'd only just dumped him. How could he be getting engaged? Ohhh, it hit me all at once. He was either back with the OG—the original girlfriend and first love he'd had before me—or he was making shit up to make me jealous. I'd go for it being the latter. Well, while that was fine, I needed him out of here quickly, because while he was getting me to show him rings I doubted he had any intention of buying, Joelle had a genuine customer who was dripping with an expensive watch and ring already and looking at bracelets. Plus, he was around sixty, so her prime real estate.

"Okay, tell me, what kind are you looking for and what price range?" I looked around me. "Oh, and I'm forgetting my manners. Come take a seat at my table. Can I get you a coffee?" *Because I fucking need one.* My swearing to not drink looked like lasting the shortest ever time because if brandy had been to hand, I'd have poured it on an 80/20 ratio of alcohol to coffee into my mug and downed it so fast I'd have taken out my oesophagus.

"Oh, you know me. I had no clue what I was looking for last time either. Could you show me a selection and help me choose?"

"Sure," I said politely. "Maybe if you could tell me a little about the lady you're buying it for, it might help me."

"Okay. Well, it's been a whirlwind romance, and she's just beautiful and everything I ever wanted. She's so pretty, so it needs to be pretty, and she's got a similar build to you, so I'll take a guess at her being a similar ring size. If it doesn't fit, we can bring it back to be sized, right?"

Jesus, was he on something or manic?

"Of course. Let me just go choose a few. Give me a moment."

I went into the storeroom at the back where I banged my head into the nearest glass cabinet.

"Is everything okay, Freya?" my boss, Eddie asked.

"If fine is your ex-boyfriend coming in to buy an engagement ring the week after you dumped him because he's had a whirlwind romance, then, yes, everything is fine."

Eddie fixed me with a look. "The last time he came in to buy a ring he left with no jewellery, but a new girlfriend. That's not going to happen this time is it, Freya? You are going to make a sale, aren't you? Because what is our private mantra?"

"Show the bling, make their finances sting." I found it very hard not to roll my eyes.

"Perfect. Now back out you go with a whole host of expensive engagement rings because his new fiancée deserves the very best, doesn't she?"

I nodded, made my selections and went back outside.

John dithered for the best part of an hour, making me put them on to show him. (I refused to put them on my engagement finger) and asking my advice, until in the end I snapped. But only inside. Outside I had to still be the perfect salesperson.

"This one, John. If it were me, I would be ecstatic to receive this ring here." I held it up and twinkled it into the light. "It's completely perfect and you will own her heart. Okay?"

"Sold," he beamed. "Thank you, Freya. You're the best."

"Okay, so how will you be paying for it?"

"Oh, erm, I'll put it on my credit card. Hopefully, my limit will be high enough."

I paused at that. No matter what Eddie said, this was my ex and at one time we'd been happy.

"John, any woman would be lucky to have you as their fiancé. You don't have to spend a stupid amount of money. Hold on a moment." I took away the tray of rings I'd shown him so far and found him another lovely and popular one in a more affordable price range.

I walked back out and sat near him. "This one. It's beautiful and affordable, and if she loves you, she'll love whatever ring you buy her."

He looked visibly relieved. "True, she would, wouldn't she? Okay. That one please, Freya."

Usually we gift-wrapped items, but John asked me to just put it in the box and in the bag. He paid and then he just hovered in the doorway.

"Erm, is everything okay, John?" I asked him, noticing he seemed a bit nervous and jumpy. *Oh no.*

My fears became reality as he walked back into the store and dropped to his knees. What was even worse was Joelle was at the side of me now having finished with her customer. My humiliation was going to be witnessed by my enemy.

John fumbled with the bag, discarding it to the floor. Customers gathered around watching as he opened the ring box.

He took a deep breath. "Will you marry me?" he said.

"John, no. Don't be ridiculous," I uttered...

...as Joelle screamed, "Yes."

I stood back and watched, stunned, as he put the ring on her finger.

A customer laughed to another as she pointed at me. "Poor girl thought he meant her."

I looked from Joelle to John and back again. Clearly, John had some jewellery fetish, and I began to wonder if there'd ever been a fiancée number one.

Joelle wagged her finger at me and grinned. "Oh look, I have your man now. That's whose pubes I was looking for in between my teeth. You didn't deserve him, ditching him to go fangirl over rock stars you'd never have a chance with."

"Good morning," a voice growled out. "I've come to buy an excessive amount of jewellery and I absolutely insist on Freya serving me."

I spun on my heel to see Rex standing at the side of me.

"Actually, Susan was our next available assistant," Eddie told him.

Rex stood up straight and flexed his biceps. "Do you know who I am?" he snarled.

Eddie almost shit his pants. He visibly shrank before glaring at me. "Freya, what are you waiting for? Serve our customer."

"Would you like to come over to my table?" I grinned at Rex. I'd never been so happy to see someone. The customers had lost all interest in the proposal and Joelle's face looked like she'd been forced to eat rabbit droppings.

"Let's say congratulations to the happy couple," I shouted to everyone left in the store. There was a muted attempt at congratulations and applause, like you'd expected Take That to cut the ribbon at a store opening and turned up to find a tribute act instead. Eddie quickly got the rest of the staff to find out who was a genuine customer and to clear out anyone who'd just rolled in to stare at Rex. I wanted to punch the air because Joelle was stuck with my ex-boyfriend and had now realised that she was wearing a bargain priced engagement ring. It was just too funny.

I sat down at the table with Rex. "So, before I offer you a drink like I do most customers, would you like to explain what you were doing outside the store?"

He sat back in the chair opposite me and unfolded his legs. They were like frikking tree trunks and stretched his jeans to the max. The bloke was big, but in a stacked and ripped way. As I compared him to my ex, I decided his cock must be three times the size and I swear my core screamed 'I'm not ready' in fear. It certainly had a little flutter.

"See, while your undies and pillow got me through the night, babe… this morning, I had to come see you for my daily fix." He shrugged. "That, and of course, I wanted to make sure you were okay after your night of indulgence."

"Hmmm. Coffee was it?" I said, and I got up and went into the back room, to the sounds of his laughter ringing in my ears.

I returned with a coffee for us each. "I apologise for um, calling you a fuckwit," I reluctantly uttered. "I don't remember, but Erica told me I did it, so I'm sorry, and thank you for getting her to call around."

"You're right. I was a fuckwit for not shagging you when I had the chance," he said.

I sat dumbstruck for a moment and then I put my hands over my eyes. "Please tell me I did not say that," I begged.

"I could, but I'd be lying."

Rex decided to save me from any further embarrassment by surreptitiously nodding over towards where Joelle stood with my ex. "So that's your ex and he just proposed to one of the other assistants?"

"Yeah, I think he's got problems." I explained how I'd met him.

"He almost had bigger problems than that," Rex replied.

"Huh?"

"I was watching outside as the guy dropped on bended knee in front of my mate. If it had been you that he'd proposed to, I'd have picked him up and thrown him back out of the store like a javelin." I watched as he took several gulps and deep breaths. "As it is, I'm having problems knowing he's been inside you."

I watched my boss over Rex's shoulder. He kissed Joelle on the cheek, shook John's hand and then steered him out of the store. Then I saw his mouth utter, 'Now get back to work'.

"So, that commission and the competitions you were telling me about." Rex stretched and showed me his stomach. I had all on not to drop to my knees and lick it, and I'm not sure I meant his stomach, but I'd start there for sure. I bet his skin would be all salty. I could lick him, take a shot of Tequila and then ride his cock. A Tequila Slam-Her.

"Hmmm, yeah, what about them...?" I no longer gave a shit to be honest. Well, until I felt eyes burning into my face and I turned and saw Joelle. All she needed was 101 Dalmatians and she'd be set.

"I think I should just buy a few really expensive pieces, don't you?" He winked. God, it would be so tempting, but it was like his saying I was his mate. If I got sales, I wanted it to be because I'd done it, that I'd beaten Joelle fair and square. My moral compass had been put in place ever since the guilt of taking someone's boyfriend from them a year ago. Mostly, anyway...

But John chose to walk back into the store then. "Freya, I realise she's not the one for me," he yelled. "I realise I was just trying to make you jealous." He walked over to a stunned Joelle, who took off her ring and threw it at him before running into the back of the store. Then he picked the discarded ring up, walked further towards me, and he started to bend down.

With the ring he'd just given someone else...

In front of the wolf shifter who said he was my mate...

Oh crap.

"Freya. Will you..."

He didn't get any further as Rex picked him up and threw him into the next table.

"She's MINE," he growled, and then he took a syringe out of his pocket, and he stabbed himself in the butt. Oh, fuck, he was gonna go furry without it. I ran up and took the discarded syringe and put it safely away in my drawer at my desk.

It was still like witnessing Bruce Banner becoming the Hulk. He roared at John.

Eddie screamed at me. "Get him out of my store. He's scaring away all the customers and causing a commotion."

I went towards John. "Not him. HIM." He pointed at Rex.

I was about to say that Rex would be willing to spend a shit-load of money to make up for the fuss, but as I stood there, I realised my career here was done. As much as I'd loved matching people with jewellery, this place would always now be tainted with what John had done, and let's face it Joelle wasn't going to get any better now after this fiasco. Instead, I walked over to Rex, and I stroked his arm. It was the only thing I could think of that might calm him down and it seemed to work as he turned to look at me.

"Let's go," I told him. "People are starting to record you on their phones."

We left the store together, climbing into his car. "I'm sorry, Freya," Rex said as he started the ignition of his Mercedes.

"You can't help your biology, Rex, whereas John can help being a dickhead." I didn't know what I'd ever seen in him now.

"I'm still sorry."

"Thanks," I said. We drove in silence back to my house.

"What the fuck?" I shouted when I looked at my front door. The words LIAR and WHORE had been painted on my brickwork and a group of teenage girls stood outside my house, one of whom was psycho bitch.

"Oh God, it looks like your fans have seen the video and worked out who I am." I felt myself well up. "What the hell am I going to do?"

"You're going to come stay with me. I have seventeen spare bedrooms," Rex said. I was about to protest but he shook his head. "It's non-negotiable because your home isn't a safe place right now. Some of the Subs are crazy. I'll get security to come and secure the place and keep it patrolled, but until it all dies down, you're not living there. Sorry."

I had no job, no home, and a man who wanted me only because of some genetic fuck-up. Plus, my hangover had decided to remind me it was still present.

"Can we have bacon butties at your place?" I asked.

He turned to me. "Sure, we can, but don't you want watermelon instead?" He winked.

Chapter 6

Rex

I'm not sure I would have been as understanding as Freya, had things been the other way around, but she was coming to stop at my house, and I was trying not to whoop and holler. As I turned to look at her, my inner celebratory trumpets lessened to that more akin of a toddler trying to blow through the hole as I saw just how tired and low she looked.

"It'll be okay," I told her.

"Will it?" she replied. "I'm happy for my friend, but I'm beginning to wish I'd never accepted her invitation to go see Britain's Best New Band."

Her phone rang and taking it from her pocket, she sighed and answered. "Hello, Mum." I could hear someone rattling away and Freya just going, "Yeah, U-hum."

Then she blew a gasket and the Freya I knew better was back. "Mum, Rex will sort it. He has people. Did it look like I was doing anything? There you go then. Oh, no. I'm not going home. Their fans are there, it's not safe. He's sending security. Nope, I don't need to, I have somewhere to stay. At Rex's. MOTHER. It's not like that. I know what it looked like, but..." She huffed loudly. "I always do. I'm not saying that out loud. Oh my god, Mother. Cross my heart and hope to die, if I tell a little lie, I will use precautions if I sleep with Rex Colton."

I sniggered and received a dirty look in return.

"It wasn't necessary because it isn't going to happen," she said snarkily.

"It will," I mumbled.

"There's more chance of a stray firework hitting him in the bollocks." More chatting. "I apologise for my language. Yes, I'll ring you every night. Yes, I'll send you the address so you can look it up on Google Street View." She ended the call. "Well done, you've now set off my mother's paranoia about my safety."

"I can assure her you're perfectly safe staying with me."

Freya raised a brow.

We'd reached the large silver gates of my estate and I radioed ahead to let my security guy know I was here. The doors opened, and I drove through, going around the large circular driveway and past a couple of the other buildings. Eventually, I turned off to the right and my house came into view.

"Holy fucking shitballs. That's your house?"

"Yup."

"Dude, that is not a house, that's like Buckingham Palace or something."

"Alas, there's no queen in my building, though I'm working on it."

She ignored me.

"I'm going to get lost. It's bigger than the hotel we just left."

"Not quite, but not far off. And I'll always know where you are because I can scent you."

"Great. That doesn't make me want to bathe in bleach at all!"

I pulled up outside and Miles, my man-who-can came out to greet us. I threw him the keys. "I'm putting Miss Steel in the

Buttercup Suite. If you could let Cath know to prepare some refreshments for the room?"

"Yes, sir." Miles turned to me. "Welcome to Oakley Manor, Miss Steel."

"Thank you," Freya said, holding out her hand.

Huh, he got the nice version. I looked at Miles, trying to picture him from a woman's point of view. He was in his early fifties, with just the slightest hint of grey sprinkles to his dark-brown hair, and thank God, happily married to Cath. He shook Freya's hand back firmly. "If you need anything just dial 1 on the phone in your room and it will be dealt with." Miles turned to me, with a haughty stare. "Though I draw the line at having to go all the way to McDonalds for one tiny carton of their curry sauce."

"You wouldn't if you tasted it," I protested.

"I would really like a bacon sarnie, a nice hot cuppa, and a bed and TV. That'll be me done for the rest of the day," Freya declared.

"I'll make that for you," I told her.

"No you bloody won't. No trying mating crap while I'm tired and vulnerable to attack."

"Does that mean I can try mating crap when you're more awake?" I joked.

That earned me a death glare.

"Your requests are noted, Miss Steel. I'll let Rex escort you to your room, where he will *leave you* to settle in. The bed and TV are already there. I'll get Cath to sort the bacon and tea."

"Will you marry me, Miles?" Freya grinned.

I growled.

"Oh for goodness' sake," Freya and Miles said at the same time.

Freya followed me up the twenty steps to the entrance of my property. As she walked in, I turned around and watched her expression as she took in the cream hallway with its marble flooring, the giant staircase in the centre, and all the rooms that veered off.

"Stairs or lift?" I asked.

"Of course your entirely-too-large-for you property has a lift," she complained.

It was time for her to realise she was wrong, and I was getting sick of her moaning now. Okay, she couldn't stay at her own house, but a mansion was hardly suffering, was it? "You haven't met my family yet. This house is ideal. For the friends and family I have and the family I will have, so why don't you shut up and tell me how fabulous my house actually is and how not being able to stay at yours isn't so bad."

I realised it was the wrong thing to say as Freya began to stomp up the stairs. As she hit the tenth of forty she began to wheeze.

"You can slow down, you know? It's not a sign of weakness."

"F-fuck you." She carried on stomping.

By the time she'd reached the top—given she'd refused to give in and take a rest or reduce her pace—she was blood red in the face.

"So fucking stubborn," I declared, and while she didn't have the energy to do anything about it, I threw her over my shoulder and marched down the corridor towards her room.

"Put me down, you arsehole bastard," she shouted, trying to beat at my back. That amused me even more. It was like cotton wool balls bouncing off me.

What I wasn't expecting was for her to reach out and grab my hair and pull it... hard. In a cross between the fact it goddamn stung, and my very distracted thoughts of if she could tug that hard I was gonna have some fun with those hands at some point before I died, I dropped her.

She screeched as she hit the floor and then she went, "Oh."

I looked down at Freya. She was fine due to the fact she'd landed on the most sumptuous rug money could buy, which was on the most luxurious carpet I'd ever come across.

"We're almost there. Two more doors. Can you walk there okay? I'm not so keen to carry you since you pulled half my hair out of my head."

"I didn't ask you to carry me in the first place," she retorted.

"For the love of all that is holy, why did I mate-match with the most infuriating woman in the world?" I was about to yank my own hair.

"Says the wanker who treated me like shit all week."

"Oh, here we go."

She stood up and tilted her right hip as she put her hands on them. "Just point to where my room is and then leave me the hell alone, Beast."

"Why are you addressing my cock? Are you not talking to me directly now?"

"Gaaahhhhhhhhhhhhhh."

I could tell she wanted to stomp again, but she didn't know where to stomp to.

"Follow me. I'll take you to your room and leave you alone."

"Thank you," she snarked.

We made our way for the next minute in total silence. I pushed open the double doors to the Buttercup suite and revealed the room to Freya in all its glory.

Floor-to-ceiling windows held pale-lemon drapes, currently pulled back to let the sunlight in. Double doors in the centre led out to a balcony with a wooden table and four chairs and there was a parasol folded and stored in the corner. The chairs had padded seat cushions covered in a buttercup design. The balcony looked out over the gardens and woodland.

The same buttercup design was on the wallpaper on the bedroom wall side of the room and the living area side. A huge king size bed with white bedside tables rested against one of these walls, then there was a few feet of space before the emerald green velvet sofa which faced the other feature wall where a widescreen TV hung.

It was a room the colour of sunshine and you just couldn't be miserable in it.

"There's a e-Reader in the top drawer that has books pre-loaded, but it's attached to an account so if there's anything else you want to read just download it," I informed her as she began to walk in.

"Which side?"

"There's one at both sides."

That earned me an eye-roll.

"In the desk/dresser in that corner there are some books too, but again I have Amazon Prime installed so feel free to get some more delivered tomorrow. The television is also set up with Netflix, Prime, and other subscription services."

"It's even better than the hotel. I can't believe this room. It's... too much, Rex." She sighed looking around her. "I feel overwhelmed."

"Look, you said yourself that you're tired and hungry. Just pretend you're back at a hotel again and tonight is for settling in. Everything will be better after food and a good night's sleep."

She lifted her shoulders up and down and I tried and failed to not watch her tits jiggle. "I guess so." She gasped and her eyes widened. "Oh, I don't have any clothes or toiletries."

"I'm going to organise someone to go pack your belongings. Do you just want your clothes, books etc, or do you want me to have the whole house packed up?"

Her jaw dropped. "Just my clothes and things like that will be fine."

I didn't bother informing her that if I had my way she may as well bring all her things here. That could wait. At least right now she was talking to me again.

"Okay. I'll leave you to settle in as I have a few errands to run. Don't forget, you can ring 1 on the phone, or you can call me on my mobile. If I don't speak to you before, I'll see you in the morning for breakfast, say nine am? The band will be here, and of course, Erica."

A grin broke out across her face. It was like the sunshine in the room had taken possession of her body.

"I forgot she'd be here. Oh, thank God. I need to see my friend more than I need air to breathe right now."

Her tummy rumbled and she looked down bashfully.

"I'll go and chase up that food," I said, and I left the room wishing I could make that smile appear across her face, rather than a scowl.

🎸

It was nice to be home after six months on the road. I hadn't actually spent that much time here, but as soon as I'd found the Poplar Height's house with its large grounds and attached woodland it had sung to me of home and settling down. The band's success following the end of the competition had been a whirlwind, making us multi-millionaires almost overnight, but we'd hardly had chance to take in the reality of it all, sucked into a constant cycle of touring, recording, guest appearances, and interviews. My plans had been to have a weekend of rest initially. That had been thwarted by the mate-calling. Later tonight, Zak, Erica, and Roman would be here. They were staying for a while. Zak and Erica had stayed at the Broadleaf Hotel until today as Zak had yet to find somewhere to live.

Roman usually slept outdoors, but he'd recently purchased an old car park and a large piece of woodland in Poplar Heights. It was at the far side of my own woods, our boundaries separated by a stream. The car park had been cleared and he was in the process of having a luxury lodge built. I'd told him he could use my woodland too whenever he liked, as long as he was okay sharing with wolves when they dropped by.

He had of course asked before purchasing something so close to my own property, saying he didn't want to be too far away, as the band were the only family he had. Suddenly, I felt sorry that I'd caused him some distress. I'd have to make it up to him... after I'd had a little more fun at his expense.

I would have told Freya that Erica was coming tonight if I'd not thought she would have kept herself awake. She needed to sleep. I'd messaged Zak to tell Erica to come over and let it be a nice surprise. Noah and Stacey had their own place and so Noah would be coming here only to record and I'd see him in the morning. Stacey was starting rehearsals for her upcoming stint in the West End. Noah knew if we ended up recording into the night there was a bed for him here. There was room for all of them and there always would be. They were my family, just as much as my real family.

And thinking of which, I'd need to tell the staff that the bedrooms needed to be aired if my family were coming.

I plodded about the house for a while. I had something to eat, looked through my mail, and drank a beer, until the doorbell rang signalling that my guests were here.

Miles showed them in and Erica came forward and hugged me. Zak gave me the middle finger and Roman stood there... shaking.

"Man, you're not still fucking scared after what happened in the hotel room, are you?" I scrunched up my nose at him. I turned to the others. "Look at his grave face. Gosh, I thought you'd be dying to get here, Roman."

As his fist swung and hit me square in the jaw, I realised my friend had not been shaking with fear after all, but rather shaking in rage. Fuck me, a satyr in a temper was strong.

Chapter 7

Freya

I was exhausted and my mind felt like Mr. Messy's body on the cover of his book. The past ten days had been crazy to the point where I was actually craving some normal. Unfortunately, while my friend was dating an ex-incubus who was best mates with a shifter, a vampire, and a satyr, I didn't think normal was intending to visit my life again anytime soon.

The week with the band had been an experience I'd embraced because when did things like that ever come up for most people to participate in? But while I'd gone there hoping for a shagathon with Rex, I'd fully expected to go home, return to my house and my job, and then eventually meet Mr Right (a human) and live a nice, happy, comfortable life.

I did not expect a shifter to declare me his mate, stalk me to the point where I lost my job and couldn't return to my home, and then end up living with him (albeit temporarily) in his eighteen bedroomed mansion. And if that wasn't bonkers enough, my ex had proposed to someone else a week after I'd ditched him and then changed his mind and proposed to me.

Right now, I really, really needed a good chat with my friend. It was a shame then that she wasn't answering her messages.

A knock came at the door, and I found a sweet looking,

smiling woman standing in the hall. She introduced herself as Cath.

I stepped aside as she pushed in the trolley she'd brought. She hadn't stuck to bacon sandwiches and as the smell of the food hit me, I was glad. I was suddenly starving.

Cath was a small lady, probably about five foot two. She had short brown hair and just exuded calm.

"I know I've gone a bit overboard, but I saw what the idiot did. It was on TikTok. He says you can't even go back to your own house. Anyway, there's tea, coffee, and fresh water with lemon. I also added Coca-Cola and Sprite, both diet and normal. Then there are pancakes and a choice of toppings, bacon sandwiches, a cheese and tomato pizza, a jacket potato with a bowl of grated cheese, and a side salad, and oh, there's a bowl of vegetable soup and a baguette. There are a few different sandwiches... and some crisps."

My mouth dropped open.

"And I'll just put these desserts in your fridge for later, shall I? There's a selection of chocolate—both bars and boxes—a slice of toffee cheesecake, a portion of tiramisu, a slice of chocolate fudge cake, and a slice of apple pie."

She busied herself putting things away and placing food on the table in front of the sofa. "There we are. Tuck in and if you need anything else, just give me a shout."

"I don't think I'd need anything else if I was staying the rest of the year." I laughed. "But thank you. It looks delicious and I am indeed ravenous."

Cath beamed. "Okay, I'll leave you to it. It's very nice to meet you, Miss Steel."

"Please, call me Freya."

She nodded. "It's lovely to meet you, Freya."

As soon as she left the room, I dived onto that food like a dog in fox poo.

It was a groaning Buddha lookalike version of myself that eventually made it to lie down on my bed. All I'd managed after eating was to load up the food trolley and place it outside of my room like they did in hotels and hope that was the right thing to do. Taking the eReader out of my drawer, I chose a book and read for a while, until my body no longer felt like it would burst open, and then I fell asleep in my clothes because my things had never arrived.

When I woke, the sunlight was coming through the windows, and someone was knocking loudly on my door. The knocks were getting ever louder and more frantic, but the person on the other side wasn't giving me a chance to wake up.

"I'm coming in," came a muffled voice and the door pushed open and in walked my best friend.

"Erica! You know I'm hopeless in a morning." I let my head flop back onto my pillow.

I heard the familiar clink of the food trolley. "That's why I brought breakfast including lots of tea and coffee, so you can get up and we'll have breakfast on the balcony."

I groaned and pulled the duvet over my head. "Five more minutes."

Erica did indeed leave me for five minutes, but only because she was opening the balcony doors and setting up breakfast. The next thing I knew, she was directing someone to place boxes down at the far side of my bed. I was actually starting to get quite hot under the duvet, but there was no way I was emerging while there were strangers in my room.

It seemed like an eternity when Erica finally said goodbye and closed the door. I pushed the duvet off myself, panting.

"Come on. Let's get breakfast and then I want you to tell me everything that's been happening with you and Rex."

I remembered I was still wearing my clothes from yesterday. I'd shower after breakfast and then go through the boxes to find myself something clean to put on. After needing to stretch and yawn a few times, I made my way out onto the balcony and fully took in the view of the gardens and woodland.

"It's simply stunning, isn't it?" Erica stated.

"Breathtaking." I sat opposite her. "But overwhelming. I mean, you're dating Zak, but it's only been a few days. What if you get used to all this and then it's over?"

"I'm just intending on making the most of every day. It's all anyone has anyway, Frey. This moment we're in right now. So I suggest you just enjoy yourself and see what happens."

"I can most definitely sit here with this amazing view and delicious breakfast and chat with my best friend. That is not a hardship." I began to butter a slice of toast. "Have you seen Rex then? How is he this morning?"

"Apart from a small bruise on his chin, he's fine."

"Huh?"

"Roman punched him for what he did to him in the hotel. And then for winding him up about it afterwards."

My brows furrowed.

"Do you not know that Roman thought he'd been buried alive?" She filled me in on the story and while I felt sorry for him, I couldn't help but laugh.

"And what's your role this week, Miss PR?"

"I'm getting the scoop on them in the recording studio and on their downtime away from the touring. I'm going to stay here until either the album is done, or I'm bored of Zak. That means you and I can spend some time together!"

I squealed and threw my arms around her. "Oh my god, I'm so happy. I didn't want to be on my own."

My hug soon turned into my clutching my friend in fear as I heard a loud thumping noise coming nearer. Was there an earthquake?

There was almost what would have looked like a joint suicide, as a brown wolf flew through the door and bounded up to the open balcony doors. How Erica and I didn't jump so high we sailed over the railings I do not know.

Noah wasn't far behind the wolf.

"Hey, you two! Erm, Freya, if you're gonna squeal, then you need to know you're gonna end up with Rex in your room, as his protective stance means he has to check you're okay and not in pain."

"Oh. Okay." I stared at the wolf who was just staring at me with hungry eyes. I didn't know whether to throw my bacon and sausages at it just in case it was eyeing me up for its own breakfast.

Zak sauntered in. "Yeah, you might want to remember that if you read anything a bit risqué on your eReader or binge on Henry Cavill movies, your 'little death' might be misinterpreted." He winked.

Noah elbowed him. "Not the right time."

"How does he, er, change back?" I queried because despite the minutes ticking past, I was no less nervous of the fact a huge hairy wolf was standing in front of me. Oh my god, it was moving nearer to me! I clung onto Erica more firmly.

"Ow, you're going to break one of my ribs," Erica complained.

I stared at her.

"Please do not tell me you are weighing up whether to throw me at Rex in order to save yourself," she added, pushing me away. "He wants you, not me."

"It's okay, erm, Rex." The wolf's eyes seemed to sparkle with their yellow hue which didn't make me feel any more comfortable about being in his proximity.

"You're fine, Freya. Rex won't harm you. You're his mate. He's here only to protect you. If you calm him down, he'll return to his human looking self."

Calm him down? Meaning I had to pet the wolf? Great. Yet another thing I didn't have on this week's to-do list.

Slowly, I inched forward, reaching out my arm. I couldn't look at him. It felt too weird and too intimate, so I just headed towards his back until I hit fur, and I began to smooth my palm down it. His fur was so soft and glossy. I found that stroking it made me feel calmer. Opening my eyes, I started to stroke the top of the wolf's head.

"It's okay, Rexy," I assured him. "I'm fine, look, as you can see. I was just excited to see my best friend and that's why I made the screaming noise. Now you can turn back into normal Rex, okay?"

"And that's my cue to leave," announced Zak. "Come on, little E, let's leave the wolf and his mate. Noah, you coming?"

"Yep."

"I can't leave Freya here alone," Erica protested, just as Rex shuddered under my hand and I found myself staring down at a completely naked drummer with an extremely huge drumstick.

"Why the hell didn't you tell me that was about to happen, Zak Jones? My eyes." Erica ran from the room, her boyfriend chuckling behind her.

Noah looked down at Rex. "We will be starting to warm up in the *heavily soundproofed* recording studio."

Rex nodded and I narrowed my eyes at his friend. "There will be no need for you to be in any *heavily soundproofed* room whatsoever. Now take this animal with you."

"No can do. He just showed you his true self. You two need to talk." With that, Noah walked out of the room and closed the door behind him, leaving us alone.

"Do you think you could put some clothes on? You're putting me off my sausages," I huffed, turning to walk back out towards my hopefully still hot breakfast.

"Please don't leave me. Not even to just step outside," Rex's voice was a plea from his lips, his voice quieter than I had ever heard it before.

I turned back around. "Are you okay?"

He shook his head. "I can't bear it, Freya. I'm mated to you. My body wants to serve you, to protect you, to own you, worship you, make love to you. It's killing me." He put his hand to his forehead and pushed his hair back from his face. "My parents are coming tomorrow, and I'm hoping my mum might be able to help work out what's happening with my mate-matching genetics, but while I'm waiting, it's just so... hard."

My eyes went to his drumstick. Wow, it really wanted to bang something.

I excuse myself for what I did next, because basically it was an act of mercy towards this poor man who was in pain at my feet.

I decided I would eat a sausage as planned. Just not the one on the table outside.

Dropping to my knees, I shuffled myself over towards Rex.

"Freya." The way he said my name was my undoing. Damn him.

He didn't give me a chance to approach his cock. Standing, he whisked me up into his arms and he stalked towards the bed.

I expected him to throw me on it and ravish me like a raw steak, but he placed me down on the mattress almost reverently before stripping me slowly, his eyes feasting on every inch of my skin, so that by the time I was finally naked, I felt I was the one in pain from longing.

I cast my eyes up to the man sat astride my thighs. His arms were thick and muscly with biceps I could swing on. In this position his thighs were taut. I ran a hand down one feeling the hard muscle. Jeeeezzzuuussss. He had an eight pack, defined pecs, and a smattering of dark hair over his chest. Not too much. Just enough for me to want to trail my fingers there and then down, down, my fingertip following the happy trail that then bushed out around the tree trunk between his legs.

Your pussy is going to be ruined. You'll need surgery. My inner voice shrieked. But my vagina was having none of her warnings.

I'm so fucking wet it's gonna slide in and out like a pen nib when the clicky bit is in the hands of a person with severe anxiety.

You'd have thought I'd be concerned about the fact my mind was having a war with my vag, but you see while they were arguing, my eyes had stolen the show. I couldn't look away from Rex. His hair, his bone structure, his taut jaw, his amber-coloured eyes, his pouty Mick-Jagger-style lips, his Adam's apple, the scruff at his jaw and top lip. Then down that perfectly sculpted body that was ready to do dirty, dirty things to me.

He leaned over me, and I felt his warm breath on my skin as his breathing increased to a deeper pace, and then his mouth closed on mine and my eyes closed.

My pussy yelled *VICTORY*.

Rex's mouth pressed down onto mine searching and sweeping. His tongue pushed insistently to gain entrance and I opened my own mouth. His right hand trailed down my body, cupping and squeezing my breast, and trailing further, making my skin goose bump as he hit my ticklish spots. As he reached the trail from my hip down to my core, I bucked as it proved too much.

But I needn't have worried. It wasn't his intention to delay things tickling my inner leg. His large digits swept across my heat, flicking and tantalising my clit and then delving deeper into my slick wetness. He pushed a finger inside me, and I groaned, two, and I almost came there and then. I didn't want to think of another man, but John's dick had only been the equivalent of two of Rex's fingers in how it had felt inside me. I was keen to continue this experiment.

Rex having been a hairy manslut and being able to understand the beat played itself out beautifully across my clit and in minutes I was convulsing around his fingers while shouting out pleas for Rex to not stop.

"I have no intention of stopping, not until we're both satisfied," he growled out.

I hoped later he'd growl against my core because I'd bet that vibration was better than any washing machine on its spin cycle.

One of those mighty thighs pushed my own further apart. He reached into my bedside drawer and opened up a black box, taking out a condom. After sheathing himself in what must have been an Extra, Extra, Extra-large size, he positioned himself between my thighs, and then pushed in.

My pussy squeezed itself in protest against this huge intrusion. An inch had gone in, and my body was trying to expel it back out. Great, cock-blocked by my own vagina.

Rex stopped, his eyes meeting mine.

"Look at me, Freya."

I did but I wasn't sure it made things any more relaxing as I realised Rex Colton was trying to fuck me.

His mouth lowered to mine again and he took his time kissing me, until I was so lost in the motion of his mouth, I hadn't realised he'd been slowly tilting his hips. He slowly sunk into me, inch by delicious inch, filling me to the hilt. It was glorious.

He kept the pace slow and kept on kissing me. My body adjusted to him, and I eventually had to break our kiss as my breaths were coming in short pants and I needed to keep my oxygen intake steady. Rex quickened his pace, picking up my calves and wrapping my legs around his body so he could sink even deeper.

Back and forth, in and out, fast and slow. He drove me crazy until eventually we were frantic, seeking our climaxes, sweat beading our brows.

As I came with the most explosive orgasm I had ever experienced, sure that the earth really had moved and had probably felled several trees in the surrounding woodland, Rex also came, and as he did, he screamed, "MIIIINNNNNNNNEEEEEEEE," as he shook and trembled within me.

It was so loud.

I wasn't sure even a soundproofed room could avoid hearing that, but I definitely knew every member of staff in the house would not have missed it.

I wanted to die of embarrassment. Zak had foreseen this earlier. From le petite mort to a huge death caused from shame.

He may as well just have shouted, 'I DID IT. I FUCKED HER GOOD', while flying a banner with the same words from a plane.

With no indication he had done anything wrong, Rex withdrew from me, and tried to pull me into his large arms. He wanted to snuggle?

I fought against him. It was tricky but luckily because he was sweaty, I was able to wriggle away from him and out of bed.

"I'm going to get a shower and when I come back out you need to have gone."

"What? W-was it not good for you?" he queried, looking ready to go for another round.

"It was fantastic, but I came and I'm good for now, so you can leave and meet the others in the recording studio. *That's if you haven't lost your voice after screaming your possessive crap at the top of your lungs,*" I snapped.

"You are mine. It was just proved how good we are together. I will claim you."

"And now you definitely need to leave before I go get my fork and stick that in your arse cheek, or your eyeball."

"How can you just walk away from me after what we just shared?" His bottom lip wobbled.

It was a good question because I figured walking was going to be a bit of a challenge after that session, but I needed to brazen it out. "It was a fuck. A good fuck, but it was just sex. Get a grip."

"Did you not feel anything for me, anything at all? Did you not catch feelings?" I swear his lip wobbled again.

"I'm going to be catching my own puke in a minute, Rex. Get cleaned up and get on with your day. I will see you later." I walked towards the bathroom.

I heard him mumble something about 'just being used for sex' before I closed the bathroom door.

Chapter 8

Rex

Huh, that had certainly not happened to me before. I had to get rid of women from whatever bed I'd slept in or get out of their room before they started making plans for our future. I did not get kicked out after I'd just rocked someone's world.

Please tell me I *had* rocked her world.

Surely, she'd not faked it?

As I made my way to my room to hit the shower, my stomach suddenly felt like it was lead lined. What if I'd not satisfied my mate? That would be a disaster. I needed my mum. I needed her advice. Otherwise, I was going to be the pack's joke.

The wolf whose mate didn't want him.

The wolf who couldn't give her o's.

No O, just no. That would be my tagline.

Thank goodness my mum would be here tomorrow.

I enjoyed the feeling of a nice hot shower and started thinking of some of the bits of melodies I'd been working on and hummed along while I got clean. I'd better go face the band. It wasn't a good start when one of the band members didn't show for the first get together to work on new material when it was his studio and he'd insisted the band be ready for nine am sharp.

With towel dried hair and casually dressed in jeans and a white Bon Jovi t-shirt, I made my way into the studio.

"Yep, he sowed his wild oats. Hand over the money, human boy." Roman held his hand out towards Zak.

Zak huffed at Erica. "I told you, but 'Oh no, Freya won't give in that easily'," he mimicked in a sarcastic voice.

"Excuse me, I'm off to see my best friend." Erica gave Zak a chin lift. "And you won't be sowing any wild oats if you do that again, human boy."

Roman sniggered and received a flinty stare from Zak.

By this time, I'd flopped onto one of the soft, sumptuous sofas in the room.

"For someone who just got some, you're not looking very... satisfied." Noah came to sit next to me leaning forward.

"I thought we'd connected." I threw up my hands in a quizzical manner. "Everything seemed to have gone *very* well." I rubbed at my chin. "And then she asked me to leave and threatened to stab me in the arse or eye with a fork."

"You should have let her do it. At least then you could have come and announced that you'd had a great fork." Zak smiled enigmatically.

Noah's head snapped towards Zak. "Not helping."

"No one appreciates me today." Zak sighed. "I shall sit quietly and write some chart-topping lyrics." He got up and sat on a different sofa taking an A4 pad and a pen from the coffee table.

Noah squeezed at my arm. "Without going into too much detail, what happened?"

"I felt bereft without my mate's contact, so I just sat on the floor, and she came over to me. We kissed and then I took her to bed. It was incredible. Well, to me anyway. She seemed happy, but then after she just got angry and chucked me out."

"Rex, you must have done something to piss her off."

"I just shouted she was mine. She got pissed off, accusing me of saying it too loudly, and then when I let her know I would be claiming her, that was it."

"Oh, Rex. One step at a time. You've leapt in with all four furry paws and bared your teeth."

"He's a wolf," Zak shouted across. "He's supposed to be all alpha, club your mate over the head, drag them to your lair, give 'em the D so hard they have no choice but to submit cos they're no longer capable of walking out anyway." He huffed. "He's not a fucking puppy."

"Yeah, but actually it was my puppy-dog-eyed expression that worked with her, so maybe I do have to be cuter and fluffier," I pondered.

"Where are your balls? And I don't mean the ones puppies chase and bring back to their owners on command," Zak scolded.

"Zak!" Noah repeated.

"Oh, am I 'not helping'," he said in the same mimicking voice that had got him in trouble with Erica. He went back to scribbling on his pad.

"What am I going to do?" I asked Noah. Realising Roman had been quiet all this time, I turned to find he was asleep on the floor in the far corner. "What's up with him?"

"He's having problems sleeping because of what you did to him."

"Oops."

"Yeah, you might want to apologise rather than laugh at him. Especially now you're experiencing someone taking the piss out of you first-hand." Noah nodded towards Zak.

"I've got the beginnings of a new song," Zak announced. "You know... if anyone wants to work today."

"Okay, fair enough. I'll leave my issues until my parents arrive tomorrow and then hopefully, they can offer me some advice.

Let's hear what you have so far." I sat up and leaned forward and Noah did the same.

"It's called *Missing You*." Zak tapped his knee starting a beat and then began to sing.

You've been in my life for so long now.
 I can't imagine my life without
 You with me

I didn't treat you right somehow
 But please do not desert me now
 Forgive me

"Loving it so far. Carry on." I smiled.

You were there
 And then you left
 And now I'm feeling so bereft

Come back to me
 I need you bad
 Cos I'm just a dick if left without...
 my gonads.

As Zak collapsed clutching his stomach, I leapt across the space between us ready to punch him in the face.

Noah pulled us apart.

"Zak Jones, get out of here until you can behave."

"Hey, it worked, didn't it? He's found his fire again. Now

stop being such a fucking pussy, Rex, and let's get some work done."

I turned to Noah and shook my shoulders. "Dude has a point. I fucking hate it when shit for brains has a point."

"Don't we all," mumbled Roman from the corner.

🎸

We worked through until early evening, only stopping for a bite of a sandwich or a quick carton of O-neg for the vamp. Roman had woken up and joined in, and I'd apologised for my behaviour. Inside, I still thought it was hilarious, but given he was my friend, I felt a little guilty about the fact he'd not been able to sleep since.

As I'd nipped out for a toilet break in the afternoon, I'd messaged Miles and asked him to sort me a little surprise out and then I'd contacted Stacey because I needed her to use some witchcraft to finish the mini project off.

We wrapped up for the day and I turned to my friends. "I've arranged for us to have a picnic on the edge of the woods. It's all prepared, so let's go eat and get some fresh air. The women should already be there," I informed Zak and Noah.

The four of us rode in a small, motorised buggy to the edge of the woods. It was next to where Roman's lodge was due to be built and near to the adjoining woodlands.

He looked wide-eyed at the bunting strewn around the trees and the large summerhouse structure that had been erected near the stream.

"What's this?" he asked as the women walked forward to meet us.

"This, my friend, is my apology for what I did to you. The summerhouse is a space you can escape to when you're fed up of us all until your home is built, and Stacey has put wards on your woodland so that no one can come onto the land unless they have your say-so. She'll tell you the wording you need to use, but you can be sure that when you go to sleep no one can disturb you.

You can, pardon my pun here, rest in peace, and sleep a good night's sleep in the firm knowledge you will not be disturbed unless you've wished it so. The summerhouse has blankets, pillows, and a sofabed."

"You're forgiven." Roman jumped up and down in excitement. "When I have my lodge, it shall be perfect." Roman looked at Freya. "How you cannot want this man as your mate is beyond me. He is one of the most genuine people I have ever met."

She bent down, picked up a handful of soil and undergrowth, and threw it at Roman's head. He shrieked and ran up to a tree, hugging it.

"Still think that, tree-hugger?" She looked around at us. "What?"

I sighed. "Let's go to the area set up for the picnic. I'll entice Roman away from the tree with the promise of hard liquor."

Although Freya was still ignoring me for the most part, the picnic was pleasant. We'd lit a small fire as it went dusk and enjoyed the food and drink. There were large cushions to sit on, trees to lean on, and camping chairs for those who wanted one. We showcased a few snippets of what we'd put together to get the women's take on them. Zak wisely chose to not sing his song about my supposed missing bollocks.

"It's lovely here." Stacey cuddled into Noah's side. "Once your lodge is built, I think you're going to be very happy here, Roman."

"Yeah, it'll be a good start on things," he said, unspoken words hanging in the air.

Our friend was a very private man. Out of all four of us he was the one we knew the least about. He was largely estranged from his family and tended to keep his cards close to his chest. The fact he trusted us meant a lot as he gave the impression he didn't trust easily and that was why I couldn't bear to have upset him with the whole buried alive thing, even if it was hilarious.

"Maybe you could invite Harley for a picnic when everything's ready? She'll be back from America in another few weeks, right?" Erica stated.

Roman shrugged. "I don't know. There's a lot I need to sort out." Reading between the lines he didn't just mean about developing the land.

I shrugged my shoulders at Erica who looked forlorn. The woman wanted everyone living their happy ever afters, but you couldn't force things. Lead a satyr to water and they'd want it murky so they could frolic in its filthy depths.

"So the family are coming tomorrow, Rex?" Erica changed the subject. "Or just your parents?"

"My parents and some of my younger siblings," I replied.

"How many do you have?" she asked.

"There are seventeen of us."

Freya and Erica's jaws dropped open in perfect synchrony.

"Has your mother spent her entire life pregnant?" Freya asked, relenting on her not speaking to me rule, her curiosity having got the better of her.

"Shifters are only pregnant for three months and tend to have large litters. For my mum she had me, then Paloma, then four, then six, and then another five."

Freya paled. "Condoms work for shifters, don't they? Like one hundred percent work?"

"They work the same as for everyone. So more or less."

"I don't like the sound of less. I don't like the sound of that *at all*." Her voice rose in pitch and volume, and she grabbed the wine bottle nearest to her and drank it like it was an oasis of water in a hot and arid desert.

"You'll harm the cubs drinking that," I announced. She dropped the bottle, looking wild-eyed.

"Leave her alone and stop tormenting her, Rex Colton, or I

will stop singing your praises and get her to call Splinter and see what he's up to."

"If she calls Splinter he'll be *up to* waiting for his arms and legs to be encased in plaster," I growled. "But thanks for having my back. Love ya, Ricci."

"Who the fuck are you pet-naming?" Zak shouted, jumping to his feet. "Stick to trying to impress your own woman. My little E is not your Ricci."

I winked at him. "Do you feel impotent not having any supernatural powers now, Zakky?"

"No, because I'm madly in love and can concentrate on my future with my beautiful girlfriend. Do you feel impotent having a mate that thinks you're a bellend?"

The next thing I knew was I couldn't move. I was glued to the spot.

"It's for your own good until you calm yourself down," Stacey informed me. "Once you're calm, you'll be able to move again, but if you try to make any moves towards Zak, you'll find yourself still again."

Zak sniggered.

"Do you want me to put a spell on your mouth? Because believe me I have been offered millions to do so."

That shut him up.

"So tell me more about who's coming later from your family," Stacey encouraged.

"My three youngest brothers and two sisters. They're six. So prepare yourselves because it could get a little wild in the house. Luckily, I have the large garden, which I also had fenced off today and warded by your lovely self." I smiled at Stacey. "Because otherwise the buggers would climb it and we'd be searching the trees."

"So many siblings must have been hectic to live around," Erica stated.

"It's all I know, remember? We're not used to having one kid like humans. We find that strange. Our litters with other wolves are like I say, usually around five or six, and with a human woman around three on average."

"Th-three?" Freya picked up the walkie-talkie I had brought in case of needing to contact Miles or Cath given there was unreliable mobile reception in the woods.

"H-hello. Can you arrange a doctor for me? N-no, I'm not ill, just a private matter. Thank you. Yes, as soon as possible though. A telephone consultation will do, yes. Thank you again."

She put it back down. "I need the morning after pill, just to be sure. My body and mind are not prepared for three wolves to descend from my vagina. Please excuse me. I need to lie down," she said. I figured the wine intake and shock had taken their toll as she curled up next to a tree, pulled a blanket over herself and closed her eyes.

Chapter 9

Freya

I now had my laptop from home, so as soon as I was back in my room, I fired it up and paid my membership for access to Frankie's database because I needed access all areas.

In particular, I wanted to ensure I was not going to have cubs anytime soon. I also wanted to fully research shifter families, because Rex's mum and dad were turning up tomorrow evening and I had no idea how they were going to react to me.

The liquor cabinet and fridge had been filled with drinks and I opened a can of mojito. Maybe instead of alcohol, I needed to do some deep breathing? Some kind of yogic exercise so I could calm down and think straight. That would be something else to look up though, so I plumped for the mojito and the laptop.

Shifter Families

(Not to be reproduced. Copyright F. Love, 2018, 2019, 2020)
Wolf shifters are extremely close to their families and quite often live in large family groups, or in commune type accommodation. If you disrespect a family member, this can cause you to be outcast from the pack.

A potential mate will be introduced to the family at the earliest opportunity in order for the family to accept them as a new member of the pack. The Alpha of the pack shall have the final say. Should the mating not be accepted, the wolf will either have to leave their pack and live with their mate pack-less or commit to a life of misery without their mate.

In recent times, some witches have developed spells which can temporarily grant reprieve from this misery, but the wolf is still never quite their old self.

Great, so if I didn't mate with him, he could have to live a life of misery? Well, no pressure there then. It seemed all I could do right now was to wait and see what happened when Rex's family turned up.

Sighing, I looked around the room. It was the most fabulous home, and my every need was catered for at present, but it wasn't *my* home. I had to find a way to get a new job and to return to my house and be safe at my earliest opportunity. This week though I'd pretend I was on holiday with my best mate. The weather was lovely and somewhere in these boxes I had bikinis. I'd send out for up-to-date suntan lotion and hope they had sun loungers, because me and my eReader had a date in that vast garden tomorrow.

※

Tuesday morning was an entirely different experience. I woke knowing where I was, and this time I showered, dressed, and made my way downstairs just before half past eight, to search out the kitchen.

"Good morning, Freya. Where is it you want to go? I'll take you." Of course, Rex was going to be three steps behind me wherever I went. Hopefully tonight it would be over once his mum had sorted things.

"I'm looking for the kitchen, but it's okay, I'm just following the scent."

"You can scent? I wonder if that's because of our coupling?" Rex said excitedly.

I rubbed at my eyes. This was too much BC—before coffee. "I can smell toast and coffee, Rex."

"Oh. Well, I was headed that way anyway." He fell into step beside me. "Did you sleep well?"

"I did, thank you. Very well." I decided to change the subject from me. "Are you ready to get back into the recording studio?"

His voice was full of enthusiasm. "I can't wait. I spent part of the night working on some new stuff. Letting the others hear it and getting their comments and corroboration is part of the fun. You should come listen."

"Maybe I will." I thought about it. Why not? See how tracks were put together. "Although my schedule is packed today. I'm planning on sunbathing and reading."

He cleared his throat. "I know you haven't accepted the position as my mate, but would you come and meet my family this evening? It won't just be you. I'm arranging a buffet on the terrace at six pm. Everyone from last night will be there, as well as my mum, dad, and younger siblings."

"As long as they don't try to pressure me in any way, I'd really like to meet them," I said honestly. "As your family, not as *my* family. Okay?"

"Understood."

He was being polite and so I decided while he was being that way, I could try to be civil too. "I know this is weird and I'm sure things will work out as they need to. I'm reading up about shifter history, just to make myself aware of your culture and traditions."

"I appreciate that."

"It's mainly so I don't accidentally do anything that means I'm stuck with you," I added.

He sighed at that. "Look, I get it. I was a complete dipshit towards you and now I've changed my mind, and you aren't feeling the same way. I'm a week too late. We'll talk to my parents tonight after the banquet buffet and take it from there, okay?"

"Okay."

"Just know that while I am being reasonable right now, the wolf inside me wants to pick you up, take you to my room, and repeat what happened yesterday." Rex's eyes hooded with lust.

Oh boy. This did not help my resistance and it wasn't helped further when Rex leaned down towards me and whispered in my ear. "My wolf can smell your desire."

I ran off into the large dining room that had appeared ahead, Cath already bustling around serving Roman. Rex ended up coming to a halt behind me, his hand on my hip and his hard-on pressing into me.

"You're not helping me resist you, Freya. You mustn't run. My wolf will chase you."

"Oh of course, sorry," I said.

Move Freya.

Move away from the anaconda in his pants.

"Morning, you two. Did I miss something? Are you together now?" Roman's voice broke up my being hypnotised by Rex's trousersnake and I whipped forward, did an about turn and walked towards the dining table where Roman and Cath's amused faces greeted me.

"No. We are *not* together." I huffed. "I am just being stalked by this idiot."

"I'm not stalking her, my wolf is." Rex said, like it was nothing to do with him.

Pulling a chair out, I dropped into a seat. "Oh, that's how we are playing it now is it? You have multiple personalities and it's your wolf who wants me?" Then I realised this was actually the truth. "Oh, shit. That *is* the truth. You didn't want me and then the mate thing clicked. It *is* the wolf that wants me. Not you. I'm calling you the idiot, but I'm the idiot. It makes so much sense now thinking of you as a divided being." My nostrils flared. "And it makes things a lot clearer for me. You're still an utter dickhead," I yelled at Rex.

"Tea, coffee, water, and juices are on the table. What can I get you to eat, Freya?" Cath asked, a little louder than usual, ending my rant.

"Anything." My shoulders slumped. "I'm not that hungry anymore."

I knew I was being ridiculous. Having received the message loud and clear last week that Rex wasn't interested, I'd said *I* wasn't interested at his sudden mate-match crap. But deep down inside, in a part of me that I'd not wanted to face, a locked-up part of my heart, I'd been happy Rex now wanted me. Happy that he was suffering, and if I admitted it to myself, after he'd suffered for a while, I'd hoped to find he genuinely wanted me. But it wasn't to be. It *was* just his wolf, not him. And it hurt more than I could let show.

So I mustn't show defeated body language and sulk.

Sitting up straighter, I reached over for the coffee pot. "Actually, is there any chance for some fresh watermelon to start, and then pancakes with lemon and sugar?" I'd been fancying watermelon since my drunken episode.

"Of course. I'll get that organised." Cath smiled.

"Oh, also. Where's the nearest place I can go to for suntan lotion and a sun lounger?"

"The pantry is stocked with all different lotions so just let me know what factor you need, and the garden store has loungers, swings, egg chairs, loveseats, chairs with storage for wine and coffee etc. There are tables too."

"Goodness me. This place is like a magical Narnia," I exclaimed. "If I could have some factor 30 and a selection of different loungers and seats and tables for in case Erica might want to join me?"

"Not a problem. I'll have them set out in the garden. If you prefer to sit by the pool, then there is already furniture there."

My mouth gaped open. It took me a few moments to close it again. "There's a pool?"

"There are two pools." Rex took a seat at the side of Roman facing me. "An indoor one and an outdoor one. As it's looking like it's going to be a beautiful day outside, then Miles will take the coverings off everything. It's heated and there's also a jacuzzi."

"The indoor one has a series of steam rooms, and we can book for someone to come and do treatments for you," Cath added before she left the room.

At that point I considered becoming Rex's mate just so I never had to leave the estate. Then common sense prevailed, and I decided to chat to Roman and ignore Rex.

"Did you sleep okay, Roman, after everything?" He looked much better than he had yesterday.

"I did. Thank you for asking, Freya. I took a weighted blanket up to a tree at the side of the stream and I slept so peacefully, drifting off while listening to the water's tinkle."

"That would just make me want to pee all night."

Roman laughed. I realised his laugh was a rare occurrence. I saw a hint of a different Roman and it was a good change. I began to notice what Harley was attracted to. I dropped my thoughts as I noted that Rex was gripping his cutlery hard while counting to ten under his breath.

"Yep, the satyr life would not do for me," I concluded, and Rex managed to put his knife and fork down on the table.

"It's not for most people, believe me," Roman answered and then he took a mighty mouthful of his scrambled eggs which I guessed was his way of communicating he was saying no more on the matter... or he was very hungry this morning after a good night's sleep. Either way, I would now concentrate on my own breakfast that Cath was bringing in and then I'd concentrate on improving my suntan. I saw a note tucked under the plate.

Doctor will call to see you at ten thirty am. He is aware of Rex's heritage.

I looked up at Cath and mouthed, 'Thank you'.

The others joined us. My best friend had arrived looking mussed up, her boyfriend smug and yawning a lot. Then Noah had turned up shortly afterwards.

"It's not yet hot enough for sunbathing and your best friend will be sitting in the recording studio making notes for the blog, so why don't you do what I suggested and come down to the recording studio and watch us in action?" Rex suggested.

"Yeah." Zak grinned. "I dropped part of a new song yesterday. I might let you hear it."

"Run," Rex drawled.

"Huh?" Zak was none the wiser.

"I think he's giving you a head start before *that* song becomes about you. He'll probably play with the detached pair if you catch my drift," Erica told him.

Zak placed his hands over his genitals. I had absolutely no idea what they were all talking about.

"Does someone want to enlighten me?" I asked. "What have I missed?"

Zak turned to me. "Nothing. Nothing at all. Come to listen though. Erica will love to have you there."

"Yes, Erica, who can speak for herself, would." Erica huffed.

"Sorry, babe. I forgot your mouth is no longer full." He winked.

Erica blushed the shade of the tomatoes on her plate.

Cath had brought me some watermelon. I picked up a slice and began to eat it. The juice dripped down my chin.

"That reminds me of good times," Zak said, squeezing my shoulder.

"Yeah?" I wiped my lips and chin with a napkin. "Summer holidays abroad? They used to sell it at the beach when we were in Greece."

"No, I meant this morning." A piece of toast was shoved straight into Zak's mouth by his better half.

"Excuse me." Rex stood up, sounding half-strangulated and he rushed out of the room.

"That'll be him late to the recording studio... again." Noah groaned.

"What's up with him?" Erica asked and I shrugged my shoulders while meeting her gaze.

"Goodness knows. Probably just another attempt at manipulating me into his bedroom. You know, I go and see if he's okay. He gives me the sad eyes again. Then he's shouting MINNEEEE again."

Zak, now free of toast, snorted.

"He's not manipulating you," Noah said matter-of-factly. "But he's in close proximity to you, and his so-called friend keeps talking about sex. I'm guessing the watermelon incident almost finished him off, so he's gone to actually finish himself off."

"Yeah, you're not my type, but watching you groaning in pleasure as you bit that melon and the juice all ran down your face. Well, I'm only... satyr." Roman added.

Reality flooded me. Rex had left because watching me eat watermelon had given him the horn. And he'd gone to jerk off. My fantasies were minutes away. I was sitting with watermelon, sugar... and a hard cock, was, if I moved fast enough, within reach.

"It might be an idea to find out if Rex and I are sexually compatible. I was too annoyed yesterday to make an informed decision," I announced, and then grabbing the remaining watermelon and the sugar, I ran out of the room. I mean, there was an hour until the doctor came. I might as well make the most of the opportunity.

Chapter 10

Rex

I kicked open the door to my room. Fucking thing went so hard it rebounded off the wall and nearly knocked me the fuck out. Throwing myself onto my bed, I let out a howl of anger and frustration. Fuck it. I was a wolf, so my friends would have to deal with hearing him. My wolf wasn't separate to me, not really. He was part of me. Yes, sometimes his presence became stronger, but that was only as that part of him wasn't being answered right now; his call to his mate ignored. He was bewildered and unsettled, and that made me bewildered and unsettled.

A knock sounded at the door. I sniffed the air. Freya? Huh, had she come to stick her kitten heel in a little harder?

"Not now," I shouted.

"Erm, are you sure?" she replied in a not-angry-at-all voice. In fact, she sounded quite... horny.

I sprung off the bed as my cock sprung against my pants. I had the door open in less than three seconds.

So fast, Freya took a few steps backwards, almost dropping

the watermelon and the sugar bowl she had on a plate in her hands.

"Wanna play?" She winked.

I took the plate from her and closed the door behind her.

"For real?" I queried.

"I have a fantasy I can make real. No strings, Rex, just lots and lots of foreplay and sex. Can you handle it?"

"If you can handle this?" I dropped my joggers.

"Can you stream music?" she asked me. "Only I have to make out to Harry Styles. It's part of my fantasy."

"You are talking about his music, aren't you? Not that we have to watch him on a video or something?"

"I want to fuck to *Watermelon Sugar*," she announced clearly.

"Kinky. Okay, your wish is my command."

I walked over to my iPod dock, chose the song, and put it on repeat.

By the time I'd turned back around, Freya was completely naked. Was this really happening, or had that door actually hit me in the head after all?

I finished taking off all my own clothes. "Tell me, what specific fantasies did you have about watermelon then?"

"W-well, erm..." She paused. "I can't remember. I was pissed as a fart," she admitted.

I laughed, picking up a slice of the melon and walking towards her slowly. I lifted it to her mouth and watched her lips part.

"Bite."

She took a bite of the melon and just like at the breakfast table, the juice ran down her chin. Only this time, I was able to reach down and lick it off. She swallowed and I claimed her mouth, tasting the watermelon on her tongue. Lifting her up, I carried her to my bed. This time she was exactly where I wanted her. In my room, on my bed.

Her eyes shone as they looked up into my own and her thighs

parted slightly. I bit another piece of the melon off above her tit and then did the same to the other. I got a spoonful of sugar and sprinkled it over each breast and then licked up the wetness that dripped off them, teasing and tasting her puckered nipples as she gasped and writhed.

"So fucking sweet."

Watermelon Sugar played out in the room, and I thanked Harry fucking Styles for making this song. He deserved a knighthood. Shame he probably didn't know about werewolves; I could have asked for him to be made an honorary member of the local pack.

Why are you thinking about Harry fucking Styles right now, dickhead?

I refocused my attention to between Freya's thighs.

"My fantasies do not involve sugar on that area," she informed me. "I once got sand in my bikini bottoms on a beach. Never again."

"Noted." I took a new piece of watermelon and turning it on its edge I got it to stand between her pussy lips and then I ate it. The juice dripped everywhere, mingling with Freya's own as I kept licking her there.

If I'd died right there and then, I'd have left the earth happy, the taste of Freya on my tongue. But I was alive and making the most of it. Watermelon time was over. Now it was time for the main event. Sheathing myself in a condom I'd had tucked under my mattress, I lay between her legs and pushed inside. There was no resistance this time, no hesitation. Just a shout from Freya of, "Oh yes."

I fucked her hard and deep, running my tongue back over her mouth and down her neck. My body was united, man and wolf, as we sought our climax, our mind and body in no doubt whatsoever that this woman belonged to us. But this time, I would silence the beast and not yell out our claim. We needed to wait, to win her over. He agreed, happy to be lost within her depths. I shuddered hard within her, my finger at her clit, pinching and flicking until she also exploded, milking my cock.

We both stopped, gasping, and I withdrew, lying next to her on the bed. This time I made no attempt to cuddle. Instead, we both panted into the otherwise silent room, trying to get our breath back.

After a few minutes, Freya turned to me. "Thank you. I'm sure that beat any drunken fantasy."

"You're welcome," I replied. "Would you like to shower now? Then we could go to the studio."

"I'll go to my room," she said. "Then I won't delay you any further. I have an appointment at half past ten, but I'll come to the studio after."

"Okay. Well, no pressure."

"No, I want to." She smiled.

Fuck me. Was I actually getting somewhere with this woman?

"Thirty-seven seconds," I said.

"Huh? We took longer than that." She giggled.

"That's how long it takes for me to walk at a normal human pace from my room to yours," I told her.

She sighed. "You shouldn't know that. You made it weird again." Climbing off the bed, she quickly dressed.

"You're going to count how long it takes, aren't you?" I smirked as she reached the doorway.

"Of course I fucking am. It's like a compulsion for me to check it out after you said that."

I laughed.

"Bollocks, you smug arsehole." She left and pulled the door firmly shut behind her while scowling at me.

Didn't matter. Right now, I felt on top of the world.

"I'm not getting here until eleven tomorrow," Noah announced. "Seeing as you're always fucking late."

"Emphasis on the fucking," added Roman.

"Miss Cath's breakfast then. See if I care. I had no idea either of these sexual escapades were going to happen," I said, humming *Pour Some Sugar on Me*.

"I'm here to watch you all create the next hit album, so if you want to actually work that'd help me a great deal," Erica shouted from the sofa where she'd clearly been reading a magazine if it lying open at the side of her was a clue.

"Sorry, Erica. I do have a few bits of a song. I'm sorry. It's about my mating dilemma. Can I sing it though? I mean you've all written songs based on your new loves." I raised my brows with a questioning gaze to my bandmates.

"Go on," Noah eye-rolled.

I didn't have an amazing voice like Zak, but I could sing, we all could, which was great for when we did these jamming sessions.

I got my portable electronic drum that I used for these sessions when we were just starting to get new music down. "This is called No Escape."

I began to sing and tap my kit a little to start a beat.

You're in my periphery
   The edge of my proximity
   There's no escape
   It's in your fate
   My intended mate.

You say it's my vanity
   I'm at the edge of insanity
   You can make me wait
   Can pretend to hate
   My fated mate.

. . .

Give in
  Give up
  Surrender to my charms
  Live here
  Love me up
  Crawl into my arms

"That's as far as I've got," I told them, holding my breath.

"I really like it," Zak said.

The others agreed and I let out an exhale.

"Let's get our instruments and put some music to it," Roman encouraged.

"I'll sing, Rex, but can we try with you leading and I'll harmonise? It's your track and your deep bass voice suits it," Zak suggested.

"Sometimes you can actually be a really good bloke." I patted his arm.

"How do you think I landed that gorgeous chick over there," he whispered.

Shaking my head, I smiled. "I'm glad you did, my friend. It's good to see you so happy."

We carried on working. Just after half past eleven, Freya joined Erica on the couch and they both watched. We immediately switched to a different track. I didn't want Freya to hear this yet, and the others knew without me having to tell them as we'd recorded their love songs before. We returned to others we'd been working on. The two women seemed to enjoy watching us do our stuff. We broke off at one pm to go get some lunch, and after that Erica and Freya said they were going to use the pool. I didn't blame them. It was hot out there.

"Okay, grab everything you want to eat and then straight back to the studio." Roman got bossy.

"Yes, Sergeant." I saluted him.

"Your family will be here soon, so let's get as much done as we can while we're in the zone."

"Oh yeah. Good thinking," I told him, and we all did as he'd asked, taking everything back to the studio.

Finally at four, we finished for the day, as my family would be here anytime now.

I slapped Roman on the back. "Thanks, my friend. You were right to call us to order and get us back in here. Great session."

"You're as stupid as him sometimes." He pointed to Zak.

"What?"

"The women were about to go to the pool. One word. Bikini."

My eyes widened as his true reasoning dawned.

"You utter bastard."

Zak turned around and shrugged. "Erica'll model hers for me later. No biggie."

"No biggie?" I shouted. "I missed seeing Freya in her bikini." I had to keep swallowing so as not to howl.

"Yeah, and then you'd have been off up to your room again with your own 'biggie' and no songs would have been recorded for another hour," Roman said.

"Just because you're not getting any." A slow smile built on my face as an image of Freya came to mind. "Hey, maybe she's still out there," I noted, and I took off at a sprint.

She wasn't. They were both long gone. Cath said they'd gone to get ready for the evening buffet.

I didn't have time to imagine what she might have looked like in her two-piece because Miles had answered the door, and five little children came stampeding through. If I hadn't known they were wolves, I'd have pegged them for a monkey/hyena hybrid as they scattered around the place.

My mum ran up to me as Dad carried all the luggage in behind her, pulling a face at me behind her back.

"Darling." She sniffed at me and then turned around to my

father. "He had sex. Eek. Does that mean your mate has accepted your coupledom?"

"How did you...? I showered."

"I'm a mother. I know everything there is to know about my children. We have a raised sense of smell of our cubs. Now answer my question."

"Not yet."

"Oh well, you're clearly making progress. I shall look forward to meeting her. In the meantime, can you arrange a glass of red wine for me, Cath?" she asked, turning around to my cook. "Only..." She pointed at the screaming banshee cubs.

"I've had you a nice bottle of Merlot breathing. Come with me. The men can take care of the children for a while, can't you?" Cath gave me a look. I sometimes wondered which of us was the staff here. Trouble was Cath and Miles knew they were indispensable and therefore they held the power in the relationship.

Miles walked over to my father. "Shall I show you to your rooms, and we can take the luggage up?"

"Thank you, Miles. That would be most kind," Dad said, and as he began to walk away, he gave me the middle finger.

Just as I realised I'd been left with my siblings. Alone.

Chapter 11

Freya

The doctor had reassured me that condoms were just as effective with shifters as they were with humans. When I'd had a bit of a panic attack regardless, he had told me he had a herbal remedy he could give me to make doubly sure. He stood next to my drinks cabinet and I heard the sound of carbonated gas escaping and then he gave me a drink.

I pointed out it smelled and tasted exactly like ginger ale, but he insisted it was a secret recipe to ward off stray sperm.

Clever bastard took the bottle away with him anyway. I'd hazard a guess there was no mention of this 'secret herbal remedy' on Frankie's database. I was suitably reassured though that I wasn't about to have three wolf cubs anytime soon. The doctor had looked quite uncomfortable at times as I tried to emphasise that Rex was very strong and very large and I wasn't entirely convinced his sperm couldn't walk up to my eggs, announce 'your mine' and claim them.

I'd gone back on the pill to make sure that if anything happened after the next couple of weeks I'd be doubly protected. I kind of wasn't acknowledging the fact that I'd accepted that I might keep shagging him. You had to keep your options open and what if Jasper from Twilight just happened to pop by? That reminded me, I must ask Noah if Jackson Rathbone was truly an actor or if he was a vampire for real. Jackson could bite me anytime.

The day had been a pretty awesome day to be fair. Gorgeous food, an amazing fantasy enacting bonk, watching a top band put together new tracks, and sunbathing by the pool with my best friend. It might just be my most favourite day of all time.

That was until I walked downstairs wondering what the hell the noise was and found myself almost knocked over by two small children.

"What the...?"

A very exhausted looking Rex stood in the middle of his living room holding one child upside down by his legs while he wriggled and protested to be freed. Others sped past me so fast I couldn't count them. He'd said there were five, it felt more like fifty.

"Help me," he pleaded.

I tried to grab one, but it was like trying to capture a cloud. It was after five minutes where I found myself sweating like a pig and empty-handed that I discovered I might be a tad pre-menstrual—or I was just downright fucked off—when I hollered at the top of my voice. "Keep still, you little bastards."

To my utter astonishment four children came to stand in front of me and the one in Rex's arms stopped wriggling, asked to be put down in a polite voice, and walked over to me too.

Rex's mouth was hung open. It reminded me of how I must have looked when I first saw his cock.

Five brown-haired, brown-eyed children stood staring at me. Now what did I do? After deciding since I'd already called them bastards, I wasn't going to have endeared myself to his parents anyway, I carried on in the same vein.

"Okay, I'm Freya. It's nice to meet you all, but you're acting like little shits. So rules. You can go outside and run around like crazy."

One turned around to set off to the garden.

"When I tell you clearly that is. Right now, turn and face me and listen."

Jesus. They were doing as I'd asked. What was this strange kid control mojo I had going on?

"There are visitors in this house, me included, and I don't want to be knocked on my arse by you kids flying about. So no running in the house until late, when *if you've behaved*, we can do races up and down the hall, okay?"

Five heads nodded excitedly. "Can we pretend there are hurdles?" one asked.

"Sure."

"I'm gonna pretend there's a deer and I'm gonna tear it apart," another boy said, looking far too enamoured with the idea for my liking.

"Well, you can probably pretend that at the buffet," I suggested.

"Yeaaaahhhh, cooooolll."

"So, we're going to walk. Hear me? WALK to the back doors, and then you can run around. You must not attempt to climb over the fence because there's a witch's spell on it and basically, you'll feel like you're getting the worst tickles every time you go up to it. No trying to get in the pool, no throwing any furniture, just run around and play. I'll see if there are any footballs or skipping ropes, and if not, I'll send for some stuff, okay?"

Five heads nodded. This was fucking weird.

"Right, follow me," I told them, and they walked, *actually walked properly*, all the way to the outside, and then when I told them they could run, they went off, back to their wayward, crazy selves.

Rex stood behind me. "What just happened? Those children do not ever do that. *Ever*."

I turned to gawp at him. "I have absolutely no idea. Maybe I have some kind of wolf mojo?"

"Makes sense. That might be why I mate-matched with you."

"Or it could be that I told the little shits that if anyone they hadn't met before spoke to them, they'd better listen and listen good, or I'd put them in a cage for a week, together." We spun around to see a woman with long, dark hair standing there.

"I can't believe you left me with them all, Mum. I'm traumatised."

Mum? She had the most amazing athletic body and looked like Courtney Cox in the later series of *Friends*. How the hell had this woman birthed seventeen children? She was dressed in blue skinny jeans and a dark-purple t-shirt that showed her midriff for Christ's sake.

"How the hell do you think I feel daily with them?" She rolled her eyes at him.

I blanched as I remembered this kick arse woman was a wolf.

"I'll introduce myself, shall I, son, while you recover from the fact you spent forty-three minutes with your brothers and sisters?" She shook her head that time and stepped forward holding out a hand. "I'm Tanya, Rex's mother, and you must be his mate?"

Oh shit. How did I answer that?

I reached out my own hand and said, "I'm Freya," to find myself yanked against Tanya's body where I was enveloped in a tight hug and... was she... sniffing me?

She let me go. "It's very nice to meet you, Freya. I won't overwhelm you, but I hope we can speak some more after we've eaten. I'd better go keep an eye on my errant youngest children. I'm glad you've been fucking though. That's a good first sign, and you smell fertile, so... so far, so good."

With that, she stepped past me, out of the door and outside, and I watched as she ran around the garden gathering up her kids ready for the buffet that was currently being placed on the terrace.

"Shall we go out to the terrace?" Rex asked me. "There's plenty of wine and whisky. I know I could sure use a scotch or two after that."

"Your siblings or your mother?"

"Both. Welcome to my family."

I side-eyed him.

"I meant welcome to having met some of my family and seeing what they're like."

"Wine. I need wine." I headed off towards the terrace.

The food was lovely as usual, and I stuck to just a couple of glasses of wine so that I could keep my wits about me. I kept feeling Tanya's eyes upon me, but I kept myself distracted by chatting to Erica, Stacey, and the band. I was introduced to Rex's father, who was very friendly and put me at ease, saying I must excuse his wife, who acted before she spoke. This was clearly a cover-all-areas statement as I'd not said a word about my meeting with her.

There was a *lot* of meat at the buffet, and I watched as the children tore it off its bones. Jesus. What if one of them got overexcited and bit me? I'd lose half my arm with those ferocious little jowls.

"Rex's family seem nice, don't they?" Erica announced.

"His mother is ready to pounce on me. I can feel it in my water."

"You have wine. And I thought you were only having two glasses? What number is that?"

"It's number 'Tanya Colton keeps looking at me and I'm close to wetting my pants like a training toddler'."

"You'll be fine." Erica smiled.

I put a hand on my hip. "Fine? Her son has told her I'm his mate. I have no idea what she's going to say to me, but I've a feeling it'll be along the lines of, 'My son is perfect, you'd be lucky to have him, and if you say no and break his heart, I'll bite out your throat'." I took yet another swig of wine. "I can't cope. Fuck, I need to get out of here for a minute."

I took off, running towards the nearest fence, but as I

approached it, I burst out laughing, grabbing my body and shouting, "No, stop," as I tried to catch my breath.

He'd had it warded against my escaping too?

The utter bastard.

When I'd managed to stop sniggering and got myself away from the fence, I stomped back to the party and headed towards Rex. He was deep in conversation with his mother who looked at me, said something, and then as Rex moved away towards the band, she came out to intercept me.

"I thought we'd have a chat now. Shall we go take a seat?"

My jaw clenched, but it wasn't as if I could say no to her. I nodded my head because I didn't trust my mouth not to say what I was truly thinking, and I wasn't ready to bleed to death.

We sat together on a swing seat that had been set out.

"I told him off for having the fence warded against you leaving. Whether or not he's mate-matched with you, he has no right to keep you here against your will. You're free to leave, although I ask you not to while we get this mate thing sorted out. I also understand it's not safe for you out there at the moment because of the jealous Subs."

"It's all very difficult to comprehend," I admitted. "I'm overwhelmed by the whole thing."

"Why don't you tell me everything from your point of view? Help me understand, and then maybe I can explain things from a wolf point of view? It might just help."

So I did. The wine had no doubt loosened my tongue, but I spoke of how I'd envisaged a potential romance with her son. How he'd spurned me. How I didn't want him to want me just because of the mate thing, and I even confessed I'd shagged him because I'd thought 'what the hell'. I really needed to quit drinking.

"Everything you've said to me makes perfect sense. I get why you're not trusting of Rex's intentions and feel it's his wolf not him, but that's not how we work. We are wolves. We talk as if the wolf is inside us because we have a human looking form, but ultimately, it's who we are. Rex is fighting against his true nature right now because his wolf will be desperate to claim you at the next full moon."

"Which is on the 5 July."

"You looked?"

"I've looked at that and I've been researching the history of wolves and how the pack works."

"Does that mean you are potentially interested in my son still?"

"It means I was making sure he didn't trick me into marrying him."

"Oh." She looked disappointed. "Rex wouldn't do that. My son is loyal."

"He might not do it on purpose, but I was nervous that I would do something that committed me to a life I'm not ready for yet."

"Yet?"

I sighed. "I know you want me to sit here and tell you I want your son and I want to be his mate, but I can't. Last week he did not want me. Not in the slightest. I have to protect myself. So, if you could look into what went wrong with Rex and how to break the mate bond, I'd be grateful. Then, if he still likes me, maybe we could see where it goes."

She put her hand over mine and I flinched because I thought she might be about to tear lumps of my skin off or something.

"Freya, there is no breaking of the mate bond. He has mate-matched with you. It's final."

"What?"

"At some point your own bond with him should kick in, but if not, on the rare occasion it doesn't, then he will likely pine until he dies."

"He can have spells to help, can't he? I read that."

"They help as much as morphine with a kidney stone, dear. They cloud your mind, but the pain is still quite excruciating.

However, you can't let that influence your decision. Either it'll come through or it won't."

She passed me a piece of paper with a telephone number written on it. "This is my direct number. You can ask me anything while we're here. Then you can ring me any time after we've left. I'll leave you for now because I'm sure you've lots to think about."

She wasn't kidding. If I didn't mate with her son he'd pine away and die? Was that the truth though, or was it more wolf trickery? Tomorrow, I was going on Frankie's database forums to ask a shitload of questions.

But I did feel like I now wanted to cut Rex some slack. We were lovers, so why not be friends for now? Try to get to know each other better, and if our clothes happened to come off at times? Well, maybe I was testing to see if I had this mate bond thing stuck inside me.

That's not what you want stuck inside you, you hussy.

I needed the bathroom. I'd had four glasses of wine now and could do with five minutes to myself and my thoughts, so I walked indoors. Rex and Zak were walking down the hall carrying equipment and so I dived behind the counter that was covered with delicious looking desserts ready for taking outside.

"If you could have the mate bond broken, would you?"

"Absofuckinglutely," I heard Rex reply.

Then he said. "Freya... are you in here?"

I stood up. Stupid wolves and their sense of smell. I'd forgotten I couldn't hide from him. Picking up a chocolate gateau, I launched it at his head.

"If we can't break the bond, maybe I can break a few of your bones, you utter, utter wanker," I screamed, launching a few more items from the side. Zak ran outside yelling for Erica.

"Let me finish my sentence." Rex held his hands up in a gesture of surrender.

"No. I'm done listening to you, you furry arsehole."

"I do actually have a furry arsehole at times, you're anatomically correct. However, I still need to finish my sentence, woman."

"Woman. *Woman!*" The trifle sailed over toward his head, and this was in a glass bowl. It shattered at his feet. Erica ran inside at that point.

"Rex, get out of here. NOW," she yelled.

He stood rooted to the spot, hands on his hips looking very much like an alpha male who had no intention of going anywhere. Until his father walked in, grabbed hold of his ear, and walked him out of the door. All I could hear was, "Ow, ow, ow, ow, ow."

Tears filled my eyes as I looked at my best friend.

"Come on. Let's go up to your room for a while." She tipped her head in the direction of the stairs.

"He said he'd break the bond if he could. 'Absofuckinglutely' he said, Erica. It cements what I thought all along. He doesn't want me, not really. I was right to keep my distance."

She put her arms around me and pulled me close. "Oh, Freya. I had hoped on a selfish level you two would get together, and also because I want to see you happy."

I admitted my truths to her. "I really, really liked him, Erica, but he's broken my heart."

"Sssh." She patted my back. "Come on, let's go to your room and get you away from everyone for a while."

I let her lead me out of the kitchen and up to my room. I saw no other option right now but to leave, and yet my stupid damn heart wanted me to stay.

Chapter 12

Freya

We sat on the sofa in my room. Erica opened a bottle of red she'd put on the coffee table along with two glasses. Fuck it. I didn't care if I got hammered now. I was done here.

Tomorrow, I would leave. It looked like I might actually have to go back and stop with my parents, and if that was the case, I definitely needed to drink.

I told Erica everything that had happened.

"Why don't you give him the chance to explain what he meant?" she asked in a soft tone.

My friend had a heart of gold, but unfortunately, she thought everyone else's was pure too, and they just weren't.

I shook my head. "I'm tired of his bullshit. It's messing with my head. I need to get away."

Erica placed a hand across the top of mine. "Oh, Freya. Don't leave. I'm enjoying having you here."

Removing my hand from underneath, I gave hers a squeeze. "I know, and the time we spend together is great, but that's not for much of the day. You have work and you have Zak, and that's okay," I added quickly as she looked like she might cry. "This is not the right place for me to be."

"But the bond…"

"Is his problem, not mine. He doesn't want me."

She exhaled loudly. "Look." She took her phone from her pocket. "I have a recording to show you from this morning. It's something the band are working on, but Rex swore them to secrecy. You must not say a word about it, but I'm going to play it for you."

She flicked to the correct video and pressed play, and I listened to the part of a song Rex had written and performed.

"Is this supposed to be romantic?" I asked her.

"He wrote you a song. Well, he is in the process of writing you a song. He's putting his feelings for you into words and music, Freya, that's huge."

"Not as huge as his fucking ego," I snapped. "Listen to the words. It's all you need to be with me. Give up. Blah, blah, blah. There is no emotion in this song like 'you complete me' or 'you're my person', or 'you're my lobster'." I stood up.

"What are you doing?"

"I'm going back downstairs. I'm not letting him know he's getting to me anymore. I'm going to go down there and enjoy myself. Why should I not eat dessert?"

Erica arched a brow. "Is there actually any left? You threw quite a lot of it."

"Meh. It's Cath. She'll have enough for the whole pack in the fridges and freezers."

I grabbed hold of my bestie's hand. "Come on. Thank you so much for having my back, but it's fine, truly. I'm okay. Oh actually," I sat back down. "Can I just listen to that song again a few more times?"

Thirty minutes later we returned. I'd changed my top into a logo one I'd bought that said Fuck off, Fuck you etc. Then I remembered there were kids present, so I put a lightweight hoodie over the top. I knew I was wearing it. It gave me an inner strength and satisfaction.

The band were jamming on stage, and Tanya told me they were playing requests after asking me if I was okay.

"I'm fine." I turned to the stage to let her know they were my final words on the matter.

"This next song is one we play on tour. The Rolling Stones' *I Can't Get No (Satisfaction)*. Roman, my friend, this one's for you, pal." Zak pointed at the lead guitarist.

Roman gave him the finger.

Rex launched into the song and changed satisfaction to satrysfaction. He dropped a drumstick and Noah burst out laughing.

"All of you can do one." Roman started a guitar solo, drowning out his bandmates and showing us his exemplary skills.

When he'd finished, we gave him a thunderous round of applause and Tanya literally wolf whistled.

Roman took to the microphone. "I just thought I'd remind my bandmates that I'm actually very, very skilled with my fingers and with my instrument." He did a solo fanfare on the guitar which had Tanya howling with laughter. A laughter howl was truly disconcerting.

"What a hoot. Shame we can't find him a mate too," she said.

"He has an admirer. Do you know Harley Davis off the TV?" I asked her.

"Seriously? Harley likes Roman? Oh my god, they would have the cutest children. We need to get them together."

"She's in America, but Stacey says she's going to try to matchmake a bit when she's back."

Tanya clapped. "Oh, I'm so pleased. You must keep me abreast of all the gossip on that one."

I nodded, pleased she was distracted by someone else's love life.

The band sang more songs, and I relaxed listening to familiar sounds I'd heard on the tour. The kids were at the front dancing, shaking their butts and making each other giggle. I had a few more glasses of wine until I felt buzzed and mellow. Finally, I was enjoying myself again. I'd forget what tomorrow would bring and enjoy the rest of the evening before, I guessed, I arranged to have my things packed once more while I phoned my mum.

I watched as Rex was fitted with a microphone around his face. He cleared his throat. "The next song is a new one I've been working on."

Oh God no. Tell me it wasn't his 'bang hard on his chest, you need to be mine' song.

But as the music started up and he began to sing, it fucking was. That was it, the straw that broke the camel's back. I didn't know if wolves ate camels, but I was taking to the stage myself, even though I couldn't really sing. I'd had wine. We all thought we were Madonna after alcohol.

I snatched Roman's microphone off his stand, glaring at him. Noah stopped playing and Rex stopped drumming.

Zak looked at Rex.

"Carry on with your backing vocals," Rex ordered him. He said to everyone watching. "This is called *No Escape*."

You're in my periphery
The edge of my proximity
There's no escape
It's in your fate
My intended mate.

Holding a hand up, I told Zak to stop a moment. "I have my own verse," I informed everyone. I was no Zak Jones, but I didn't give a fuck. In fact, sod it. I pulled off my hoodie and turned to Rex so he could see my t-shirt. I pointed to the 'Fuck You' bit in particular. I'd aced English at school, and alongside my inner sarcastic bitch, it meant I could put together insults faster than the speed of light. I started to sing.

> *I was in your vicinity*
> *You didn't want a bar of me*
> *Like put out trash*
> *Or a STD rash*
> *So you're too late.*

Rex lifted his chin at me as if to say, 'bring it'. Looked like the wolf didn't want to lose face and run off with its tail between its legs. He carried on.

> *You say it's my vanity*
> *I'm at the edge of insanity*
> *You can make me wait*
> *Can pretend to hate*
> *My fated mate.*

Fucking arsehole. I had another verse.

> *It really is your vanity*
> *That thinks you can now have at, at me*
> *You can fuck off, mate*
> *That's your fate*
> *Because you're too late.*

The bastard smirked. Smirked! Then sang.

> *Give in*
> *Give up*
> *Surrender to my charms*
> *Live here*
> *Love me up*
> *Crawl into my arms.*

Like hell, I snarled, and I gave him the last of what I'd managed to make up in my head between seeing the video and hearing the song a few times, and standing making up tunes in my head while they played their set.

> *Give up*
> *Give in*
> *You aren't gonna win*
> *Fuck the bond*
> *I'm moving on*
> *I'm not falling for your charms.*

I threw the microphone at him. He dashed from his seat and ran around to me. Dickhead was still miked up so when he spoke everyone heard.

"You called me mate!" he beamed.

"Are you on drugs? I did not."

"You did. You said 'fuck off mate'."

Damn and blast. "I didn't mean mate like your wolf crap. I meant mate as in pal. It's a colloquialism."

"You called me, mate. It means you're at least my girlfriend now. Look it up."

"You're cheating and I will look it up, you can be sure of that, but it makes no difference. I'm out of here."

I turned to stomp off the stage. Rex tried to get hold of me, but his father had jumped up onto the stage and grabbed him, this time by the arm. "Let her go, son. This isn't how we do things."

Erica approached me, but I shook my head at her. "I'm sorry. They'll know you showed me the song. I hope I don't get you in bother with Zak and the rest of them."

"I don't give a shit about that. I care about you, Freya. If you need me. I'm here. I'll be just a minute down the hall from you."

Not thirty-seven seconds away then, I thought, and then I left, and this time I wasn't coming out of my room until I'd packed.

There had been a couple of holdalls in my boxed belongings, and I filled those with everything I needed for a week or so at my parents' house. Then I began to box up anything else I'd taken out, so that it could be easily sent onwards—once I knew where onwards was. I couldn't stay at my parents' house for long. They'd drive me insane. I needed a new rental, and maybe a new identity so the errant Subs couldn't find me.

It was amazing how quickly I'd sobered up once back in my room. A couple of coffees had helped, but mainly it was the realisation that I couldn't stay there.

I rang my mum and asked if it was okay if I came to stay, and I reassured her I was okay, but would explain when I got there.

Then I called for a taxi, sent a message to Erica that I was leaving, and I made my way downstairs to the entrance hall. Stacey had taken the ward off that prevented me from leaving. It seemed she'd refused to put it there, but Rex had found another way. I'd put money on it being Donna from The Seven who'd done it. I popped into the kitchen and found Cath. I hugged and thanked her and asked her to say thanks to Miles. She huffed at me, called him on her mobile and asked him to come help me carry my bags to the taxi when it arrived.

Finally, the taxi began making its way up the long driveway. Zak had kept Rex away, pretending he'd come up with part of a track he needed to get down right now, and so Rex was safely away in a soundproofed room.

Tanya walked over to me. "Won't you stay? Let us try to figure things out."

"No. I'm sorry, Tanya, but the thing is before this weekend, I had a house, and I had a job and now I have neither. Because of Rex. I need some time to figure out where I go from here and I need to do that on my own. Even if I did accept Rex as a mate in future or that mate-bond kicked in, I don't want someone claiming me unless I can claim them right back."

"Okay. I understand," she said sadly. "Well, I hope we meet again, Freya. I truly do."

Erica hugged me. "Text me to let me know you're at your parents' safely, and then call me tomorrow if your mum gives you a chance to get a word in edgeways."

"I will." I turned to Miles. "I'm ready."

He picked up my cases and I followed him down the steps, where he passed my cases to the taxi driver to put in the boot. After thanking him, I climbed in the rear of the car and closed the door. As it pulled away and began its journey down the long winding driveway, I was glad to be getting away from Rex Colton, even if I could acknowledge that part of me wished things could have worked out differently.

By the time I reached my parents' semi, my mother had the door half open. As the cab pulled up, she ran out in her dressing gown.

I opened the rear door. "Mum, get in the house. You're making a show of us."

"I'm making sure you're okay. I mean my daughter rings up at almost midnight telling me she needs to come home. What do you think I've been doing but imagining all the things that might have happened to you since you went to stop with that bloke?"

"Sssh." I thrust a pile of notes at the taxi driver and told him to keep the change. We'd be lucky if he didn't ring a tabloid later saying there'd been a ruckus at Rex Colton's house and he'd had to rescue a damsel in distress.

Mum launched into the sentence I'd heard so many times I might have it put on her gravestone. "When you're a parent, you'll understand."

"If you'll let me get through the door with my bags then I can tell you what's been happening, and you can calm down," I said, exasperated.

She picked up one of my bags and carried it inside.

After checking me over with a quick visual once-over and giving me a chance to hang up my coat, eventually she stuck the kettle on and we sat at the kitchen table, a place familiar to me from childhood. A place where I'd always told my mum everything, and the place where I'd once said I'd been followed home from school. It had led to a man's arrest, and my mum had been over-protective of me ever since.

"Okay. I want you to tell me everything," she said. Inside, I smirked because I could just imagine her face if I said I'd been selected as a mate by a wolf. The psychiatrists would have to come to treat my mother's nerves before they got anywhere near me.

"The thing is... Rex wanted me to be, not only his girlfriend, but his partner for life," I began. "And not only have I only just met him. I mean, I've known him just over a week... but he was acting really caveman-ish. You know, all 'you belong to me and I will fight to the death for your honour' kind of crap."

My mum's eyes widened.

"I know. My eyes did that too. I mean, how ridiculous."

"Freya, you mean to tell me you've met a man who wants to keep you loved and safe, and your response was to walk out. Are you crazy?"

Hmm. That wasn't quite the response I'd expected.

"Can I chat to you some more about all this in the morning, Mum? It's more complicated than someone ensuring my safety. I mean I could hire a security guard for that. I'm absolutely shattered and I'm just not able to communicate things articulately to you right now," I said, while wanting to smack myself upside the head for actually being articulate for the first time in my twenty-one years on this earth.

But she let me go up to my old room, now redecorated as a guest room, and finally, after my mind got the message it was time to quieten down, I managed to sleep.

Chapter 13

Rex

Inspiration had caught Zak after our garden gig and so we'd followed him into the recording studio. To find he only had one sentence of 'inspiration' had been a little frustrating.

"I thought you said you were inspired? Don't you think you could have thought of a little more of the song before bringing us all in here?" I huffed.

"I don't want to lose it. Now work with me. Think of where we can go from here."

It was after a painful hour of trying to get this very average sentence into a song that Zak declared he felt it 'didn't work after all' and we should pack in for the evening. He'd just received a text, so I'd hazard a guess Erica was ready for him to play her.

Turned out he'd been playing me.

Because when I finally returned to the house, I discovered that Freya had gone.

I ran outside, turning into my wolf, and then I took off into the woods. I howled and whined. My family joined me, having also changed into their wolf selves and they stayed nearby. We stayed out all night. I missed my mate. When I finally slept, my family had closed in around me, encircling me to let me know I was safe. That may have been the case, but even within the woods I knew I was lost.

In the morning, we went back to the house. Mum and Cath fussed around me. Stacey had performed a spell that would dull the ache of my mate not being around and prevent me from running after her. Freya had told my mum she needed time to figure things out and my mother had pulled me to one side and insisted I give her that time.

"Do you want us to stay around, son, or would you rather we left?" my father asked as we ate breakfast.

"It's been lovely to see you all, but I'm okay. You can go back home," I answered. "My time will be better spent in the recording studio with the guys. It's what will distract me the most while I figure things out."

"Look, Rex. Last night, that song you sang. It was a true song of a wolf. I got it, I really did, and if your mate-match was a female wolf, she'd have adored it. But she's not. Your mate is a human and you've got to handle that accordingly," Dad said.

"How?"

"Damned if I know, son. I married another wolf."

Huh that was helpful. I felt much better now.

"Freya told me that she felt lost and needed time to figure things out. Give her some space, some time to herself, and then show her she's not lost at all. Show her she was just on a crazy path to happiness with you." Mum lifted my chin and looked up at me. "Woo her. There are so many romantic movies out there. Watch a few and get some ideas, hey?"

"I could do that," I said, beginning to warm up to the idea. I had a home cinema room after all.

"We'll get going after breakfast, but know we are only a phone call away. We'll come back if you need us. You're our son and we want to see you happy." Mum squeezed my shoulder. "I can tell she likes you, Rex. She just needs reminding of it."

"And that's why I married your mother," Dad said proudly, hugging her in close to him. "Because she's a fucking superstar and the best wife and mother anyone could have."

"You are so getting some when we get home." She squeezed his thigh.

"I have to wait until we're home? There's a perfectly good bedroom upstairs. I'll give you a head start of five, four…"

Mum squealed and ran out of the kitchen.

Cath walked in with a sausage sandwich for me, but I'd lost my appetite. Thank goodness, I'd put my parents right at the other side of the mansion.

I then realised I'd been left with my siblings again. Fuck my life.

The band joined me for breakfast. After making sure I was okay, we fell into the usual banter of our brotherhood. Thank God, Stacey had worked her craft with me, so I didn't spend the day howling in the woods. I still felt bereft, but in an amicable end of a relationship way, rather than a completely and utterly devastated one.

"At least this morning you're not boning the girl so we can all get straight into the recording studio." Zak helpfully pointed out.

"Yeah, about that." I gestured around me. "I'm babysitting until my dad's bone…"

"Do not finish that sentence." Zak put a hand over his ears. "No one wants that mental image in their head. No one."

"Can we go out to play?" my little sister Betty asked.

"If you stick to the rules and remember the garden has the tickling fence."

She giggled. "I like it. It feels funny."

And that was the moment I looked down at my baby sister and then looked at all my other siblings and realised that one day I wanted my own family. Because no matter how much of a pain in the arse they could be, they were also a reminder of how good life could be, where even a protective wall could be seen as a thing of amusement and joy. Negatives into positives. I could learn a lot from Betty. Right now, I had to see Freya not being here as a negative I could turn into a positive.

"Do you want me to chase you?" I asked Betty. Her eyes lit up with delight.

"Yes!" she squeaked as she jumped down and ran towards the door. I looked at my bandmates.

"We'll be waiting for you. One day, we might have families and you might be waiting for us," Noah said.

I looked quizzically at my bandmate. He and Stacey couldn't have biological children. Vampires were made not born.

"We decided to look into adoption. There are children out there who've been turned, and their parents killed. Some rogue vampires find it amusing to do that."

"You'll be a great father, Noah." I smiled.

"Rexxxxxxx," my sister yelled, and I took off after her, telling my other siblings to follow me.

I actually had a great time with the kids, and when my parents finally came back downstairs, it looked like they'd had a great time too if their smug expressions were anything to go by.

They rounded up my siblings and with hugs, kisses, and several more minutes of advice, they finally left, and I made my way to the recording studio.

Tomorrow, I needed to make sure I started on time, or my bandmates were gonna get pissed off.

When I walked through the doorway, I sniffed the air. "Can I smell... burning?"

Roman looked at me. "We didn't want to bother you, but when we walked in, that smell was around and look at your drumsticks." He picked one up. It had singe marks on it, the mark of fingerprints burned into it.

"I think your recording studio might be haunted," he said. "Or possessed."

"Don't be absurd. There's a whole mansion over there to haunt. Why would someone choose a recording studio?"

"Well, I've been on Google to do some research on it," Roman said. "It would appear this land once held a cottage dwelling on it. The father of the house went insane due to syphilis affecting his brain and he burned the house down with his wife and children in it. Maybe he still haunts the place?

My mouth downturned. "I don't want a haunted recording studio. I don't like ghosts."

Noah snorted. "You're friends with a whole host of paranormal creatures and you still don't like ghosts?"

"I was afraid of the dark when I was about ten, and my bastard younger brothers used to run around dressed in sheets with the eyes cut out. It's left a deep, psychological scar," I confessed.

"Oh God, yeah. I remember you telling me that," Roman said. "I'm sure it's nothing. We haven't seen any other evidence. Maybe one of the kids got in here, or your dad had a crafty cigarette somewhere where your mum wouldn't find him?"

I nodded my head. "Yes, that'll be it. It'll have been Dad." I exhaled, my relief palpable. Then a fiery skeleton appeared sitting on my drumkit. I screamed at the top of my lungs. Though I wanted to run away, I was frozen to the spot, watching as the grinning aflame skeleton banged on my drumkit and laughed menacingly.

And then the demon skeleton turned into Aaron, the security guy from Abaddon, and my bandmates creased with laughter.

"You total utter bastards. I'm gonna kill you all," I roared. But they were too busy being hysterical to care.

Eventually, Roman caught my eye and I understood. "Well played, Roman, well played," I told him. "We'll call us even but do that again and you'd better run fast."

Aaron got off my drum kit and came forward. "My apologies, but it was nice to have a little fun. There hasn't been much of that lately in the seventh dimension."

Aaron was Abaddon the destroyer's right-hand man. A seemingly cool, calm, and collected guy who did his best to keep Don in check while making him think it was all his own idea.

"How is the big bad?" I asked. Zak's expression was wary, but then again it hadn't been a week yet since he'd been free of the deal he'd made with Don to supply him with souls.

"He's fine." Aaron looked at Zak. "Don't look so scared. He's forgotten all about you. That's how he works. You were a very small cog in his wheel of evil."

"Thank fuck for that," Zak choked out.

"Well, thank you for portalling over to help us out. I appreciate you have much better things to do with your time," Roman said.

"Hey, it was no problem at all. Like I said, fun is not in plentiful supply in this job, so it made a very pleasant change."

"Want to hang around for the rest of the morning with us?" I asked him.

"I'd absolutely love to," he replied.

"But singe my drumsticks again and I'll make Don look like a fluffy kitten."

Aaron just laughed. I guessed when you worked for a major demon, threats from a wolf were like the miaow of a cute kitten.

"Right, guys," I said. "I'm going to scrap the song I wrote for Freya."

"Wise move, man," Zak said and Noah and Roman nodded their agreement.

"I'm starting again. I spent some of this morning humming a new tune, one I think will be much more suited as a song for the woman you want to make yours forever. It's called Thirty-Seven Seconds."

This time when I sang the lyrics I'd managed so far, the band and Aaron just sat in silence and listened. And then they applauded.

"Really? It's okay?" I sought reassurance.

"If that doesn't get her to mate-bond with you, nothing will," Roman said. "It's amazing. Let's focus on that track so you can get back on yours with Freya."

Chapter 14

Freya

It was my fourth room change in two weeks, so when I woke up, I didn't know where the hell I was. Until I heard my mum shouting at my younger brother, telling him he was going to be late for school. Ferdie was fifteen and so laid back you needed to check he had a pulse. I got up, put a robe around myself and went downstairs.

"It's only science, Mum, this morning, and seeing as I'm an entrepreneur, I don't need to pass that."

"Making fake IDs for your schoolfriends to get served in off-licences, and selling fags for a premium to them is not being an entrepreneur; it's being a criminal in training," Mum scolded. "Now get your arse moving and get to school, or I'll drive you there, give you a big kiss at the school gates, and yell, 'I love you, Ferdiwerdy'."

"Fine." He got up and stomped out of the room without even saying good morning to me or asking me why I was home. Sulky teenagers were a law unto themselves. I knew first-hand; it hadn't been that long ago I'd been one myself.

"Tea or coffee?"

"I'd love a cuppa this morning please, Mum."

She switched the kettle on and got a teabag out of her jar, placing it in a mug.

"You sleep, okay, baby?"

"Yeah, actually. Once my mind settled, I seemed to sleep well."

"And how are you feeling about things today? Does a life with a caring, millionaire rock star still sound unappealing?"

"I like him, Mum," I admitted honestly. "I like him a lot, when he's not being an arsehole alpha, and even then, at times it's not so bad." I thought of us in the bedroom. "But he can't just click his fingers without any effort and expect me to jump. So, I feel the same way this morning. That being away from him is the right thing to do. I need time to myself to think about what I want, because he's saying he's all in, Mum, and that's an overwhelming statement by someone who, just days ago, didn't want to know me."

"It sounds wise, lovely. Just don't cut your nose off to spite your face, okay? If you do like him, then make your own demands. Tell him he needs to make an effort to show you how much he wants you."

I nodded. "Yeah, maybe, but for the next few days, I'm not thinking about romance, Mum. I'm just going to think about myself and what I'm going to do. I have no job now, and I loved working with jewellery."

"Go ask for your job back."

I shook my head. "No, I didn't like the staff I had to work with. I've been thinking about becoming my own boss. Do you remember how I made you those earrings once, the ones with the little charms on them?"

"Of course I remember. They're in my keepsake box."

"They are?"

"I treasure them, Freya. You put on a heart, a mum charm, and an ice cream cone because we both loved strawberry Cornettos. They bring me wonderful memories when I look at them."

"That makes me so happy." I got up and hugged her. "I'm

going to open an Etsy store and sell handmade jewellery, things like that, where I'll have base earrings, chains, and bracelets and then people can pick memory pieces for them. I'll start from there and see how it goes."

Ferdie walked in. "You want to do band ones. Use your connections with The Paranormals. Guitar charms, plectrums, microphones. You think too small, sister."

"Ferdie, you little genius. You might be onto something there. I'll have to ask the band though because I reckon I'll need to form some agreement with them. I could have lines from their songs engraved." I started to get excited. "Little discs with things like, 'my heart beats for Rex', 'my soul sings for Zak', 'my heart thrums for Noah', and 'Roman rocks my world'."

Ferdie grinned. "Ask them about doing full merch: t-shirts etc. I could do that part. Those slogans you just said would work across t-shirts, hoodies, sweatshirts, totes, mugs." He looked at Mum. "Do I seriously have to go to science, you just know we're quids in here if she gets permission for this. Family business, Mum. You won't need to teach little bastards anymore either."

"It'll be very embarrassing for me to turn up to school and find my own child isn't in my class. Now get a move on or you're getting that lift." Mum's voice rose. "However, it does sound like a very promising idea." She smiled at me. "Enjoy your day. Your dad's already at work, but he's looking forward to seeing you tonight. You have the place to yourself. Enjoy it."

They left, and looking around the kitchen, I sighed in contentment, welcoming the chance to have some time completely alone. I'd start with a nice hot bath and take it from there.

The hot bath turned into a long, hot bath. I was a wrinkled prune by the time I'd emerged, but I was buzzing with excitement about my possible new business venture. I called Erica and asked her to find out if they'd give me permission to run with the idea and what cut of the profits the band would want. Erica was almost as excited as I was.

While blow drying my hair, it did occur to me that while I'd started off with an idea about my own business, thanks to my brother's brainwave, I was about to connect myself back to the band. *Oh, it's only a tenuous connection,* I reassured myself. *You'll be selling other things.* I mean if I were printing off t-shirts, I might as well think of some other styles and go the whole hog with selling jewellery, tees and hoodies, plus gifts. I was the Queen of Sass. This girl could think up some humdinger slogans.

I'd been home less than a day and my future was already looking brighter. I got on my phone and started looking for information that would help me set up my business. I had a purpose and it felt darn bloody good.

The rest of the week passed quickly. I spent my days doing research, making samples, and ordering supplies, and my evenings with my younger brother who showed me Photoshop, other sites where you could sell stuff, and a whole host of other useful websites. I'd known my brother was tech savvy, but I did think he was a future millionaire in the making now. For all he was a gobshite teen, he really did know his stuff, and so right now, his big sister was in awe and proud of him.

It was the following Sunday night, and we were in the kitchen while Mum and Dad watched some TV.

"You do realise if you marry Rex you'll not need to work at all, right? And if you keep me in a line of credit I might not have to either," Ferdie announced.

"It's good to have self-worth," I told him.

"That's the right answer," Ferdie said. "I was just checking. Even if you do end up together, the fact you know you can earn your own cash will make you not feel so powerless if he's being all macho."

"Ferdie, are you some re-incarnation of an old soul, because that's very wise?"

"Nah, I just eavesdrop on the folks," he admitted, grinning.

"Thank you for all your help, bro," I said truthfully. "I couldn't have done this without you."

"And I couldn't do this without you. Without you having a contract being drawn up with the band, I couldn't help you with designing items that are going to fly off your website."

"You mean Etsy?"

"Nope." He logged into the computer and showed me a page.

Freya Steel Designs.

He'd thought of everything. There was an introduction about me, space for photos of the work, and a direct store linked up for purchasing.

"Mum helped with the 'about me' bit, because I'll be honest, I don't really listen to you when you're just rabbiting on. The areas that are currently blank are things I need to ask you questions about, or that you need to decide on."

I started to cry.

"Oh shit. Don't you like it?"

"I bl-bloody love it, and you, Ferdie."

"Ugh, don't cry, it weirds me out."

"I c-can't help it. It's awesome." I sniffled.

"If you look across the buttons on the top you can see this one says THE PARANORMALS. You click it and look..."

He clicked and it went through to another page set out for the products connected to the band.

"This keeps it as part of your collections, but also separate, so if Freya Steel Designs takes off on her own, or you decided you didn't want anything else to do with The Paranormals, it can be separated."

"You've thought of everything."

"Hey, I'm not being altruistic here. I'm ready to get this show on the road and make a shitload of cash, sis. If it's okay with you, I want to get cracking with the t-shirts and other branded items, leave the jewellery to you. So, is that good? Can I take The Paranormals and get started?"

"As long as you still go to school and pass your exams."

He sighed. "God, okay. It's like having another mother around the place. Can't you go have your own kids with Rex Colton and sod off now? It's been great and all, but we can have a biz meeting once a week. Only, I was using your room to keep my fags and printers in. I could do with it back."

He'd set me off thinking. The sad fact was that after being in Rex's close proximity for almost two weeks, I was missing him. I kept thinking of the nice moments we'd shared, the fantastic sex, and even when he'd been an annoying alpha, he'd just been being him. If only I felt he liked me. If I could be confident he wanted me and it wasn't all down to this bloody bond. Until then I just didn't see how I could give him a chance. I'd always wonder if he really loved me, or whether it was just the wolf bond that made him think he did.

On Monday morning at eleven I had a surprise visitor.

John.

I opened the front door to find him standing on the doorstep.

"Oh God. What do you want?" I sagged against the doorframe.

"Just to apologise and talk, Freya. I texted your mum and she told me you were here."

"I don't know…"

"We were together for a year, Freya, and you just ended things so quickly. I'd really like an opportunity to talk to you. Maybe then I can accept we're through and not do ridiculous declarations in shopping centres."

"Fiiiiine. Come in."

I made us both a drink and got a packet of biscuits out and we sat at the kitchen table. For someone who I'd thought I was in love with, as John sat in front of me, I realised that I'd felt more for Rex—even when he was ignoring me—in that short time, than I'd ever felt for this man sat here.

"I'm sorry, John. I didn't treat you right, and I apologise. You're right. I ended things abruptly and I should have done it better."

"I'd thought things were good."

Running a hand through my hair, I looked him directly in his eyes. "They were. They were good. They just weren't great. Not when I actually sat and thought about how I felt. The truth is I'd not finished things between us because I did enjoy your company and I did think a lot about you—"

"—you said you loved me," he interrupted.

"I thought I did," I admitted.

His shoulders slumped. "But now you realise you didn't. It's because of *him*, isn't it?"

"It is, but Rex and I aren't together, John. I don't know if we ever will be, but there's something there, some chemistry, that me and you just didn't have. And you can't blame Rex because I realised that and ended us before I went on to spend the week with them."

"Have you slept with him?" John stared at me and turned away. "Don't answer that. It's not my business. I can see that. Not anymore."

I placed my hand over his. "We just weren't enough, and I need you to know that one day hopefully we'll both find someone who is enough."

"I thought I'd found someone before, was getting engaged to them," he said. Guilt consumed me that I'd let this man flirt with me in my job and stole him from a potential future wife. It was like John had read my mind because he said:

"Oh fuck it. You might as well know. There was never any fiancée. I just fancied you and thought that was a way in."

"What?"

"I thought I'd show my interest while playing hard to get and it worked, didn't it?"

I ran my hand through my hair. "John, I've spent so much time feeling guilty about my actions. That I'd taken another woman's man. The only reason I continued was because I'd thought you would have split up anyway given you were clearly not that interested in her if you'd been flirting so heavily with me." I finished the last of my drink. "Our relationship was based on a lie, and I came to it with a part of myself I didn't like. A mistake. I would never do that to another woman now. It's made me feel sick to my stomach about having hurt someone else."

"See, you can get over it now, because there never was anyone."

I huff-laughed. "You don't get it, do you? Whether they were real or not, I made the wrong decision, and I know now that being with you was a total wrong decision. Especially after the fiasco with Joelle and the double proposal."

He looked down at the floor.

I stood up. "Thank you for coming, John. It's really helped me to clarify what we had and put things in perspective. I hope you do meet the right woman soon. Maybe if you don't lie to her, and don't act like an idiot, you'll have more success. I know I've certainly learned lessons from this relationship."

He stood up himself. "I came here hoping for another chance, but I know now we're completely over. Your heart belongs with Rex. I can see it clear as day. Why can't you?"

I let him out of the house and closed the door behind him. I was left feeling a sense of sadness and regret about me and John, and with a yearning inside me to see Rex again. But he'd not been in contact with me. His message was clear.

Out of sight, out of mind.

Chapter 15

Rex

I'd spent my days in the recording studio, sometimes evenings too, and any spare time was spent in my cinema room watching romantic movies. I'd done them all. *Sleepless in Seattle*. *Dirty Dancing*. You name it. And I now had a song and a series of plans which I hoped would get me the girl.

Erica had sneakily got in touch with Mrs Steel, Freya's mum, and so I was set to turn up at eight pm, ready to wear my heart on my sleeve for the woman I wanted in my life. Yes, she was my mate, but I needed to show her I wanted her anyway.

I'd confessed my true feelings to the band. How I had found her attractive but had pushed her away because I hadn't wanted to give her false hope, not when I would find a true mate. I just knew Freya was the kind of girl who threw her heart and soul at you. She was full on Freya. It was actually a testament to the respect I had for her and for Erica that I'd not fucked her six ways from Sunday and then ditched her. Freya may say she'd have been okay with that, but I'd argue differently.

And now I needed to communicate all this. I was dressed in a sharp, navy-blue suit which my mum had told me over video-chat was the best colour for bringing out my natural colouring of my amber eyes and reddish-brown hair, and I was ready to do this.

That was a half-truth. I was ready in that I was prepared ready, but inside I felt like an army of ants were stampeding around my guts, and truthfully, I felt nervous and faint. I mean, think about it. I was off to try to tell Freya how much I needed her, for life. And would it be okay if at some point soon I bit her neck and made her a wolf. Not too much pressure then.

Roman passed me a paper bag.

"That's not nice," Zak stated. "I think he looks quite handsome."

"It's for him to breathe into, not for over his head."

"I know, couldn't resist though." Zak nudged me. "Go on, you sexy beast. Go get your girl."

I took a few deep breaths and then I left my house, walking to the driveway where Miles sat behind the steering wheel of my car, because even though I could drive myself, my shaking hands right now would make that very difficult. With Freya's mum's address in the SatNav he set off.

This was it.

Freya

My brother had insisted that we work from my bedroom after my mum had said she was fed up of us hogging the kitchen. He'd already complained my room was too hot and had demanded I open my window, and he seemed very distracted. He was showing me some potential designs he'd put together, when Mum yelled up the stairs to him that she needed his help urgently.

"Coming," he shouted, which struck me as odd because he

always groaned whenever he was asked to do something. It had my suspicious nature alerted to my family's current actions. I'd stood up and was just about to go see what they were up to, when I heard a deep voice from under my bedroom window.

"Freya Steel."

My heart skipped a beat. Rex Colton was in my parents' back garden?

I hung my head out of the window. When I saw him in his suited and booted glory, I swear my heart beat twice as fast as normal.

What was he doing here?

"Miss Freya Steel, you seem to not be fully aware of my feelings for you. So allow me to demonstrate." He did a little nervous cough. "I have been researching romantic movies for inspiration and I would like to start by serenading you under your window. Would that be okay with you? I can clarify it is a brand-new song."

"Okay, you may." I smiled, leaning as far forward as I could go without plummeting to my death.

"This song is dedicated to my love, Freya Alberta Steel. It's called Thirty-Seven Seconds."

Fuck. I just knew before he even sang a note that this song was going to be *everything*.

> *"I told you no*
> *When my soul said yes*
> *In my defence*
> *I had your happiness*
> *In mind*
> *In mind*

> *I thought that you and I*

Andie M. Long

Could never work
That's the reason why
I was a stupid jerk
All the time
All the time

But come on
We're 37 seconds from love
37 seconds from us
It's no time at all
But I can't wait that long for you

So get up
We're 37 seconds from love
37 seconds from us
I'm moving fast
Don't let me run on past you

I didn't want to hurt you then
And that was why I had to pretend
To not want you
But I wanted you

I thought my true love laid in wait
And so I was awaiting fate
But I saw you
I really saw you

Thought someone else would be my mate
Turned out it just switched on too late
But it was you
It always was you

So come on
We're 37 seconds from love
37 seconds from us
It's no time at all
But I can't wait that long for you

So set off
We're 37 seconds from love
37 seconds from us
I'm moving fast
Don't let me run on past you."

As he finished, he handed the microphone to my scheming father who now came into view. My dad looked up at my window and winked, and then I heard footsteps in the house. Rex was moving fast, and I didn't want him to 'run on past'.

I yanked open my bedroom door and he was there, out of breath.

I was about to launch myself at him, but he smiled and shook his head.

"Miss Freya Steel, would you accompany me on a date this evening?"

Now I knew why my mum had told me off earlier for 'letting myself go' and saying that being in the house all day wasn't an excuse for not bathing. She'd made me have a wash and then passed me some clean jeans and a top I'd thought was far too dressy for home, but the look on her face had made me just eye-roll and stomp off, putting them on anyway.

"I'd like that," I answered.

"Okay, well I know I'm not dressed as one, but in *An Officer and a Gentleman* style, I shall now pick you up and carry you to the car, if... that is okay with you?" He lowered his voice. "I thought that one might appear a bit alpha."

I walked closer to him. "I give you permission to carry out any part of your date night plans. Pick me up, Rex."

He did. He lifted me into his arms, and he walked me down the stairs past my mum, who was embarrassingly clapping and whooping, and he walked us out of the front door and up to a Mercedes being driven by Miles. Miles stood leaning against the car, smiled at me, and then opened the rear door. "Your carriage awaits, Miss," he said with a wink.

I climbed into the back. "So where are we going?" I asked.

"You'll see," Rex told me.

We ended up in the Oxo Tower Restaurant with its fantastic views over the London skyline.

"This is the closest I could get to *Sleepless in Seattle*. I didn't want to send you wandering around a building, but I wanted iconic views, so I settled on this. I hope it's okay?"

"Rex, it's amazing. Thank you for inviting me out tonight."

When the waiter had poured us some champagne, Rex spoke. "I needed to explain myself and I hope the song went some way to doing that. I'm sorry I pushed you away, Freya. It's just I've had many women throw themselves at me, and then when I can't commit to them, they turn nasty. With your friendship with Erica..." He looked at me earnestly. "You couldn't be a quick fuck, Freya. I'm sorry."

"I understand. And I know I can be full on. I threw myself at you and basically didn't give you a chance to catch your breath."

"And that's what our groupies are like. I'm afraid, at first, I just put you down as being like those. Thought you were simply after getting me into bed to say you slept with a Paranormal."

"That was my exact aim. But not *a* paranormal, *YOU*," I admitted.

"It seemed fate decided to turn everything on its arse when the bond hit. Then I was throwing myself at you." He laughed.

I laughed with him. This was good. We were talking. Not arguing. Not bossing each other about. It was a proper date.

He lifted his glass. "To possibilities," he said, and I chinked my glass with his.

We chatted throughout the meal about our families, the new business I was setting up, and how the band were getting on with recording their new album. The conversation flowed easily. I was enjoying his company. The real Rex sat in front of me, and he was fucking HOT.

By the time we were on dessert, not touching him was killing me.

But the night wasn't finished... I hoped.

Rex

So far, so good. I'd relaxed a bit now she was here in the restaurant. I still felt a little foolish about what was next on the agenda, but it wasn't for me. It was all for her.

"Is this meal the end of our date?" she asked. "Are you being a perfect gentleman?"

I grinned. She was plainly horny AF, but we'd given in to our carnal desires twice before. This time we weren't falling into bed through need alone. This evening had taken a lot of preparation, and it wasn't over.

So next we went on the Thames. Being a millionaire had its benefits and being able to hire a boat solely for us and for the purpose of this date was one of them. We rode up and down the river enjoying the views and the ambience. When I had her positioned at the front of the boat, suddenly *My Heart Will Go On*, Celine Dion's iconic song from *Titanic* came out of the speakers.

"Please tell me you're not planning on this boat capsizing?" Freya laughed.

I moved in behind her, put my hands around her waist and told her to hold out her arms.

And then I leaned in, and she leaned towards me, and we kissed. Turning her in my arms, I held her close and tried in my kiss to tell her everything that I felt.

We broke off.

"Freya," I said. "I know my being a wolf and saying you're my mate is scary, and wolves do rush headlong into things, but if you'll date me, I will try my best to take things slow."

"Okay," she replied. "Let's see how this goes."

"Really?" I grinned like an idiot.

"Yeah, really," she said, and then we kissed a whole lot more.

Freya

I was officially dating Rex Colton with a promise from him that he would go slow. Despite wolves immediately wanting to claim their mate, he'd agreed to slow things down for me. This date had been perfect, and I was excited for where things went in the future.

"So was this the last of our date?" I checked.

"No. There's one more thing."

"Oooh, which film is it from? Give me a clue," I begged.

"As soon as we're back on dry land." Rex smiled. "Until then, I think we should do more of this." His lips brushed against mine. "Only I think we've seen the views on the way out, we don't need to look again on the way back, do we?"

I had to agree with him.

🎸

After a quick bathroom break, we departed onto the riverbank. Rex was carrying a large bag but wouldn't explain what was in it.

"So the final movie is *Dirty Dancing*," he declared.

The iconic scene from the movie played across my mind's eye. I imagined jumping into Rex's strong arms, him holding me aloft while the passers-by watched enviously wishing it was them.

And then he went into the bag and brought out a watermelon.

He walked towards me. "I'm guessing you thought of a different scene?" He smirked.

"Yup, 'I carried a watermelon' was not the one I'd plumped for, but—" I stopped in midsentence as suddenly my body became overwhelmed in sensation. For a moment I couldn't breathe, and then I found myself staring at Rex. It was as if my eyes were committing every cell of his to my memory. His scent hit my nostrils: smoky, heady, virile, *MINE*! I couldn't look away from him, overwhelmed by his presence at this moment in time. My heart palpitated wildly. I realised I was absolutely in love with Rex Colton.

"Freya? Freya, are you okay?" Rex took a step closer to me and that broke the staring spell I appeared to be under.

"I love you. I want you to be my mate," I screamed out.

"Pardon. What did you just say?"

It might have been more romantic had he not got a watermelon in his hands, but it was our moment, and we'd remember it for the rest of our lives.

"Rex, you're my mate," I yelled again, my voice full of utter joy, as my mind and body rejoiced over the fact that my forever was right in front of me.

He dropped the watermelon to the ground as I ran at him. Then he spun me around and kissed me over and over.

"Seriously? You love me?"

"Yes. I want us to be together. Fated mates..."

"I love you too, Freya."

I stared up into his eyes. "Take me home," I said.

"To your parents' house, do you mean?" He waited for my reply with bated breath.

"No." I shook my head. "I mean to our home, mate."

Chapter 16

Rex

I could never have foreseen how the night would end, but as we ran back to Miles and the car and told him that we were happily mated and ready to go back to our home, I was bursting with joy. All seemed right in the world. I swear Miles shed a little tear and I knew Cath would.

But I only had eyes for my mate and the minute we were through the front door, I picked her up, took her to my bedroom and claimed her several times over.

No recording took place the following day. Not in the music studio anyway...

July 5th...

"Are you sure about this, Freya. Because it's only been a few weeks."

"Rex. If you ask me one more time, I'm going bop you on the

nose. Are we, or are we not fated mates who will be together forever?"

"Yes, we are."

"Then there's no point waiting any longer to bite me and make me your wolf wife, is there?"

"But we can wait."

"I don't want to wait, unless... you do?"

"Hell, no. I want to unleash my other beast on you." I winked.

She laughed, but it was all husky and dirrrttyy.

"So it's me, you, and the full moon. What happens exactly?"

"I chase you, you run. I catch you, we make love. I bite you, you become a wolf. We fuck like animals because we *will* be animals, and then you're my true mate, forever more."

She stared over my shoulder. "What's that?" she asked. I turned around, but there was nothing there. I turned back. "What are...? Oh."

Freya was running out of the door.

I took off after her.

Roman

The architects were drawing up the final plans for the lodge, but for now I was perfectly happy in my own little piece of heaven in the woods. Sometimes I worked on music here, either in the summerhouse or near the stream. It was a quiet place away from the main house. Rex had said I could get my meals and have a room there for as long as I liked, and while I was grateful, I only wanted the room for its washing facilities. I preferred to sleep outdoors.

I heard shrieks and smiled. Rex had forewarned me of tonight, but we all knew the nights of the full moon anyway. We kept an eye on our shifter friend. I was pleased for him. He and

Freya had gone from hate to mate in a very short space of time, but that was the shifter way.

I was sitting in a swing seat outside of the summerhouse, gently rocking to and fro as I thought about my friends and how happy they all were. Noah and Stacey were married and now thinking of adopting, Zak and Erica were new but so happy, and soon, *very soon* if the noises coming from the woods were anything to go by, Rex and Freya would be man and wife in wolf terms, if not in human ones.

I felt the melancholia hit me and shook my head as if I could shake it away. While I was truly happy for them, the fact there was no significant other in my life was now apparent more than ever before. Because the band were my family and now they were moving on with their lives, and I was still the same.

I wasn't stupid. I knew Stacey had some crazy idea that me and Harley would get together in the future, but Harley was—though still unaware of it—a Nephilim. A half-angel. I was a satyr and while I did my best to stay good and keep clean, most of my kind were womanising, drunken tricksters, not to be trusted and not all that fond of bathing. How could a man who was part goat date a woman who didn't know such things existed?

He couldn't.

I would just have to accept my solitary existence, because I certainly didn't want to end up with one of my own kind. Nymphs didn't like to be refused by a male and were known to wreak revenge if rejected. No, I'd rather stay far away from them. My turning my back against what my family saw as my inheritance was why I no longer saw and had barely any contact with them. They didn't approve of me being in a band, said I was trying to be a human and forgetting my heritage.

So they forgot they had a son.

I heard the roaring of wolves and raised my bottle of scotch in the air.

"To Rex and Freya. I wish you both happiness," I toasted, although they'd not hear it.

My phone began to ring then and putting my bottle down, I picked it up. Harley Davis was ringing me on FaceTime at one am. What the hell? Also, WiFi was sketchy as shit here, so I hoped the signal stayed.

I pressed answer.

Harley's tearstained face came on the screen. Her usually pristine eye make-up ran down her face in black track marks and the smile that normally lit up her whole face was gone.

"R-Roman. I'm sorry to call you. I t-tried Stacey but she didn't pick up and I honestly don't know what to do and who to call."

"What's the matter, Harley? What's happened?"

"I think something is wrong w-with me, but the th-thing is, do you remember the final of the concert?"

"Yes...," I said a little hesitantly because her co-presenter possessing bodies was what had happened at that concert. While we'd thought Harley was a human, we'd assumed her mind had been wiped by Noah in a compulsion, but of course... turned out she wasn't completely human.

"I just put it down to too much showbiz bubbly because as you know, it's in plentiful supply at these events, but I'm beginning to think now that maybe what I saw that night: Bill acting weird as if he'd been possessed because he sounded just like D-Dan was real. C-can you please tell me, Roman, did you see that?"

She was rambling and distraught, and too far away. "Harley, look at me. What's making you think something is wrong with you, exactly? Spell it out to me so I can understand and help."

"I'll sh-show you," she said. "It's easier." She panned the camera so that I could see her top half. Behind her were two huge, white angel wings.

"I can see them, and I can feel them. Are they real, Roman, or am I crazy?"

"Fuck, Harley. You're not crazy. Goddamn it, why do you

have to be in the States when you need my help? I can get on a plane but it's going to take hours. Can you sit tight?"

"I'm not in America," she confessed. "They made me pretend we'd gone there. I'm in a seedy hotel room in Soho."

"Tell me which and then sit tight. I'm on my way," I told her. She managed to give me the hotel name before the connection severed.

THE END

Can Roman help Harley to come to terms with the truth of what she is, and just maybe, show her his own true self? Find out in the final book in the series, Satyrday Night Fever.

To keep up with latest release news and receive an exclusive subscriber only ebook DATING SUCKS: A Supernatural Dating Agency prequel short story, sign up here: geni.us/andiemlongparanormal

Playlist

Def Leppard, *Pour Some Sugar On Me*
Alice Cooper, *Schools out*
Whitesnake, *Is this Love?*
Thunder, *Love Walked In.*
Rolling Stones, *(I can't get no) Satisfaction*
Harry Styles, *Watermelon Sugar*
Celine Dion, *My Heart Will Go On*
Bill Medley & Jennifer Warnes, *(I've Had) The Time Of My Life*

SATYRDAY NIGHT FEVER

To everyone with a difficult to pronounce Christian name. A character told me their name in this book was Saoirse. It's pronounced Seer-sha.

I'm taking bets that while you read the book you make up your own pronunciation, hahaha.
Andie xo

Chapter 1

Harley

I looked in the mirror and then attempted to flop onto my dressing room sofa. Except I couldn't because I had weird protrusions coming out of my back. If I'd thought I might be having visual hallucinations, the fact remained that they must also be sensory hallucinations because I could *feel* them.

Wings.

Two large, glowing white wings.

Taking a deep inhale, I peered over one shoulder and then the other. Yep, they were still there.

What on earth was I supposed to do?

Trying, and mainly failing not to panic, I bit on the tips of my expertly manicured fingernails while I tried to figure out what to do.

There was a chance this—as in my current hallucination—had been coming for a while now. Back when I'd been hired to co-present the television show *Britain's Best New Band* with a guy called Dan Trent, there had been a few things happen that I'd done my best to overlook, but I now noted could have been the beginnings of psychological distress.

When my co-presenter went missing it had understandably been a majorly stressful time. I'd been worrying about what had happened to him—even though I disliked him intensely because of how he treated me—as I would never wish a person harm. The guy still had family who loved him, and I'd also like to think people could be redeemed. Unfortunately, though, his going missing caused me a lot of bad press because of how he'd badmouthed me. Some people actually thought I could have been responsible for his disappearance, saying I wanted the job of presenting all to myself, and I'd been interviewed by the police. I wasn't the only one, but still, it hadn't been nice.

Then as we got ready to announce the winners of the competition at the final, the big boss behind the competition, Bill Traynor of Deep Heat records, had acted strangely out of character and like... well... Dan.

My bottom lip wobbled, and I started to cry as I let myself picture what I thought had happened.

Bill had tried to push me off the stage.

My friend Stacey had fallen off the stage.

Noah, her now-husband and the bass guitarist of The Paranormals had moved at an impossible speed. Stacey had been thrown on the stage and Noah had landed on a piece of wood. Which had gone *through* him.

I was now shaking as I'd never fully allowed myself to think of this before.

His friend had gone over to him, pulled out the piece of wood and he'd just healed up. Not one scratch had remained. I'd been on the stage watching and wondering if I was seeing things.

Noah had taken to the stage and hypnotised the audience. Everyone left not knowing what had happened. I knew because I'd gone to say hello to Erica, who ran the band's fan club and she'd not known what I was talking about. She'd told me she'd clearly had too much to drink as the evening was a bit of a blur and how great was it that the two final bands had won in a dead heat.

Maybe Dan's disappearance had affected me more than I'd originally believed?

I needed to speak to someone who might not think I was having a breakdown, although it was possible *I might be having a breakdown*. In which case, I realised, I needed to speak to someone who'd take care of me anyway. Picking up my phone, I rang Stacey's number. It just rang out though until the answering machine service kicked in. Damn!

Who else could I reach out to?

In the end, I plumped for the man who I felt a connection with. Roman Idiri, the mysterious lead guitarist of The Paranormals, the biggest band on the planet right now. He was probably screwing a groupie though I thought as I hovered over the keypad. The thought annoyed me and made me press his number on Facetime without further delay. If he was, then I was interrupting any such shenanigans because truth was, I wanted him for myself.

"Hello?" he answered immediately which made me so relieved I burst into tears. His tone gave away his confusion about my ringing him. *Again, it is one am*, I reminded myself.

"R-Roman. I'm sorry to call you. I t-tried Stacey but she didn't pick up and I honestly don't know what to do and who to contact."

"What's the matter, Harley? What's happened?"

The concern in his voice just made my tears run down my cheeks faster.

"I think something is wrong w-with me, but the th-thing is, do you remember the final of the concert?"

"Yesss," he said a little hesitantly. As I looked at his face staring back at me on screen, there was a crease between his brows.

"I just put it down to too much showbiz bubbly. Because as you know, it's in plentiful supply at these events. But, I'm beginning to think now that maybe what I saw that night: Bill acting weird as if he'd been possessed as he sounded just like D-Dan was real. C-can you please tell me, Roman, did you see that?"

Concern was clear in his face now. He obviously thought I'd

cracked up. "Harley, look at me. What's making you think something is wrong with you, exactly? Spell it out to me so I can understand and help."

"I'll sh-show you," I said. "It's easier." I panned the camera so he could see my top half, including my two huge, white wings. "I can see them, and I can feel them. Are they real, Roman, or am I crazy?"

"Fuck, Harley. You're not crazy. Goddamn it. Why do you have to be in the States when you need my help? I can get on a plane but it's going to take hours. Can you sit tight?"

He would help me. Oh, thank goodness.

"I'm not in America," I confessed. "They made me pretend we'd gone there. I'm in a seedy hotel room in Soho."

"Tell me which and then sit tight. I'm on my way," he told me.

I'd just managed to tell him the name of the hotel when the line went dead. All I could do now was hope and pray that he came here soon.

As I thought the word *pray* my wings widened. Huh? I thought it again.

Pray.

Standing proud.

And again.

Pray.

Another flicker, standing out and proud.

What would be the opposite of that? Erm, satanic rituals?

I pictured the devil in my head and my wings closed up and disappeared with an abrupt snap, wrongfooting me so I faceplanted the sofa.

Feeling at my back, there was no longer any evidence of any wings. I thought the word *pray* again.

Nothing.

Great, now Roman was on his way here and I had no wings to show him. Perhaps it would be easier if I just said it was a prank? I walked back over to the mirror to look at myself. All that stared back at me was a woman whose eye make-up was smeared halfway down her face, making me appear even more batshit.

Sighing, I walked out of my dressing room—which in reality was a converted small meeting room—down the corridor and into the bathroom.

🎸

"Hey, are you okay?" Saoirse, one of the assistants on the show, came out of a toilet cubicle and stood next to me.

"Yeah. I was just thinking about one of the families. You know, the sister, Leonie, was so up for being reunited, but then she died before it happened, and—"

"It led to the brother changing his mind," she finished off for me. "I know, it was so sad. And after all that research too. But that's how it goes on *Relatives Reunited*. Some we get, some don't work out."

"I know. Just I'm a little bit sensitive."

She squeezed my arm. "And that's why you were perfect for the job. Still, it would have been better if we'd actually managed to travel to Los Angeles wouldn't it, instead of having to pretend we were there? Do you believe they double-booked the venue?"

"No. I just believe the budget was cut," I said, wanting to put my hand straight across my mouth. Since when did I share what I truly felt with the staff of the show? If Saoirse shared my thoughts, I could get in serious trouble. "Please don't tell anyone I said that," I begged her.

"Of course I won't," she reassured me. "That's what we love about you, Harley. You're so down to earth. Not like most of the presenters we come across, thank God."

As she said the word 'God', I felt my back tingle. "Oh no," I yelped, as I dived for the toilet cubicle where I promptly threw up.

Saoirse knocked on the door. "Oh, Harley. I'll get you some tablets and leave them on your dressing table. Sorry, you're feeling ill. Good job we've finished filming for the day, hey? I'll leave you in peace. No one needs an audience when they have a dicky tummy, do they?"

The door banged shut as she exited. I pulled off some toilet tissue from the roll, wiped my mouth and stood up. I'd pictured the red horned one again to see if that stopped the tingles becoming another explosion of white wings and it appeared to have worked.

Come on, Roman. I thought. *Please help me make sense of what's happening to me.*

After washing and cleaning up my face, I checked there was no one on the corridor and dashed back to my dressing room. Saoirse had left me some diarrhoea tablets on the dressing table as she'd promised. Huh, a dicky tummy would have been much preferable to a dicky brain.

A knock came to the door, and I swung it open eagerly ready to see Roman, but it was Saoirse again.

"Oh, you're looking a bit brighter. I just came to check on you, because if it was a bug you'd need to go home for forty-eight hours."

Of course! It might cause a few problems with recording, but it couldn't be helped. Couldn't have a TV crew coming down with the shits. This was my way of escape until I worked out what was going on.

"Yeah, I'm thinking I may need to go home for a couple of days, just to be on the safe side."

"Malcolm said if you did need to go off sick, could you stay with a friend who'd keep their mouth shut that we weren't in the US?"

I sighed. Of course that would be Malcolm's concern. Not that his presenter was sick.

"Tell him I'll find somewhere and not to worry." I rolled my eyes.

"Typical Malcolm, right? We're just part of his meal ticket. And if he's not bothered about you, think how he is with us," she said.

I parked that thought for later. Right now, I didn't have time to look into what she meant, but I would. Just at the moment I couldn't afford to be doing any more good deeds.

That's what had led to my spontaneous wing eruption in the first place.

"I'll leave you to gather your things, but are you expecting someone? Because I'll not take offence, but you looked disappointed when I turned up."

I bit my bottom lip. "I'm so sorry. I would never win at poker," I told her. "I'm expecting a friend. I should have said really. He's called Roman."

"Okay, I'll go look out for him. You sure you should meet someone when you're sick though?"

"He knows. He's come to help take care of me."

She smiled. "Oh that's good then. Right, take care and I'll see you when you're better."

I said goodbye and hoped Roman wouldn't be too much longer. In the meantime, I gathered my things together, ready to leave the hotel.

Chapter 2

Roman

Harley had reached out to me, and now I was going to have to be the one to tell her the truth. Her mother had obviously hoped to keep the fact she'd shagged an angel quiet, but the wings were now out of the back and Harley was going to need support.

Hell, I'd been a satyr for all of my twenty-five years, and I still had issues with it.

There would be another elephant in the room though, and that would be the fact Harley and I liked each other. We'd admitted it but had agreed while she was filming in the States there was no point in attempting to pursue anything.

Now though, she was here. Hadn't been in the States after all. The thought of being vulnerable to anyone made my skin crawl. I preferred to live in denial about my life while being permanently in a state of inebriation. The only time I liked to be sober was when I was performing or rehearsing.

Being drunk was the satyr way, and while I kept a large distance between myself, my family and other satyrs and nymphs, much preferring to be alone, it now looked like I'd be telling Harley the truth, and nothing but the truth. I only hoped her mental state was otherwise strong, because this was huge. Her being a Nephilim, me confessing my truths, and her wings. HUGE.

The driver I'd called dropped me off at the entrance to the hotel. Jesus, it was a hovel. There was a woman of the night looking at me hopefully from a few shop doorways down, so I dashed into the reception as fast as I could. The last thing I needed was the press getting an opportunity to take a photo of me near a prostitute on the seedier side of town. They were already always posting about the 'mysterious party and playboy of The Paranormals', no fuel needed adding to that fire.

I walked over to the receptionist. A young girl with lip and nose piercings, she looked up with a narrowed gaze as I tore her away from whatever she was staring at on her phone. As her eyes widened as she realised who I was, I saw she'd been looking at Ashley Banjo flashing his pecs on TikTok. The guy was goals, I had to say. If anyone could entice me to a gym it was Ashley Banjo. I knew far more than I should about his TikTok performances due to the fact my bandmate, Zak, was always moaning about his girlfriend watching them and asking him if he'd thought of asking Diversity to teach The Paranormals some moves.

"C-can I help you?" The receptionist asked.

"I've come to meet Harley Davies."

"There's no Harley Davies here," she said firmly.

What? Had I got the wrong place? I got my phone out and dialled.

"Hey, Harley. I'm in reception but she says you're not here."

"Oh, that's because of the heavy secrecy about the fact we're filming here. Sorry. I should have given you the codeword. It's Los Angeles. That's where we were supposed to be."

"Okay, I'll be there shortly."

"Los Angeles," I told the receptionist.

She smiled. "If you go in the lift or take the stairs to the first floor, she's in room 111."

"Of course she is." I laughed to myself.

"Pardon?" The receptionist looked bewildered, not being aware that my angelic friend was in a room numbered with the main angelic numbers.

"Nothing. Thanks so much for your assistance...?"

"Mandy. Amanda Huffington."

"Thank you, Mandy."

"Erm, could you sign this piece of paper for me?" she asked. "Only no-one will believe I met you. I'm not allowed to take pictures with Harley because she's not supposed to be here."

"I tell you what." I leaned in closer to her, passing her a business card. "If you can arrange for this driver to come for us when I call down and direct him on how to get us out of here without the press being alerted, I'll arrange for you to come meet the band and have your photo taken with us all." I nodded at the paper. "Write your details on there."

She scribbled them down and I put them in my shirt pocket.

"We have a very small private car park. I'll let him come get you from there. Leave it with me."

"You're a star, Mandy. Okay, catch you later," I said, then I ran up the stairs and hurried to find Room 111.

I only had to knock once, and the door flew open. It took me by surprise when Harley basically threw herself at me shouting, "Oh thank God." And then whoooomph, two massive angel wings sprouted out of her back, and she lifted us off the floor as they flickered.

We hovered up around the ceiling for a split second before crashing down onto the sofa as her wings disappeared again. I landed on my back; Harley laid out on top of me.

As I looked at the bewildered, vulnerable looking woman lying on me, all I wanted to do was to rise up and close the gap between us and let my mouth meet hers. But that wasn't what she needed right now. She needed my support. Harley scrambled off me as if she was on fire.

"Oh my... nothing. No deity at all. At all. See, Roman? Did you see them? I have wings, don't I? Please tell me I'm not imagining it?"

I sat up. "You're not imagining it, Harley."

She stood still for a second and then she slumped onto the sofa at the side of me, relief etched onto her face so heavy it looked almost permanent.

"I'm not? How do you know?"

"Promise you won't get mad?"

She nodded her head. "Just tell me."

"I thought there was something strange about you. You always seemed so... vibrant. But when you healed my wrist in the dining room that time and you were talking about your family, it just came to me that you were probably..." I swallowed nervously, "half-angel."

Harley started laughing. What started out gentle soon turned into a full-blown belly laugh where she was having to hold her stomach. Then her hands went to her face.

"Oh my cheeks. They hurt. What are you talking about? I can't be half-angel. That would mean my mum or my dad was an angel and my mum is certainly no angel and my dad's dead."

I grabbed hold of Harley's hand and placed it on her knee, keeping mine on top of hers, and I looked seriously into her eyes. "Has your mum ever actually told you that your father is dead?"

"Duh, she said he's in..." Her eyes widened, "Heaven."

I took my hand off hers and patted it. "He's an angel. Remy, you said his name was. I looked him up because I didn't know much about angels and he's one of the seven main archangels of God, known as Ramiel, the angel of hope. He's responsible for divine visions and for guiding people to heaven."

"Oh, that's good then."

"But he's also known as Remiel, a fallen watcher, one of two-hundred angels who fornicated with human women and told them the secrets of being angels."

"And that's how he managed to be my dad." Harley sighed.

"Looks that way."

Harley reached behind her for a cushion, and I made the mistake of thinking she was trying to make herself more comfortable. I was therefore a little shocked when the cushion smacked me hard in the face.

"You knew and you didn't tell me? What sort of a friend are you?" she yelled.

I'd never seen Harley mad before. Looked like I was getting a glimpse of her human half as she continued to batter me with the cushion.

I got a cushion pasting for each word that came out of her mouth.

"How." Whack.

"Could." Whack.

"You?" Whack.

I grabbed the cushion, throwing it to the floor, and I held her wrists. She tried to wriggle out of my hold, but I held firm.

"Harley, I am not the enemy here. I am your friend. I didn't think it was my place to tell you. I figured your mother was surely keeping an eye on things. Maybe even your father?"

She sat on the sofa shaking her head. "I can't believe what I'm hearing and seeing. You're telling me I'm a half-angel and I keep sprouting wings. It's just all too much."

I opened my jacket up and reached inside my pocket, bringing out a bottle of scotch.

"I'm always prepared with inappropriate coping mechanisms." I passed her the bottle after opening the screw cap. "This'll take the edge off. I know it's usually sweet tea for shock, but I've got a feeling we need to go a bit more hardcore on your new revelation."

Bang. Her wings came back out, knocking us both off the sofa again.

"Don't mention the 'r' word, or any other word connected to the big book," she said, taking a swig of the scotch and coughing. Her face went pensive for a moment and then the wings went back in.

"How'd you do that?" I asked her.

"Think sinful thoughts," Harley answered. "It's not ideal, but it gets them to go back in. I need to find out how to handle them though. I can't just be showing my feathered side willy-nilly."

"So any good thoughts bring them out?"

"Yes, not every time, but most of the time, and then I have to think of bad things to make them disappear. I don't know what I'm going to do. This is crazy."

I looked around her dressing room. "Look, I can't get hold of Rex right now because he's busy tonight." I thought about all the howling in the woods I'd been having to endure just before Harley called me, as he mated with Freya under the full moon. "But I know he'd be okay with you staying with us, with me. He has the mansion and I have a very unglamorous summerhouse with a sofa in it on the edge of the woods."

"Oh, Stacey said you were having a place built near Rex's."

"Yup. I am. So if you're in agreement, I think it would be a good idea to go there while you get used to your new, *identity*. A driver will pick us up from the hotel car park to take us there, and Miles and Cath will get us settled for the night. I have a guest suite there with two bedrooms, so I can stay with you if you like until we can call your mum, because ultimately she's the one with the answers."

"Yeah, okay. To be honest I'll just let you guide me because I don't know what to do for the best right now."

She really did look shellshocked still.

I hit the reception button on the phone on the table in front of us. "Hey, Mandy, it's Roman. If you could call that number I gave you now and tell Rod we're ready."

"I certainly will. If you come down to the reception, I'll show you how to leave via the back so you can get to the car unseen."

"Thanks, Mandy."

I stood up. "Okay, let's gather your things as Rod won't take long to get here. I've had him on standby."

Harley packed some things up into a holdall. "I don't have much here in my dressing room, but I don't want to go to my hotel room right now as it's right at the other side of the hotel and ten floors up. Too many opportunities to reveal myself. I'll sleep in my clothes for a night. It won't hurt."

"We can organise anything you need. I'm a millionaire remember?"

Harley stared at me. "The others act like millionaires with their massive houses and lavish lifestyles, but you don't. Why is that?"

I smiled. "We've no time to go into the story of Roman right now. That will have to be a tale for another time."

Her eyes on mine, she tilted her head. "I really would like to hear it one day," she said.

Then Mandy called to say my driver was here.

"Put this throw around you." I picked up the gold-coloured blanket from her sofa. "And keep thinking sinful thoughts all the way into the car, okay?"

"Okay," Harley said, and we made our way down through reception.

"Take care." Mandy waved and smiled as we walked past. "See you soon."

"Absolutely. Looking forward to it," I told her, patting my pocket to let her know I still had her info, and then we left the building and got Harley safely into the back of the car.

Chapter 3

Harley

I was clutching the bottle of scotch under the blanket. Once I was in the back of the car, the throw removed and my seatbelt safely fastened, I took a few more swigs from the bottle. I could be a party girl at times, but scotch had never been my poison of choice. However, the burn down my throat and the buzz in my brain as I mellowed under the influence meant a girl could be persuaded towards the hotter side of life.

You're half-angel. I thought as I shut my eyes. It was the early hours of the morning. I'd been filming all day, and I was bone-weary tired. I could feel my eyes closing and my arm slipping. Then I'd remember the bottle in it and jerk back awake again.

The bottle was removed from my hand and then an arm came around me, pulling me close. I melted into Roman's chest. He smelled of earth and grass and a cedar-based aftershave. His chest rumbled under my cheek, and I realised I'd been sniffing him like I was a hound. It was clearly amusing him. I let my eyes close, and I thought of how lovely this was, and wished Roman felt the same way about me, but it was clear he didn't.

I mean I'd been thinking sinful thoughts to keep my wings in all the way to the car and they'd been about me, Roman, and a bed. Yet as we'd passed the reception, the woman behind the desk had said she'd see him soon and he'd tapped his pocket. He clearly had her phone number in there. That meant that on his way to come help me, he'd scored the phone number of another woman.

My next thoughts—and the last I remembered—definitely would keep my wings in. I don't think my father or his peers would be impressed with what exactly I thought about the woman on reception.

"Harley, we're here at Rex's." I was shaken gently awake and as I got my bearings, I realised we were indeed outside a large house and there was a middle-aged man and a woman looking in.

"Wow, she's even more beautiful in the flesh," the woman said to Roman. "Just give her a minute to wake up. It'll have been quite the evening for her."

I woke up rather quickly while three people watched me and waited. Sitting up and undoing my seatbelt, I stared at the couple.

"Oh hello, I'm Harley. Sorry for turning up at this time of the morning. I hope I've not disturbed you too much?"

"You'll soon realise when you come inside that it's not you disturbing us." Miles raised a brow.

My own forehead crinkled in confusion. Jesus, I'd need a top facialist when I'd worked all this angel stuff out. Wrinkles were not welcome in my world. I'd be cast aside for the next, new tight-faced presenter.

I stepped outside the car, Roman grabbing my elbow to steady me.

Miles took my holdall and as we made our way inside, Cath asked if we wanted anything to eat and drink. I realised I'd not eaten for hours, and I actually felt quite famished. "I'm hungry, but I'm not sure what I fancy at this time in a morning," I said honestly.

"How about a couple of slices of toast with some butter, and maybe some jam, and a nice warm drink? Do you like cocoa?"

"Oh, that sounds lovely," I answered honestly.

"Okay, well, I'll get on with that, and, Roman, you'll be glad your room is far away from Rex's." She turned to me. "I'm sorry. It means it's quite a walk, but you'll soon realise why it's worth it." Cath rolled her eyes heavenward.

Just as I was about to query what she meant, I heard a female voice shouting, "Oh my fucking god. Yes. Yes. Yeaaassss."

I quickly battled to think evil thoughts, which were of me holding a pillow over Freya's face to quieten her down.

It was followed by a male voice which I immediately recognised, also shouting. "You're so fucking mine." A guttural groan followed.

Cath picked a box of earplugs out of her pocket. "There are some in your room just in case. I really hope they quieten down somewhat and it's only due to the mating ritual."

"M-mating ritual?"

Cath's eyes fixed on Roman's.

"I've still a lot to explain," he told her.

"Ah. Well in that case, let's get you taken to the suite immediately." She nodded to Miles, who gestured towards, and then led us up the grand staircase and along a vast landing. Though Roman told Miles he knew where his room was, Miles insisted on doing his job of escorting us there.

"Mr Colton's rooms are that way," Miles said to me as he pointed to the other side of the stairs. "And we are going right over this side. Follow me." He wore a smirk as he began walking. "My missus seems to have forgotten we were young and newly-weds once. Think I might have to remind her what I'm still capable of." He chuckled and Roman laughed back. I was too busy taking in the interior of the huge mansion to join in the hilarity.

By the time we reached the suite, I thought my legs were

going to give way. It was harder work than my personal trainer put me through five times a week.

"My wife will be up with your food and drink soon. You need anything else, just call for us," he said and then he left us to it.

Walking into the suite almost took my breath away. I'd stayed in swanky hotels many times, but after being in the seedy Soho one for almost a month it was a refreshing and welcome change to see luxury. The double doors had opened up to reveal a sitting room that had floor-to-ceiling windows to the front and the right-hand side, with a grey wall with black glossy doors on the left.

It was so very opulent.

Roman pushed open one of the bedroom doors and I peeked in. "There's an en suite. If you want me to send for any clothing for you or you need anything else let me know. I'll be sleeping in the room next door if you need me."

"Are the rooms the same? Because I'd rather you took the better one otherwise," I told him.

"They're the same, but thanks anyway."

I moved away from the bedroom and took a seat on the bottle green sofa in the room. The décor was of cream wallpaper with a palm leaves pattern and the furniture was all natural wood. "This room is gorgeous."

"I think so," Roman said. "I've stayed in this one a few times."

After Cath had brought up the cocoa and toast and left us to it, I sat back on the sofa and took a bite, groaning in satisfaction.

"Mmm, that's divine," I said and sure enough my wings popped out again. "This is getting on my every damn nerve." Back in they went, but of course I'd been ejected off the sofa with the force of their eruption and had to get up and sit back down again.

I looked over at Roman to see he was chuckling once more.

"Funny, yeah?" I snarked.

"I'm sorry, I thought it was men who had the problem with premature ejection of white stuff." He creased up.

I couldn't help but giggle alongside him.

Once we'd managed to stop, he looked at me more seriously.

"So what caused it to happen the first time?" he asked.

I thought back to earlier that evening.

"We had a reunion episode we were due to film and Leonie, the sister of the siblings died. Although there was a niece and nephew that Patrick, the brother, could have met, he pulled out of the show. I just felt like reaching out to him, regardless of the show and so I'd called. He was in America and although it was half past twelve in London it was only early evening there. We chatted and he'd told me how he had social anxiety and he'd finally plucked up the courage to travel to see his sister and then she'd passed and he'd taken it as a sign it wasn't meant to be. When I said that maybe the fact they'd found each other meant that he was supposed to enter his niece and nephew's lives when they'd lost their mum, he like had some kind of epiphany and said he'd rethink things, and that's when it happened. Ping. Out popped my wings. I had to make up an excuse to get off the line and then you know the rest. I didn't know if this was real, or I was having a breakdown."

"Been quite eventful, hasn't it?" Roman smiled.

"Indeed, and now can you tell me what the heck is going on with Rex?"

"Are you sure you're ready to hear the truth about everyone? It will mean you have a whole other heap of questions, and you'll look at life differently for a while until you get used to your new normal."

"Yep, hit me with it," I told him.

"Okay, so our band is called The Paranormals for a reason. Rex is a wolf shifter. He can turn into a wolf at any time, and has to have injections handy so he doesn't get tufty in front of people, so maybe there's an antidote for your wings in the same way?"

"He's part-wolf?" I double checked.

"Yes. On a full moon he has to turn and go run around the woods and hunt, so that's why he bought this place with its large woodland."

"Ohhhh. Makes sense now."

"At midnight, he and Freya mated on the full moon, so in wolf terms they're now husband and wife. As you've heard he's doing more than just kissing the bride."

My jaw dropped. "But it was only last week that she liked him and he didn't like her."

"And then he liked her and she didn't like him."

"But now they very much like each other?"

"He wooed her. Grand romantic gestures and now she's also a wolf shifter. He bit her as the moon went full."

I rubbed at my eye. "What about the others?"

"Zak is human, but he was an incubus. That's why he couldn't understand how you didn't fall for his charm because everyone was guaranteed to. That was part of his deal with a demon from the seventh dimension of Hell called Abaddon."

It took me a few minutes to run back through all my encounters with Zak during the competition and the couple of occasions I'd met him afterwards, and now it made a whole lot more sense.

"So it wasn't that he particularly wanted to get me into bed. It was because I wasn't susceptible to his charms?"

"Yup, and he told me that your soul shone so bright that sex with you would have been the equivalent of maybe ten other women's souls."

"He wanted to drain my soul?"

"That's what incubi do. Just run your battery down, and the woman would need to sleep a day or two to charge back up."

"I'm going to kick him in the balls."

Roman laughed. "He was tricked into the deal. He actually

hated most of it. Sex became a chore. Now he's human and with Erica and he's happy. So for Erica's sake, leave his balls alone."

"Fair enough, but only for Erica," I joked.

"Noah and Stacey are vampires," he announced.

I fell off the sofa that time without my wings having caused it.

Chapter 4

Roman

It was a good job Harley had a backside a Kardashian would envy because it was going to get super bruised with the amount of times she was ending up on it.

I helped her up and back onto the sofa.

"Are you okay?" I checked.

"I might be a bit sore later, but right now I'm a little distracted from the potential pain of falling onto my arse due to your recent statement that one of my friends is a vampire."

I grimaced. "I guess I really should have let Stacey tell you herself."

"I knew she was a witch, but that's just like creating herbal potions and things isn't it?"

"Erm."

"Why are you staring at the carpet? Eyes on mine, Roman Idiri. Is Stacey also a broomstick flying witch?"

"No."

"Phew."

"But she can do proper spells."

"Whaaat? Like turn me into a toad?"

"Yup. Do you remember the whole lead singer of Flame-Grilled Steak saga where Drayton dressed as Stacey?"

"Yesssss."

"Donna did that. She shouldn't have. You're supposed to cause no harm, but she said he brought it on himself by stealing their thunder with the dance off."

"Can I have the scotch back, Roman? Because there's a lot for me to try to get my head around here."

I passed her my bottle again and she took a mighty glug. Seemed she was becoming more accustomed to the burn.

"So Stacey is a witch and a vampire?"

"She was a witch and then, when they got married, Noah made her a vampire. With her blessing, that is. Otherwise, she would age and he wouldn't. Now they'll be together for all eternity."

"Whoa. So Rex is a wolf shifter, Freya is now a wolf shifter, and Zak is now human but was an incubus. Erica is human, right?"

I nodded.

"I'm a Neliphim."

"Nephilim," I corrected.

"Half-angel. Noah is a vampire, and Stacey is half-vampire, and a witch. Anything else?"

"The Seven's females are witches from the same coven as Stacey and the males are bear shifters."

"Ohhhhkayyy. And... anyone else?"

"Can't think of anyone."

"I mean you, dufus." She pointed her finger hard into my chest and I realised at that point that since meeting in her dressing room she'd drunk a serious amount of my scotch. "Are you human or a paranormal?" She scrunched up her eyes. "And I don't mean a band member."

I took a deep breath. "I'm a satyr," I confessed.

"What's a satyr?" She sat up straight and gave me a once over as if she was looking for clues.

"We're male nature spirits," I began to explain. "Mainly known for being extremely promiscuous and drunk."

"Oh."

"In my natural state I share some characteristics of a goat."

Whisky shot out of Harley's nose.

"A goat? Tell me you have horns." She held her sides with mirth.

"And this is funny is it? My being part-goat?" I was starting to get a little rattled by her finding this all amusing.

"Yes! Because I'm half-angel, right? I'm half-good and I have wings. And you're part-goat and you're naughty and you have horns. We're like opposites."

"The opposite of an angel is a devil, not a goat," I corrected her.

"Potatoe-Pohtahto," she sing-songed. "Now I know why I feel a connection to you. We're both good and bad at the same time."

"I'm not bad. Satyrs are badly behaved, but I gave up being around those kinds of people a long time ago," I protested.

"Soon, I have to face my mother and find out the truth about my angelic side." Harley pouted. "So right now," she crawled along the sofa towards me, "let's both be bad." Her mouth met mine and the deep carnal part of me I did my best to control unfurled from the pit of my stomach in a *holy hell YES* fanfare. If it were visible it would have looked like an Olympic acrobat with a ribbon. But then her mouth slid down and off my chin as she succumbed to alcohol and exhaustion. Staring down at the beautiful woman laid on me once more, I knew that once I'd put her down in her room, I was going to have to have a serious session with my cock.

In the end, I left her on the sofa and covered her with the throw she'd come home with and another from a chair in the living room. Making my way to my room, I longed for my bed out in the woodland, but Rex had made this a comfortable alternative. I climbed beneath the duvet of the wooden bed, dealt with my hard-on, and then I stared through the skylight at the stars until I fell asleep.

Knock. Knock. Knock.

What was that?

Knock. KNOCK. KNOCK.

I sat up, suddenly remembering where I was and what had happened in the earlier hours of the morning.

"Hello?" I called out.

My door pushed open slightly and a blonde head appeared around the corner.

"Hey, Roman. Sorry to disturb you, but do I call down for coffee and breakfast or is there a set time to eat? Only I have a bit of a headache and food might help."

I rubbed at my face.

"Shit, you were sleeping. I'll leave you. Sorry."

"Hey, hey," I called out, looking at the clock on my bedside table and realising it was past nine am. "I should be up by now. Forgot to set the alarm so it's good you woke me."

Finally getting my thoughts in order, I remembered that Harley had fallen asleep in her clothes. "Look, why don't I order some hot drinks and some breakfast to the room, and if I lend you one of my shirts which would I reckon come down past your knees, then we can get your clothes laundered. There'll be no one around until later apart from the wailing wolves, so how about while we send for someone to collect your belongings from the hotel, telling them you're ill and taking some time off, we get a picnic packed up and go spend some time in the woods? I can show you where I'm having my lodge built."

"That sounds lovely."

"Okay, well, why don't you hit the shower first? There are fresh robes and towels in the bathroom cupboard. I'll leave you a shirt in your room to put on, and I'll be ordering our breakfast before I grab a shower myself. I'll ask Cath to come get your clothes, so drop them outside the bathroom door. I'll meet you out in the living room when breakfast arrives. Say for in twenty minutes or so? In the meantime, I can fix you a quick coffee or a water as there are provisions in the room."

"I can't thank you enough for looking out for me like you have, Roman," Harley said. "I need to contact Stacey again as she's messaged me back, but I really feel I can talk to you, so will you help me still? Like be there when I talk to my mum? I know it's a lot to ask..."

"Of course, I will. I have your back, Harley. I know what it's like to feel you don't fully know yourself."

"If you ever want to talk to me, you know I'll listen."

That made me smile. Even though Harley was going through her own crap, she was still worried about me.

"Let's concentrate on you for now. I'm fine." I threw the duvet back off my chest to indicate I was getting up. "I'll get you that coffee."

Harley stared at me for a beat too long and I realised she was distracted by my now naked chest. She shook her head. "Shower. Right now."

She disappeared and I heard her soft footfalls carry her quickly away from my door.

While Harley showered, I did as I'd said, and I called down to Cath to ask her for some breakfast and to pick up Harley's clothes to get them laundered so we could go out. Then I rang our PA, Vikki, and asked her to arrange for someone to collect Harley's belongings from the Soho hotel.

Vikki called back to say she'd spoken with the hotel and a woman called Saoirse had agreed to pack up Harley's belongings and had passed on her best wishes that she hoped Harley would feel better soon.

After we were both showered and dressed, we sat in the living room with fresh coffee and pastries. I felt a little awkward as I didn't know Harley that well, and yet, here she was, sharing the same bedroom suite as me. It was tempting to start drinking my scotch, but I made myself stick to a strong, black coffee instead.

"I guess I need to call my mum," Harley sighed. "I hope she'll tell me the truth about my father, because she's not the good one, is she?"

"I don't think she'll have a choice once she sees your wings."

Harley let out a groan. "If my sister has to know the truth, she'll be a nightmare. She already acts out because she's jealous about my career. It's not my fault she's only seventeen and still at college."

"One step at a time, Harley. Let's find out what your mother has to say first and take it from there."

She nodded. "You're right. Do you have any brothers or sisters?"

I felt my shoulders stiffen. "I have two brothers, one older and one younger, but I've not seen them for a long time now."

"Because of them or because of you?" Harley probed.

"Because of my parents and the satyr ways," I admitted. "But let's get back to you. Stop changing the subject. You need to make the call."

"Who knew you had a bossy side? There I was thinking you were all laid back." Harley picked up her phone and began to scroll until she hit a button and held the phone to her ear.

"Hello, Hyacinth. Is Mummy there?"

She took her phone away from her ear. "That's Mum's cleaner."

"Hey, Mum. I've finished filming and I thought we could catch up."

She listened for a while. "I know you have a busy schedule, but I'm your daughter, so a week on Thursday will not do, no. Tomorrow afternoon? No, a ten-minute window will not suffice. I'm your daughter, not a dental check-up. You can skip meeting Patty Jenkins. She can tell you about her new toy boy next week. Okay, bye."

"My mother will begrudgingly fit me in at three pm tomorrow afternoon at the house."

"What's your relationship with her like?" I probed.

"It's okay. She's a chameleon."

My eyes widened.

Harley noted my expression. "Oh, no. Not a real one. Just a person who adapts to her surroundings. She's currently living in a nice house that was part of her divorce deal from Des, husband number two. She still has times when she disappears off for a week or two with my sister's father. He only appears when he needs something, but I guess she takes what she needs from him and vice-versa. The whole 'she had an affair with a you-know-what' is hard to get my head around. Fancy corrupting a good being!"

"Hmm, I don't think your father was particularly well-behaved at that time since he ended up cast out of you-know-where for a while."

"True."

"So how are the wings today? Not appeared so far?"

"No. I'm trying to avoid anything that could set them off." She poured another coffee. "I don't usually drink this much caffeine, but all the wing opening and closing yesterday was exhausting."

"Yes, physiological changes can be tiring, and you've yet to get used to it."

She bit on her bottom lip and looked into the room before bringing her attention back to me.

"What do you look like in your true state, Roman?"

"You don't want to see that. It's not the best paranormal deal in town. Not like your pretty white wings."

"Huh. They might be pretty, but they're a little over-the-top. I showed you mine, now you show me yours," she quipped.

Harley might be half-angel, but right now I was getting her naughty side.

"I'll show you my horns and you'll have to be satisfied with that for a while." I wiggled my brows. I was flirting and I needed to quit. Harley needed me as a friend right now. Trouble was, my true nature loved women, loved everything about them. I'd see every one for their skin, their hair, their eyes, their bodies, their smells, their essence. Satyrs were deeply passionate lovers and as dirty within the sheets as they usually were around the swamps. I felt my dick engorge. Wrong kind of horn, mate. Pipe down.

And that made my mind up, because concentrating on my head horns' emergence would take the strain away from my dick.

Closing my eyes, I imagined the protrusions coming out of the top of my head. I could feel the push on my skin, knowing that my skin would open like a trap door at both sides, letting my horns emerge. They were no small stubs. My horns were around three inches wide each and about seven inches long. Cream coloured, they rose up for about three inches at the front and then curved backwards and to each side.

When I opened my eyes, Harley was staring like I'd just shown her my bare arse.

"D-did that hurt?"

I shook my head. "No, not at all. It's a natural process for me. Same as I guess your wings don't hurt when they emerge because I only heard you scream in surprise, not pain."

"True. What a pair, hey?" She looked down at my shirt on her body and smoothed it over her thighs.

My dick would be off again in a minute. Desperate, I blurted out. "Would you like to feel them?"

What?

What the actual fuck?

Why on earth did I ask her that?

Socially awkward weirdo. That's what I was.

I might be amazing at fornicating with women, but communicating with them was another thing entirely.

"Erm, okay," she said as her hand fluttered to her lips. She clearly wanted to say no.

"It's okay. Forget I asked you. I'm just not used to talking to women."

Her brow raised at that. "Yeah, I'm guessing there's no goody-goody wings for you with the salacious stories I've read about you in the papers."

"The media exaggerate things, but, yes, I'm no sai—"

Harley rushed over to me, her hand going across my lips. "Don't say it."

Her hand had been wrapped around her warm drink and it felt nice against my lips. I wanted to kiss her fingers and then progress on from there, but then she moved her hand to one of my horns.

It felt so good. My horns weren't connected to my dick or anything; the pleasure wasn't of a sexual nature. It was more akin to that of a scalp massage, tingly and nice. I pushed my horn further into her hand.

"Oh, is that nice?"

"Yeah, it's relaxing," I confessed.

She continued to run her hand across my horn. It felt like she was trailing her fingernails down it. Then she changed to the other one.

I was in a strange place because satyrs didn't do this. They just pleasured women and took their own. We didn't do intimate massage type manoeuvres. This was new territory for me. This woman was touching my body and getting under my skin.

I pulled away from her. "Nothing special, is it? Just an everyday animal horn." Standing up, I began to make my way towards the door. "I'm going to go and have a word with Cath about our picnic. See you downstairs in half an hour or so? Once your clothes are back."

"Yeah, okay," Harley said, and she smiled at me. But I noticed it didn't reach her eyes.

Chapter 5

Harley

You'd think I'd be fully pre-occupied with the fact I'd just discovered I was a half-angel and some of my friends were paranormal beings, but no, instead I was crushing on Roman Idiri.

The man clearly isn't that into you, I scolded myself.

I'd landed on top of him and he'd done nothing. I'd stroked his horn which seemed kind of intimate, and he'd moved away from me and left the room.

Remembering what I'd seen yesterday, I quickly walked into his room, and spotted the shirt he'd been wearing the previous day lying discarded on the floor. Before I could question my actions, I grabbed it and went in the right pocket. Sure enough, there was a piece of paper. Unfolding it revealed the name Mandy and a phone number. It was just as I'd thought. He'd taken the telephone number of another woman on his way up to rescue me.

He sees you as a friend and that's all. Sadness overwhelmed me. Yet, as much as I should go and hide away in a rental property and lick my wounds, my determined nature said no. That we would show Roman just how good we could be together. I had a chance of spending a week in his company and I was going to take it.

The thought of a week off was also enticing. It had been so long since I'd not worked around the clock filming different TV shows in my quest to be the top woman television presenter. I'd signed a massive deal during the Britain's Best New Band filming and it was taking its toll. I'd always had this feeling that I needed to shine, and it drove me to pursue my career with ferocity. Now I was questioning everything and wondering whether it was all about the part of myself I was unaware of, that had been trying to show itself.

I folded the piece of paper back up and replaced it in Roman's pocket and put it back on the floor. Hopefully it would be collected for laundry and the pockets not checked and then it would be goodbye Mandy. I was glad I didn't have to go back to the hotel. My non-angelic side might have emerged as I scratched her eyes out. Hmm, visions of Freya turning wolf and doing exactly that flickered through my head. I was doomed. My crush would be crushed.

After my clean clothes were delivered back to my room, I dressed and made my way downstairs. The place was huge and trying to remember the way I'd come in last night, I retraced my steps until I reached the front entrance. I'd grab some fresh air while I waited for someone to appear.

Opening the front door, it made a chiming noise, but if that made me jump a little, watching two wolves stretched out next to each other on the front lawn made me jump a *lot*.

Footsteps came behind me and I turned to find Roman, Cath, and Miles approaching.

"Morning, Harley. I thought maybe Dave might be arriving with your things," Miles said.

"Dave's one of the drivers," Cath explained.

"Oh, no, it's just me. I didn't know where anyone would be, so I thought if I hung around the front entrance, Roman would find me."

Cath clipped Roman around the ear. "You left the woman on her own in this massive house? We could have found her skeleton in a year's time."

Roman rubbed his ear while looking a cross between shocked and bemused.

Cath looked horrified. "Oh, Roman, I'm so sorry. Sometimes I forget you lot aren't my sons."

A very strange thing happened then. Roman stepped towards Cath and hugged her. She looked at me over his shoulder as she held him tight with a quizzical look. After a minute or so, he stepped back.

"Thanks, Cath. That felt good. Now I have an idea what it's like to have a mother who cares."

I saw the tears that sprang to her eyes, and I think my own heart broke clean in two.

"Okay, I'll go grab the picnic basket, and then we can walk out to the woods. It's a lovely day for a stroll," he told me, and then he walked down the hall, disappearing into a side room I presumed led to the kitchen.

"Oh my heart." Cath clutched at her chest. "That boy just needs love."

I didn't miss the glance she gave me. Miles elbowed his wife. "You can stop that. We don't know if Harley here already has a fella, or whether she has any interest in Roman."

Now they were both looking at me.

Awkward much?

"We're just friends. He doesn't have romantic ideas about me. He scored a woman's phone number from the hotel when he came to fetch me yesterday," I explained, though why my mouth was running away and spouting out everything I didn't know. I put it down to my awkwardness around these people I hardly knew.

"The boy's an idiot then. When he comes back past, I might smack him around the head a second time. Might knock some sense into him." Cath folded her arms across her chest.

"It's fine. I have a lot of things on my plate at the moment and romantic complications are something I can do without."

Cath came over and opened out her arms. "You want a hug too, girly?"

"Yes please," I said, and I let her squeeze me tight.

"One day that boy will realise that while he might be able to score with other women, he has a complete angel right in front of him."

It was good she'd let go by then as my angel wings made their appearance.

"Not a complete angel. Just half of one." I grimace-smiled and shrugged my shoulders.

Cath and Miles stood there for at least ten seconds before Miles managed to speak.

"There's one I didn't think I'd ever see. I mean there are two werewolves sunbathing on the front lawn, so you'd reckon nothing would faze me by now, but I think that one did it. An angel right in front of me. Wow."

"You are simply even more beautiful than I first thought." Cath's bottom lip trembled. "I feel blessed to be in your presence."

Roman appeared and dashed towards us with his hands full. The sound of liquids sloshing from bottles accompanied him.

"Don't say the good words around her. Not until she's got herself under control," Roman said, then he turned to me. "Satan, devil, sin, evil, Beelzebub."

My wings folded away.

Cath's hand went to her chin. "I wonder if you need a special shampoo for them?"

"There's a lot we need to find out about it all and the first thing we're doing is seeing Harley's mother tomorrow to find out how Harley came to be a Nephilim. In the meantime, we're just going to chill out while she gets used to it as she's only discovered she was one in the early hours of this morning."

"Oh ble—"

"Cath!" Miles put a hand over her mouth.

"You two go enjoy your picnic and don't forget to call us if you need anything. The house bleep's in the basket." She pointed to the picnic basket, like we needed clarification. Maybe because I was a basket case?

"Thank you so much for putting that together. I'm looking forward to getting some fresh air and seeing where Roman's having his new home built," I went on, feeling a desperate need to get away from their sympathetic stares.

I took a step towards the doorway and then stopped when I remembered the rather large wolves on the lawn. I didn't much fancy being their breakfast.

"Too busy eating each other to worry about you," Miles said, receiving a hard elbow to the ribs from his wife.

He broke into guffaws and we laughed along with him, possibly as much at his wife's embarrassed face as at his joke. Then we stepped through the door and began walking up the edge of the lawn, away from the animals, and heading towards the woodland.

It was a gorgeous July day, and I was glad I'd been wearing a white t-shirt and beige cargo pants after filming. The cargo pants could be rolled up to long shorts and that was the first thing I'd be doing once we'd reached our destination.

We walked around the perimeter of the woodland making polite conversation, and after about twenty minutes, Roman pointed ahead to where there was clearly ground clearing works in progress. I could see fork-lift trucks and mounds of gravel.

"That's where my lodge will be," he explained and so we carried on walking in that direction.

"So tell me all about it. What's it going to look like?" I couldn't imagine what Roman's ideal home would be given I now knew he was a woodland creature.

"It's going to be all natural wood. All the furniture inside will be the same. The front of the house will face the woods so that the views from the windows will be all woodland. Then there will be a back entrance and all the parking, and accessibility for anyone staying or delivering will be behind the house. There'll be a formal garden to the rear with lots of shrubbery and trees planted at the back to disguise the concrete because I need to see nature not manmade materials where I can."

"Makes sense."

"I'll make sure I have guest bedrooms for people to stay over, but I'm likely to spend most of my own time in the woods. I'll show you where I've been sleeping and working on music when we make our way over there."

"So really, this lodge is more for when you have visitors than for yourself?" I queried.

He nodded. "Sometimes I like to be indoors, but I'm mainly at my happiest in my natural habitat. You can't expect visitors to camp outside though, and I'm hoping that the guys will come stay sometimes. They've offered their hospitality to me so much and I want somewhere to return the favour."

I smiled, but inside I was thinking that really what he wanted was somewhere to shag Mandy and any other groupie because they'd expect the millionaire lifestyle, not a quick fuck against a tree.

"Right, let's go find that picnic spot." He smiled and I could plainly see that it was the woodland where his heart laid, not this lodge.

We crossed into the edge of the woodland, and I followed Roman down a sweeping path. Dusty with dried dirt and with bits of tree roots and lost branches embedded, I was glad I had my trainers on and not a pair of high heels. Sunshine dappled through the trees, but not like when you were driving, and it hit you like strobe lighting. It was just... right. Birds sang and flew around, and the odd squirrel ran up the trunk of a tree at the side of us.

And then I heard the tinkle of water and Roman led me over to a stream.

"This side of the stream and the woodland we stand on now

is my part of the woods and the other side is Rex's. He says I can go there too if I like, but I think I have enough for what I need."

I span around taking in the complete 360-degree view. The light danced on the water, and it was so hypnotic to look at and listen to.

"Roman, it's beautiful."

We reached his summerhouse. It was only quite basic, but he had a table and some chairs in front of it on some decking and he placed the picnic basket and backpack with drinks in at the side of the table.

I pulled out a chair and sat down and Roman followed suit.

"Roman, I don't think you should build the lodge," I told him. I kind of blurted the words out, but I couldn't keep these thoughts to myself because I felt them deep in my gut.

"What? I thought you liked the idea when I explained it." His expression slackened.

"I do, but it's not really you, is it?" I gestured to the woodland around us. "Last year I stayed in Center Parcs and they had treehouses. That's what you should do. Build some treehouses. One for yourself and a few for guests. You could have some lodges on the ground too. They can have all necessary amenities run to them. Maybe where you were having your lodge you could build some type of office/business space instead because I know Wi-Fi is not great here." I'd been chattering on and realised Roman had stayed silent.

Guiltily, I paused for a second. "Sorry. That was rude of me; to dismiss your own plans and announce what I think you should do."

"Are you kidding?" he replied. "I'm loving every single thing you've said and could kick myself for not thinking of it first. Carry on."

"Really?" I smiled.

He nodded enthusiastically. "Really. Keep talking and I'll be pouring us some drinks. Is water okay?"

"Please." I was so happy he liked my ideas. I had just felt they were a lot more Roman. Not that I knew him well. I accepted the plastic tumbler full of cooled water.

"You could have subdued lighting hanging between the trees. And for any tree you have to fell to develop the area, you could not only plant a couple more in their place—I mean you have the whole car park area you can develop—but also you can use the wood for your furniture."

"I'm just going to grab my pad and pen from inside the summerhouse and sketch all this." Roman jumped up and reappeared a minute later. Then he sat and began sketching what I'd described.

"Wow. You can draw. Those sketches are incredible."

"Yeah, I like to sketch and paint. I find it therapeutic. You know, if I'm not being creative writing lyrics, it's a different creative outlet."

My eyes lit up and I became even more animated, gesturing with my hands. "That's it! The building you can have on the cleared car park. Landscaped grounds with like sculptures or something, maybe carved wood, and your building can not only be some all mod cons desk space, but a studio. Somewhere you can draw and paint."

"And it can have a large kitchen because I've always wanted to learn to cook, to get creative with food." Roman was warming to the idea.

"Yes! Oh, Roman, that's perfect."

He stared at me, his gaze lingering on my face, and then he looked back down to his notebook and the moment was lost.

My deluded, romantic heart thought he'd been going to announce that I was perfect too. Instead, he put down his pen and reached for the picnic basket.

"I'm getting hungry. Are you?"

I nodded, but it wasn't food I was admitting being hungry for.

I was hungry for Roman's attention.

Chapter 6

Roman

I had to change the subject quickly, because I almost blurted out that Harley was perfect. Thank goodness I was able to hide my face down by the chair leg as I reached for the picnic basket and busied myself arranging food.

It's her divine birth that's making you think she's perfect, Roman. She's too pure for you. Our kind are mired in sin and that's not what this woman needs.

I kept my conversation around Harley's ideas and decided that the moment we got back to Rex's place, I was calling my architects and changing all my plans. Then I was throwing money at it to get this new set of dwellings erected as quickly as possible because I couldn't wait to live there.

As we were walking back from the woods to the house, Harley startled, looking behind herself. "Oh. I was sure there was someone behind me then."

"It'll be shadows from the sun and the trees."

She looked behind herself again. "Okay. Only with there being wolves loose, I don't want to take chances on being leaped on."

At that moment I thanked God I wasn't in the company of

Zak because he would not have let the opportunity to turn that into an innuendo laden statement just lie there.

When we got back to the house, Cath greeted us, taking the picnic blanket from my hand. "Did you have a good time?"

"The food was delicious, Cath. Thank you," Harley said.

"Your belongings from the hotel arrived while you were out. They're in your room. If you need anything laundering, let me know."

"I'm starting to think you're the... thing that I half am."

Cath beamed.

"So what did you two get up to while you were out? Just enjoyed the views?"

Hmmm, I was beginning to think Cath wasn't as angelic as she made out, if the mischief in her features was any indication.

"Harley came up with the most amazing idea about how I can develop the land I bought while we were out," I told her.

I thought I was seeing things myself then as Rex appeared from a doorway. He was chewing a large piece of meat. "Roman, my friend. And Harley. Come join us at the dining table and regale us with tales of your life enhancing journey to the woodland."

I sneered at him as I approached. "Why are you speaking like Thor?"

He actually began to look bashful, an expression which my cocky shifter friend rarely wore.

"Seems I am still in role-play." He went back into the dining room.

I turned to meet Harley's amused gaze. "Do you want to go and join them? We might need sick buckets?"

She laughed. "Come on. We can laugh and bitch about them both afterwards," she whispered.

"Deal."

For the first few minutes I think we both just stared in shock and bewilderment as they ate more food than rugby players after a game.

And then they licked the sauce from around each other's mouths.

Finally, with their bellies satisfied, Rex and Freya managed to sit and offer us both some attention, albeit Freya was sat on Rex's lap, and kept doing a grinding motion.

Harley had had enough. "Freya, can you stop lapdancing your wolf husband for just ten minutes, or give up and just go back to your room? I love you dearly but it's not so much a public display of affection, but a public dickplay of affection."

"Sorry." Freya blushed a little. "It's just, you know, it's Rex Colton. And he's minnnneee." Their lips locked again, and Harley stood up. As her chair scraped back, Freya reluctantly broke off. "Sorry, Rexy. Normal service shall resume soon." She winked.

"Well, I guess you two are enjoying your wolfymoon," I said with a voice laced with sarcasm.

"Jealous, mate?" Rex smirked.

"You can't call him your mate now. You'll have to say pal. I'm your mate," Freya said.

They grinned at each other. It was truly nauseating.

"I'd better just check with you that I'm okay to stay here for a few days. Only you were otherwise occupied when I turned up," Harley stated.

"Of course," Rex answered. "Cath said you're going through some things and needed a time out. Stay as long as you want. He does."

"*He* is getting his new home built PDQ and even more quickly now I've just had to endure your own personal lap dance."

"Roman, stop acting all innocent. I've burst in on you with actual lapdancers. And that's plural," he confirmed to Harley.

Great, now Harley wouldn't feel safe in my manwhore company.

"Oooh, tell all about the plans for the house." Freya sat forward looking genuinely interested and so we got them up to speed with what I intended to do with the woods.

"And is there anything we can help you with Harley? If you want to talk about whatever's bothering you, we're here to help," Rex said.

"Absolutely," Freya added.

Harley took a deep breath, stood up and away from the table and said, "So help me God."

And he did, because her wings appeared.

"Fucking hell," yelled Freya, and that caused Harley's wings to retract.

"Any 'you know what' words, *good* ones, often bring them out and bad devilish words make them go back in. I'm seeing my mum tomorrow to see if she can shed any light as to what I need to do next."

"And you had no clue? None whatsoever?" Freya checked.

Harley shook her head. "I can make people's hurts better, like Roman's wrist hurt once and well, I feel heat come through my hands and it stops the hurting, but other than that, no. I just did something that was obviously a bit too helpful and there they were."

"Wow." Freya's eyes were still wide. "Get me a pad and pen, honey," she told Rex.

He pulled a face looking ready to tell her to get one herself and then she folded her arms across her chest and narrowed her eyes at him.

"Of course, darling. Two seconds." He shouted for Cath to bring him a pad and pen, then turned to Freya and shrugged. "I'm an alpha male. I like to demand things."

Freya thanked Cath and began writing on the paper. "This is a website I'm a member of. I can give you this code to recommend you and it gives you a discount. Get an account set up there and you'll be able to read up on the angelic realm. It might just help before you see your mum tomorrow. Stop her telling you any more half-truths and lies." She passed the paper to Harley.

"Thank you so much. I'm going to get on this right now," Harley answered.

"Are you going to get on this right now?" Rex asked Freya.

"Okay, we're going back to our room to enjoy the rest of the afternoon. So we'll see you both later?" Freya said the words, but it was more a statement than a question as they disappeared through the door at top speed.

"I'm glad we already ate, because I think I just lost my appetite," Harley announced. "Anyway, I'm going to go back to the room and see what I can find on this website."

"Okay. I need to make a call to my architect. I'll go do that from the living room so that you can have some privacy."

Cath came in to begin clearing up. "I'm going to do a barbecue on the patio outside at about eight. I'll do some cold salad-like things as well so if you don't want to come down, just dial 1 and I'll send a tray up to your room."

"I'm going to leave here three stones heavier." Harley patted her stomach.

"Huh. I know what those TV folks are like. I've read in the magazines. Making you eat tissue paper because the camera adds pounds. You get proper food and nourishment here."

"I can assure you the only paper I've had near my food has been what my fish and chips were wrapped in." Harley smiled.

Then she excused herself and left the room.

"Hey, Cath. Do you think I could ask the others along to tonight's barbecue?" I asked her. "Only Stacey is one of Harley's friends, so it would be nice for her to have some female company."

"Of course, love. You know I love entertaining. The more the merrier."

"Thank you," I said. Cath was fast becoming one of my favourite people.

I called Noah and then Zak and both said they'd love to come over for a barbecue. Then I called my architect. He was just as enthusiastic about my new plans. Whether that was because it appealed to his creativity or whether it was because it was a shit-load more work and therefore more money to be earned wasn't clear. I phoned my builders too, to warn them to anticipate a lot of changes and that a requirement for an increased crew was likely. We talked money and I assured them I had it covered.

This was going to be my home, and I just knew now that it was going to be everything I wanted and more. Any reservations I'd felt about the previous plans were gone. I looked at my drawings of my potential new treehouse. The glass fronted large building had a wraparound deck that was vast enough to house a jacuzzi and outdoor patio furniture. The left-hand side of the house held the kitchen and dining room, and a sliding door brought the inside outside. At the other side was the living room and that had the same glass sliding doors. It was all on one floor and at the other side was a bathroom and two bedrooms. One bedroom and the bathroom had normal sized windows, but the other bedroom had skylights and the glass sliding window/doors. I could open them at night if I wished and within the woodland, I'd be halfway between my natural habitat and luxury. It was perfection.

The other lodges would also have balconies and the sliding patio doors but not on such a grand scale.

Cath came bustling in with her trolley. On it was coffee and a selection of slices of cake.

"Can I tempt you with a little afternoon treat?"

I stared with longing at the assortment of treats. Being a sinful satyr at heart, decadence was my middle name, and desserts were my weakness. "Can I take a fruit and cherry scone please with clotted cream and strawberry jam, and also a slice of the chocolate fudge cake?"

Her eyes twinkled at me with mischief. "Shall I go warm that up and serve it with a little vanilla ice cream and some cherries on the side?"

"Why are you already married, Cath?" I whimpered.

She laughed as she prepared my scone. "How do you think I got Miles? The saying 'a way to a man's heart is through his stomach' is right, as long as now and again you get lost on your way to their stomach, if you catch my drift."

My jaw dropped and Cath hooted with laughter as she went out of the room. "I'll be back in a minute with your chocolate cake."

When she returned, she asked to look at my house plans and oohed and aahed and then she made me add a steam room and make the bath fit two people. "Oh and I think you should add a walk-in-wardrobe with places for shoes and bags as well as clothes."

"Are you planning on moving in, Cath?" I joked.

She shook her head at me, laughing again. "No, but you just should be prepared for if you ever do want to move a nice young lady in," she said. Then she lowered her voice. "You know, one like Harley for instance."

I opened my mouth, and she shoved a forkful of chocolate cake in it.

"I know, you're just friends," she said, and as she left the room, she seemed to mumble something that sounded a lot like, 'bloody idiot'.

Chapter 7

Harley

Once I got back to the room, I sorted through my belongings, placing my clothes on hangers in the wardrobe. Gosh it would feel good to sleep in my silk pyjamas tonight instead of my t-shirt and cargo pants. Plus, I might actually sleep in the bed, rather than pass out drunk on the sofa.

Then again, Cath was throwing a barbecue. I might end up falling asleep drunk under a garden bench.

I poured myself a glass of water from the mini fridge in the room, and then sitting on the sofa, I opened my laptop and caught up with some messages. I sent one to Malcolm explaining that I wouldn't be at work for at least the next week and that I'd get my physician to send him a note tomorrow.

Following that, I put my laptop down on the coffee table and phoned my agent to let her know where I was and what I was doing. Carol hadn't wanted me to do the job in the first place once the travel part had 'fallen through'.

"Why don't you let me get you out of the contract? Malcolm's a dick and he never had any intention of flying you anywhere. I'll bet you a hundred quid that all those relatives have had to fund the trips themselves."

That horrified me. "Tell me he wouldn't do that."

"Honey, I could lie, but I reckon all he's doing is getting his research team to find and reunite the families and then he'll give them some kind of sweetener and that'll be it."

"I'm going to find out," I told her, feeling determined. "I'm not sure how yet, but I'm going to find out and if that's the case I will fund the trips myself, and help the families meet up privately."

Boom. Out came my wings and once more I was sitting on my arse on the floor.

"Suck a dick," I yelled, my wings going back in.

"Pardon?" Carol's shocked voice came down the line.

"I said Malcolm is such a dick," I lied, thankful it had a) come quickly and b) my body had allowed me to tell the lie. Maybe because my statement actually wasn't one?

After ending the call, I sat back against the sofa and closed my eyes for a moment. Everything was giving me a headache. I had the ridiculous TV production, my new normal half-angel self, and my unrequited crush on Roman. Add my mum to the mix tomorrow and I'd be in the Priory by Tuesday getting counselling. Especially if my sister was home too.

"Thank you," a voice whispered in my ear and my eyes shot open. I sat up and turned to look behind me to where the voice had come from, but there was no one there.

I was actually going mad.

"Is someone here?" I asked hesitantly as I edged towards the door, because I knew if a voice said 'yes', I'd be running out of this room screaming. But there was nothing.

I'd clearly fallen half to sleep and was experiencing a hypnogogic reaction. That stage between awake and asleep where you could imagine things. I'd once seen a spider run down my bedside table. It had disappeared before my eyes as I'd started to scream, so I was aware of what could happen.

After taking a few deep breaths, I grabbed my laptop and moved to my bedroom, sitting on the edge of my bed. I logged in to the website Freya had written down for me, *Supernaturals Uncovered*.

I read all the introductory posts. There was so much information on here. I could look up satyrs and learn more about Roman. But before I did any of that I needed to look up what I was. I made sure I allowed plenty of room for my wings, which came out just as I typed in the word Nephilim.

Nephilim
Copyright Frankie Love.
Nephilim are the children of a human mother and an angel father. They look like humans in appearance, but usually are noted for their beauty and their grace.
Nephilim used to be seen as a disgrace, but in these modern times are now judged according to individual merit. Most Nephilim fathers are fallen angels cast out of heaven, although some swore to work off their sins and were returned to the hierarchy.
Many Nephilim never know their true identity. While they may show a gift for healing or for being helpful, this is not enough to reveal their true self.
Usually there will be an inciting incident, an act of selflessness, that will lead to the first display of angel wings. This can be a great shock to a person who thought they were human and many Nephilim enter mental institutions. Luckily, due to a cosmic 'ping', when a Nephilim gains their wings, an earth-angel usually engages with the Nephilim within the first few days of their change and takes them out of the psychiatric facilities.
All Nephilim can mate with humans and the females will carry human children with no angelic qualities. A similar thing happens with any pregnancy with another species. The half-angel side of a Nephilim does not dilute further, so any such pregnancies, eg Vampire and Nephilim would result in a Vampire/Human mix.

So I'd have half-human, half-satyr children with Roman, I

thought, and then I scolded myself for having such a vivid imagination. I carried on reading.

Nephilim live to what would in human terms be called a 'ripe old age'. When you hear of humans living into their late nineties or early hundreds they are likely to be Nephilim.

Many Nephilim work within the caring and counselling services or seek the spotlight as their own natural angelic light is dimmed.

There was a lot of information and I carried on reading for a while. Then I typed into the search bar:

How to stop angel wings from spontaneously appearing.

The following appeared:

Angels can control their wings at all times, but for newly-winged Nephilim, they will appear at the mention of many divine words and close away once the Nephilim's mind is clear of this. The earth-angel will perform a short ceremony to stop this from occurring and give the Nephilim the power to fold and unfold their wings at their discretion.

Oh thank goodness. The sooner this earth-angel appeared, the better. It was a shame there wasn't a helpline number.

I read further and then went, "Oh."

Should you need to get in touch with an earth-angel urgently, you can send a text to angelsophia@heaven.org. Replies guaranteed within twenty-four hours.

I clicked the link so that it opened a blank email and I began to type.

To: angelsophia@heaven.org
From: HarleyDaviesOfficial@mail.com
Date: 3 July 2023
Subject: Query about earth-angel allocation
Dear Angel Sophia

I recently discovered that I am a Nephilim. At the moment my wings are causing me discomfort due to the fact that their surprise arrival makes me overbalance. I would be grateful if you could let me know when I might expect a visit from an earth-angel as at present I am not living at my own address.

I am currently staying at Oakley Manor, Poplar Heights, London. My apologies that I'm not sure of the postcode.

Looking forward to hearing from you.

Harley xo

I received a confirmation email. I was just about to begin to research satyrs when the man himself sent me a text.

Roman: You might want to come downstairs. Erica and Zak just arrived, ready for the evening's barbecue.

Harley: Be right down!

My friends were here! I'd met Stacey at the competition that she entered with her band, and I'd got to know Erica and Freya when they'd spent a week with the band a few weeks ago. Gosh, it would be nice to see some friends!

Shame my wings would no doubt keep popping in and out all night. It was so weird how they just managed to appear through any outfit without tearing the material. I guess it was similar to how Roman's horns didn't puncture his scalp.

I got up from my bed and began to stroll out of the room. Just as I turned to walk out of the door a shiny spinning circle appeared in front of me. *Oh, way to go, Harley. Start with a migraine just as your friends arrive.*

But it wasn't a migraine, because a woman with ginger, bobbed hair stepped out of it.

"I *was* in the middle of seducing my husband, but Angel Sophia said your need was greater than mine." She sighed heavily. "I'm Lucy." She held out a hand. I went to shake it and she pulled it back.

"On second thoughts, I've not washed my hand since it was around Frankie's cock. Can I use your bathroom?"

Unable to actually form coherent words to reply, I just nodded and pointed to the bathroom door.

I don't know what I'd expected an earth-angel to act like, but it wasn't like Lucy. When she explained she used to be a demon it made a lot more sense. She told me that she did earth-angel duties occasionally as well as helping her husband Frankie to keep his database up to date.

"Oh." I smiled. "You're Frankie from Supernaturals Uncovered's wife."

"Yup, that's me, Mrs Love. No one cares I do good deeds now, just that I'm married to the genius that is Frank," she said, her voice laced in heavy sarcasm. "Anyway, new Nephilim. Let's check you over."

She stood in front of me.

"Angel half, show thy wings. Feathers white and strong."

My wings appeared, but this time they came out softly and gradually and fluttered as if in a soft breeze.

"Beautiful." A genuine smile appeared on Lucy's bright red lips. "There's nothing finer than the pureness of an angel wing."

I returned her smile.

"Angel half, hide your wings. Feathers away and calm."

In they went. Again, carefully.

"I'm going to place my hands either side of your temples and although I will outwardly say nothing, I am communicating with your wings that they do your bidding."

"Okay."

She touched my temples with her fingers, and I felt a feeling of love and peace wash through me.

"All done," she said, passing me a card. "If you need me for anything else, my contact details are on there." She took another card out of her pocket. "And if you ever have problems getting a date, my friend runs a dating agency for supernaturals, so you might want to keep that handy."

"Er, thanks." I took the card.

"Any other questions before I go?"

"Can I fly?"

Lucy laughed at that. "No, lovely, you can't fly, so don't worry, you're not going to fly off up to heaven."

"I did end up on the ceiling the other day."

"You can float a bit, but it's parlour trick stuff, nothing that's going to save you paying for *Virgin Atlantic* or *RyanAir*."

"Ah, okay."

"Unlike me, who can just draw a portal in the air and off I go," she said, doing exactly that. "Ciao, darling." She winked as she climbed through it and disappeared.

I was having the strangest twenty-four hours of my entire life and as I took a moment to sit on the sofa and reflect before I headed downstairs for the get-together, it came to me that it was only probably going to get weirder.

Chapter 8

Roman

"You're sharing a suite with a hot blonde, and you haven't tapped that yet? Who are you and what have you done with my womanising bandmate?" Zak guffawed.

"Leave him alone. He's being respectful. It sounds like Harley is going through a lot right now," Erica scolded him.

"She grows wings. Big fucking deal. Our knobs grow every day. Don't see men the world over harping on about how hard it is to deal with. Oh hard. Hahahahaha."

My eyes met Erica's. She must really be in love, or ever so slightly deaf.

"So I gather from Cath that my best friend and her new boyfriend have been very vocal. She always has been a gobby cow."

"Now she's a gobby wolf," Zak replied.

"Yes, I'd expect to see them both yawning a lot tomorrow."

"You do realise now that you're the only single dude, man. Subs are going to be turning their attentions on you. You're going to have pussy for miles."

"Hi everyone."

I whipped around to find Harley standing behind me. She came and joined me, Zak, and Erica. The doorbell rang.

"That'll be the other two," I said to make conversation.

Sure enough, Noah and Stacey walked through the double doors and onto the back garden a few minutes later. After air kisses, the women went off in a huddle of their own—no doubt to catch up on what Harley had just discovered about herself, and for Harley to question Stacey about her own supernatural abilities—and I was left with my bandmates.

"So how come Harley is staying here?" Noah asked.

"She was recording a television show about reuniting families, and it was supposed to be filmed in LA," I explained. "But something went awry, and they ended up holed up in a two-star hotel in Soho. She can't have anyone in the U.K. know she's here, so she's hiding out for now and has told the show's producer that she's ill."

"I'm sure Stacey will be able to come up with some cloaking spell, or Harley could just say she's returned to the U.K. because she's not well," Noah said.

"Er, no, it's fine, it's sorted."

He arched a brow. "Hmm, do I detect that you're actually wanting Harley to be here?"

I rocked on the balls of my feet a little. "It's been nice, having someone to hang around with. It's easy. There's no pressure. No expectations. She's someone I get on well with. You're all busy these days and it's nice to not be on my own right now."

"Oh, mate." Zak flung his arms around me. "I didn't realise we were neglecting you. Come have a snuggle."

"Get off me, you lunatic." I unfastened his arms from around me and pushed him away.

"Charming. That's probably why you end up on your own so much," he huffed. "I'm going to go suck up to Cath so I get the largest piece of chocolate cake." He wandered off, leaving me with Noah.

"So you like her, huh?" he pushed.

"Yeah, I do, but you know me. I'm not one to form an attachment because people just let you down when you let them in.

She's got a lot of things going on, and I'm there to support her through it. While that's happening, she doesn't know it, but it's helping me too."

"I know your relationship with your family broke down, but are there not other satyrs you could hang with?" Noah queried.

"There's not a social club if that's what you mean. Satyrs are mainly selfish creatures who lounge around drunk and fornicating all day, every day. For some reason, I'm a little different. It is what it is."

He squeezed the top of my arm. "Perhaps it's time to let someone in, Roman. You let us three in back at college. You can do it again."

His eyes flickered over to Harley.

"She keeps looking over here. You know she likes you too."

"Yeah, but I've told you. Right now, she doesn't even understand herself and who she is. That's where her focus needs to be. So right now, I'll just be the friend she needs. But," I shrugged, "after she's got used to things, feels more settled, maybe I will ask her out."

Noah smiled. "You do that, my friend. It's a step in the right direction. And I don't want to get mega soppy, but I think the right woman and a family would give you what you clearly desire, Roman. Roots."

I mulled over what he was saying. Was that what I was craving? I was having a home built, placing myself in one location so that when we weren't on tour, I had a home to come back to. Did I want a partner and family with that? To admit that to myself though meant admitting that I deeply missed the family who had rejected me. As I felt a pressure behind my eyes, I swallowed and reached in my pocket for my scotch. Sometimes it was easier to call on my satyr genetics and get rip-roaringly drunk, than face up to my reality.

We ate and drank, and just being around my friends made me realise that I had let the others in and although they now had wives and girlfriends, it only meant in the long run, that I was actually expanding my own circle. I was fond of Stacey, Erica, and Freya. Maybe I just did need to let myself follow my heart a little? Alcohol had loosened me up and I decided I might go try a little flirting with Harley after all.

She was sitting on a swing seat with a glass of wine and was gently rocking on it. The other four were chatting near the table. "Hey, you okay?"

Harley smiled at me, and my heart fluttered a little. "I am. It's lovely out here. I'm just enjoying being out in the fresh air, relaxing with a drink and taking in what's around me, you know? Looking at the sky and the trees. A bit like earlier outside your summerhouse."

"Nature is wonderful," I acknowledged.

"Yeah, it really is, and you know, I've been so busy pursuing my career that I've forgotten what life is really about. I mean, just seeing those families who have been separated and for whatever reason haven't been able to reconnect, it's made me realise how lucky I am to have my mum and sister." She looked at me and clapped a hand over her mouth. "Oh, Roman. Shit, I just put my foot in it once more."

"May I sit?"

She nodded and I took the seat next to her. "It's fine. You don't have to avoid talking about my family. They were clear that my leaving the swamp and rejecting the woman they had chosen for me in order to pursue a rock career, was an insult to them and to my upbringing. I was told if I left then I was never to return. I've tried in the past to mend fences but ultimately, they don't bend from their rigid ways. They're waiting for me to 'get it out of my system' and then I can return and beg for forgiveness."

"I'm so sorry. I couldn't imagine being a parent and sending my child away, no matter what they wanted to do with their life. I wonder if my own dad thinks about me at all?"

"Hopefully you'll get some answers tomorrow when we go and see your mum."

"I hope so. I've always felt like I was looking for something and never knew what it was. Maybe all along it's been the other side of me trying to tell me it was there?" She exhaled loudly. "I'm rambling, ignore me."

"You're not rambling. It's more than likely true. You have a side to you that's been trying to shine and now you can realise your whole potential."

"You don't think I'll have to go live up in heaven, do you? Lucy was an earth-angel. Maybe I'll have to be one of those."

"Lucy?"

"Oh, yeah, I've not had chance to tell you yet. An earth-angel called Lucy visited me in our room and she did some weird temple healing thing that meant I now will only have wings appear if I ask them to. No spontaneous eruptions."

"I thought it was strange I'd not seen them appear."

"I owe Lucy because Zak would not have been able to help himself."

I laughed. It was true. He'd have been shouting about God and devils and watching Harley's wings appear and disappear until either Erica or Harley punched him.

We rocked on the seat for a few minutes enjoying the ambience.

"This is nice isn't it?" I stated.

"Yeah, it really is," Harley replied.

I turned to her, and we stopped swinging.

"I know you've only been here a day, but it's great having you around."

She smiled coyly and looked at me from under her lashes. "I like being around you, Roman."

Time seemed to stand still. My eyes flicked over to where my friends were watching Zak try to escape a wasp. No one was looking at what we were doing. What I was doing.

I leaned over towards Harley, shortening the gap between us, and she moved closer to me until our lips were only a whisper apart. My mouth landed on hers, and I took in the feel of her soft warm lips against my own. I reached my hand around her neck and held her firm as I opened my mouth and deepened the kiss.

She tasted of white wine and strawberries, and as I kissed her a feeling of peace and everything being right with the world flooded through me. This kiss, such a delicate first meeting of our mouths, was perfection, and something I'd never felt before and I had kissed many women in my life. Many, many women.

I couldn't put it down to the alcohol swimming around my system because I'd been much drunker than this when lustily pursuing women. It was just her, Harley.

Then the sound of the front doorbell echoed. I broke the kiss, backing up. Harley and I just stared at each other, until Cath eventually came out of the door and walked over to us.

"Erm, Roman. There's a woman at the door to see you?"

I felt my brow crease. I wasn't expecting anyone.

Cath looked at Harley and then back at me. "She says she's your wife."

Harley threw her white wine in my face. "Wife? You utter, utter bastard." She got up and ran across to the others, while I sighed and made my way to the front door.

Chapter 9

Harley

"What the hell just happened?" Stacey asked me as I stomped over towards them with tears in my eyes. "I saw you just throw your drink at Roman. What's he done?"

"What h-has h-he d-d-done?" I trembled as a tear ran down my cheek. "He k-kissed me and then Cath came over and said that his w-*wife* is at the door."

I was greeted with four slackened jaws.

"His what?" Noah asked. "Did you say wife?"

"He kissed you?" Erica said. "Oh my god, what was it like?"

"Babe, that's not the focus right now, Mrs Romantic. He's kissed her and apparently has a missus. Which I for one didn't know about."

"Me neither," added Noah. "When the fuck did he get married?"

"I'm going to my room. I need to get out of here. There's no way I can meet his w-wife." More tears spilled down my cheeks.

"Come on. I'll go up to your room with you for a while. I know a way around the back so we can avoid the front door and go up the back staircase," Stacey said.

"I'll come too," Erica added.

"I'll stay here so I can fully appraise myself of the situation and report back," Zak told Erica.

She rolled her eyes at him. "I'll have my phone. You keep me updated on *everything.*"

"Yes, Boss." He saluted her. "Oooh, can we role-play female CEO later?" he shouted to our retreating backs. Then I heard an, "Ooof." That made me smile a little as he'd clearly just been physically reprimanded by Noah.

I managed to keep it all together apart from a few stray tears until I walked into the suite. Then I flopped down on the sofa and burst into tears. Stacey and Erica sat either side of me and I felt arms come around me as I let out all my upset, disappointment, and frustrations.

When I stopped and started sniffling, Erica got up and grabbed a box of tissues, taking a couple from the box and passing them to me. I blew my nose on one and wiped my eyes on the other and held them scrunched in my hand.

"I really like him, and I'd thought something might finally be happening between us, and then I find out he has a wife?" I sniffled and wiped my eyes again.

"Everyone's as shocked as you are. No one knew." Stacey stroked my hair.

"He's a lying dirtbag. I mean, he got the hotel receptionist's phone number on the way to coming to help me. I should have known not to trust him. He said he was ex-communicated from his tribe or whatever they call themselves for not being a true satyr, but he seems to be a fully-fledged womanising trickster from where I'm sitting," I spat out.

"Huh, I think it's time Roman had a taste of his own medicine." Stacey sat folding her arms across her chest. "I need to think like Donna. How can I do no harm and so not break my oath, but also have a little revenge against Mr Idiri..."

She sucked on her top lip.

"Okay. Just give me a minute here." She reached into her pocket and took out a pinch of what looked like tiny green flecks which she threw in front of her. "Sage," she said, meeting my inquisitive stare. "Now for the spell." She cleared her throat.

> *"Roman hid his truth from all.*
> *Now it's time to topple his wall.*
> *For every time he tells a lie*
> *Out of his mouth shall come a fly."*

"Ew, that's a bit mean," Erica said. "Flies land on shit. Who'd want them in your mouth?"

"If he speaks shit then they'll be right at home. Anyway, they aren't real, although they'll appear real. It will cause no true harm, but it will mean he'll think twice about not being completely honest," Stacey said.

"Oh, that's fine then. As long as he can't catch any weird disease."

"He's p-probably already got a ton of diseases from all the women he's been with," I uttered. Even thinking about flies coming out of his mouth wasn't cheering me up. I'd been crushing on him big time, and he'd destroyed me by actually making me think he might like me, only to have neglected to tell me he was married. I couldn't stay here after all. I needed to leave.

"I should pack my stuff."

"NO," the other two women said together.

"He can fuck off," Erica said. "Not you."

"Yeah, he can go back to his summerhouse."

"He'll probably go back to wherever his wife lives. Maybe he has a home with her. It's like those men you read about that have secret families. Oh nooooo. He might even have children," I wailed.

"Oh, Harley." Stacey hugged me close to her again. "He's had us all fooled. I honestly thought Roman was quiet, sensitive, and misunderstood. But Erica's right. You stay here and let him leave."

"I'm just going to freshen up," I told the others, standing up. "Then let's go and see what she looks like, hey? I want to watch the flies come out as he tries to explain himself."

After washing my face and then splashing it with cold water, I went into Roman's room and picking the discarded shirt up again, I took the paper out and put it in my own trouser pocket.

Coming out, I stood straight and faced the other two. "Let's go."

"Proud of you, lady. Let's go see the charlatan and if you want to yell at him, go for it," Erica said.

"I don't know what I want to do," I replied honestly, "but I can't help but want to see what she looks like. What he married."

What I, and the other two women with me did not expect, was for all four of the others to be sitting on patio furniture laughing away together.

I took in the features of the woman who I'd just seen rest her head on Roman's shoulder. Her long, reddish-brown hair waved past her shoulders. She was wearing a black vest top and black jeans with converse. She was athletically built with pale skin with freckles. She was gorgeous. As she sat back up chatting and waved her arms around gesticulating, I could see her muscled forearms. I had to keep fit and toned as part of my career, but she looked like an athlete. I hated her already. Zak and Noah sat on the adjacent sofa and looked captivated, and as I took in my female friends' expressions they looked about as happy with the situation as I did.

Zak grinned at Erica. "Little E. Come meet Sasha."

As everyone walked over, there was room for Erica and Stacey to sit with their partners. I just stood there like an idiot while Sasha clearly looked me up and down.

"Want to sit here?" Roman asked, patting the seat at the other side of him.

I honestly didn't know what I wanted to do. Though it wasn't stand in front of everyone like I was in Madame Tussauds.

"So, Sasha. How long have you been married to Roman?" Stacey asked through gritted teeth.

"Oh, we aren't really married. That was just my little joke." Sasha laughed and pushed at Roman's arm. I realised where I wanted to sit... right in between them.

"Pardon?" Stacey said. Sasha seemed oblivious to the fact that Stacey's jaw was tightening further by the second.

"We used to call each other husband and wife as a joke when we were younger. Our parents would think it was cute and we'd be rolling our eyes. Our parents wanted us to get together. Betrothed us as kids. Only problem was, Roman wanted to go be in a band, and I fancied his older brother, not him. Anyway, I got his whereabouts out of his mum, although it took me a while. I'm now marrying his brother, and I want Roman to be at the wedding. I know that's a difficult situation, but we've always been close, and I want him to give me away. My father died last year."

Fuck, now I had difficulty hating her because she'd just lost her dad. Also, she wasn't Roman's wife. Finally, being able to move my feet, I went and sat at the other side of Roman. He wasn't married! I felt giddy and relieved and then I remembered the phone number in my pocket. Ratbag.

He turned to me and grinned. He actually looked a little shy. Gosh, he should be an actor. No wonder he had women throwing themselves at him. I gave him a smile that I reckoned came across as more of a grimace as his expression turned to one of confusion.

I could just make out Erica telling Zak off under her breath for not texting or phoning her while we were in my room.

Never mind all that. I was still pissed at Roman, even if everyone else was suddenly all pally pally again.

"Roman," I interrupted the conversation going on around me. "Have you ever farted and stuck your head under the blankets to sniff it?"

"No." He looked at me weirdly and then his eyes went wide,

his expression turned to one of confusion and horror and his mouth opened and out came a fly.

"Liar," I shouted.

Roman stood up, his mouth open. He began heaving slightly. "What the hell? When did I swallow that? How long has it been in there?" His skin had turned green.

"Have you ever scratched your bum and sniffed your finger?" I asked him.

"What on earth is wrong with you? Are you drunk?" he asked me, then stuck his tongue out and scraped it with his teeth.

"Well, have you?"

"NO."

Buzzzzzzz.

"Help me. What the fuck is happening?" Roman ran to the table to get some water. Stacey came over to me. "I need to lift the spell. He's not married. He didn't lie."

Roman walked back. He was sloshing water around his mouth and spitting it onto the grass.

"Did you, or did you not take a woman's phone number when you came to see me at the hotel?"

"No."

Buzzzz.

"Help me. Help me please. Phone a doctor. I must have swallowed fly eggs."

I took the piece of paper from my pocket.

"Mandy. That's the number of the woman you took." I thrust the piece of paper out. "Here. It almost went in the laundry. Thought you might need it."

"Ohhh," he said, then he turned to the others. "I forgot about this. This receptionist at the hotel. I said if she helped me get Harley out of the building unseen, she could come get her photo taken with us all. That okay with you guys, if I ask her to pop up while we're recording this week?"

In horror I realised no flies had come out of his mouth. He was telling the truth.

He wasn't married.

He'd not taken another woman's phone number with lust-fuelled intentions.

He'd kissed me.

I needed a drink. Walking over to him, I opened his jacket, reached into his inner pocket and took out his bottle of scotch.

"I'll be over there," I announced, and I walked back over to the swing seat out of the way of everyone. I didn't care what Sasha thought. I'd just made an absolute fool out of myself and Roman was still thinking he'd had a fly lay eggs in his mouth. Why couldn't I fly? I'd have done it now. Flown right bloody off and away.

The longer I sat there, the more I drank as I thought about the things I'd asked Roman. I mean I asked him about smelling his own farts and sniffing his fingers after scratching his bum. He must have thought I was a complete lunatic.

With a sigh, I stumbled off the seat and went back up to my room. None of them even noticed. All too busy talking to Sasha or dealing with a still hysterical Roman.

Guilt flooded through me. I needed to leave. To get away from here too. There was no way I could go to my mother's. My sanity would completely leave there. I'd have to go back to the cheap hotel. I needed to sleep anyway. I'd been awake over twenty-four hours, nothing but adrenaline keeping me going. I could control my wings now. I'd just say I felt a lot better after all. Get back to filming and back to my own life. The one without Roman in it.

Chapter 10

Roman

At first, I'd not had a clue what Cath had been talking about when she'd said my wife was at the door. I'd been completely captivated by Harley's soft lips.

If it had been a disturbed fan at the door, I may not have been able to hold in my temper, but instead, my old best friend was there. And we'd used to joke, calling each other wife and hubby, as we rolled our eyes at our parents saying they wanted us together. We'd just never felt attracted to each other in the slightest. We'd looked out for each other as friends, but that was it. One day Sasha had confessed to a crush on my older brother. I'd laughed at her of course and then not long after that, I'd left.

"Sasha!" I launched myself in her direction, throwing my arms around her and hugging her tightly.

"Ow, you're hurting me, you oaf," Sasha squealed.

Letting her go and apologising, I looked her over. "You look so well. How did you know where to find me?"

"Your mum. Eventually. Anyway, are you leaving me on the doorstep all night?"

"Sorry. I'm just so shocked. Come in, come in. I'm just eating with some friends out the back. Come and meet them all." She walked in behind me, and we passed Cath. "Cath, this is my childhood friend, Sasha."

"I thought you were his wife?" Cath questioned; her eyes narrowed.

"It's an in-joke," Sasha said, reaching across and rubbing the top of my head.

"Oh, would you like a drink, lovely? I have most things." Cath had suddenly adopted a much friendlier demeanour. Goodness knows what had got into her tonight.

"I'd love a gin and tonic if you have it?"

"Ice and a slice?"

"Please."

"Okay. Well, you both go out back into the garden and you introduce your *friend* to *everybody*," Cath said.

"Come on. I can't wait for you to meet everyone."

But when I got back outside the women had all disappeared. "Zak, Noah. This is Sasha. She's my bestie from back home."

"Not really his wife. That was a joke." Sasha held up her hands.

"Aww, I thought it was going to be some large and juicy gossip," Zak whined.

"Oh, I can still regale you with lots of tales about Roman." Sasha grinned.

"Come sit with us and tell us all." Zak guided her to the patio seats.

"It's fantastic to see you, but I'm guessing there's a reason to this visit?" I asked my friend.

"Yes, big and surprising news. I'm getting married... to Augustus."

"Whaaaaattt? When did that happen?"

"Last year. He finally realised I was his ideal woman."

I laughed. "What did you do?"

"Well... I may have pretended to be drunk and walked naked into his bedroom."

"*Sasha.*"

"*What*? Other than clubbing him over the head, I was running out of options. Anyway, it worked. The wedding is in a month's time, and I very much want you there. So, I made your mother tell me where you'd been living."

"Let me guess. She doesn't want me there as I'll embarrass the family."

"I told your mother that either you were both there or neither of you were."

"You're a brave woman."

"I am, and there are lots more like me, Roman. We intend to change things. No more satyr men thinking they can just drink and frolic and not pull their weight around the place. Times are a changing. It might be a hard slog, but I'm starting by having who I want at my wedding, and you will be welcomed with open arms by me and your brothers."

"How is Marcellus?" I asked her.

"He misses his other brother, so say you'll come to our wedding."

"I'll consider it," I told her.

"And you can bring a guest. Tell me, is there anyone special in your life?"

"Funnily enough, he thinks no one spotted him and Harley playing tonsil tennis earlier, but I was just about to shout, 'Look at those two go', when you arrived," Zak announced.

Noah's head snapped to me. "You kissed Harley?"

"I may have, but seeing as Cath then announced my wife had turned up, I'm sure you can imagine what happened next."

"Oh, Roman, shit. I never thought." Sasha bit her bottom lip.

"It's fine. I'll explain. Oh, here they come now."

Sasha started telling the others stories of things I'd got up to when we were younger while I watched the women make their way over. Every one of them looked really pissed off.

It all became a little awkward as Harley just stood in the middle of us all, and then it went from awkward to weird as she asked me a series of strange questions and flies started coming out of my mouth.

While I was having a breakdown over the fact flies eggs had somehow embedded themselves in my mouth, she handed me the piece of paper with Mandy's name on it, after which she took my scotch and walked off.

I was confused. She knew now that Sasha wasn't my wife, but she was still acting pissed off and weird. I'd have to ask her if she was okay later, but for now, I needed to phone a doctor about my mouth.

Moments later, an apologetic Stacey confessed to a spell after thinking Sasha really was my wife and I was finally able to laugh about it.

Harley had gone to sit on the swing seat again and I kept an eye on her from a distance. I'd check in with her later but right now my friend was here, and I had to give Sasha my attention.

Harley had been sitting there for about thirty minutes and then the next time I looked she'd gone.

"Fuck," I said, gaining Sasha's attention.

"What's up?"

"Just that Harley's gone. She seemed in a weird mood. Maybe she regrets me kissing her."

"There's only one way to find out, isn't there?" Sasha said. "Go and find out."

"But you've come to visit."

"Mate, you aren't getting rid of me now I've found you again. Not now I've finally stood up to those idiots back at the swamp. Plus, actually, I should be on my way home myself. I'll say goodbye to everyone, and I'll leave my contact number with Cath, okay?" We stood and hugged, then kissed on both cheeks. "Speak soon, now go see what's wrong with your girl."

My girl. I liked the sound of that.

I dashed up to the room, stopping outside our door and trying to get my breath back, both from running and from nervousness. What was I supposed to say?

I'd just decided to open the door regardless when it opened in front of me and Harley halted there. I saw the holdall in her hand.

"Where are you going?"

"I'm going back to the hotel, Roman. You're busy, and well, I need to be on my own."

"No. I don't think so," I replied.

She took a step back. "Pardon?"

I took the bag out of her hand. "You're not going back to that crummy hotel. You're staying here with me."

She cocked a hip out. "Who made you the boss?"

I actually didn't know what to say in reply. She might be the angel, but I was winging it. So, dropping her holdall down to the floor, I strode towards her, pulled her into my arms and kissed her again.

At first, she stiffened in my embrace and for a split-second I thought I'd made a mistake. But then she gave in, and her arms wrapped around my neck as her mouth slanted against my own. There was more passion to this kiss though and it went on for quite some time, until gasping for breath, we broke apart.

"So. To make it clear. I don't have a wife."

"I'm sorry for making flies come out of your mouth."

"Harls, it was certainly something I'll never forget. Remind me never to get on the wrong side of you."

"I guess that would be the part I got from my mum." She smirked.

"Luckily, Stacey was still here to remove the spell she'd put on me. And she had to apologise seeing as I'd done nothing wrong. Why on earth did you think I'd taken that receptionist's phone number for a future date?"

"You said see you later to her and patted your pocket. I saw the phone number."

"Harley, I ran across town at one am to come to see you. If I wanted a quick hook up, I could have phoned one of the women who email me nudes."

"I hate your Inbox now."

"Harley, Harley, Harley. When are you going to realise that the only woman I want is the one stood in front of me right now?"

"Really?"

"Really. So just so you know, you aren't going anywhere." I picked up her holdall and threw it back on the bed in her room.

"You shouldn't have done that," she said.

"Why, do you still want to leave?" I asked.

"No. I want you to take me to bed and now there's a holdall in the way," she announced.

"Yes, but there's nothing on mine." I waggled my brows and then I lifted her up and walked her to my room, kicking open my door, and laying her on my bed.

I slowly stripped her of all her clothes. Harley's skin was soft and smooth and perfect for my lips to run over every inch. I felt her skin goose bump beneath me as I trailed wet kisses down her arms, and her nipples puckered under the lave of my tongue. Her skin was salty and sweet, and I couldn't wait to find out how her pussy tasted. My cock almost punched out of my own jeans at the thought. But right now, it was all about her. Letting her nipple fall from my mouth, I kissed down her belly, and I trailed my nose down her landing strip, taking in the musky scents mixed with vanilla scented shower gel that emanated from her. I situated myself below her and pushed her thighs apart, taking in the glistening skin that showed how wet and ready for me she was. Running my tongue up her seam, she sighed in ecstasy as I finally got a taste of her. She tasted heavenly, and it was nothing to do with her genetics. Adding my finger to her clit, I played and teased her like she was my most prized guitar until she was clutching my pillow as she arched off the bed. Her pussy detonated against my face as she screamed my name. I rested on one elbow and just watched her from my position at the end of the bed as she caught her breath. She was running her hands through her blonde hair and her chest fall and rose with urgency.

"Fuck, Roman, that was..."

I climbed off the bed, stripped out of my clothes, sheathed myself in a condom from my wallet, and then climbed back on. Harley's eyes looked me over from head to toe and then back up, her eyes alighting on what she had coming... literally.

Her tongue swept across her bottom lip, and it was my undoing. I pushed inside her as my mouth swept over where she'd just wet her lip.

"What were you saying?" I whispered in her ear as I then lightly nibbled her lobe.

"I don't even know my own name right now," she replied.

Moving slowly in and out of her, I smirked against her mouth as I swept her up in a kiss again. She'd seen nothing yet. Once you'd been satyrsfied, you were never going to look at another species.

As I thrust within her and took her over into a second orgasm while claiming my first, all I could think was this was everything I'd been searching for and never found before. And while it was exhilarating, it also scared the hell out of me.

Chapter 11

Harley

Wow. Wow. Wow. Wow. Wow.

Last night had been *everything*.

When I'd first woken up, I'd wondered for a moment where I was, especially as I had warm arms wrapped around me and a warm and solid body against my back. I'd never been as comfortable in my life. I didn't want to move. Because as soon as I did, or as soon as Roman woke up, then we'd have to talk about what happened. What if he said he'd made a mistake?

He'd said the only woman he wanted was me.

But he was a satyr. He probably said that to every woman he met in order to get them into bed. And it would work, every time. It had certainly worked on me. There was a delicious ache between my thighs to remind me of the fact.

"Keep wriggling like that and I'm going to spread you wide and do naughty things to you," Roman groaned in my ear, now fully awake, hard and beginning to grind against me. I pushed back against him and found myself pushed onto my back.

And then he did exactly what he'd threatened to do and my doubts about him thinking this was a mistake faded away as he worshipped every part of my body.

Roman sat up, leaning against the headboard, rubbing at his

eyes and yawning. "After breakfast I'll be in the studio with the guys until we need to set off to see your mum, okay?"

"Yeah, that's fine. I'm going to go check out the indoor pool, sauna and steam room, while I figure out what questions I want to ask her."

"Big day."

"I guess. Though at the side of yesterday where I found out I was a half-angel and then rode a rock star all night, it'll probably seem quite normal."

A slow, lazy smirk crossed Roman's face before it became a full-on beaming smile. He ran a hand over the covers and over the outline of his cock.

"You sure did," he drawled. "Now go get in the shower before I drag you back to this bed."

It was only the fact I knew the band were all meeting for breakfast at eight am sharp that had me reluctantly heading for the shower. Reluctant until the door opened, and a dark-haired hottie slid open the double shower stall door and stepped inside.

"I figured seeing as I need a shower too, and I'm running a little late, it would be in our best interests if we showered together." His mouth ran down my neck making me shiver despite the heat of the water. Roman took my hands and put them against the wall of the shower, my back to him, and then he nudged my thighs apart with a knee. His fingers trailed through my wet heat, not just damp from the shower, and it wasn't long before my body was pressed against the shower wall as he thrust inside me.

We were late to breakfast.

As we walked into the dining room where the others were chatting and enjoying the food lovingly prepared by Cath, silence descended and seven pairs of eyes looked us over. Cath actually winked at me. I felt a deep burn start from my chest. It rose up and over my cheeks.

Then Roman reached for my hand, walked me over to an empty chair, and pulled it out for me to sit on.

"Like you lot haven't been doing the same all night," he addressed the others, before taking a seat at the side of me, smiling at me in reassurance and squeezing my knee.

Cath took our breakfast orders and left the room.

"So are you together now?" Zak asked. Erica elbowed him in the ribs.

He turned to her while rubbing his middle. "Ow. What was that for?"

"Maybe they don't want to dissect the morning after in front of everyone? Just because you give a news update of every bit of our relationship."

I was mortified. We'd not said anything about what happened next beyond my going to see my mum. Where we maybe should have been talking, we'd been fucking instead.

But then a hand wrapped around mine again under the table. "Harley is now my girlfriend. That's all you need to know," Roman announced, squeezing my fingers.

Zak whooped. "Yaaaayyy. Congratulations, guys. Now we're all loved up."

Finally, I found my voice. "Never mind about us two, anyway. What about the newlyweds we have among us?"

Freya beamed. "Rex and I are very happy. And... he proposed this morning."

Erica squealed. "Oh my god, oh my god."

"I don't have a ring yet of course, but it makes sense for us to get married even though it's fast as we're committed for life as wolves anyway."

Rex and Freya were glowing. That's the only word for it. It was lovely to see. Zak meanwhile had gone a bit green. Roman had noticed.

"You okay, pal?" he asked him.

"Y-yeah. Fine. Totally peachy over here."

"You look more limey than peachy right now, my friend."

He fixed Roman with a glare and did a throat slicing action across his neck. Luckily, Erica was too engrossed in chatting with Freya to notice. And then I realised. He was feeling the pressure to do the same with Erica. But they were both human and had only been going out for a few weeks.

"I'm so very happy for you both," I announced. "Though it's super-fast, it seems it's the right thing for you both seeing as you're already married in the eyes of the pack anyway. It's funny really. You did it so fast and although Noah and Stacey seemed to get married quickly, their relationship spanned many years. I think somewhere in the middle is about right."

Zak smiled at me. "I agree. Somewhere in the middle."

Erica turned to him. "What? You want that one day? Marriage?"

"Of course, babe. Don't you?"

"Yes."

"Oh my god. Did you like just propose?" Roman said. Zak's eyes went so wide I fully expected his eyeballs to fall out and roll across the top of the table.

"Wh-what?"

"He's messing with you, Zak." I punched Roman in the arm. "Stop that. It's not funny."

"She's laughing," he said, rubbing his arm and pointing to Erica.

She was full-on belly laughing.

"Zak's face! I'll not start buying *Brides* magazine anytime soon." She turned to her boyfriend. "Zak, I hope one day we get there, but we just started dating, okay. So chill your boots. Anyway, I'm only with you for sex."

Calm swept across Zak's features, and he wiggled his brows as his eyes flashed with mischief. "Understandable, darlin'."

After breakfast, Stacey left to go to the theatre, Freya excused herself as she said she was organising an office for her new business today, and Erica had work to do as part of the band's PR. I realised how much I was looking forward to a few hours all by myself in the indoor spa. This would be the first time in so long that I could relax, think my own thoughts, and not have a make-up team coating my face with products, stylists on my hair, wardrobe putting me in outfits, and hot cameras on me. There were times I absolutely loved my job, but I was way overdue a holiday and these next few hours were all mine.

They went way too fast. I'd spent most of the time replaying my sexfest with Roman in my mind, but thanks to the many orgasms of the night and the morning, and the effects of the sauna, steam room, and jacuzzi, I felt as relaxed as I could as I got re-showered to get rid of the chlorine from my skin and then dried and dressed to make my way over to my mother's house.

🎸

Roman entered the suite about ten minutes before we were due to leave. His eyes trailed over my face and down my blouse with hunger.

"Damn real life," he announced. "I'll just go and get changed into something smarter."

I knew what he meant. Chemistry was addictive. I wanted nothing more but to have my mouth and hands on Roman Idiri, but they were more likely to be going around my mother's neck than his cock in the upcoming hours.

🎸

We pulled up outside my mother's mock Georgian home. Hyacinth greeted us at the door and told us my mum was in the front sitting room.

She rose as Hyacinth announced our arrival and swept over to us, a heavy waft of floral perfume following her.

"Darling." She air-kissed me. I thought I might choke on the fumes. "So good to see you." She stepped away from me and over to Roman. "And you brought a fine young man with you. I approve, darling. Ten out of ten."

"Mother!" I scolded as she air-kissed Roman too, lingering a little longer on either cheek than she had on mine.

He stepped back and held out his hand. "I'm Roman, Harley's boyfriend."

"I'm Lilith. Come take a seat both of you. What would you like to drink? Tea, coffee? Is it too early for sherry?"

"Just a water please," Roman addressed Hyacinth.

"Same please," I said.

My mum looked disappointed. "I suppose I'd better have that too then. Bring plain water and a lemon infused one please, Hyacinth."

Hyacinth nodded and left the room.

"So, what brings you here?" Mum blinked her eyes at me a few times fast. "Only, call me cynical, but usually you don't actually visit unless I use some form of coercion." She smacked her lips together. "Are you getting married? Are you pregnant?"

"No. If we could get the drinks first, that might be best," I told her.

The first tells of my mum being on her guard now showed. She scratched at her collarbone and her lips pursed.

The awkward silence between us all was broken by the sounds of a tea trolley rattling, the noise getting louder as it neared the room. There was a general squeak on it from one wheel. Hyacinth returned, placed the drinks out on the coffee table, poured us a glass each and then left.

I took a sip of my drink to quench the arid desert that was my current inner mouth situation and then I stood up. "I just wondered if you could explain this," I said, and I let my angel wings fly out.

My mother gasped. "Oh fuck!" she exclaimed, her real accent breaking through the airs and graces one she'd been conversing in so far. "I was hoping we'd escaped this, and you'd dodged Remy's DNA bullet."

Standing up, she came towards me and looked deeply at my wings. "Can I touch them?"

"Sure, why not?" I answered.

As she did, I got a wave of her feelings through my body. Enthralled. Apprehensive. Sorrow. I knew then that my mum had deeply loved Remy and his loss had had a severe impact on her. My feelings towards my mother instantly changed. The way she appeared was a front to how she really felt: lost.

"Wow. It's the same as when I knew your father. You transmit a feeling of peace through your wings. A connection to the higher plane. To the pure and the good. You're beautiful, daughter, although I'm sorry that this happened as it means you can't live a normal life."

At that point my younger sister burst through the door.

"What the actual fuck? I know these designers who dress you can get a bit weird and wonderful, Sis, but I think this one is slightly impractical for a Monday afternoon."

"Why are you wearing that extremely short skirt, Bonnie? I thought you wanted to look different from your friends and not be a sheep?" Mum said.

"Oh my god, Mum. I saw Roman getting out of the car. Thought he might like to see a bit of leg." She turned around and wiggled her bum.

"Bonnie!" Mum and I shouted at the same time.

She fell about laughing. "Oh, Christ. I'm only joking. Hahahaha, I saw you two holding hands from my window. Your face, Roman. You look like you're going to bring up your lunch. Good job I don't actually fancy you, or I might slit my wrists. Anyway, Sis, what are you doing here?"

I looked at my mum because I didn't know how to answer.

"Sit down, dear. I have something to tell you."

Bonnie slowly lowered herself onto a chair. I stayed put. "Yeah?"

"Harley's father was an angel, Bonnie. And I hoped to have

dodged a heavenly bullet, but it seems it really did fertilise my egg. Your sister is a Nephilim."

Bonnie scrunched up her nose. "A what? She's a what?"

"She's a half-angel."

"Hahahahahahahaha. Hilarious. Fuck off. Why are you really here?" She stared at me.

I watched as Roman moved closer to Bonnie. He knelt down at the side of her chair, took her hand and said, "It's hard to believe, but it's real, Bonnie. Go feel the wings and you'll receive the truth."

She shook her head. "Right. Go feel the wings. Then, what? I get an electric shock? Ohhhkaaay, here I go, feeling the wings because it's completely real that my sister is a half-angel." She strode forward and placed a hand on my wing.

Two things happened at once.

"You really are an angel," she announced as the truth pulsed out from my wings and into her mind. But her thoughts in reverse pulsed back through me.

Jealousy. Resentment. Inferiority.

My sister had always thought I was the lucky one, and it seemed this had just made it a whole lot worse.

Chapter 12

Roman

Bonnie was clearly in shock, so I jumped up to assist her, but she shook me off. "I'm okay. I don't need help. You know I'm not a baby, right? I'm seventeen."

"Yeah, but it's a shock when people find out there are paranormal beings among them."

Bonnie sat back down in the armchair. "How the fuck did she become an angel? Is she that much of a goody two-shoes that God like knighted her or something?"

"Yes," Lilith answered.

"No," I corrected. Lilith huffed out a breath above her top lip.

"I only discovered I had wings in the early hours of Sunday morning, so you aren't the only one in shock, Bonnie." Harley spoke in a soothing tone and then put her wings back in and sat down. "That's why I'm here today with Roman. I want Mum to explain how this came to be."

We all turned to look at Lilith.

Lilith looked heavenward, probably hoping someone from up there was going to help her with her confession. "Oh, very well. I had a job cleaning the local church. It wasn't very glamorous as you can imagine, but it was my first job after leaving college and it was a start. I made a big effort to impress, and the vicar was so pleased. Said the place had never looked as good and that God would be delighted with me. It was the first time in my life anyone had ever made me feel of any worth at all, so I didn't look for another job. I stayed there a while. One day, I saw a guy hanging around the place. He had pale brown hair and looked in his mid-twenties. I felt drawn to him." Her eyes went dreamy, and she looked towards the doorway, no longer focused on us but on her story. "However, something strange was happening. He'd speak to people as they left the congregation and then I'd hear they'd died. It happened too many times to be a coincidence and I decided he must be a serial killer. I told the vicar, who denied the man's existence, so I challenged the man directly when I next saw him."

"And this was my dad? Remy?"

"Yes. He was stunned because I shouldn't have been able to see him. He explained he was an angel and that his job was to show people the way to heaven. As you can imagine, I laughed at him. Until he showed me his wings. He was mesmerised by the fact I could see him, and I was enthralled by everything he was. After a time, we slept together, and then we found it had all been a test of angels on earth. He was cast out of heaven for a time, and I found out I was pregnant. I rented a very cheap and basic house and Remy stayed with me, but it was clear he was deeply unhappy. Not with us. He loved me and he loved our unborn child. But his place was with God, and it was like he was living on the wrong blood type. He had a chance to speak with God and he pledged to never see me again and to do God's work forever more. That was it."

We all sat in silence for a moment and processed her words.

"So I can't ever meet him?" Harley said.

"I don't know. All I know is he can't see me again."

"How do I get in touch with him?"

"I don't know the answer to that either, Harley. I'm sorry.

I've told you everything I know. You were born a normal human baby and I thought that was it. Until you just came and showed me your wings. It must have been a shock."

Harley explained what had happened before her wings had appeared.

"Roman, you seem to be taking all this rather well. It must have shocked you too?" Lilith queried.

"Erm, not really," I said, and I showed her my horns.

"Holy fucking shitballs," Bonnie exclaimed.

We stayed with Harley's mum and sister for another hour and then we left. Bonnie seemed to have calmed down a little, especially after I'd told her she could come and hang with the band. I'd explained about arranging for Mandy to come and have her photo taken and said Bonnie could come at the same time and I'd let her know the arrangements.

After saying goodbye, I climbed back into the driver's seat of my Porsche after holding the door open for Harley to take the passenger seat.

"Bonnie's not happy."

"She seemed okay after I said she could come hang with the band."

Harley's face was sullen, her shoulders slumped. "She's always been jealous of me. Thinks everything has been perfect for me and shit for her. When she touched my wings, it all came through them. Her jealousy that I was now angelic. She puts a brave face on things, but she craves acceptance and to be more than who she is. I worry about her."

I put my hand over hers. "She'll come around. Can she sing? Maybe she could do the backing vocals for a track or be in a video or something."

"It won't be enough. I'm a half-angel, dating a band member of The Paranormals. My sister will be go big or go home. It's a good job everyone else is spoken for or she'd be turning up in the mini skirt again, but with no knickers."

"She'll find her own path, I'm sure. Now, how about we go back to our room and enjoy room service tonight?"

"That sounds lovely." Harley smiled. "I'd like to get to know you better, Roman Idiri."

"Then it's a date," I told her. "Our first."

🎸

Harley did nothing but yawn while we drove home, and so when we got back I insisted she went to bed for a nap. Let's face it, we hadn't slept a lot last night, and then she'd been relaxing in the spa, followed by having an emotional meet up with her mother and sister. She needed the mental rest as much as the physical one.

I didn't need a nap. Satyrs were used to fucking all night—it was part of our genetic make up—so while she napped, I ordered a meal from my favourite Italian restaurant to be delivered, and got Cath involved in helping me set a table in the suite with roses and candles.

"I am beyond pleased you and Harley have got together," she whispered. "I could see how perfect you were for each other from the start."

"It's our first date, so don't buy a hat for the wedding yet, okay?" I winked.

"Shoot, you mean I have to return the one I bought this afternoon." She chuckled.

"You know, Cath. Your sons are really very lucky to have you as a mum," I told her.

She audibly swallowed and I noticed a tear in her eye. "Roman, I don't know your family background and I don't need to, but if your mum doesn't recognise the beautiful son she has, well, she's the one missing out, my boy, and more fool her. If you need a mum figure to support you, or to whoop your arse, I'm here. You only have to ask. And hey, sometimes you won't even have to ask, I'll just step in and mother you anyway. Just let me know if I need to back off." She stepped forward and pulled me into a hug and once more I took everything I could out of it because I missed my own mum. Mine had been a great one until I'd started to become independent. Then she'd turned her back on me and it hurt more than I could ever have imagined. Because mums didn't do that, right? They loved unconditionally like the woman hugging me now. But I'd not been enough for my own. Had embarrassed her by not being a true satyr. By moving away from my tribe. To her, I'd brought shame and couldn't be forgiven. It was why I decided I wouldn't go to my best friend and brother's wedding, even though Sasha wanted me there.

We broke off the embrace. "My hugs are free, Roman. You come grab one whenever you like." Cath rubbed a hand through my hair. "Just straightening you up a bit for your date night." She smiled. "Have a fab evening. Miles will bring up the food when it's delivered. I've even got him to dress up in his best suit."

"You didn't have to do that."

"Hey, it's as much for me as for you." She did her dirty chuckle again. "All I'm saying is double-o-heaven."

She left, once more almost hysterical with laughter as she saw my face.

"You young ones underestimate us older ones. We're fifty, not dead." She closed the door behind her.

Then I felt eyes on me and saw Harley was standing in the doorway to her room.

"How long have you been there?" I asked softly.

"Long enough to see the hug and the beautiful friendship between you and Cath." Harley walked out of the room, dressed in cream silk pyjamas adorned with a crimson rose pattern. She stepped into my personal space, the top of her head against my chest, fitting under my chin, her arms reaching around my waist. I pulled her in closer, my hands going around her back. I smelled the shampoo in her hair, undertones of strawberry and vanilla. Her look and her smell was like ice cream and strawberry sauce and I wanted a taste. But I also wanted us to have a proper date, so although it almost killed me, I settled for just a kiss.

I lowered my head down, and lifted Harley's face up, and pressing my lips to hers I kissed her firmly. Moving my lips over hers, once, twice, three times, nibbling and tasting her, I then broke our embrace and looked down at her wondering if my craving for her showed on my face. Her blue gaze almost hypnotised me and it was at that point I realised I was falling hard for this woman. She'd somehow got through my defences, broken down my walls of protection, and she had no idea that I stood before her raw and vulnerable.

"Now if you'll excuse me, I need to get dressed into my finest clothes. Only I have a date tonight."

"Really? Me too. Well, have fun on yours. Hope it goes well." She laughed, a little tinkle, and strutted back into her room, swinging her hips as she went and humming a tune to herself.

We'd been getting to know each other better over the starter and the main and everything had just been so easy and comfortable. Miles helped serve the desserts and I told him I could handle the coffees. He bade us both a good night and left the room.

"I didn't think you were interested in me, you know?" Harley said after taking a sip of Merlot. "I mean, I'd thought I'd been a bit obvious with showing I liked you, but then you said we should be friends."

"Well, you were going to America, and I thought you could do better than me. I'm not someone who usually opens up. I can be surly, moody, obstinate, and I'm clearly deranged to have turned you down. But also, I've slept with so many women. I didn't think I was the ideal boyfriend for you, or someone to take to introduce to your parents."

"Ha. That was one thing you didn't need to worry about." Harley laughed.

I laughed along with her. "I was a dickhead. I nearly didn't face up to what was right in front of me. You. My beautiful, stunning, wonderful girlfriend. I'm so very sorry."

"Hey, you got there eventually."

"I did." Jumping up from my seat, I ran around the room whooping and hollering and shouting that I got the girl. After she got over the shock, Harley giggled as I thrust my chest out, then wiggled my butt, did the floss, and finished off with my arms waved high in the air in victory.

"You're mad," Harley declared.

"Mad about you, yeah," I said, and then I picked her up and took her to bed.

We were in Harley's room this time. The room had that slight scent of the strawberries and vanilla, mixed with the citrus tones of the perfume she'd worn tonight.

I'd taken my time re-acquainting myself with her body and Harley herself had got bolder, moving down the bed and enveloping her mouth around my cock. I thought she was going to take me to her father's homeplace via orgasm.

Now we were wrapped around each other talking about her parentage.

"It just doesn't seem right, that I got these wings and yet I can't meet my dad. But I guess that's why the earth-angels are there. To teach us why we might be here. Although mine was too busy wanting to sleep with her husband to give me much information."

"You can contact her if you need to, but I had a thought." I kissed her forehead. "It will probably lead to nothing, but why don't you go hang around the church for a bit where your dad met your mum?"

"I don't think lurking around a church building is going to entice an angel from heaven."

"Maybe not, but perhaps praying in there might reach him? It's worth a shot, isn't it?"

She chewed on her top lip.

"I guess so. I'll go tomorrow. If nothing's happened by the

end of the week, I'll contact Lucy and see if there is any way I can meet my dad, even just once." She sighed against my chest. "I wish your family realised how wonderful their son is."

"There's more chance of you meeting Archangel Ramiel than that. You really are wishing for a miracle there," I told her.

Chapter 13

Harley

I had not expected praying in the church to work, and yet I was bitterly disappointed that it hadn't. It was now Friday morning. I'd been and prayed for the last two afternoons and yesterday the vicar had even asked me if I was all right, given he'd never seen me there before and I'd suddenly turned up twice. I'd told him I was new to the area, which wasn't a lie; I was travelling to a London parish I'd never been to before. Then after telling him I was fine, I'd basically run out of church. So today, I was on guard wondering if he'd come seeking me out again.

I sat three rows from the back on the left-hand side of the pews, my head bowed as I tried saying the same thing I had the previous days in a different way, as if that might make my father appear. I sighed. Maybe I had to speak my prayers, not think them. I just had to hope no one heard me and shot me with a sedative before carting me away. I cleared my throat and whispered. As far as I knew I was the only person in the church right now.

"Dear Father. I mean, Dear God, our father in heaven." This was complicated.

"My name is Harley and I'm sorry if my prayer to you is unclear, but you see I actually do have a father in heaven. My real dad. His name is Remy and I know you threw him out of heaven for a while because he shouldn't have fathered me, but you know, if you set these tests then you have to expect a percentage of failure right? I'm not being critical, just realistic. I mean, I'm mostly a good person, but I can have my moments, especially at a certain time of the month, and you created that too, didn't you?" I didn't realise how much my prayers consisted of rambling on until I said them aloud.

"Anyway, I am praying today, at the church where my mother met my dad, to ask if there is any chance that I could meet him. Just even one time. So thank you for listening, and if you need me to do any good deeds just let me know, okay?"

I felt I'd said everything I needed to say, so I added an, "Amen," and rose to my feet. And turned to find the vicar sat behind me but on the back seat. I startled.

"Sorry, Harley. But I must confess that I do snoop on my visitors if I have any concerns about them. I'm Father Desmond. I know you're not from around here. When I'd seen you over the last few days, I'd thought you looked familiar and then I realised why. I Googled you and it said you were in America. Knowing you weren't and that you'd seemed a bit distressed, I decided I'd wear my soft *Hush Puppies* today. Totally silent against the floor, so I could have a little eavesdrop." He scratched his chin. "So your mother met your dad at my church? Were they in the choir together or something?"

I shrugged my shoulders and was intending to say that I wasn't sure, but instead I blurted out. "He was an archangel." I placed a hand across my mouth. "I didn't mean to say that. I meant to say, he was an archangel." I tried again. "He was an archangel. Oh my goodness, what is going on here? I'm trying to say something else entirely."

"It would appear that the only thing you're able to say to me in here is the truth, Harley." The grey-haired old man scratched at his whiskered chin again. "Can I ask you a random question?"

"I guess so."

"Did your mum work here, a long time ago? As a cleaner?"

I nodded and he nodded in return. "I should have made the connection earlier with you having the same surname, but you look quite different. Lili Davies. Your mum was an asset to the staff here and then she quickly left. It was a strange time. She'd told me there was a serial killer taking my parishioners."

"She told me about it all recently. I understand you not believing her. It was a reach."

"I didn't understand because I'd not reached that level of enlightenment at that time. I was newly qualified, and it was my first parish. My journey took me a while, but I got there in the end. Your father came to me and explained what he did."

"Pardon?"

"Your father. Remy. He walked in one day and revealed himself in all his glory. It was quite a sight to behold. He told me about what he'd done, and he explained that Lili had seen him preparing to escort people to heaven. And he said that one day, if the truth was revealed, you might come looking, back to the place where it had all began, and if so, I was to let him know."

"L-let him know? H-how?" I couldn't believe my ears.

"By taking a large white feather from your wing and letting go of it outside." He stood up. "So the question is, when do you want me to do it?"

I took a deep breath and standing up and moving to meet him at the back of the pews and near the entrance of the church, I said, "Now, please," and then I let my wings unfold and showed Father Desmond my true self.

"It's only the second time I've seen true wings and it's no less magnificent than when I saw your father's."

I noticed his face had a white glow and I heard in my mind that this was the glory of God pouring through my wings and being reflected in this messenger.

"Now angels don't lose feathers. You have to decide to shed one," he explained. I reached around my back, closed my eyes and asked for a feather to give itself to me. The next thing I knew

I had one in my hands. It seemed today, in this church, I was more in tune with the angelic side of myself. I passed Father Desmond the feather and he crooked his arm open for me to thread mine through. "Shall we?" he asked, nodding to the entrance.

We walked outside. It was a cloudy summer's day, but it had been dry. Father Desmond led me around the back of the church and then he turned his palm up, the feather upon it.

"Your daughter sends you a message, Remy," he said, and the feather floated from his hand, up into the air, swinging and swaying and then was gone.

"Now what?" I asked him.

"It's time to go back inside to chat."

I tried to mask my disappointment. I'd thought my father might just appear, like when Lucy had stepped through the portal. I chastised myself for being so stupid. Of course, an archangel wasn't just going to drop all his duties and come down to earth. He'd no doubt send some kind of message through Father Desmond.

We walked back around and through the doors of the church, where the vicar pointed to the front. There was a man sitting on the front row with his back to us.

"That's your father," the vicar said, tapping me lightly on the back, and then he walked away, leaving me standing there dumbstruck.

It took me a moment to collect myself, but then I couldn't get to the front of the church fast enough. Because I didn't want my father to disappear before I had a chance to see him and to ask him my questions.

The middle-aged man with pale-brown hair and vivid green eyes looked at me and smiled. "Hello, Harley. Daughter." Standing up, he beckoned me into his arms and as I stood within them, I felt so much love and peace sweep through me that I burst into heavy sobs and fell to my knees.

My fall had not been a glamorous one and I'd hit my knee on the edge of the seat on my way down before falling onto the prayer cushions. My eyes were stinging and I felt faint. Taking deep breaths, I focused on my healing feeling until my fingers tingled and my hand was warm and then I placed it on my knee. The pain disappeared and helped by my father, I got up from the floor and took a seat at the side of him on the pew.

"I didn't actually expect this day to ever come," he said. His voice sounded like the feeling you have when you open the curtains to a warm summer day.

"I can't say I expected this myself."

He smiled at that. "Quite."

There was an awkward silence for a minute. Now he was here, I appeared to have lost the ability to speak. To ask him the questions I'd had ruminating over in my mind.

"I guess I should start from the beginning and tell you what I think you need to know, and then if you have any questions, I'll answer them." His last words trailed off like a question.

"Okay."

"We were sent down to earth for a short time as an experiment to see if we could work more closely with humans. To guide those who were approaching the end of their time on earth and work to ease their transition to heaven. And that's what I'd been doing. Except then I came across your mother. In heaven, we don't have proper bodies. We are a manifestation of energy. There is love, but there is no sex, no procreation. Angels just are. We are the children of God. He didn't expect for us to be tempted. He knew it was a possibility, but He didn't expect us to yield to the temptation." He sighed. "I guess it was Eve and the apple all over again. I, and other angels did indeed, shall we say, 'romance' women and when it was discovered, many of us were cast out of heaven."

"Mum said you couldn't cope with being on earth."

"That's right. I am a child of God and on earth I didn't thrive. Your mum could see that. I got a voluntary job counselling people at the end of their lives, and I was invited back. But there were terms to being brought back home."

His voice made a sense of foreboding drop like a rock in a puddle in my stomach.

"If you ever got in touch. If you were in fact a Nephilim... then you could see me, but only once."

"Oh." I felt crushed. "So this is it? The only time?"

"I'm afraid so, but actually, it's not as bad as you think, because it's just human time. When your time on earth is done and you join us in heaven, then we'll have all eternity, because then you'll be welcomed as part of us all. Your human soul will have gone, and your angel self will reign."

I gave him a half-smile. "Oh. That's not so bad then. It's like a date to meet up in the future."

He nodded. "I regret my behaviour on earth. It was not a representation of who I am, who I was born to be, but I don't regret you, Harley. You are as beautiful as I imagined you would be. Now tell me, what happened to make your wings appear?"

I told him about speaking to the families. About how Leonie had died, and I felt Patrick should come meet his niece and nephew.

My father placed a hand on my forearm and squeezed. "Your angel wings appeared because you have an opportunity to heal a family. This is something you must pursue. The message is clear."

I thought about his words. Was this true? I was being directed to do something for God? *No pressure there then.*

"Wow, okay. I'd better give that some thought then and decide how to proceed with arranging their reunion. Not that I expect Malcolm to be helpful."

"Malcolm?"

"The show's producer. I'm not totally sure he's being legit about everything."

"Then you have another task, don't you? To discover what is

happening behind the scenes of this show and to work to provide the healing these families need."

My dad's words hit home. Inside, it felt 'right'. Totally hard to explain, but a gut instinct that this was indeed what I needed to be focusing on.

I shot around to look behind me as I felt sure someone had just sat in the pew behind.

"Something the matter?"

"I thought someone was there. I keep imagining things. I need more sleep. Voices. Seeing shadows. I keep making myself jump."

"Or maybe you're not actually seeing things clearly yet and need to slow down and pay attention to what's around you." Remy sighed wistfully. "I have to go now, Harley. I'm sorry, but rest assured we will meet again, just not until after the end of your human years. You have a long, happy, and healthy life ahead of you and can do great things. Live life to the full and enjoy every moment, because you have the best of both worlds. You have God's essence within you to heal, but you also have a human life to experience and to live. You're truly blessed, my daughter."

He leaned over and kissed my forehead. I'd remember that majestic and enormous deep feeling of love for the rest of my human life.

My eyes had closed as he had kissed my forehead and placed his arms around me, holding me close, and then I felt him leave. When I opened my eyes again I was sitting on the bench by myself.

Well, I thought I was by myself.

Until a voice from behind softly whispered, "Help me."

Chapter 14

Harley

When I turned around, again there was no one there. But I now realised that someone was trying to communicate with me, and I had the intuition that this was in some way connected to reuniting the family where the sister had died, and maybe helping the other families too.

I knew where I needed to go next. Back to the hotel in Soho.

It was time to go back to work.

I looked for Father Desmond to say goodbye, but he wasn't around, so I headed out of church and then took my mobile phone out of my bag.

"Hey, Carol?"

"Hi, Harley, hun."

"Did you look over my contract and see how I could get out of it?"

"Babe, you can just tell him to sit on your middle finger and swivel around on it. It's all about a show in Los Angeles, not one in London. He's not fulfilling his side of the contract; you can just walk away."

"Great, because I'm going over there now to kick his arse."

"Oooohhh. I want to come see."

"Come on then. I'll meet you in the reception in like thirty minutes?"

"It's tight, but I like tight. Contracts, men's trousers, my vagina."

I laughed and ended the call.

My taxi dropped me off outside the hotel and as I walked into the lobby and caught sight of Mandy behind the desk, I was relieved that I now knew she was a Paranormals fan and hadn't slipped into Roman's DMs.

"Good morning, Miss Davies. Are you feeling better?" she said, followed by a grin that displayed her tongue piercing.

"I feel amazing, Mandy, thank you. Are you looking forward to spending time with the band tomorrow?"

She nodded her head so enthusiastically that all her piercings made their own musical arrangement as they tinkled together. "I can't wait. I can't believe I am actually going to see them in the studio and get my photograph taken with them all. My friends might actually believe me then, that I meet famous people."

"They think you lie?"

"There's never any evidence. Like how Malcolm said I couldn't take a photograph with you because of the secrecy of you being in Soho and not LA."

"Is that so?" I did a gesturing motion. "Come on, get your phone out. Snap a pic and get that shit shown wherever you like."

She scrabbled around for her phone, beaming from ear to ear. Then she walked around the front desk and took a selfie of us.

"You can say exactly where it is. I'm not hiding from the press anymore. We were supposed to be in Los Angeles and we aren't and Malcolm is running a shit show here. It's time for all that to change."

The door opened and Carol came hurtling through it, all

wild, mid-length, brown corkscrew curls. She blew her hair away from her face.

"Tell me I didn't miss anything good yet."

"Nope. Nothing. I'm just chatting to Mandy."

Carol rubbed her hands together with glee.

"Come on, let's go."

Smiling as I headed towards the large events room where the filming so far had taken place, I realised I really did have the best of both worlds as a Nephilim. Because while I was ultimately here to do good, I could also cause a little mischief along the way.

As I headed towards the events room, I passed Saoirse on the corridor, rushing like her tush was on fire. "Hey, I didn't know we were expecting you back today," she said, out of breath.

"No, Malcolm doesn't know."

"I figured he'd be in a better mood if he did. He's in arsehole mode."

"Is that so? Well, I think it's time for him to be better reacquainted with his own shit. Where's he got you running off to?"

"The LA backdrop has ripped. I need to go pick up a new one from the photo place pronto."

"No you don't." Carol told her. "Come with us. I'm happy to go over all your contracts if you need me to. Can be my good deed of the day."

She stopped and looked down at herself.

"What the fuck? I don't do good deeds. I'm a ballbusting agent. What's happening to me?"

I wanted to laugh. Looked like hanging around with a half-angel rubbed off on some people.

"It's a nice thing to do. These people have been treated like crap, and you'll probably get some future business out of it."

Carol sucked on her top lip. "Yeah, that's true. Phew. Thought I was going soft in my old age."

I let Saoirse go on ahead through the door to the room, and watched from behind the door as Malcolm bellowed, "What are you doing back here already? Unless that backdrop is being carried up your arse, get back to the shop."

I stepped through the door with Carol. "Hello, Malcolm."

"Oh, thank fuck. We can get this show wrapped up now you're back. Then I won't have to deal with these idiots any longer."

"Yes, I'm much better now. Thanks for asking," I said sarcastically. I walked up to one of the sound guys and got him to mic me up.

"Can everyone gather around," I asked them.

Malcolm appeared at my side. "That's it, Harls. Tell them you're back. That they'll be staying until we've finished filming, so they need to cancel all their evening plans."

The show's staff all gathered around. I could see in every person's demeanour that they were desperately unhappy. I was annoyed with myself that I'd not noticed this before, too self-absorbed in my own misery at the job.

"Hi, everyone. I'm pleased to tell you that I'm back, and that filming on this show is finished."

"No it's not. I—"

Carol pulled Malcolm into a headlock and wrestled his microphone off him. "Shut the fuck up or I'll put this mic up your rectum seeing as that's what you talk out of most anyway."

I continued. "I apologise for not doing this sooner. You will all be paid for the work you were signed up to do, and I will be talking to all of the families to ensure they are recompensed for travel and expenses. It's my intention to set up my own production company, Halo Productions, and to record this show as it should have been done. That's in a decent studio, with cast and crew treated with respect. Carol will re-negotiate with the TV execs, explaining that Malcolm had misled them."

"You can't do this," Malcolm screeched, though not many heard as he no longer had his mic.

"Do you know who I am?" Carol said to him. "I'm one of the best agents in this business. You have two choices now, mate.

SATYRDAY NIGHT FEVER

One, you crawl in a hole and die, which'd be my preference; or two, you start making decent programmes where people are treated properly. If you don't choose one or the other, I'll badmouth you so hard you'll always be looking behind you because someone will be ready to put the knife from their back into yours. You'll be ruined."

"Fuck you. Fuck all of you." Malcolm stormed out of the room trying to slam the door behind him. Unfortunately, it had a self-closing mechanism, so he just looked even more of a dick.

Then one of the people standing around me began to clap, and before I knew it everyone was clapping and hollering.

Carol asked for everyone's contracts, and I gave them a long weekend off. I told them Carol and I would be in touch with the television executives about taking over the contract and then we'd need to find a new studio, but we'd be in touch as soon as we could.

"I got this handled, babe. This is so much my jam that between my thighs is creaming. Go have a nice weekend, but keep your phone on, just in case. Halo Productions, huh? Never mentioned that to me before."

"That's because I thought of it while I was speaking. So I need to know how to set all that up too."

"It's going to be golden, kiddo. Your company is going to shine. I'll contact all the families over the next few days, see what they signed up to and whether they want to carry on if we get the go ahead for taking over, but expenses paid this time and a decent hotel and hospitality."

"Yeah, you do all that, but not Patrick Rivers, okay? I'm going to speak to him myself because I've had some contact with him already."

"Okidoki, you take Mr Rivers. Right," She air kissed me on both cheeks. "I'd better get out of here. I suddenly have a shit ton more work to do." She shimmied. "God, it gets me all hot thinking about it." Then she walked out of the hotel doors and into a waiting taxi.

I'd arranged to use my old hotel room for an hour or so while I sorted a few things out. I called Roman.

"Hey. How's it all going? You've been gone a long time. I missed you."

"Shut up. You've been recording and I know how you lose yourself in music."

"Yeah, but I want to lose myself in you, so hurry back."

"I'll be another couple of hours yet, but you be arranging for a nice meal we can eat cold if necessary, and for that double bathtub to be filled for later. It's been quite the day and I want to tell you everything, but let's do it in comfort, hey?"

"You got it."

"Anyway, is Rex with you, or do you have his number?"

"Oh, yeah, bored of me already? Freya will claw your eyes out though if you try for her man."

"Yeah, yeah, yeah. I want to ask him if he'll let me use some of his downstairs rooms if needed to help a family reunite."

"Two secs." I heard muffled voices.

"Yeah, not a problem."

"Really? He said it was okay?"

"His actual words were he couldn't give a fuck cos he only needs his bedroom and the kitchen."

"Fair enough." I giggled. "Tell him thanks, and I'll see you soon."

"I'll be waiting," he replied. "And probably naked."

The silence of my hotel room hit me then. It had been such a busy afternoon. I picked up a bottle of lukewarm water from the desk, opened it, and enjoyed the feel of it coating my mouth and throat. Then I picked up The Rivers family's file and called Patrick Rivers.

"Hello."

"Hey, Pat. It's Harley."

"Hello there, lovely. I've still not booked a flight, but I have been in telephone contact with my niece. She's twenty-seven and a law student," he told me. I knew all this from the research documents, but I let him ramble on, filling me in on his conversations with his niece.

"I'm phoning because there's been a change with the programme management, Pat. I'm taking over. Malcolm's been sacked. Now, I know you were keener on the reunion than being on television, and I also know how nervous you are about coming over, but I want to make you a deal."

"Oh yeah?"

"How does staying over at Rex Colton from The Paranormals' house sound? I'm staying there at the moment. All your expenses and meals covered. And we get your niece and nephew here. Your meet up would be private and not for television. All you have to do is get brave and say yes. I'll book you first class so it will be complete luxury."

"And when would this be?"

"I've checked out flights and I can get you here Sunday?"

"Can I think about it?"

"You can, but what's to think about? Are you going to let a fear of flying stop you from meeting your family? Or are you going to take a leap into the unknown and get on that plane?"

Pat paused for a second or two. "Oh, go on. I'll do it. I'll just make the most of the free liquor on the flight. Don't expect me to be able to walk off the flight. Either my legs will be jelly or I'll be physically incapable because of the free liquor."

I laughed. "I'm sorting out your tickets, Pat. I'll be in touch, and I'll see you on Sunday."

I put the phone down and rang his niece.

It took me some time, but everything was sorted for a get-together on Sunday afternoon. I laid back on the bed and closed my eyes. It was such a shame he didn't get the chance to meet his sister. That would have been the icing on the cake. I wondered if they wanted to try a séance, but it was Relatives Reunited, not Ghosts Get-together.

"Harley."

I shot up again, my eyes wide open but there was nothing there. Or was there? Was I just not seeing what was right in front of me? The talk of ghosts and spirits came to the forefront of my mind. My father, Remy. His job was to prepare people for heaven. What if I had been given my wings because I had a task of my own to do with this family?

Taking a deep breath, I said out loud, "I am ready to see with clear vision. If there is someone trying to contact me, please show yourself."

A shimmer came to the edge of my bed, and it became clearer with my resolve to not fear my sight and to know it wasn't malevolent but meant to be.

A middle-aged woman with short blonde hair appeared, sitting on the edge of the bed dressed in a leopard print top and a brown skirt. She smiled at me. "Finally. I thought you were never going to notice me. I'm Leonie Rivers. I'd like you to reunite me with my brother as promised before I have to travel on up to heaven, please."

I smiled at her. "Hello, Leonie. I'm happy to help."

Chapter 15

Roman

Saturday morning came.

After a lovely evening and an amazingly relaxing bath, followed by ravishing sex, we'd both slept in until mid-morning. Tempted though I'd been to wake Harley up, I felt with what she'd been through over the last week, she needed to catch up on some much-deserved rest. There were lots of strange happenings at the moment and none more so than the fact that when I was with Harley, I didn't feel the need to sleep outside. Yes, I craved my outdoor space and the fresh air, and I spent time outdoors each day, but I was sleeping better than I ever had. When we got to sleep that was.

She stirred and I waited for her to fully awaken.

"Hey." She smiled up at me.

"Hey. Oh, I forgot to tell you, the architect finished my revised plans for the woods and has submitted them. I have a copy to show you later."

"That's fantastic. You'll feel so much better when you have your own place. I guess I should be making my way back to my own apartment now."

Harley lived in a small one-bedroomed apartment right in the heart of London, in Chelsea, where prices were large and so property ended up being small.

"Now I've stayed in this mansion for a week, I don't know how I'll face my lovely but tiny place."

"Yes, I have to admit, Rex's place is amazing, and it's become the base of all of us really. Mainly because the recording studio is here, but I'm glad my own home won't be too far away from here. Once he and Freya start having cubs, they'll need some extra hands to help, and I can assist."

"Your brother and Sasha might have some kids too."

"Yeah."

"You don't sound very enthusiastic. Have you been in touch with Sasha since she came here?"

Harley knew Sasha had told me she understood I needed time to think things over, but that she hoped I'd make the wedding because she wanted me to be there.

"I haven't. But I have decided I'm not going."

"Roman!"

"If my family starts lecturing me or being difficult, it will spoil Sasha's day. If they wanted me to be there... if they wanted to see me, they'd have got in touch with me themselves."

Harley folded her arms across her chest. "You're being stubborn. Sasha made the first move, and you should at least go visit her at the swamp and see what happens."

"Don't you think you've enough going on in your own life without worrying about mine?" I knew I was being a little sharp, but I didn't feel like thinking about this right now.

She spoke more softly. "I do, but I just don't want you regretting your decisions."

"I won't. My decisions lately have been pretty damn amazing." I dipped my head down to kiss Harley and then distracted her from talking about my family by continuing to trail kisses down her body.

Cath had prepared a buffet lunch for outside ready for Bonnie and Mandy coming over. Rex had sent a driver to pick both girls up and by the time they got out of the car to join us they seemed like firm friends.

"Hey, guys." Bonnie wandered over like she'd known us for years. No doubt she'd told Mandy she had. "This is Mandy. She's a bit shy to be around you all, so gently does it, okay?"

After introductions, we went to get food so that Mandy could get used to being around us. Zak and Erica took her under their wing. Erica was a very caring woman and Zak made goofy jokes that put Mandy at ease. Soon she was laughing and joining in with the rest of us. Bonnie had had no such inhibitions. The main thing we needed to do with Bonnie was to make sure she didn't blurt out anything about our paranormalness.

We had the photographs taken and then went into the recording studio.

"We're going to just sing a few tracks we're currently working on, okay? You can tell us what you think." I smiled at Mandy, who beamed back.

Bonnie was sitting behind her on her phone where I could see her posing for selfies. After meeting us a couple of times, she was clearly over the whole thing other than using it for bragging rights. Harley went to sit next to her.

"This track is called *Someone to Love*," Zak said.

Never thought there'd come a time
When I craved you like the finest wine
I've been around, I've been all over town
But I'll tell you I've done looking now.

Never thought this would happen to me
A love that hit me so perfectly

I've travelled the world, been all over town
But I'm ready now to settle down.

It was youuuuu
You're amazing
It is yoouuuu
You daze me
If there was ever a message from up above
It was that I'd been sent... someone to love.

I'd written the song over the last couple of days, without thinking too much of Harley being my muse for it. We wrote rock ballads and rock anthems, and the ideas for them and the words could be inspired from everything. Not every song meant something. Some just sounded right and some words just belonged to that particular piece of music.

So I'd tell myself that the lyrics had just complemented the tune I'd strummed on my guitar and that I wasn't feeling the first stirrings of love at all.

"Who wrote this one?" Mandy asked.

"Everyone kind of came up with it," I said quickly.

Zak gave me a weird look, and then smiled at Mandy. "Sometimes we can't remember who came up with what. A lot of it is a group effort."

After another hour, Mandy went home thanking us profusely, but Bonnie stayed to 'hang with her sister'. Bonnie actually stayed so she could ask us about our supernatural powers.

We were all sitting at the dinner table that evening and Bonnie was quizzing us all. It was like when little kids ask 'Why?' Entirely bloody annoying.

"I wish I was a paranormal, instead of a regular boring teenager. All I have to look forward to now is college. My mother went from shagging an angel to shagging a pisshead. I mean, thanks a bunch. She could have at least found another good guy. He's a right waster."

She took a drink of the beer her sister had allowed her to have. "Then again, you're an angel. Maybe I'm supposed to be a devil."

"You don't want to go anywhere near that side of things," Zak told her, being harsh of tone and unlike the Zak she'd got to know. "I've been there, done that, and it almost ruined my life."

"Yeah, but you just didn't think it through, did you? No disrespect, but you were horny, and Don offered you a ton of sex. All I want is red wings. Harley's are white and that goes with her blonde hair, but I'd suit red, or black even."

"Go to the fancy dress shop," I told her. "Or Etsy. They take money, not your soul."

She nodded and huffed, "Okayyyy, demons bad, stay away. I get it."

"So congrats on your new production company, Harley," Rex said. "Roman's been telling me about it. Any thoughts beyond taking over the reunion show?"

"No, not at the moment. I'll start slow." She turned to her sister. "Hey, Bon. If you did media studies instead of retail, you could come join my new business as an intern."

Bonnie side-eyed her. "I'll make my own way in life, thanks very much. I don't intend to sit in your shadow like a charity case or the poor sister all my life."

"Well, the offer is there," Harley said, looking at me and shrugging.

Bonnie just needed to mature a bit. She'd find her way eventually. But I knew Harley felt guilty. She shouldn't. She had no need to. But she clearly did. Guilty for her success and now for her ancestry. But she needed to allow herself to take centre stage. You shouldn't dim your light for other people. They'd never thank you for it. They'd just moan about the dark.

"You staying over tonight, Bonnie? We've loads of spare rooms," Rex asked her.

"Can I?" she asked Harley. "Please. And can I have a huge room all to myself?"

Cath appeared. "I can make sure there's no access to alcohol."

Bonnie sighed.

"But lots of access to fizzy pop, chocolate, and any other goodies."

Her eyes lit up. "Like a whole bowl full of orange smarties?"

"Oh, that's easily done."

"So can I, Harley?"

"Sure, as long as you behave, or you're straight back home. You'll have to borrow one of my nightshirts."

"Funnily enough they're all clean, because she's not been wearing any." Zak sniggered.

Bonnie pulled up her backpack. "I brought my own. And my toothbrush and toiletries. I was going to ask if I could stop anyway."

"You can be an extra pair of hands for your sister tomorrow," I told her.

"Why? What's happening then?"

"She's organising for a family to be reunited."

"That sounds entirely dull." Bonnie puffed out her cheeks and then pulled out a swimsuit. "There's a pool, right?"

After the meal, Bonnie went to have fun in her room. Cath told Harley and I not to worry and that she'd keep a close eye on her and would make sure she had fun, but within reason, and she'd ensure she went to bed at a reasonable hour. As I saw her chatting with Stacey in the kitchen doorway, I reckoned there was going to be a little bit of magic involved in keeping Bonnie out of mischief.

Harley and I had decided to go for a walk to my woods, to get some fresh air and walk off our dinner. It was a mild evening, and the birds were doing their evening song.

"Are you nervous about tomorrow?" I asked her.

"Yeah, I have to admit I am a bit. I mean, when I saw Leonie in my room, I agreed I would get Pat here, but it didn't mean he'd see her. I'd only just seen her. If he doesn't believe, it won't happen."

"But you'll be giving it a chance, and his niece and nephew will get to meet their uncle. It's still good."

"It is. But I really hope it works out and Leonie can make her way to Heaven. It's funny. I always feared death, but now I don't. Now I know what's there."

"Hey, you're going nowhere." I pulled her into my arms.

"That's actually true. My dad told me I would live a long and happy life," she informed me.

"We'll be at the stream soon, and I have lots of comfy blankets. I could work on the happy bit if you agree to lie on them."

"You make me happy anyway, Roman." She reached up and put her lips to mine. "But I've never made out under the stars, so come on, let's go."

Chapter 16

Harley

Knowing my sister was here, but in another room, made me feel a bit strange. Like, she should want to share a room with me and do a sleepover or something. I sent her a text from my own room when I got back, although by then it was ten pm.

Harley: If you fancy some company, I'm free. We could watch a movie and eat popcorn?

Bonnie: Thanks, but I'm enjoying being on my own so raincheck? Cath's making me a midnight feast with what she says is the best tasting hot chocolate ever!

Harley: As long as you're okay. Enjoy! If you need me, just message, no matter what time.

Bonnie: Thanks, Sis. But you enjoy a night of shagging. I'll be fine.

I sighed heavily.

"Everything okay?" Roman joined me on the sofa after getting changed into some loungewear.

"Yeah. I guess I just need to accept that Bonnie's her own person, fiercely independent and stubborn and determined to spend the night on her own, even though her sister's nearby."

"She's having fun, and no doubt pretending she's in her own place. It'll be exciting for her."

"I know. I just wished we got along better."

"It'll come as she grows up."

"Maybe. Do you think that's why I'm so invested in this show? In getting families to reunite? Because of my failure to unite my own?"

"What are you talking about? Your family is fine. You all speak to one another. You might not be best friends with Bonnie, but there's a large age gap between you that won't seem so obvious as she gets older. At the side of a lot of families, yours is probably a decent one."

"I just wish she realised how much I love her." A tear slipped down my cheek. I was being an idiot, I knew. "Sorry, Roman. It's just I try so hard and—"

"Maybe don't? Why don't you pull back a bit and let her get on with her life? She'll realise how much a part of her life you are. I mean where did she come today and want to stay? Near you."

"Pffft. Near The Paranormals more like. Did you hear her with Mandy? You'd have thought she was your PR person, not Erica."

"She's seventeen and around famous rock stars. It could be worse. We could be the guys from The Seven. She's over the age of consent. They'd be sniffing around her saying she was fresh meat."

"If any of them take a step near her, I will... s... s..."

"What?"

"It won't let me say it." I mimed doing a stabbing motion.

"Toss them off yourself?"

"No. Eeee, eeee, eeee." I did the motion again.

"Stab them?"

I nodded. "Darn angelic side. It won't let me threaten bodily harm."

Roman belly-laughed at that.

"Stop it. It's not funny."

He held his stomach. "It is."

I went to punch his arm, but my hand stopped partway towards him.

He pointed and laughed even louder, now actually rolling about on the sofa.

"How can I protect my sister from these infidels if I can't hit anyone?" I screeched.

But I was talking to myself because Roman couldn't hear me above the noise of his bellows.

Having got into bed, I sat up against the headboard. "I'm not going to be able to sleep tonight because I'll be worrying that my sister's out of bed and up to no good."

Roman passed me the telephone. "Dial Cath on 1. It's after half twelve. She works until one am on a Saturday night."

"Why do I need to ring Cath?"

He dialled the number himself.

"Hey, Cath. It's Roman. No, I don't want anything except information. Did Bonnie enjoy her midnight feast? Harley's just worrying she might go wandering around the house." He nodded his head. "Yeah, I thought as much. You're a genius as always. Night."

He put the phone down.

"Stacey put a charm on the hot chocolate. Your sister is fast asleep."

Relief flooded through my body.

"Cath had you covered. I saw her talking to Stacey earlier. I figured she'd done something like that. No way will she want a teenager wandering around upsetting the household. Cath runs a tight ship."

"She's a superstar."

"Yeah, she is," he said. "She's been more of a mother to me in the short time I've known her than the one who birthed me has been in the last few years."

"But she's not your mum."

Roman yawned. "Gosh, it's getting late. We'd better grab some sleep because we don't know how much of your energy you'll use tomorrow with your mediumship skills."

He pulled me towards him and settled us down under the covers, but I couldn't help but think his going to sleep was more about shutting down talk about his family than my needing energy.

It was our first undercurrent of tension, and I didn't like it one bit. He'd told me he could be a stubborn man, but sometimes you had to lead a goat by the horns, right?

I'd give it all some thought. After I'd attempted to reunite a brother and his family with an earthbound ghost.

Chapter 17

Roman

Despite having Harley in my arms, I couldn't sleep. The truth was that I missed my brothers and my best friend. I even missed my parents despite their rejection of me, but why should I try to build fences? My parents should be inviting me back.

In the end I got out of bed, and I walked out of the house and down to the stream. I finally fell asleep listening to the relaxing sounds of the water trickling by.

"Hey, you." Harley's voice registered in my ear. I opened my eyes to see her sitting next to me.

"Hey," I croaked out, my mouth dry.

"It was weird waking up without you. Funny that," she said.

"I couldn't sleep. I would have disturbed you. Figured I needed to be near nature, so I came here."

"Yeah, I get that." She paused. "I'm going back to my own place tonight, Roman. There's no reason why I shouldn't now."

I sat up and scrubbed at my face. "Oh, okay."

"We can date like normal people, right?"

I shrugged. "I guess. Though we aren't normal, are we?"

There was an awkward silence. I hated it and yet my stubborn arse wouldn't do anything about it. I was basically having a tantrum about her going home and was still sore about her mentioning my family. I couldn't seem to help myself though.

"Well, I'm in dire need of coffee. I just wanted to check if you were here, seeing as I woke up to an empty room and no note. Now I can see you're fine, I'll go back. I want to make sure my sister is okay and I've a lot to do before the Rivers arrive."

I nodded my head. "I'm fine. You don't need to worry about me."

She stood up, hurt in her eyes, but fire in her stance. "I won't then. See you around, kid."

It was the ultimate insult, and she knew it, a hint of regret crossing her features before she turned on her heel and left.

Kid. A baby goat. She was calling me a child. I was acting infantile though.

But why, Roman? Why are you being like this with the woman you've fallen for? My inner voice questioned.

And I figured that was exactly why I was acting like a complete idiot. Because I had fallen for her hard. In fact, I was in the beginning stages of falling in love with her and that scared the absolute hell out of me, because every time I loved someone hard, they hurt me. It was my default setting to protect myself and back away.

If I didn't change, I was going to lose another important person in my life.

Chapter 18

Harley

I wiped away a tear as I left Roman where he was sat. Stubborn idiot. When I'd woken up this morning to find he wasn't there, I had craved him with such longing. It had made me realise that I'd developed strong feelings for him.

Now the feelings I had were ones of wanting to kick him in the balls. Was this all just a tantrum because I'd mentioned him making amends with his family? I mean, okay, perhaps it wasn't the right thing for him to do, but surely if we were a couple, we should be able to have an adult conversation about these things without him walking away. Because that's what he'd done. He'd withdrawn from me last night and left and he was still harbouring a grudge today, when it was one of the most important days of my life.

I would be using my angel powers for good today. I could have really used his support. But stuff him. If he wanted to stay out in the woods, then he could. And after I'd finished with the Rivers family, I'd leave with Bonnie. We'd have a cab to drop her off at home and then I'd go on to my flat.

It was time for me to focus on myself. I'd been relying on Roman far too much since I'd discovered my heritage. No more. I was a strong, independent woman, and I would do this on my own. Help a family, then go home and start making the changes to my career that would lead to me being who I was born to be.

With a newly fired up determination, I carried on out of the woods, across the garden, and back into the house.

"Everything okay?" Cath said as she let me back into the house.

"Fine," I replied.

"Oh dear. Your sister's in the dining room having a cooked breakfast. You want anything?"

"I've not much of an appetite to be honest, but today could be a hard day, so maybe just some toast?"

"How about some jam with it? A bit of sugar for energy?"

"That sounds great. Thanks, Cath."

"He's not used to depending on anyone," she said softly. "People let him down. The route to Roman's heart won't be easy, but he's shown you the way and that's a lot more than he does for most people."

"Yeah, well at the moment he's put up a roadblock, and I'm too busy to deal with his maintenance." I pursed my lips. Cath said no more on it, just saying she'd go fix my breakfast.

My sister was tucking heartily into a massive plate of bacon and eggs when I walked in. I almost fell over in shock when I was greeted with an ear-splitting smile. Had Roman and Bonnie swapped bodies?

"Morning, Sis."

I took the seat opposite her. "You look..." I pondered the correct word for how she did appear. "Content."

"Harls, I had the best sleep of my entire life. It must have been the luxury of that bed. It's clear I need to marry a rich man, so I can live like this. I wonder if I could sell myself as a virgin bride?"

"You need to spend your life with someone who you love. Don't do a mother and marry for money all the time."

"Mum got hurt by both our fathers. I've been thinking about it. She was rejected by your dad and the good side, so whether she realised it or not, she then chose a bad boy. Then when that didn't work out either, she chose money. I reckon she gets what she needs fucking my dad when he turns up, but has basically put a freeze on her heart because she doesn't want to get hurt again."

My mouth dropped open and I stared at my sister for about ten seconds straight.

"You are so wise. When did you get so wise?"

I realised Roman was doing something very similar to our mum.

"You can love someone though. You're not closed off to it like Mum, are you?" I questioned.

"Nah. I'm just young and not ready for all that crap. And don't worry. I can't be a virgin bride because I'm not a virgin."

I put a hand to my forehead. Talking to Bonnie was like playing a game of Fortnite. You thought you were doing well and then something would appear out of nowhere and Game Over, leaving you wanting to, or actually swearing very loudly.

"Bonnie."

"Oh don't start trying to mother me. You're my *sister*, not my mum. I am fine. I just lost my v-card to Harvey because I wanted rid."

"Harvey, your maths tutor, Harvey?"

"Yeah, he taught me a few extra equations. Like input equals O."

"What?"

Bonnie put her left thumb and forefinger together and poked her index finger of her right hand through. "Input."

"Arrgghhh. Okay, I get it."

"Equals, ohhhhhhhhh." She faked an orgasm sound just as Zak and Erica walked in.

"Cath," he bellowed. "I want what's she's having."

Unsurprisingly, Bonnie had no problem with the idea of hanging around the rock star mansion for another day.

At lunchtime, Patrick Rivers arrived. His appearance belied his age. Though he'd just turned seventy, he was sprightly, had a blonde rinse, a tan, and perfect white teeth.

He grinned as we met at the door and hugged.

"I did it! There's no stopping me now. Might just become an international jetsetter!"

"Well done! I knew you could do it." I introduced him to Cath, Miles, and my sister. Cath and Miles took him off to show him to a room with a bathroom where he could freshen up, and then they said they would get him something to eat and drink.

Bonnie told me the band had gone to the recording studio because Zak was in the zone right now and coming up with genius lyrics.

"Is that according to Zak?"

"Yeah. He's right though. He sang me some. He might be full on sometimes and cocky, but he really is talented."

"You got a crush?"

"Eww, no. He's a good laugh though. He gets me. It's nice to meet someone who gets me. And I love Erica. She actually said if I wanted to hang with him anytime to let her know because sometimes she needs a Zakectomy. And he didn't even get annoyed with her. He agreed. Then he said he planned to shag her bare on a regular basis, so she always carried a bit of him wherever she went. He's hilarious."

"He's something."

"What's happened with you and Romanio, Juliet?"

"He's got family things to think about."

"Ooh, do they not approve of you?"

"We are not the Montagues and Capulets. This is a mardy-arsed goat boy who's decided to have a strop. I'm too busy today to change his nappy so I'm letting him get on with it."

"Trouble in Paradise."

I sighed with sadness. "Yep, maybe I rushed into things.

Anyway, that's something to think about later. Right now, I'm concentrating on the reunion. I'm going to head to the room and work on my laptop until everyone arrives."

"Okay, sis. I'm sorry about you and Roman. You make a cute couple. Not as cute as Zak and Erica, but close."

"Thanks. I think." I headed off, needing some time to myself.

Only of course that wasn't what I got at all.

Leonie shimmered into appearance in the formal sitting room. This time she sat in front of the grand piano.

"He's here. I'm so excited. I'm afraid I got so overexcited I tried to appear to him in his room, but he didn't see me."

"Leonie! If he had, you might have caused him a heart attack. Are you trying to reunite on the other side?"

She pouted. Leonie was dressed today in a t-shirt with a large, cute kitten on it and a pair of pink sparkly leggings. She was short, plump, and had died aged sixty-four from smoking. Not the actual amount of fags, but the fact she was lighting one and not looking where she was going when she stepped out in front of a car.

"It's just I waited so long to see him again and he's here."

"I know, honey." I really did have every sympathy for this family, and I think that's why I'd wanted to go over and above for them. They'd not known about each other. Their mum had had Patrick adopted and then moved to the U.K. It had been Leonie doing an Ancestry check that had reunited them, only for her to be cruelly taken away before they could meet.

"I'll conserve my energy now though until you call for me," Leonie assured me.

"You do know that this might not happen? You might not be able to be seen?" I worried the woman was headed toward disappointment.

"Yeah. I've told myself that even so, I'll be able to watch Patrick meet my babies, and that will be enough for me to move on."

I smiled. "I'll call for you soon."

Leonie's 'babies' were twenty-seven and twenty-eight. Lizzie and Leon looked nervous, but once again Miles and Cath took over and put them at ease. By now, I'd been chatting to Patrick for a while in the sitting room. He seemed like a great man. Polite, fun, and so excited to meet his family.

There were tears as they were finally reunited and a lot of them came from me.

"Oh my goodness. I can't believe it. You look like my own daughter. She has two small children so couldn't come, but maybe you could both visit us sometime?" Patrick said to Lizzie.

"I'd love that," she answered.

I left them for a while to catch up. I opened the French doors to the patio and sat just outside. While they nattered at a million miles an hour trying to fit in years of missed history, I wondered how I would broach them seeing Leonie. I mean, 'Oh by the way, your dead relative is now a ghost and wants to say hi' was going to be met with, 'the woman is batshit, especially if I couldn't get them to see her.

When a lull came in the conversation, I walked back in. Lizzie's eyes were filled with tears as she said. "Oh, if only Mum could have been here. She so wanted to meet you. Life can be so unfair."

That was my cue. I took a seat back on the sofa.

"I'm going to broach something with you now, and to be honest, you're going to think me crazy when I say it, but I'm going to say it anyway." Three sets of eyes looked at me. "Hear me out and then if you all just think I'm batshit, I'll have the driver come to take you to the hotel we booked for you all."

I'd paid for a central London hotel for them all for four nights so they could spend time together before Patrick's return flight home, and so that Patrick could also explore the city if he wished.

"Harley, you've been nothing but amazing to me so I'm all ears." Patrick turned to me, and Lizzie and Leon followed suit.

"Okay. So the thing is, I recently discovered I could, erm, see ghosts. Well, one ghost actually, just one. Leonie."

There was a stunned silence before Leon yelled out. "Oh hahaha. I knew there'd be something else going on. No one funds a reunion without wanting anything in return. You've got hidden cameras, haven't you?"

Patrick though stared at me. "You're not kidding? You see Leonie?"

"Only since yesterday. Since I started to relax and allow myself to believe and not be scared of something *other*. If you want to see her, that's the only way you can too." I called for her and watched her shimmer and stand right in front of Patrick. "She's there. Can you see her?"

"Oh my god," Leon gasped. "I can."

He'd been the one I'd least expected to do so, but he leapt over and was able to hold his mum in his arms telling her he loved her. And with his belief she got stronger. As Patrick and Lizzie also suddenly gained the sight, Leonie was as solid and there as any of us. But although I could speak with her, she couldn't speak to them. Well, not with words. Her hugs and facial expressions told them all they needed to know.

"She won't be able to maintain this for long," I told them, "and then she'll move on to heaven."

"Okay." Leon stepped back. "I'd better let you two have your time then before it's too late."

His eyes were drenched with tears, and I was startled when he threw his own arms around me. "I never, ever, expected this. I can't thank you enough."

I saw when Leonie began to shimmer again, and I told them that she didn't have much strength left to maintain her presence, so they all crowded around for one last family hug.

And then she was gone, and the words, "Thank you," were whispered in my ear before I felt her absence in the room.

"I'll give you a moment and then when you're ready I'll arrange your transport," I told them, and then I walked out of the room. As I walked down the corridor sobbing with the deep emotions coursing through me from what had just happened, a familiar body walked over to me and enveloped me in a hug.

"Come here, I got you," Cath said.

And I cried harder because I wanted the arms to have been Roman's.

Chapter 19

Roman

I'd gone straight to the recording studio and waited for the rest of the band there so that I didn't have to bump into Harley or any of the others.

I knew I was just being a stubborn idiot, and that I needed to apologise, but now Harley would be busy with the family she was reuniting. Hopefully after working in the studio, my mood would improve, and then I could go find her and say sorry for being an arsehole.

I was fine until Zak started talking about *Someone to Love*, and then I realised I wasn't in the mood to stay in the studio any longer.

"I was thinking about these lyrics," he said and began singing.

> *"It was youuuuu*
> *You're amazing*
> *It is yoouuuu*
> *You daze me"*

He sucked on his bottom lip. "I think we should swap daze out for saved. Listen.

> *It was youuuuu*
> *You're amazing*
> *It was yoouuuu*
> *You saved me.*

What do you think?"

He specifically looked at me, but then again it was my song.

What did I think?

I thought I needed to be on my own because I'd not finished sulking.

Getting to my feet, I walked out of the studio, and...

Into a *lasso*?

"What the fuck?" I said, as I grasped at my neck so as not to be strangled.

"Let's go, motherfucker," Bonnie snarled.

"Now, Bonnie. Remember what we agreed. You have to be gentle as he does perform some of the vocals occasionally so no damaged vocal cords." Zak's voice came from behind me and then he walked to the side of Bonnie and they both stared at me.

"We're going to go sit in Rex's garage where it's nice and quiet." Zak took a remote out of his pocket.

Bonnie tilted her head. "And where I can start some car engines, so you won't be heard screaming if I need to twist your fucking nuts off."

Bonnie was scaring me. She wouldn't be able to find my nuts to twist off, they were retreating so far up my body. Was she absolutely certain she wasn't demonic after all?

She tugged on the rope around my neck. As I walked alongside her, agreeing that I wouldn't try any sudden moves, she mouthed, "You hurt my sister anymore and you'll be found hung from one of these. I'll make it look like kinky sex play gone wrong."

Jesus. I'd only had a bit of a sulk. We'd not even argued. I was going to have to ask Stacey to fix me a protection spell against this teenager.

I looked at Zak and he was laughing under his breath.

We reached the large garage and Zak pressed the remote to open one of the garage doors and then we all stepped inside. An interior light came on automatically. Bonnie took in the luxury motors in front of her: lambos, Porsche, Mercedes, an Aston Martin. Rex had eight cars in his collection so far.

"Niiiiccccccceee." Bonnie looked them over. "Real nice. Do you think he'd miss one?"

"I think he would, but I also think he wouldn't mind us sitting in this classic VW campervan. It's set up in the back with a small table. Perfect for an intimate conversation." Zak pulled a key out of his pocket and opened the door. "Shall we?"

Once I was sitting safely inside, Zak took the noose from my neck. Bonnie had wanted to keep it on me and tie it to the table leg.

"There's something very wrong with you," I told her.

"Yeah, it's called being protective of my older sister. So you'd better tell me why she's upset and what you intend to do about it."

I huffed. "For God's sake. I can't believe I'm having to talk to a seventeen-year-old about my relationship."

"And a twenty-five-year-old," Zak added helpfully.

"With the mental age of seventeen." I crossed my arms. "It's like being cross examined by Shaggy and Velma."

"I suppose my pretty sister is Daphne? I'm always second best. You'd better be even nicer now you've called me Velma."

"She's the brainy one if that helps?" I tried to get out of my error.

"What. Did. You. Do?" Bonnie screamed as she smacked her fist down hard on the small Formica table. Even Zak jumped.

"Okay. Okay. I just got annoyed that she was trying to convince me to go see my family when I don't want to. I just ended up in a bit of a strop. It's the satyr way."

"Did you like my performance? I watch lots of detective shows. Especially *Lucifer*. I wish I could do that 'What do you desire?' mojo, oh and also show a red burned out face to scare people. That would be hilarious."

"Not sure I've heard of being demonic as 'hilarious' before," Zak mumbled. "You'll be making friends with Don next."

"Oh I bet he's not so bad when you get to know him."

I fixed Zak with a look. "Do you really think my love life is the biggest problem at this table right now when the teenager is saying she might friend the ruler of the seventh dimension of hell?"

"She's just messing. Aren't you, Bonnie? Because otherwise I'm going to have you sent to an all girls boarding school until you're eighteen. I'll offer your mum a million pounds to send you there."

"Huh, she fucking would as well." She clenched her teeth. "Okay, I'll stop threatening to go befriend Don the Demon, but, Roman, you've hurt my sister who I love dearly even if I wind her up ninety percent of the time. Now you have a choice. You go make a grand romantic gesture of apology tonight, or you end things and live a sad, lonely, solo life."

I felt very uncomfortable under the dual gaze and so looked at the tabletop and the faint pattern within it as if it were the most fascinating thing I'd ever seen.

"Eyes up, Roman. I need to know you've heard me, and you understand."

I looked up from a bowed head. My dark hair was hanging over my eyes slightly this way, so I was looking at Bonnie, just through my fringe where I felt safer.

"I know I've been an idiot, and I was going to apologise anyway. I just didn't want to do it while I knew she was busy with the Rivers."

"That was something she needed your support with. Her first angelic job, and you let her down. You do that again and you'll only wish I'd hung you with a rope."

"Bonnie." I was annoyed now. "I can't promise not to upset Harley again because that's what happens in relationships. You have tough times. But I will do my best to make sure we get through them as quickly as possible."

She cracked a grin. "And that's the correct answer. You sound like a man who knows he's met his woman. Go forth and apologise. Zak and I wish you every happiness, don't we, Zak?"

"We do." Zak's eyes mocked me.

"So I'm free to go now? You're not going to lead me back by the noose?"

Zak turned to Bonnie and pouted. "Can we?"

"No, Zak. He said the right thing. I need him to be able to speak his apology to my sister very clearly and eloquently."

Zak huffed but opened the van door. I climbed out, stretched, and then made my way into the house to find Harley and apologise.

But she wasn't there.

Miles met Bonnie at the door to tell her that Harley had gone home. That she was sorry for not waiting, but she needed some space and would be in touch and that a car would be called for whenever Bonnie was ready to go home.

"I'll just get my things together and I'll go now," Bonnie said. Then she turned to me, put a hand around her neck mimicking strangulation, and promptly strode off upstairs.

I needed to go see Harley, to apologise, and to admit I'd been an idiot.

I also wanted to note my concerns about her sister's disturbing personality.

"Zak?" I asked him. "Would you come back into the studio to work on that song with me? Only, it worked for Rex. Maybe I need to confess my feelings in a song?"

"No," Zak said, and for once he was being serious. He even

placed a hand on my shoulder. "You need to actually stand in front of Harley and tell her exactly how you feel. No more hiding. No more retreating. No more avoiding. Step up from the shadows, Roman. It's like when you're on stage. You're always nervous before the show, but once you hit that first chord, you come alive and then your performance is exemplary."

He mimed playing the guitar.

"Go prepare for a solo spotlight performance for Ms Harley Davies and do not hit a dud note," he warned.

"Zak. Thank you," I told him. "That's really helpful."

"Well, like I wanna be back in the studio with you when I could be boning Erica," he said.

I got changed into a nice clean pair of dark blue chinos and a grey linen shirt. I even brushed my hair through although it just sprang back unruly. A spritz of aftershave and I was ready. As I headed out of the door, I wondered if I should stop by anywhere for flowers, but then I remembered Zak's words. What I needed instead was a large bunch of honesty. Leaving a message for Cath, Miles, Rex, Freya, or whoever else saw it on the sideboard near the door, I stepped into the car I'd ordered to take me to Harley's apartment.

Someone was going into the apartment complex as I arrived and so I shimmied in after them. The guy who let me in did a double take, doing the expression I saw often, the 'I know you from somewhere but can't place you' look. I just smiled and followed him in, and then I took the back stairs two at a time until I was outside Harley's apartment door. She needed better security. That was one thing I'd be helping her sort out.

I rang the doorbell and waited. After a moment, Harley opened the door slightly and met my gaze. Her mouth was down-turned, and she looked upset.

SATYRDAY NIGHT FEVER

Then I heard a noise, and I looked behind her. Where I saw a naked male standing there.

"Unfuckingbelievable. I came here to apologise. Didn't take you long to get over me, did it?" I said, and turning, I stomped off back in the direction of the stairs.

Chapter 20

Roman

I reached the bottom of the second set of stairs and a stairwell, when I jumped about six feet in the air as the naked man appeared right in front of me.

"What the...? How the...?" I spluttered.

"I heard her sister on the speakerphone saying you were coming to apologise, and that if you messed up, she was going to castrate you so that you'd still be able to sing on stage, but it would be a lot higher," the guy said in a gruff voice. "So, you'd better get back up there, mate. Don't do what I did."

"I'm sorry, who are you? How did you get here? And what are you talking about?"

"Have you not worked it out yet? I'm a ghost. I've been in that apartment since I let the love of my life leave and killed myself. I don't know what's changed, but Harley walked through the door, and she could see me. We've been talking. She's helped me see that I made a mistake, but it's done, and I need to move on. I'm making my peace with my decision, and I hope that reincarnation is true, and I get a chance to make better decisions next time. So, mate. If you don't want to live an afterlife of regret, I suggest you come back upstairs with me."

I walked back up with him. It was very difficult when

engaging in conversation to keep my eyes up from his hairy bollocks.

"I'll be out of your hair soon. I just need Harley to show me the way forward and out of here. Gimme two secs, yeah? I'll ask her to answer the door when we're done and then you'll be able to have the place to yourselves."

I nodded in agreement, thanked him, and wished him the best.

Him giving me a moment outside meant I had a chance to get my words right because I'd managed to fuck up yet again.

Indeed, when the door swung open this time, Harley knelt against the doorframe and gave me a look so arctic it was probably capable of freezing my balls off.

"What do you want, Roman?"

I was ready with my speech about how I wanted to say sorry, but in the end, I figured I had just a few short words to say before she closed that door in my face. Remembering what Zak said about the right notes, I simply said.

"I want you, Harley. I think I'm falling in love with you."

Harley's mouth opened and closed as she attempted to speak and then lost her words. In the end she gestured for me to come in instead.

I followed her, going through a tiny entrance hall and through a door that led to an open plan living/dining/kitchen area. It was all pale white walls and a black gloss floor, but she'd accessorised with lots of colour. It was very Skandi looking and modern. She indicated towards a bright yellow sofa and I took a seat. Harley went to a white gloss cabinet, opened it, removed a bottle of scotch and poured herself a glassful, taking a swig before passing me the bottle and sitting down next to me.

"What did you just say to me, Roman?"

It was time for all my words now.

"Before I repeat my opening sentence, I just want you to know that last night and this morning, I was an idiot. I'm not trying to make excuses, but it is very satyr to sulk. However, I realise that's not an excuse to hide behind when actually I'm just being a dickhead. So, I'm sorry. I felt the pressure of maybe having to confront my parents when it's a lot easier to be avoidant, and so I distanced myself from you as well. It was a gross error, but it's been my default setting for a long, long time. I apologise, and I promise I will do my best to change, but sometimes I might be a sulky, mardy-arsed bastard who needs pulling up on it." I paused for a second or two. "Please don't send Bonnie to do that though, or your boyfriend might end up haunting your apartment naked like that other bloke."

She smirked at that.

"Did you have a temperature at all last night?" she asked me.

My brows creased. "No, why?"

"I'd just wondered if your hotheadness could be put down to a Satyrday Night Fever?" She began giggling.

"How long have you been saving that joke up for?" I asked.

"Ever since you said you were a satyr." She sniggered.

"Am I forgiven for being an idiot?"

"You are, but also, I'm sorry. I've been reuniting families for the show and in real life, and I went too far. We've only just got together. I shouldn't be pressuring you. I know little about you really."

"I intend for that to change, because like I said, Harley Alexandra Davies, I'm falling in love with you."

She beamed. So brightly I really could have used some sunglasses.

"Really?"

"Really."

I leaned forward and she moved in closer so I could sweep my lips over hers.

"I might like you a bit too," she mumbled against my mouth.

And then we ceased talking until the next morning.

Chapter 21

Harley

Things between Roman and I had gone from strength to strength. I was busy progressing with my production company plans and he was busy in the studio, so we were dating around that and getting to know each other better.

I'd not seen any more ghosts, but fully expected that it would be part of me now to come across them and help guide them home. I was my father's daughter after all.

Bonnie had decided she wanted to be a singer and performer and had made my mum enrol her in singing and dance lessons. Alongside college it was keeping her out of mischief, so I was happy for her. She seemed enthusiastic over the whole thing, and she could sing, so who knew what the future held for her?

And Roman had decided that he'd go and see his parents to talk to them about his plans to attend Sasha and Augustus' wedding. He was due back at any moment, and I had been crossing my fingers and praying up to my ancestors for it to all have gone okay.

Finally, he called around to my apartment where I'd arranged to cook him dinner.

He walked in and I took his coat from him, hung it in the

hallway, and then I gestured for him to take a seat at the table where I brought in two steaming bowls of freshly made tomato and basil soup.

"So, how did it go?" I asked him.

"Well, funnily enough, it went better than I expected because—and you won't believe this—but my parents were apparently visited by an angel who told them that it was their destiny to embrace change and bring satyrs into modern times." He raised a brow.

"That's very strange." I tried not to laugh.

"Now I don't know which angel this was because apparently, she had black glossy hair and deep brown eyes, but she got my parents thinking about how stupid they had acted putting the ways of the tribe above their love for their middle son. Then they broke down in tears and apologised profusely, admitting all the errors of their ways and begging my forgiveness."

I smiled.

"It will take time, but we're willing to work towards spending time together as a family, so I'd be very honoured if you would accompany me to Sasha and Augustus' wedding as my plus one. I'm guessing my parents might find you bear a striking resemblance to the visiting angel?"

"I doubt it," I said smirking, because I'd asked for a favour from one of the make-up artists I knew who did theatre work. I hadn't recognised myself when she'd done with me—thinking it was for a new TV show where I went undercover.

"You're a minx," he said, "but thank you."

"I've no idea what you're talking about, but if you want to punish me for disobedience, I'm game," I winked.

"Does this dinner reheat?" he asked me.

"No, but pizza delivers, and I seem to have lost my appetite for food."

As he picked me up and carried me into my bedroom, he looked around the room and laughed.

I'd bought forest style bedding and curtains and had changed all the furniture to real wood, including the flooring.

"I'm not sure I'm ever going to leave your room now," he said.

"Good, that was the plan," I replied as he kicked the door closed behind us.

Chapter 22

Roman

One year later, July 2024

Everyone gathered at the picnic area outside of my completed treehouses and lodges with a glass of champagne in their hands.

The band was all there with their significant others, and I was there with mine. I had my arm around Harley's shoulder and hers was around my waist.

It had been an amazing year. My relationship with my family, was, while far from perfect, much improved, and I could now visit and spend time with my brothers, and my best friend—who was now pregnant with my brother's baby. I couldn't wait to be an uncle. Their wedding had been incredible. They were so in love, and it was making the elders of the tribe realise that arranged marriages were becoming outdated. Of course, there were also the younger ones who were glued to watching episodes of *Married at First Sight* and who were happy to be instantly betrothed to a satyr they'd never seen before. I guessed it was about balance.

Harley's production company had won the contract for *Relatives Reunited* and ironically the press had termed her 'a true angel'. If only they knew...

Harley had approached Mandy and asked if she was happy at the seedy Soho hotel or whether she would like to work as her personal assistant. I'm not saying Mandy jumped at the chance but there's probably a Mandy's head shaped hole in the hotel ceiling.

The upshot of everything had been that Harley had spoken about moving to a larger place now she had the money to buy something bigger. And that led us to tonight.

I stood holding a microphone as I asked for everyone's attention. There was a large group of us: Harley's mum and sister, some of my family, Mandy and a friend, Cath and Miles, and a few others including some of the people who'd worked on the project, and The Seven.

"Thank you all for gathering here tonight. It's been a long time coming, but I have finally put down some roots, and so will you celebrate with me as I cut the ribbon to declare my new pad and my guest pads open."

I snipped the ribbon that hung suspended between two trees and after I made a speech thanking everyone, I raised a toast, and everyone cheered and joined in.

"Now of course, it wouldn't be a celebratory evening without a performance by the band, so, if my bandmates could come to the front, we'd like to open the party here this evening with our next song from the new album."

We were back on tour from next week which was ironic. Just as I'd put down roots we were off again for six months. But I knew my new home was here when I got back. I also knew that Harley and I would work around our schedules to make sure we were together as much as possible. We were also independent enough to survive when we couldn't. I mean there was video messaging these days after all.

SATYRDAY NIGHT FEVER

The band stepped forward and all mic'd up we began *Someone to Love*.

I cleared my throat. "This is a song I wrote for the album, and for the love of my life. Harley."

I heard her gasp, and I could see her eyes twinkling with tears as Bonnie and her mum hugged her from either side. I'd never confessed to having written it before. I'd been waiting for now. Zak sang backing as I sang the song.

> "Never thought there'd come a time
> When I craved you like the finest wine
> I've been around, I've been all over town
> But I'll tell you I've done looking now.
>
> Never thought this would happen to me
> A love that hit me so perfectly
> I've travelled the world, been all over town
> But I'm ready now to settle down.
>
> It was youuuuu
> You're amazing
> It was yoouuuu
> You saved me
> If there was ever a message from up above
> It was that I'd been sent... someone to love.
>
> Right from the start, I knew that I
> Had never fallen so hard, yet I felt so high

*I've made mistakes, I've been around
But I know that our song is the perfect sound,"*

I walked over to Harley, standing in front of her and singing the words while I looked deep into her eyes. Ones filled with such love and emotion I knew they mirrored my own.

*"It is youuuuu
You're amazing
It is yoouuuu
I'm craving
If there was ever a message from up above,"*

I dropped down on one knee in front of Harley.

"It was to marry the girl I was born to love."

Reaching into my pocket, I pulled out a ring box, opened it, and said, "Harley Davies. Will you marry me?"

She nodded her head as tears escaped her eyes.

"Yes. Yes. I will marry you."

Zak immediately launched into Bruno Mars' *Marry You*, a song we'd sang at the *Britain's Best New Band* competition that had led to every one of us meeting our other halves.

I'd never felt so happy as I took my new fiancée in my arms and kissed and danced with her along to the track.

Our celebrations went deep into the night, and then when everyone had left, I carried Harley over the threshold of our new home.

"Don't you think that's a tad early?" Harley laughed.

"Never too early to practice. Being in a band means I'm all about the practice and how it makes perfect, so, quick question. Will you want kids one day?"

"Yes."

"Excellent." I moved into the bedroom and lowered Harley gently onto the bed. "Then I figure we should practice that too."

She giggled and it was music to my ears. She was the heaven to my earth and together I knew we were utter perfection.

THE END

Take a look at my series featuring Mya, Noah Granger's sire in:

SUCK MY LIFE.

geni.us/Suckmylife

To keep up with latest release news and receive an exclusive subscriber only ebook DATING SUCKS: A Supernatural Dating Agency prequel short story, sign up here: geni.us/andiemlongparanormal

Playlist

Eurythmics, *There Must Be An Angel (Playing With My Heart)*
Harry Styles, *Lights Up*
Bruno Mars, *Marry You*
Robbie Williams, *Angels*
24KGoldn ft Iann Dior, *Mood*
Iann Dior, *Shameless*
Taylor Swift, *Bad Blood*
Take That, *Rule The World*
Lady Gaga, *Heal Me*

Suck My Life
Mya

One minute I'm working in a bookshop and the next minute a vampire decides to kill me.

Enter the tall, dark, handsome stranger who's been hanging around the store lately. He has a deal he says I can't refuse. I can either a) die or b) become a vampire and Queen of the Damned.

Great choices there, hey? Obviously, I choose option b.

So here I am, trying to get used to not only being undead, but to my new royal role where I'm in charge of the Home of Wayward Souls. Yep, any newly dead spirits that are wild, unhappy, and out to cause trouble. All mine.

Oh, and there's another tiny thing I need to get my head around. The guy who prevented my demise? He's Death himself. The grim reaper took a shine to me and wants to take me on a date.

Suck. My. Life.
geni.us/Suckmylife

The Vampire Wants A Wife

SUPERNATURAL DATING AGENCY BOOK ONE

Running a dating agency can be a killer...

Shelley Linley is sick of sickos. Yet another prankster has applied to her dating agency. This one says he's a vampire and he wants Shelley to help him find a wife.

Meeting him for a second interview against all her better judgement, Shelley discovers that he has no clue about women. A shame because he's super-hot, amusing, and has a lot of single friends he could recommend her struggling business to, even if he does say they're werewolves and demons. She has to help him, even if he's crazy.

If she can ignore his delusions, she's sure she can help him meet someone. But when death threats start arriving on her doorstep, Shelley's not sure she's cut out for the job...then her dating algorithm states she's his ideal partner. Now she's not sure if she should take the risk for love, or run like hell.

The Vampire Wants A Wife

books2read.com/u/m0v7k0

About Andie

Andie M. Long's love of vampires, reading, and her wicked sense of humour resulted in her creating her own paranormal comedy worlds.

She lives in Sheffield.

When not being partner, mother, or writer, she can usually be found on social media, at her allotment, or walking her whippet, Bella. She's addicted to coffee, chocolate, and Vinted.

Andie also writes contemporary romance under the penname Angel Devlin and psychological suspense as Andrea M. Long.

SOCIAL MEDIA LINKS

Follow me on TikTok and Instagram: @andieandangelbooks

Join my reader group on Facebook:
www.facebook.com/groups/haloandhornshangout

Paranormal Romance By Andie M. Long

PARANORMAL ROMANTIC COMEDY TITLES

SUPERNATURAL DATING AGENCY

The Vampire wants a Wife
A Devil of a Date
Hate, Date, or Mate
Here for the Seer
Didn't Sea it Coming
Phwoar and Peace
Acting Cupid
Cupid Fools
Dead and Breakfast
A Fae Worse than Death

Also on audio, paperback, and series bundles available.

THE SUPERNATURALS

Hex Factor
Rock 'n' Souls
We Wolf Rock You
Satyrday Night Fever

Also in paperback. Complete series volume available.

SUCKING DEAD

Suck My Life – available on audio.
My Vampire Boyfriend Sucks – available on audio.
Sucking Hell – available on audio
Suck it Up
Hot as Suck
Just my Suck
Too Many Sucks
Sucking Nightmare

OTHER PARANORMAL ROMANCE TITLES

DARK AND TWISTED FAIRY TALES

Caging Ella
Sharing Snow

Filthy Rich Vampires – Reverse Harem
Royal Rebellion (Last Rites/First Rules duet) – Time Travel
Young Adult Fantasy
Immortal Bite – Gothic romance

Printed in Great Britain
by Amazon